For Duck's Sake

ALSO BY DONNA ANDREWS

Rockin' Around the Chickadee

Between a Flock and a Hard Place

Let It Crow! Let It Crow! Let It Crow!

Birder, She Wrote

Dashing Through the Snowbirds

Round Up the Usual Peacocks

The Twelve Jays of Christmas

Murder Most Fowl

The Gift of the Magpie

The Falcon Always Wings Twice

Terns of Endearment

Owl Be Home for Christmas

Lark! The Herald Angels Sing

Toucan Keep a Secret

How the Finch Stole Christmas!

Gone Gull

Die Like an Eagle

The Lord of the Wings

The Nightingale Before Christmas

The Good, the Bad, and the Emus

Duck the Halls

The Hen of the Baskervilles

Some Like It Hawk

The Real Macaw

Stork Raving Mad

Swan for the Money

Six Geese A-Slaying

Cockatiels at Seven

The Penguin Who Knew Too Much

No Nest for the Wicket

Owls Well That Ends Well

We'll Always Have Parrots

Crouching Buzzard, Leaping Loon

Revenge of the Wrought-Iron Flamingos

Murder with Puffins

Murder with Peacocks

For Duck's Sake

A Meg Langslow Mystery

Donna Andrews

MINOTAUR BOOKS
NEW YORK

This is a work of fiction. All of the characters, organizations, and events portrayed in this novel are either products of the author's imagination or are used fictitiously.

First published in the United States by Minotaur Books, an imprint of St. Martin's Publishing Group

EU Representative: Macmillan Publishers Ireland Ltd, 1st Floor, The Liffey Trust Centre, 117–126 Sheriff Street Upper, Dublin 1, DO1 YC43

FOR DUCK'S SAKE. Copyright © 2025 by Donna Andrews. All rights reserved. Printed in the United States of America. For information, address St. Martin's Publishing Group, 120 Broadway, New York, NY 10271.

www.minotaurbooks.com

Title page illustration by Gabriel Guma

The Library of Congress Cataloging-in-Publication Data is available upon request.

ISBN 978-1-250-89438-0 (hardcover)
ISBN 978-1-250-89439-7 (ebook)

The publisher of this book does not authorize the use or reproduction of any part of this book in any manner for the purpose of training artificial intelligence technologies or systems. The publisher of this book expressly reserves this book from the Text and Data Mining exception in accordance with Article 4(3) of the European Union Digital Single Market Directive 2019/790.

Our books may be purchased in bulk for specialty retail/wholesale, literacy, corporate/premium, educational, and subscription box use. Please contact MacmillanSpecialMarkets@macmillan.com.

First Edition: 2025

10 9 8 7 6 5 4 3 2 1

For Duck's Sake

THURSDAY, JUNE 8

Chapter 1

"This is the life," Iris Rafferty exclaimed, taking a long pull on her glass. "Eileen, give Meg a refill on those Arnold Palmers."

At least I think that's what she said—it was hard to hear over the noise of the bulldozer in the backyard. But Eileen, Iris's daughter, must have heard the same thing I had. She lifted up the pitcher, so I held out my tumbler.

"Just what is he doing?" Eileen shouted, gesturing in the direction of the bulldozer.

"Putting in a duck pond," Iris bellowed back. "Isn't that going to be fun?"

I was relieved that Iris sounded enthusiastic about the duck pond. A few months ago she'd sold her house to my brother, Rob, and his wife, Delaney. But part of the deal was that she had life rights to stay in the mother-in-law suite she and her husband had built onto the ground floor of the century-old farmhouse. Technically, it was a mother-in-law apartment, since it was equipped with a compact but fully functional kitchen. I'd been worried at first that she'd resent any changes they made to the house where she'd lived for more than sixty years, ever since her marriage to the late Joseph Rafferty. But instead, she'd encouraged them to make as many changes as they wanted, both to modernize the place and to make it more to their taste.

"I enjoy the excitement," she'd said, and I'd been relieved to realize she was telling the truth. Iris had been bored. Having Rob, Delaney, and their newborn daughter, Brynn, move in had given her the proverbial new lease on life.

"Why a duck pond?" Eileen asked, shading her eyes as she peered through the back of the screened porch to get a better view of what the bulldozer was doing. "Are Rob and Delaney going into duck farming? I thought they both worked for Mutant Wizards."

Actually, Rob and Delaney owned Mutant Wizards, the company that had been founded on Rob's curious ability to come up with ideas for successful computer games—which had now grown into a software empire, thanks to the wizardry of programmers like Delaney. But I'd let Iris explain that later. I focused on the duck angle.

"Delaney wants to have duck eggs for the family," I said.

"You don't get enough eggs from all those chickens of yours?" Eileen looked puzzled. "You must have several dozen by now."

"She wants duck eggs," I explained. "Apparently, ounce for ounce they contain more B12, iron, selenium, and omega-3 fatty acids than chicken eggs. And they can be hard to find in the stores, so she wants to have a good supply of them from their own ducks by the time little Brynn is old enough for solid foods."

"Which will be any day now," Iris said. "About time that young whippersnapper got started digging the pond."

We all glanced over to where Aaron Shiffley, atop a blue-and-white Shiffley Construction Company bulldozer, was dumping another load of rich, black earth onto the pile a few yards away from the future pond's location.

"And you're here to keep an eye on him, I assume," Eileen said.

"Actually, I'm just hiding out here," I said. "As soon as I go home, I'll get sucked into preparations for the Mutt March."

"The what?" Eileen looked baffled.

"Mutt March," I said, a little louder. "It's a combination animal adoption event and fundraiser for the local shelter. Clarence Rutledge, our local vet, has collected hundreds of adoptable dogs from all over the state—"

"Make that all over the East Coast," Iris said, with a chuckle. She wasn't exactly exaggerating.

"And they're going to have a big parade in town on Saturday," I went on. "All the dogs will be marching in it, and they'll all end up in the town square for a dog-themed festival for the tourists. We'll be having a dog agility contest and several sheepherding demonstrations and all kinds of dog-related entertainment."

"And there will be lots of booths selling food and dog gear," Iris said. "That's why we've been baking all those gingerbread dogs."

"And of course, people can adopt the dogs," I added.

"You're not just going to let random strangers walk off with the dogs!" Eileen exclaimed.

"Of course not," I said. "Clarence has been taking applications and prescreening people for weeks. Anyone who has already done that can fall in love with a dog and take it home the same day. Anyone else can put in dibs on a dog and start the screening process at the fair."

"Only dogs, I assume," Eileen said. "We cat lovers will be out in the cold."

"We'll have some cats," I said. "Not as many, and they won't be marching, of course. We'll have floats full of cages for the cats, rabbits, parakeets, geckos, and whatever else the shelter happens to have. And for any senior dogs or puppies who can't march quite as far."

"Sounds like quite an event," Eileen said. "But what does that have to do with why you're over here today?"

"The dogs are at our house," I said. "They've been arriving in batches over the last two weeks. And today and tomorrow are when they're all getting washed and groomed and fitted with their costumes."

"Costumes?" Iris echoed. "They're marching in costumes? Wonderful!"

"Sounds like a lot of work." Eileen was the practical type. "Please tell me you and your family aren't doing it all."

"We have a lot of volunteers helping out today," I said, "including a whole bunch of school kids who are getting today and tomorrow off, thanks to our not using up most of the snow days that were built into this year's school calendar. Several Scout troops, in fact, plus the Ladies' Interfaith Council, and the Jaycees, and—well, pretty much every volunteer organization in the county, plus a whole lot of unaffiliated animal lovers."

"About time more people pitched in to help Meg," Iris said to Eileen. "Every day for almost two weeks, Clarence has shown up with more dogs that need feeding and walking and such. It's been running her ragged."

"Everyone in the family has been pitching in," I said. "I haven't been doing it all myself."

"But you're in charge," Iris pointed out.

"Not today," I said. "Mother took pity on me and volunteered to supervise the three prep days and marshal the event itself. Yesterday was the first sane day I've had in weeks."

"Still, I bet she finds plenty for you to do," Iris said.

"But only as a worker bee," I said. "I'd forgotten how relaxing that can be."

"And they're in your yard," Iris went on. "The rest of the

volunteers, including your mother, can go home to get away from the chaos—you're living in it. No wonder you came over here to escape. And I bet the Small Evil One's glad to be over here, too."

I glanced down at my feet where Spike, our eight-and-a-half-pound furball was dozing. Yes, Spike was relieved to be away from the Mutt March preparations. He'd long since lost his voice barking at all the canine intruders, and currently could only utter faint wheezing sounds. I was thinking of asking Rob and Delaney if he could stay with them tonight.

"It will all be over by Monday," I said. And then I flinched at how loud my words sounded. Not because I'd shouted them—we'd all been shouting. But the bulldozer's engine had just sputtered to a stop.

"That's so much nicer," Eileen said with a sigh. "Peace and quiet—at least for a few moments."

I glanced over at the bulldozer. Aaron had climbed down and was standing beside the blade, staring at something in front of it.

"Peace and quiet's all very well," Iris said, "but we don't want too much of it just now. The sooner he finishes excavating for the pond, the sooner we can get all the construction over with and bring home the ducks."

Aaron didn't seem ready to remount his bulldozer. As we watched, he squatted down as if to take a closer look at something.

"Maybe I should go out and see what the problem is." I set down my glass and headed for the porch door. Spike looked up, as if wondering whether to follow, then set his head back on his paws and closed his eyes again.

I strode across the yard toward the bulldozer. The spot Rob and Delaney had chosen for the duck pond was at the very back part of the yard—in fact, arguably not so much in the yard as in a clearing in the patch of woods that surrounded the house on three sides, separating it from the farm's fields and pastures.

When I got close, Aaron must have heard me. He stood up and turned around.

"Complication," he said.

"Problem with your bulldozer?" I asked.

He shook his head, turned back to where he'd been digging, and pointed. I took a step forward so I could see what he was indicating.

Bones. A scattering of bones mixed in with the rich dark soil. Maybe it was my imagination but—no. If you laid them out a little more neatly, they'd add up to a human arm.

Chapter 2

"This is bad," I said.

"Happens sometimes." Aaron shrugged. He was trying for nonchalance, but I wasn't quite buying it. He was young—in his early twenties—and looked younger, possibly because he was tall, like most Shiffleys, and hadn't yet grown into his height. Young and more than a little shaken.

"You've had this happen before?" I asked. "Digging up a dead body when you're excavating for a duck pond?"

"Unearthing a skeleton," he said. "Nothing left but the skeleton, and you can tell it's been in the ground for a while." He pointed to a place where a bone had been snapped off—probably by his bulldozer's blade. The newly broken end stood out paler against the faded ivory of the other bones. He frowned slightly, and I found myself thinking that he wasn't really taking this quite as calmly as he was pretending to. Probably good to help him out by staying calm myself.

"Definitely not recent," I said.

"But it's still going to mess up our construction schedule. Got to report it to Chief Burke. Get him to check it out."

"In case it turns out to be a murder victim."

"Right, but I'm pretty sure it won't," he said. "That's just what you have to do when you find a skeleton at a build site. Never found one before myself, but I know it happens sometimes. Happened to one of my uncles last summer when he was digging for someone's swimming pool. Usually turns out to be someone's private backyard burying grounds. We've had a couple of those in the family. My great-uncle Cephas, for example. He was so wild the preacher didn't want him anywhere near the First Presbyterian churchyard. We planted him at the far end of the peach orchard. We put up a marker, and if anything happens to that, there's plenty of us who know where he is, but if a family did that and then died out or moved away, it could be all forgotten."

I nodded. We should ask Iris about this. Her husband's family had farmed this land for more than a century. Maybe a century and a half. If this was a wayward Rafferty who hadn't been welcome in the churchyard, she'd know about it.

"Or an Indian burial," Aaron said. "That's what my uncle found last summer, digging for that pool."

"Looks kind of new for that," I said. "I mean, those bones look old, but not centuries old."

"You never know," Aaron said. "Depends on the soil chemistry and stuff. The chief will know what to do. Probably call in scientists from the college. That's what they usually do." He glanced up at me. "Could you maybe be the one to call him? They'll take you seriously. Me, they'll probably think I'm making up an excuse to slack off, or trying to pull a practical joke."

"Sure." I pulled out my cell phone. I hesitated for a moment. Obviously calling 911 would be overkill. This wasn't any kind of an emergency. The scattered bones looked very peaceful in the bits of sunlight that filtered through the oak and tulip trees.

But did I even have the Caerphilly PD's nonemergency number in my phone?

I dialed Chief Burke's cell phone. Since his youngest grandson was best friends with Josh and Jamie, my just-barely teenage twins, I practically had his number on speed dial.

"What's up, Meg? Adam ready for pickup?" The boys were taking advantage of their days off from school to help with the Mutt March preparations.

"Last I heard, he was still making *Star Wars* costumes for the dogs," I said. "I called to ask you what to do about something else. I'm over at Rob and Delaney's. Aaron Shiffley started digging for the duck pond and turned up a skeleton."

"Oh, dear." He didn't sound happy at the news.

"Not very recent, by the look of it," I said.

"That's good," he said. "But we still have a lot to do. First I have to come out and see if it looks as if the deceased was the victim of a crime."

"You're probably going to need to dig up a bit more of him to do that," I said. "All we can see at the moment is an arm. Left arm, I think," I added. "Dad could probably tell for sure."

"Yes," the chief said. "Can you call and ask him to meet me there? I need to track down Dr. McAuslan-Crine, the college's main archaeology expert. If the skeleton's only partially excavated, we need to see how soon we can get someone to come out to finish the job, and she's the one to organize that. And I'll send Horace over, too, in case the professor unearths anything to suggest that someone bumped off our bony friend. Aaron still there?"

"Yes." I glanced over at where Aaron was making a phone call of his own. With luck he'd be telling Randall Shiffley, his boss at the construction company, that the duck pond was on hold and he was available for another assignment, not spreading the news to his friends about his find.

"Keep him there till I arrive," the chief said. "I'll need him to make a short statement."

"Will do."

"He doing okay with this?"

I studied Aaron's face for a few moments.

"I think he's over any initial shock," I said. "I'll keep an eye on him."

"Good."

We hung up. Aaron rejoined me by the bulldozer.

"Randall says I should stay here till the chief comes," he said. "And offer to stick around in case he needs me to do anything with the bulldozer, although that's unlikely. Last year when my uncle found that Indian burial, they had to shut down for weeks while some professors from the college dug it up with teaspoons."

"The chief's already calling Dr. McAuslan-Crine to finish uncovering the body," I said.

"The little old lady with the British accent?" His face brightened. "I remember her from last time. She's pretty cool."

Yes, the professor was pretty cool, and remarkably patient with kibitzers at her digs. Like Dad, who could never resist the opportunity to watch archaeologists at work. The "little old lady" phrase was slightly jarring, since she was at most ten years older than me, but I let it pass.

"And I'm calling my dad to come over," I said, as I dialed.

"To pronounce our guy officially dead?" Aaron sounded almost amused. But just then Dad answered the phone, so I didn't get the chance to point out to Aaron that the job of medical examiner also involved figuring out who the skeleton belonged to, how long it had been there, and whether his manner of death was natural, accident, suicide, or homicide.

"What's up, Meg?" Dad asked. "And yes, I know I should have

been there by now. I had to drop by the hospital to check on a patient, but I should be at your house in another five minutes."

"Keep on going past our house to Delaney and Rob's," I said. "We need you here. Aaron Shiffley started digging the duck pond and turned up a skeleton."

"A skeleton! What kind of skeleton?"

"Human," I said. "Anything beyond that is what we need you to figure out."

"I'll be there as soon as I can."

"Don't hurry too much," I said. "The dead guy's not going anywhere, and I expect a deputy or two will be showing up to help the chief process what could be a crime scene, so stick to the speed limit. The chief could be cracking down on letting you off with a warning."

"It was only that one time," Dad protested. "And it really was—well, maybe not an actual emergency, but arguably rather urgent, and—"

"I'm sure the chief understands. Just don't push it."

"Roger. Can you send me some pictures of the crime scene?"

"No," I said. "You can see it yourself in five minutes, and I don't want to make your driving any more distracted than it already is."

And I ended the call in the hope that he'd focus on the road.

I glanced back at the house. Iris and Eileen were watching us. Iris had even gotten out her binoculars. But the bulk of the bulldozer was between them and the skeleton.

"I should let them know what's going on," I said to Aaron. "So they won't panic when the yard starts filling up with cops and archaeologists. You stay here and guard the bones."

"Roger." He gave the skeleton arm a sidelong glance that made me wonder if he minded being left behind with it.

"But keep well clear of them," I said. "Potential crime scene, you know."

"Right." He put another ten feet or so between himself and the bones, and looked happier.

"Iris has fixed Arnold Palmers," I said. "You want me to bring you a glass?"

"Um . . . I'm not supposed to drink alcohol on the job." He sounded regretful. "Not even a cold beer."

"An Arnold Palmer is what you call a half-and-half mix of lemonade and iced tea," I said.

"Oh, cool," he said. "Then I'd be glad of a glass. Thirsty work."

I was halfway to the porch when Horace showed up, trotting through the side yard. The gym bag in which he hauled his forensic gear was slung over one shoulder. He waved at me in passing.

Back on the porch, Iris and Eileen were watching my approach with visible impatience. And I suspected the unseasonable warmth was starting to affect Eileen's mood. She was patting her forehead with a napkin, and lifting up her sleek but heavy chignon so she could pat the back of her neck. Iris's short, tousled haircut was just as elegant and a lot more comfortable in weather like this.

"What's going on?" Iris asked, when I got close enough that she didn't have to shout. "And what's Horace up to?"

"Checking out the skeleton Aaron just found in the backyard," I said. "And just so's you know, Dad and Chief Burke and an archaeologist from the college will be following close on his heels."

"A skeleton?" Iris echoed. "Somebody dumped a skeleton in our backyard?"

"Buried it in your backyard," I said. "And it probably didn't start out as a skeleton."

"That's crazy," Iris said. "How the heck did they manage that?"

"Oh, dear," Eileen said. "This is going to cause all kinds of problems, isn't it?"

"Well, at least it should be interesting," Iris said. "Eileen, refill her glass."

"Thanks," I said. "And can you fill a glass for Aaron?"

"Let me get the new batch," Iris said. "And you can take a tray and some glasses out. I expect we'll have a deal more company before this is over, and the day's not getting any cooler."

Trust Iris to turn our gruesome find into a social occasion. Mother would be doing the same if she were here.

Iris went inside. Eileen and I watched in silence as Aaron indicated the finer points of the skeleton to Horace, who began taking pictures of it. Then Aaron started his bulldozer again and drove it out of the way of what would soon become a dig site, giving us a much better view of what was going on. Iris would be pleased. Dad and Chief Burke arrived together and waved to us on their way to inspect the skeleton.

I watched their faces. Dad's showed the kaleidoscope of emotions I'd seen before when he'd had to deal with a dead body. The calm, professional manner of a doctor and medical examiner fought with his sorrow at the illness or death of another human being and the half-guilty fascination of a lover of both mysteries and true crime.

The chief looked calm and professional, but I noticed that when he first arrived at the excavation area, he bowed his head ever so slightly and closed his eyes for a few seconds. Centering himself for the investigation ahead? Or did Baptists do prayers for the dead?

A few minutes later, another duo arrived—a short, plump gray-haired woman whom I recognized as Dr. McAuslan-Crine, and a tall young man with a buzz cut and a beard so closely trimmed it could almost pass for a mere five o'clock shadow. A grad student, I deduced. They were both visibly prepared to get down to work, clad in picturesquely disheveled clothes with bulging backpacks and a selection of shovels and other tools over their shoulders.

"Here you are." Iris emerged from her suite with a tray that contained a pitcher and half a dozen tumblers. "I think I've just barely got enough glasses."

"Thanks." I set down my own glass and took the tray from her. "I'll deliver this and make sure they have everything they need."

"And find out what they're saying," Iris said. "So you can come back and fill us in."

"Mother." Eileen rolled her eyes, which looked odd and a little amusing coming from a dignified, gray-haired woman in her sixties. Strange how often parents cause someone to revert to childish behavior.

I winked at Iris, then strolled across the yard to join the semicircle that had formed around the bulldozer and the skeleton.

Chapter 3

Aaron saw me approaching and hastened to drag over a sturdy metal equipment case so I'd have a place to set down the tray.

"—definitely not that old," Dr. McAuslan-Crine was saying. "I'm thinking fifty, sixty years at the outside. More likely thirty to forty. Our soil around here tends to be relatively acidic, and that does a number on bones."

"I agree," Dad said. "Definitely modern remains."

"And can you tell if the deceased is male or female?" The chief was scribbling in his pocket notebook as he followed their conversation.

"Not yet." Dr. McAuslan-Crine shook her head decisively. "If I had to bet on it, I'd say male, from the size of the hands."

"Yes," Dad said. "And the length of the ulna and the radius."

"Exactly." The professor used a little laser pointer to indicate the bones in question, the upper and lower arm bones. "But there are plenty of women with hands and arms that size. We'll be able to tell for sure if we can find the pelvic bones. So if Horace is finished taking pictures of how it looked when we got here—"

"I'm good," Horace said.

"Then let's get started."

Of course, getting started didn't mean that they were about to put shovel to dirt anytime soon. They began a lengthy discussion of where the rest of the skeleton was most likely to be found, based on the position of the arm and what little Aaron could tell them about exactly which patch of dirt the bulldozer blade had been plowing up when he'd unearthed it. Then they took out stakes, strings, and tape measures and began mapping out the site and setting up a grid system—a series of one-meter-square patches of ground outlined with string. I was torn between admiration for their precision and methodology, and frustration that we were probably in for a lengthy delay in creating the duck pond. I remembered when Aaron's uncle had found the Indian burial ground last summer. Last I'd heard, Dr. McAuslan-Crine and her students were still excavating that site and the homeowners were facing yet another pool-free summer.

I was about to go back to the screened porch to bring Iris and Eileen up to date when I spotted two more figures approaching: Grandfather, striding purposefully across the lawn, with the much shorter figure of Manoj, one of his zoo staff, half running along behind him. Since Grandfather had given up his driver's license a few years ago, he relied on relatives and staff to chauffeur him around, and the mild-mannered Manoj was often the one he drafted.

"Should we maybe recruit someone to keep lookie-loos from showing up and interfering with what might be a crime scene?" I asked the chief.

"Probably a good idea," he said, pulling out his phone. "Although your grandfather's here by invitation. Identifying the deceased is probably going to be pretty difficult. We might be able to use dental records—"

"Assuming we find the skull," the professor chimed in from where she was hammering in a stake. She didn't have to sound so cheerful about the possibility that they wouldn't. "No guarantee. You'd be amazed how far predators carry body parts sometimes. Entirely possible we won't find any more bones here."

She and Dad were going to get along like a house afire.

"And there's always the chance that he—he or she—might have some kind of identification on or near the rest of his body," the chief went on. "Assuming we find any more of it," he added, before Dr. McAuslan-Crine could. "But I've asked your grandfather if there's any chance he could do a DNA analysis on our John or Jane Doe."

"Is this our murder victim?" Grandfather had joined us and was studying the bones that were now at the center of the archaeologists' web of string.

"We don't yet know the deceased was murdered," the chief said. "Could simply be a natural death."

"And then someone came along and buried the poor sod, instead of calling the cops and reporting it?" Grandfather asked.

"We don't yet know if that's what happened," the chief said. "I need to talk to Iris Rafferty. Find out if she's aware of any legitimate private burials here."

"I think she'd have mentioned it if there were," I said. "As soon as she heard Aaron had uncovered human bones, she'd have said something like 'Oh, damn, it's probably Great-Uncle Cyrus. I should have mentioned that we buried him back there at the edge of the woods.'"

"Could have been the previous owners that did it," Dr. McAuslan-Crine put in. "And then didn't mention it when they sold, in case it hurt the sale. Not everyone wants somebody else's great-uncle in their flower beds."

"Iris is around ninety," I said. "She's lived here since she married Joe Rafferty, in her twenties, and she and her husband were the third or fourth generation of the family to farm this land."

"Ah." The professor shook her head. "Skeleton's a lot newer than that."

We all fell silent for a moment, and I wondered if they were thinking the same thing I was: that Iris had definitely been living here when the body was buried. Iris and her late husband. But not necessarily their three children, if Dr. McAuslan-Crine was correct in estimating that the skeleton was thirty to forty years old. Mary Catherine, her youngest, was around fifty, so she'd have been here forty years ago, but I suspected thirty years ago they'd all have left home.

But Iris and Joe had definitely been around then. So either Iris knew about the burial, and would soon have to tell the chief about it, or she was about to find out that she'd been living for the last thirty or forty years with a dead body buried in her backyard.

"Always possible that Mrs. Rafferty will be able to shed some light on the identity of our skeleton," the chief said, as if reading my thoughts.

"But just in case she can't, we can get my scientists working on a DNA profile," Grandfather said. "So let me have one of those finger bones, and I'll get the ball rolling."

"We can't just hand you a bone," the chief said. "We need to preserve the chain of custody. You let me know which one you think would work, and I can have a deputy bring it over with all the proper paperwork—assuming you think any of them is in good enough shape for you to get DNA from it."

"My guys can get DNA out of bones a couple of centuries old," Grandfather said. "Guys and gals," he added, before anyone could correct him. "They should have no trouble working with relatively well-preserved bones like those."

"Then point out a likely-looking one," the chief said. "And as soon as one of my deputies gets here— Aha! Here's Vern. He can do the transfer."

Vern Shiffley, the chief's senior deputy, nodded genially to everyone as he joined us. Grandfather, Dad, Horace, and Dr. McAuslan-Crine began to discuss the enthralling issue of which bone to send—particularly whether any of them would be more likely than the others to yield a clue to the skeleton's identity by mere inspection, without resorting to DNA, and should thus be retained with the rest of the skeleton. Meanwhile the chief brought Vern up to speed on the case.

Because it was a case, I realized. Even if Dad found conclusive evidence that the skeleton had died of natural causes, there would still be a John or Jane Doe case. Not to mention the troubling question of who'd buried the body.

For a moment, I rather envied them all. They all had a professional reason to be here and practical tasks to be done. If at any point it hit them that we were dealing with the death of another human being, they could fall back on routine and necessity. Well, with the possible exception of Aaron, and even he seemed to find it reassuring that the experts were here, dealing calmly and professionally with the situation. Or maybe he was taking comfort in the likelihood that they'd let him leave pretty soon.

Eventually, to the chief's relief, the experts agreed on which bone to send, and we all watched solemnly as Horace packed it up.

"The *proximal phalanx* of the *digitus medius*," Dad proclaimed, as he watched it disappear into the brown paper evidence bag.

"That's the bottom bone of the middle finger—the one closest to the palm," Horace translated as he carefully printed several lines of identifying information on a form attached to the bag.

"Does this mean you're giving my DNA team the middle finger?" Grandfather said, with a cackle.

Horace then handed the evidence bag to Vern.

"So, I take this over to Dr. Blake's lab?" Vern said.

"Perhaps you could take Dr. Blake there as well," Manoj suggested. "We are having a very busy day in the small mammal house, and I would like to run some important errands before I go back—unless you want to stay here to observe the excavation," he added in an anxious tone, turning to Grandfather.

"No, I should get back and make sure my DNA team jumps on this," Grandfather said. "I'm fine riding with Vern—unless he plans to lock me up in the back seat of his cruiser like a felon."

"You can sit up front and play with the siren if you've a mind to," Vern said. "Let's make tracks."

Grandfather, Vern, and Manoj hurried off. The chief watched them go. Then he turned back to the excavation site, where Horace and the archaeologists were beginning what promised to be a very slow search for the rest of the skeleton.

"I'll leave you folks to it," he said. "If you need me, I'll be up at the house, talking to the Raffertys."

"Mind if I come with you?" I asked, as he turned to leave. "I should head back before long to see how the Mutt March preparations are going, and I want to ask Iris if it's okay to leave Spike here for the day. Having so many other dogs invading his turf is hard on him."

"No problem," he said. "In fact, I'd appreciate it if you give me a little background before I tackle Ms. Rafferty." He paused, took off his glasses, and began polishing them with his pocket handkerchief, making it seem as if that was the reason for stopping. "Eileen—is that the one who's a nun? I know they don't always wear a uniform these days."

"They call it a habit, actually," I said. "And I don't think Iris's daughter wears one. But it's Mary Catherine who's the nun. Eileen's the lawyer."

"Good to know," he said.

"I think she practices civil law," I said. "Contract stuff. Not criminal, anyway."

"Still good to mind my p's and q's." He smiled, then replaced his glasses and resumed walking toward the house.

I was tempted to ask "when do you ever *not* mind your p's and q's?" But of course his comment was a joke. Chief Burke was nothing if not precise and by the book. If I'd identified Eileen as the nun, he'd probably have made a similar joke about watching his language, even though very few people had ever heard him utter anything as scandalous as "damn." He usually stuck to "blast" or "tarnation."

"And it might not be a bad thing if you stuck around, just for a few minutes," he said in an undertone as we drew near the house. "If you don't have to hurry back. Might make our conversation feel more like a social call than an interrogation."

"Can do," I said. I wasn't sure which made me happier—the possibility that Iris would reveal some information about the skeleton, or the thought of avoiding the Mutt March preparations for a little longer.

Chapter 4

As the chief and I approached the house, I saw the porch was empty. Apparently Iris and her daughter had retreated to the mother-in-law suite, but they'd left the door between it and the porch open—the better to keep an eye on what was happening in the backyard.

The porch screen door squeaked slightly as we opened it, so I pulled out my notebook-that-tells-me-when-to-breathe—a combination calendar and to-do list—and jotted down a note to bring some oil the next time I came over so I could take care of the hinges. And another note to buy a can of oil for Delaney and Rob, who seemed oblivious to the need to keep things like that around.

While I was scribbling, Iris peered out, then came out to join us. Eileen followed her, looking anxious. Iris just looked annoyed.

"So have you figured out who the heck someone buried in my backyard?" She glanced at me. "In my former backyard, of course—but it would have been mine when they buried him. It wasn't my idea, dumping a dead body on Delaney and Rob. So who is he? And what the dickens is he doing there?"

"I was hoping you could tell me," the chief said. "I take it you have no idea who he is."

"No idea at all," Iris said. "Not family, for sure. We've got a nice family plot down at St. Byblig's. If he was a Rafferty, he'd be down there."

"What if it was someone they wouldn't let you bury there?" the chief asked.

"Someone who'd been excommunicated, you mean?" Iris looked insulted. "We haven't had anything like that happen in my memory, in Joe's family or mine. And even if we did, we'd have bought him a nice plot somewhere else."

"What if you couldn't find anyplace willing to take him?" the chief persisted.

"Might not have been in Caerphilly, but I'm sure we could have found him something somewhere," Iris said. "And if we couldn't, we wouldn't have just dumped him in a hole in the backyard like a rabid raccoon. We'd have at least given him a headstone. Maybe a little fence around the plot. And nothing like that has happened since I've been living here, which will be sixty-two years next month."

"Do we have any idea how long he's been there?" Eileen asked.

"So far we don't even know for sure he's a he," the chief said. "About all we do know is that Horace, Dr. Langslow, and Dr. McAuslan-Crine agree that the remains have been there around thirty to forty years."

"Dr. McAuslan-Crime?" Iris repeated. "Who's he?"

"McAuslan-*Crine*," the chief corrected. "She's an archaeologist from the college."

"She was appointed to the college's new Ivor Noël Hume Chair in Archaeology last year," I explained. "She's British. Came from Cambridge University."

"Well, she should know her stuff, then," Iris said. "Although don't ask me why a British archaeologist would want to go slumming over here when there are so many more really old things to dig up back home."

"I know this is an impossibly vague question," the chief said, "but can you recall noticing a disturbance back there at any time? Probably in the eighties or nineties—certainly no later than the early part of this century."

"Like coming home from the state fair and finding a six-by-three-foot patch of fresh dirt in the woods behind the far end of the backyard?" Iris asked. "I think we'd have reported it."

"You would have if they just left a freshly dug grave there," I said. "But what if they covered it up again with leaves? Most of the time there would be a lot of leaves back there—Aaron Shiffley took a leaf blower to the area before he started digging, to make sure he wasn't going to run into any big rocks or abandoned farm equipment or anything else that might damage his bulldozer."

We all glanced over at the dig site. I noted, with a bit of annoyance, that the press had arrived, in the form of a journalism student who wrote for both the college paper and the weekly *Caerphilly Clarion*. He had his phone out and was taking pictures.

"Should have told my deputies to stick to cell phones," the chief said. "I think that young man must spend every waking minute listening to the police band radio."

"In a slow news period, he probably sleeps with it on," I said.

"Him and your dad," the chief said.

"Meg's right about the leaves," Iris said. "If we noticed they were a bit scuffled, we'd have just assumed it was deer or something. Still a puzzle, when they could have done it. Thirty, forty years ago, we didn't travel that much. We had livestock back then. Chickens for sure, maybe cows and pigs if you're talking closer to the forty-year mark. And with the kids all going off to college, we had less and less help. If we wanted to get away, even for just an overnight trip to the fair, we'd usually have to hire someone to take care of the critters, so we didn't do it that often."

As she spoke, Iris was fiddling with one of her hearing aids.

Had she worn them thirty or forty years ago? She'd have been between fifty and sixty—some people got hearing aids at that age, didn't they? And what about her late husband? If they had both worn hearing aids, and had taken them off to go to bed, could someone have sneaked into their yard to bury the body without their realizing it?

Maybe—but why *their* yard? There were plenty of more isolated places nearby, fields or stretches of wood that weren't anywhere near an occupied house. To me, that seemed a much more important question than when the body had been buried. Was whoever buried it trying to implicate the Raffertys? Send them an ominous message? A message whose impact had been seriously blunted by the decades it had taken to deliver it?

"I do *not* like this," Iris said. "Someone sneaks into our yard and buries a dead body? And manages to do it without us even noticing?" Her voice started to take on a slight edge that suggested that she wasn't as calm as she was trying to appear.

"After all this time, it's probably not going to be all that important to figure out precisely when the deceased was buried," the chief said in his most soothing tone. "I was just wondering if you remembered a time when you came home to find that part of your yard wasn't quite as you'd left it."

"Not offhand," Iris said. "But I'll think about it."

"That would be helpful." The chief stood, and I followed suit.

"Mind if I leave the Small Evil One here for the time being?" I gestured to where Spike was asleep in a quiet corner of the porch. "I should make sure everything's going well back at the house, but I don't want him getting overstimulated again. I can send the boys over to bring him home before bedtime."

"He can stay as long as he likes," Iris said. "Heck, he can sleep right there if he likes. He and I know enough to leave each other in peace. If that young reporter fellow tries to bother me, I'll let Spike chase him off."

"He's met Spike before," I said. "Odds are he'll leave you alone."

"Then not only *may* you leave him with me, I implore you to," Iris said.

"Let me know if you think of anything that might be useful," the chief said.

"Will do." Iris nodded. She adjusted her rocking chair slightly, so she had a better view of the ongoing excavation.

The chief headed back to the dig. Dad was standing outside the web of string but clearly intent on watching everything the archaeologists were doing.

I turned toward the path that led through a small stretch of woods to our backyard. This path, joining our two households, was already becoming well worn. On weekdays, either Rob and Delaney would drop off Brynn at our house for Rose Noire to watch, or Rose Noire would trot over early to pick up her charge. But at some point during most days, either Iris would hike over to visit with her honorary granddaughter or Rose Noire would bring the baby over to see Iris. Sometimes both. And in the evenings and on weekends, the extended family flowed back and forth between the two households.

I'd overheard an interesting bit of conversation from Josh and Jamie recently, when they wanted to invite a school friend over for a family social event.

"Just drop by our house," Josh had said into his phone.

"We'll be over at Delaney and Rob's," Jamie had pointed out.

"Oh, right." Josh nodded. "Our other house," he'd said, into the phone.

I stepped out of the woods into our backyard and came to a full stop. In the short time I'd been over at Delaney and Rob's, I'd forgotten how chaotic things were back here. Forgotten, or maybe shoved the whole thing out of my mind.

Dogs. So many dogs. Who even knew there were this many dogs on the whole planet?

Chapter 5

The entire yard was filled with dogs and people doing things with, to, or for dogs. Ten or twelve people were washing dogs in a variety of containers, ranging from dishpans for the toy breeds to a couple of defunct hot tubs and bathtubs for the bigger ones. People were brushing dogs, giving them haircuts, and trimming their nails. A small posse of people, led by Rose Noire, was performing massage therapy on some of the more stressed and excitable dogs. Or maybe she was using the available dogs as test subjects for people who wanted to learn canine massage. Either way, both dogs and humans were starting to look enviably mellow.

People were testing dogs to see if they knew the basic "sit!" and "stay!" commands, and whether they had good leash manners. People were shepherding dogs over to the designated doggy bathroom area. People were patiently fitting costumes on wriggling dogs. And across the fence, in a field that was part of Mother and Dad's pasture, people were gathering around the dozens of temporary chain-link dog runs, most of them occupied not by individual dogs but by batches of them.

I spotted dogs that looked like purebred poodles or goldens and dogs whose ancestry was probably too diverse ever to be untangled. St. Bernard– and Great Dane–sized dogs and feisty little Yorkies and chihuahuas. Shaggy dogs and dogs with short, sleek coats. Exuberant dogs, jumping up to lick the faces of their groomers, and shy dogs being gently coaxed out of the crates in which they'd taken refuge. The Westminster dog show had nothing on us.

We were also doing right by our many human volunteers. Our already large collection of picnic tables had been augmented with half a dozen folding tables Mother had borrowed from Trinity Episcopal. Rose Noire and her kitchen crew regularly refilled the five-gallon dispensers of water, lemonade, and iced tea that occupied one of them. Another table offered supplies of sunscreen and Rose Noire's surprisingly effective all-natural insect repellent. And I wasn't the only person gazing eagerly at the several tables where the kitchen crew was starting to set out food in containers bearing the familiar logo of The Shack, Caerphilly's premiere barbecue venue.

Mother had also arranged for Randall Shiffley to lend us one of what he referred to as his gold-plated porta potties—actually a small trailer that looked like the portable dressing rooms provided to actors when they were filming on location, containing two regular toilet cubicles and one ADA-compliant one. Nothing about them was actually made of gold, but they boasted porcelain flushing toilets, sinks with running water, and air-conditioning, making them so far superior to the typical porta potty that tourists had started mentioning them in online reviews of the various outdoor events that Caerphilly sponsored. Since I'd been the one to talk Randall into buying a couple of them, as an experiment, these days it was all I could do to refrain from saying "I told you so."

I waved to my good friend Aida Butler, who was looking neat and professional in her perfectly laundered deputy's uniform, with her long braids pulled back into a sleek bun. I'd thought it wise of the chief to have a deputy on duty here, just as a precaution. But Aida looked stern. I wondered if she'd already had to deal with some kind of malefactor, or if she was just doing her best to discourage any trouble before it got started. And was duty here a reward or a punishment? I'd ask her later. We were overdue for one of our "girls only" movie nights. One of these days Michael and the boys would figure out that instead of chick flicks, we watched bad martial arts movies and occasionally old favorites like *Raiders of the Lost Ark,* and they'd start clamoring to join us, but so far our secret was safe.

I headed for the barn, where Clarence Rutledge had set up his veterinary headquarters. Not in the former tack room that now served as my home office—I'd kept that safely locked. I knew even if Clarence promised to keep the dogs outside, he'd forget, and I didn't want my books and papers peed on, chewed on, or napped on. But I'd dragged out my comfy desk chair and set up a large folding table for him in the middle of the barn.

He was sitting there now. And hovering by the table was Kevin, my cyber-savvy nephew. What was he doing here, out of his familiar computer-infested lair in our basement? And in the daylight?

"Meg! Thank goodness you came!" Clarence started, as if about to dash over and give me his customary bear hug, but then remembered that he had a pair of sleeping puppies in his lap and kept his seat.

"What's the problem?" I asked.

"We've picked up a possible threat to the dogs!" Clarence sounded stressed, and his voice woke one of the puppies. It yipped and whined softly, and he patted it apologetically.

"A threat to the dogs?" I kept my tone quiet to avoid alarming the nearby volunteers. "Some group of dog haters threatening the parade?"

"I picked up some chatter online," Kevin said. "I monitor a lot of social media places where people involved in dogfighting hang out. If I get any useful intel, I give it to Chief Burke, and he tries to get local law enforcement involved."

I nodded. I had deduced that Kevin did this from time to time. In fact, I could usually figure out when he'd been doing too much of it. Occasionally he'd emerge from his subterranean lair looking gloomy, cradling Widget, his Pomeranian, on one shoulder, and hand out liver treats and head scratches to every other dog he could find.

"There's this bunch I've kind of been keeping my eyes on," Kevin continues. "They're smart enough not to use words like 'dogfight' or even 'fight' online. But they're always talking about tailgating parties and karaoke parties, and I'm pretty sure they're using those as code words for dogfighting matches."

I frowned slightly, wondering if Kevin was getting a little too paranoid about the dogfighting thing.

He must have seen my expression and deduced my skepticism.

"I mean, they're way too hyped up about keeping the locations secret and not bringing anyone who can't be vouched for," he said. "And when was the last time you heard of the police raiding a karaoke party?"

"Well, if Caerphilly's finest ever heard your rendition of 'Another One Bites the Dust,' I'm sure they'd intervene in the interest of public safety," I said. "But I see your point. Just what did this suspected thug say?"

"He mentioned the Mutt March," Kevin said. "Really innocent-like. And said something like 'we have an in. You-know-who is going to go down there, and I'm sure she can come back with a few likely prospects.'"

"Likely prospects?" I echoed. "You think they'd come to the Mutt March looking for fighting dogs?"

"Probably not," Clarence said. "And they wouldn't find any hot prospects if they did. I didn't want to bring any dogs to the march that had been badly mistreated or had aggression issues. I found a few of those, but I took them down to Caroline's for treatment."

"To Caroline Willner's?" Our friend Caroline ran a wildlife sanctuary. I wasn't sure how problem dogs were expected to coexist with her motley collection of wounded raptors, former pet tigers, and over-the-hill racehorses. "What kind of treatment are we talking about?"

"A friend of hers is really good at rehabilitating problem dogs," Clarence said. "Dogs that have developed bad behaviors due to abuse. But his neighbors kicked up such a fuss about him having too many dogs that he had to move—for the dogs' safety as much as anything else. So Caroline let him move into one of the houses on her land in return for keeping an eye on the place when she travels. Any dog I wasn't sure about, I took down to him for evaluation. And rehabilitation, if necessary. And of course, I've had Rose Noire checking their auras, too, to catch any problems I might have missed."

I wasn't sure I believed in human auras, much less canine ones. I tended to think Rose Noire was merely a good judge of character—in dogs as well as humans. But either way, I thought it a good idea, sending any pup she had doubts about to doggie rehab.

"So whoever the dogfight organizers are sending to the Mutt March isn't likely to find a fighting dog here," I said.

"But we have plenty of dogs that they might want to use as bait dogs," Clarence said. "They throw them into the ring with their fighting dogs as part of their training."

"Or maybe just because they like seeing animals hurt," Kevin muttered.

"So there is, or will be, a woman here who has ties to dogfighting and shouldn't be allowed to take home a dog," I said. "Have you told Chief Burke about this?"

"Of course," Kevin said. "And briefed Aida on it."

No wonder she'd been looking stern.

"And the chief will do what he can to figure out who she is," Clarence said. "But he was already pretty swamped with the Mutt March—his whole department is, and the same with your dad. And from the look of it, they're going to be even busier with all the complications from that dead body you found."

"Not my find," I said. "And I'd say skeleton rather than dead body. But what do you mean, 'from the look of it'?"

By way of an answer, Kevin tapped on his phone and then held it up for me to see what was on his screen. I saw a shot of Aaron Shiffley, posing beside his bulldozer. And then the shot changed to one of the excavation, with the skeletal arm standing out sharply against the black earth.

"The *Clarion*'s website?" I asked.

"Yeah." Kevin nodded. "But it's all over the internet by now. All the conspiracy theorists are already busy trying to connect it with their favorite missing person. Jimmy Hoffa, Judge Crater, D. B. Cooper—"

"Why not Ambrose Bierce while you're at it?" I saw Kevin frown, and wondered if the reference was too obscure for him. However celebrated Bierce had been in his heyday as a writer, that heyday had been more than a hundred years ago. No one my age or Clarence's escaped high school without having read his oft-anthologized "An Occurrence at Owl Creek Bridge"—but Kevin was a generation younger.

I shouldn't have doubted him. After all, he was a true-crime podcaster, and Bierce's disappearance was a famous historical case.

"I don't think the skeleton's old enough to be Bierce," Kevin said. "Dude fought in the Civil War, right? Wouldn't he have disappeared in the eighteen hundreds?"

"More like nineteen fourteen," I said. "During the Mexican Revolution. And the skeleton isn't old enough to be any of those others, either."

"Too bad," Kevin said. "And it's definitely male? No hope of Amelia Earhart?"

"I'm sure Chief Burke will figure out who the skeleton belongs to," Clarence began.

"Especially with Grandfather's lab doing DNA testing," I said.

Kevin gave that a thumbs-up.

"But we need to do what we can to protect our dogs!" Clarence swept his arms wide in an expansive gesture that took in all the crates and cages stacked around us.

"And to do that we need to uncover the mole in our midst." I turned to Kevin. "Any clue to whether she's coming as a dog adopter or whether she might already be here, as a volunteer?"

"A volunteer?" Clarence's face paled. "I never thought of that."

"Probably a buyer," Kevin said. "Because we know most of the volunteers. Don't we?"

"Good question." I jerked my thumb over my shoulder, toward the barn door. "Do you know every single person out there?"

They looked at each other and shook their heads.

"I figured the ones I didn't know probably belong to Blake's Brigade," Kevin said. "Grandfather put out a call to them."

I nodded. Blake's Brigade was the name Grandfather had given to the loosely organized group of volunteers he could call on when he needed help with one of his projects, like a protest march against a corporate polluter or an animal rescue expedition. Helping get dozens of dogs adopted would definitely appeal to the Brigade.

"Okay, stupid question, but do you have any way of making sure this woman, whoever she is, hasn't already made off with some dogs?" I asked.

"I've had people watching all the dog runs," Clarence said, "in case any of the dogs escaped, or got aggressive, or anything. And we have a complete inventory!"

"An inventory? Of the dogs?" This didn't sound like something Clarence would have thought of. He had the proverbial heart as big as all outdoors, but his organizational skills were on a par with a toddler's.

"Yeah, I know," Clarence said. "Remember I didn't say *I* had an inventory. I got Ms. Ellie to do it. She has them all logged into her database."

"Excellent," I said. Ms. Ellie Draper, the town's head librarian, was one of the most organized people I'd ever met. If any human on the planet could keep track of several hundred assorted stray dogs, it would be her. "I'll let her know about the threat to the dogs. And I have an idea about how to uncover our mole, if she's here. I'll fill you in later."

"I told you Meg would know how to handle it," Kevin said. "I should get back to those adoption applications."

"I'm having Kevin vet them all, just in case," Clarence explained as he handed over an inch-thick sheaf of paper.

Kevin winced as he took the stack. Clearly he had his work cut out for him.

"Laters." He lifted the sheaf of papers to his temple in a mock salute, then ambled out.

"If I'd known I'd be putting any of the dogs in danger I would never have organized the Mutt March," Clarence fretted.

"They're in no more danger here than they would be at whatever shelter they came from," I said. "Probably less, since the shelter dogs don't have Ms. Ellie watching over them. And don't worry. I know someone who will take the danger to the dogs as seriously as you do."

"Another dog lover." He nodded. "You can always tell a person's character by how they treat dogs."

"And animals in general," I added, as I left the barn.

Actually, Mother preferred cats to dogs—with the possible exception of a few breeds she considered truly elegant, like borzois, salukis, and Italian greyhounds. But I knew she'd never stand by and let even our scruffiest and worst-behaved mutts come to harm. That was why I'd been so relieved that she'd agreed to take charge of wrangling the several days of parade preparation— well, that and the fact that I knew she'd adore bossing around all our volunteers.

I gazed around and spotted her, seated in an Adirondack chair on our back stoop, with a clipboard in her hand and a cup of tea on a small side table at her elbow. Her right leg was elevated on a footstool, and as I drew near I could smell the aroma of one of Rose Noire's healing herbal salves—strong, but not unpleasant, unless you had something against camphor, menthol, and eucalyptus.

I wasn't entirely sure Mother's ankle injury was even real. "Just a slight strain, dear," she'd said when I'd asked her what was wrong. "Your father thinks it will heal up in no time if I'm careful." But the salve and the slight, elegant limp eliminated the need to explain to newcomers that Mother's volunteer responsibilities were purely supervisory.

I strode across the yard to join her.

Chapter 6

"How is your father holding up?" Mother asked, as soon as I got close enough for conversation. "So tiresome, having two things he adores being involved in happening at the same time. I know he must be frustrated. And he'll run himself ragged, dashing back and forth between here and his crime scene."

"Probably." I wondered if I should warn her, if she happened to be talking to Chief Burke, not to refer to it as Dad's crime scene. But no—this was Mother. She'd know that. "Something has come up that you can help with. Something that will help keep the Mutt March from interfering with the murder investigation . . . on top of protecting the dogs from a possible danger," I added, to ensure that I had enlisted her sympathy.

"Of course, dear." She lifted her clipboard, as if to signal that we were about to focus on the business at hand. "What can I do?"

"Find out who all these people are." I waved my hand to indicate the human and canine throngs behind me.

"I'm sure you know most of them, dear." A slight, puzzled frown crossed her face.

"'Most of them' isn't good enough." I explained about the possible threat that Kevin had uncovered.

"Horrible," she murmured. "And I see your point. We need to make sure none of these people have evil designs on our poor helpless little doggies!"

Since the nearest canines at the moment were a brace of shaggy behemoths only slightly smaller than our llamas, I had to suppress a chuckle at the "poor helpless little" part. But she definitely understood the problem.

"Of course, a great many of the people here are well known to us." She surveyed the crowd with an expression of suspicion and distaste she normally reserved for flower beds that had suddenly revealed themselves as afflicted with garlic mustard and Japanese stilt weed. "Volunteers from the Ladies' Interfaith Council and the Garden Club."

"And SPOOR," I reminded her. Stop Poisoning Our Owls and Raptors was the leading local environmental group. "And some of the unfamiliar faces may be new recruits from Blake's Brigades. We need to be careful and not insult any of them."

"Of course, dear," she said. "We don't want to discourage anyone who came to help out of genuine concern for the dogs. But we will be finding out who they all are."

"If you come across any suspicious characters, Kevin can probably help you check them out," I suggested.

She nodded, almost absently. She had pulled out her phone and was studying her contacts list. Then she tapped on the screen, and her face assumed an expression I'd seen all too often—the pleasant yet firm expression she used when about to talk someone into doing something for her.

"Emma, dear," she said. "May I ask you to take on a little project?"

I left her to it and went in search of Ms. Ellie.

I found her in the front yard, inspecting a squadron of dogs dressed in glitter-flecked pink or lavender tutus.

"Can you swap the costumes on those two?" She pointed to two dogs at one end of the line. "I think the pink would look better on the bulldog."

While the humans performed the desired costume change, she turned to me.

"What's wrong, Meg?" she asked.

"Clearly I need a better poker face," I said. "I'm all in favor of the Mutt March, believe me—but it's rather taken over the whole house and yard, and when I went next door to take a much-needed dog-free break—"

"I heard about the dead body they dug up," Ms. Ellie said. "Do they have any idea who it is?"

"Amazing how fast news travels here," I said. "Not yet. They've sent a bone to Grandfather's DNA lab to see what they can find out. And it's not exactly a dead body—just a skeleton, and only part of one, so far. As Dr. McAuslan-Crine reminded us, it's always possible some predator dragged the arm there from someplace else. But that's not what's bothering me. Well, not the only thing."

I quickly outlined Kevin and Clarence's fears that dogfighters might have designs on the Mutt March dogs.

"Horrible," she said, with a shudder. "What's wrong with people, anyway?"

"So is Clarence right that you have an inventory that will let us make sure the dogs he's rounded up are all present and accounted for?" I decided not to ask why nobody had told me about the system—after all, I'd made it pretty clear I wanted someone else to be in charge, for a change.

"Absolutely," she said. "Luckily, I was there when Clarence and Randall presented the Mutt March idea to the town council, and I convinced them that it'd be a disaster unless we had a way to keep track of the dogs. So I created an inventory system. Every time

Clarence gets back to town with another batch of dogs, they're logged into the system." She tapped her iPad for emphasis.

"And you actually got Clarence to do this?" It struck me that no matter how good Ms. Ellie's system was, if it required consistent effort from Clarence, it wasn't likely to succeed.

"Of course not." She chuckled at the thought. "Clarence couldn't organize his way out of a wet paper bag. I enlisted Ezekiel, that new assistant of his. Since he's living in the little apartment over the shelter, Clarence can't possibly bring in any dogs without Ezekiel knowing about it. Ezekiel has been logging in all the dogs—he's quite efficient."

"But how's that system working now that all the dogs are over here?"

"Pretty well. Here, I'll show you. Got a customer here."

A small boy in rather damp clothes, leading a shaggy, wet, medium-sized tan dog had been waiting politely nearby.

"Who's that you've got, Owen?" Ms. Ellie pulled out her iPad and tapped on its screen.

"Fruitcake," Owen said. "Dog number 25297. He's had his bath and Dr. Clarence checked that his fleas are gone."

"Excellent," Ms. Ellie said. "How's he doing? Seem happy?"

"He's doing great." Owen leaned over to hug Fruitcake, who responded by wagging his tail and licking Owen's face. "I think he actually likes baths."

"Good. Can you take him back to Run Thirty-Three? Make a stop at the bathroom area on your way, and you can let me know what if anything he's done there when you come back for your next assignment." She looked over her glasses. "And you don't have to hurry back if you think he or any of the other dogs in the run could use a little petting. Making the dogs happy is also an important part of our job."

"Yes, ma'am." Owen hurried off, with Fruitcake running beside him.

"Fruitcake was picked up as a stray in Pocahontas County, West Virginia, the first week of March," Ms. Ellie said, looking at her iPad. "And arrived in town on Monday. He's fixed, up-to-date in his vaccinations, and pretty good at 'sit' and 'stay.' He'll be marching in an Ewok costume in the Rebel Alliance formation—the *Star Wars* group Josh and Jamie and Adam will be wrangling."

"How come he's dog 25297?" I asked. "I know it feels as if we have at least twenty-five thousand dogs—"

"The first two numbers tell me on which of his trips Clarence picked up each particular dog," she said.

"That's a relief," I said. "But I assume that means we have at least two hundred and ninety-seven dogs to worry about."

"Three hundred and seventy-four, actually," she said. "Fruitcake is one of our more recent arrivals, when we were going a little batty thinking of names for them all. And while I'm not saying we shouldn't worry about someone stealing dogs, we already do have some security. It occurred to me that if someone applied to be approved as an adopter and got rejected, they might show up and try to abscond with a dog. Or some people might resent the whole idea of having to get approved. So, in addition to having the chief assign a deputy or two here, your mother and I enlisted some volunteer help."

She pointed to the spot across the road from our house where a small open-sided picnic tent stood. A sign that read INFORMATION was pinned to one of the top flaps—probably printed by Kevin, who had a curious fondness for the much-maligned Comic Sans typeface. A small table held a scattering of papers, but the tent was deserted except for two gray-haired women in canvas folding chairs, busily knitting. I recognized them as stalwarts from the Ladies' Interfaith Council.

"Are they knitting some kind of record of who's coming and going?" I asked. "Like Madame Defarge in *A Tale of Two Cities*?"

"I'm sure they would if we wanted them to," Ms. Ellie said. "But their main job is to make sure no dogs leave. Only people. And, of course, they can also answer any questions people have."

"I'm reassured," I said.

"But if it would make you feel better, we can do a check on all of the dogs. See where each and every one is right now."

"I'm game if you are," I said. "And you've probably got plenty of other things to do, so I guess it's up to me. Can you print me out a list or something?"

"Don't worry," she said, with a chuckle. "No paper required, and we'll sic the specialists on it." She did something on her phone, then leaned back in her chair.

My son Josh showed up almost immediately, shortly followed by Jamie, his twin, and their best friend, Adam. Each boy had two or three leashes draped around his neck, and I could see Adam stuffing a batch of treats into the pocket of his jeans.

"Remember the missing dog drill?" Ms. Ellie asked.

The boys nodded.

"We've detected a dognapping threat," she went on. "Condition red! Make sure each and every dog is safe!"

"Roger!" Josh saluted as he said it, and all three boys pulled their phones out of their pockets. Josh and Adam dashed off. Jamie went over to check the collars of the tutu-wearing dogs lined up in front of us before following them.

"We've got bar codes on all the dogs' collars," Ms. Ellie said. "They can scan them with their phones and mark them as found in my database. And if there are any dogs they can't immediately locate, we'll track them down with the GPS devices on their collars."

"You put GPS devices on all the dogs? When did that happen?" Maybe I'd been too uninvolved in the Mutt March planning.

"Yesterday," she said. "I decided we'd need them for all the prep work, so I made your grandfather lend me a huge batch of the ones he uses for tracking wildlife. Seemed like a good idea at the time."

"It's a brilliant idea. But what if the dognappers realize what the GPS devices are and take them off the dogs?"

"Then we'll track down the discarded GPS device, and my database will give us a good description of the dog who should be wearing it," she said. "And the chief will put out a BOLO for the dog. And for whoever took it—which we should be able to figure out from Kevin's security cameras. He put up a bunch more this morning—enough to cover the whole yard."

I nodded, and took a step forward so I could look over her shoulder at the database. It was impressive. There were columns showing which shelter or rescue organization the dogs had come from. Columns with their height, weight, and Clarence's best guess as to their ancestry. Columns confirming that they'd been vaccinated and were negative for heartworm and noting whether they'd already been spayed or neutered. Columns tracking where they were in the bathing/grooming/costume-fitting process. A column containing Rose Noire's comments on their auras. Even a column noting when they had last produced a bowel movement. And each entry included a picture of the dog in question—a carefully staged and highly flattering studio-quality picture.

"Impressive," I said.

"So why don't you let me worry about the dogs for a bit?" she said. "Me and the boys. And then you could go back and see how Iris is holding up with all that excitement in her backyard."

"And fill you in while I'm at it."

"I wouldn't object to the occasional update," she said. "And I'll let you know when we've confirmed that all the dogs are safe. Or if we have to raise an alarm to find one."

"Sounds great to me."

Ms. Ellie turned to approve the new configuration of tutus, and I returned to the backyard, which was more than ever a site of frenzied activity. But now, instead of chaos, I saw organization—complicated organization, but still. Structure. Order. Organization.

I'd been so busy for the past two weeks making sure we took care of the physical needs of the steadily growing dog population that I'd missed seeing what Ms. Ellie had been up to. Now I noticed the GPS devices and number tags hanging from the dogs' collars. I realized that two of Ms. Ellie's assistant librarians were also striding about with iPads in hand, and that the dog washers, groomers, and costumers regularly checked in with one or another of them. I saw the boys darting about, checking dogs' tag numbers and tapping things into their phones, with an enthusiasm that suggested they were racing to see who could account for the greatest number of dogs.

And while I still saw the occasional unfamiliar face among the volunteers, nearly everyone I didn't recognize seemed to be engaged in animated conversation with someone I did know. Garden Club members. Members of the Ladies' Interfaith Council. Visiting members of Mother's enormous family. Familiar faces of trusted allies. Mother had deployed her troops.

I watched as Josh darted into one of our two chicken coops and led out a sleepy-looking hound dog who seemed oblivious to the chime of the GPS device on his collar. About then, Adam and Jamie came out of the kitchen, each carrying a brace of beagle puppies, followed by what I presumed was the protective mother beagle.

When Clarence had first asked if he could use our house and yard as the staging area for the Mutt March, I'd been torn. On the one hand, it was a wonderful project, and I wanted to do everything I could to support it. But on the other hand, my schedule was already overloaded. I had blacksmithing commissions to complete. In my job as Mayor Randall Shiffley's executive assistant in charge of special projects, I was overseeing an unusually packed agenda of summer tourism events. And Rob and Delaney had recruited me to be the on-site contact for all the work they were having done at their new house. I had been afraid that if the Mutt March preparations were happening in our backyard, I'd get sucked into organizing all of it. In fact, not just would I get sucked in—I'd be unable to stand aside and watch someone else do a bad job.

Which was why I'd begged Mother to take it on. I knew myself well enough to know I was much better at doing than delegating. Mother was one of the few people to whom I could hand over a project without worrying. With her in charge, I could rest easy that if something wasn't being done exactly the way I'd have done it, it was probably because she'd come up with something better. And when you added Rose Noire, Aida, and Ms. Ellie to the mix . . .

Things were under control here, I decided. I set out on the path through the woods that would lead me back to Delaney and Rob's.

Chapter 7

When I emerged from the woods I glanced over at the dig. Dad and Chief Burke were sitting in lawn chairs just outside the maze of string, with a pitcher of Arnold Palmers and another of plain lemonade set on a small wrought iron table between them. Chief Burke was talking on his cell phone and scribbling in his pocket notebook, but he looked focused rather than stressed, and I deduced that he was managing to have a productive day in spite of the skeleton's discovery. Or at least giving it a good try. Dad was watching the digging with the rapt attention of a dog underfoot at a barbecue. He spotted me and waved.

I strolled closer so I could see for myself how the excavation was going.

"Dr. McAuslan-Crine found the jawbone!" Dad exclaimed. "The teeth could be very helpful in identifying our skeleton."

"The teeth themselves?" I asked. "Or does the skeleton have some kind of unusual dental work?"

"Nothing that unusual in the dental work that I can see," Dad admitted. "Though we're planning to have Dr. Ffollett take a look."

I nodded. Until he'd met Dr. Dwight Ffollett, a neighbor and good friend of Cordelia, my grandmother, Dad had been frustrated that none of the local dentists had shared his passion for the forensic aspects of their profession. Now, when Cordelia wanted to visit us and needed transportation from her home in Riverton, a town in the foothills of the Blue Ridge, Dr. Ffollett would often volunteer to bring her for the fun of getting together with Dad to dissect the dental aspects of recent true-crime cases.

"But our skeleton has definitely had rather a lot of dental work, so if we get a clue to who he might be, his dental records should be useful in establishing his identity. He or she," he added. "Though 'he' is looking more likely all the time. We'll know for sure when we can see the whole of the pelvic bone."

"I'm working on it," the grad student growled.

"It's okay," Dad said. "We're not impatient."

"Yes, we are," Dr. McAuslan-Crine said. "But we'll have to live with our impatience. Just ignore us."

I glanced down at where the professor was gently brushing dirt away from the jawbone. Yes, our bony visitor had undoubtedly had a lot of dental work. The silvery gray of the fillings was almost more prominent than the enamel of the teeth themselves.

"Wow," I said. "You're not kidding. Someone should have flossed more."

"I've dug up Civil War–era skeletons with better teeth," Dr. McAuslan-Crine said. "But those amalgam fillings will help us figure out how long this one's been here."

"Amalgam fillings aren't that new, are they?" I asked.

"Good heavens, no," she said. "The Chinese were using them in the Tang dynasty—in the six hundreds. And their use has been documented in Germany in the fifteen hundreds. But they've fallen out of favor here in the twenty-first century, because of the mercury content. I'm not saying you don't sometimes see someone nowadays with that much amalgam in their mouth, but if you do, it's usually older fillings. In an older person. And you can clearly see a couple of places where these fillings are relatively new—not much wear." She pulled out her little laser pointer and highlighted a couple of the fillings in question. "So I'm betting our subject took his last breath in the nineties. Maybe even the eighties. Even by the nineties, the tide had started turning against amalgam fillings."

She focused back on her digging and we all fell silent.

I glanced back at the house. Iris was sitting in her rocking chair on the screened porch, watching the digging through her vintage Zeiss binoculars. She waved and beckoned me over, so I joined her.

"How's it going?" she asked. "Anything exciting?"

"They found the jawbone," I said.

"You call that exciting?"

"It could go a long way to help identify the skeleton."

"Not very entertaining, though." She shook her head and snorted in derision. "Like watching paint dry. I have to say, I can't recommend archaeology as a spectator sport."

I was tempted to say that after the excitement of the Mutt March preparations, watching paint dry sounded heavenly to me. But just then Dad stood up abruptly and stepped forward until he was pressing against the outermost line of string. The chief kept his seat but leaned forward intently. They weren't focused on where Dr. McAuslan-Crine was working, but at the other end of the excavation, where Horace had been digging.

"Hot damn," Iris said. "Looks like something's finally happening."

"They haven't done that before?"

She shook her head, and raised her binoculars to her eyes.

"Horace is taking a lot of photos of something," she said. "Can't tell what."

I nodded, and sipped my Arnold Palmer.

"It's definitely interesting, whatever they found," Iris said. "Maybe you should go back and take a closer look."

"And come back and fill you in," I said. "Can do."

So I set down my glass and strolled down to the dig site. When I was halfway there, I got the text I'd been hoping for—Ms. Ellie, letting me know that all the dogs were present and accounted for. I thanked her and felt a moment of relief that I could stop fretting about the dogs. At least for now. I continued on to where Dad and the chief had been joined by Vern Shiffley. They were all on their feet and staring down at . . . something.

"What's up?" I asked when I drew near.

"We found a shoe," Horace said. "At least the remnants of a shoe."

He pointed to where he'd been digging. I made out what appeared to be the back half of a shoe sole, sticking out of the ground. It was red and white, the white parts looking faded and grungy, but the red parts vivid against the black soil.

"Way too modern for me to have any expertise on it," Dr. McAuslan-Crine said. "In the movies they're always identifying what kind of shoe the criminal was wearing from footprints—is that something you can actually do in real life?"

"Well, it's not as easy as they make it look in the movies," Horace said. "But a lot of times it is possible. There are databases of sole- and tire-tread impressions you can use. Not sure how far back they go, though." He frowned, took a few more pictures of the half-excavated sole, and resumed his slow, meticulous work, removing dirt from around the sole by the teaspoonful.

"If this one's not in your database, get in touch with the Nike company," Vern said. "Because I'd bet a week's pay that's an Air Jordan. One of the early ones, from the late 1980s."

"I didn't know you were a sole impression expert." Horace sounded a little annoyed, as if resenting Vern's intrusion into his domain.

"I'm not." Vern shrugged. "I pay close attention to footprints when I'm tracking someone, but matching them to the shoe that made them? That's your baby. Only this particular sole... it looks just like the sole of a shoe I spent months coveting, back in junior high. One of those early Air Jordans. Red, black, and white, with that Jumpman logo—you know, the one that looks like a silhouette of Jordan going up for a dunk. All the cool kids were wearing them. I made such a fuss over them that for once my parents had no trouble figuring out what to get me for Christmas. First time I put them on, I could have sworn they made me a foot taller. Yeah. Air Jordans."

Horace studied Vern's intent face, then nodded slightly.

"Good to know," he said. "You can take another look when I've fully excavated it. See if it still looks familiar."

"Happy to." Vern didn't look all that happy. He looked distracted and worried.

"What's up?" the chief asked. "Dr. Blake drive you crazy when you took him over to his lab?"

"No, that went fine," Vern said. "He told me all about the sex life of his naked mole rats on the way, but it was kind of interesting. I came back here because one of his scientists wants some samples of the soil from around where we found the bone. They want to analyze its chemistry and see what that tells them about the age of the bones. They tried to explain the process for collecting it, but I told them not to try teaching this old dog new tricks— I'd get Horace to do it."

"No problem." Horace stood, dusted off his pants, and trotted over to his forensic kit. He pulled out a handful of test tubes and returned to the skeleton. It was starting to look more like a skeleton instead of just a single arm. The grad student had made good progress on where the torso had been—I could see ribs and a bit of spine. And under Dr. McAuslan-Crine's deft hands, the skull was beginning to appear.

Although something about the way the skull was positioned in relation to the hand made it look as if the skeleton was thumbing his nose at us. I hoped that wasn't an omen.

After a discussion with the professor about where the samples should be taken, Horace filled half a dozen test tubes with small amounts of dirt. He labeled them, tucked them all in a brown paper evidence bag, and handed the bag to Vern with a flourish.

"I'll run these right over to Dr. Blake," Vern said.

"And then get some shut-eye," the chief replied. "Or have you forgotten your shift ended two hours ago?"

"Yeah," Vern said. "But I didn't want to just vanish if this turned out to be a homicide and there was anything you wanted me to do."

"If it's a homicide, it's a pretty cold one," the chief said. "I think we can afford to give you enough time to get some sleep. And a meal, if you haven't bothered with that."

"I'll be fine," Vern said. Which the chief and I both knew meant he hadn't eaten all that recently—if he had, he'd have reassured us by mentioning when and what.

"You can drop by our house for the meal," I said. "Mother had food brought in for all the volunteers. From the Shack," I added, by way of inducement. Few people turned up their noses at the barbecue Vern's cousins dished up at the Shack.

"I couldn't eat up all your food when I haven't yet lifted a finger to help with the march," Vern protested.

"You can help, then, while you're there, and in a way not many people can, just by being there and taking a brief stroll through the crowd." I explained—briefly—the possible threat to the dogs. "So before you pack yourself a doggie bag, check in with Mother. If her troops have identified any suspicious persons, she can point them out and you can glower threateningly at them. Even if she hasn't, you could just inspect the premises with a stern look on your face. Between that and your uniform, it might be enough to scare off anyone with sinister designs on the dogs."

"Now that I can do, and gladly," Vern said. "Although if they're more scared of me than Aida, they must not be from around here. The only thing I have a black belt in is sarcasm."

"A lot of out-of-towners there," the chief said. "So go make yourself useful, and then get some rest. We could be in for a lot of work on this, whether or not it's a homicide. But we can afford to pace ourselves. It's not as if we have a crazed killer on the loose in town."

"Or if we do," I added, "he's probably slowed down considerably in the thirty to forty years since our friend here met his end."

The chief chuckled and nodded at that.

"Roger." Vern nodded and touched his temple in a casual salute, then turned and headed toward his parked cruiser. But before he'd gone too far, Iris waved and called to him. He obligingly changed course toward her, and I followed. I figured it was time to brief Iris anyway.

"What'd they find?" Iris demanded.

Chapter 8

"Horace dug up part of a shoe," Vern said.

"The sole," I added. "Looked to me as if the leather and cloth parts of the shoe—all the organic parts—have rotted away."

"Not going to be much help, then," she said. "In identifying him, that is."

"No, ma'am," Vern said. "Good thing we've got Dr. Blake and his DNA lab on the case for that."

"Dr. Blake and his DNA lab?" Iris cocked her head. "But there's nothing left except the skeleton."

"I gather they can work with bones these days," Vern said.

"Really?" Iris frowned, and glanced over at me.

I nodded.

"That's unsettling," she said. "It's like there's no privacy anywhere anymore. I had this crazy cousin who saved all her shed hairs and fingernail parings. At least we thought she was crazy. Maybe she was just ahead of her time. Can they get DNA from hair and fingernails?"

"I think for hair you need a root," I said. "And Grandfather's lab can definitely get DNA from fingernails, but I gather it's complicated. Takes more time."

"Even more time than regular DNA?" She chuckled. "I hope I live to see the results on our skeleton. Takes months, doesn't it?"

"Not anymore," I said. "If you can hang on till this afternoon, we should hear something by then. Grandfather's lab is one of the places that has developed fast DNA technology. It doesn't give you the full human genome, but it's enough to see if someone's a match in CODIS—the FBI's DNA database."

"And that's a real boon for law enforcement," Vern said. "Say we pick someone up for a relatively minor offense, something he's bound to get bail on, but we think maybe he might be good for a more serious beef. With Dr. Blake's fast DNA system, Horace can tell us if our dude is in CODIS before we have to let him out on bail. But I doubt if we'll find this guy in CODIS."

"Why not?" Iris asked. "Just because he's a victim of this crime doesn't mean he might not have committed others."

"CODIS wasn't around at all in the 1980s," Vern said. "The pilot program didn't start till 1990, and they didn't implement it on a national basis until 1998. And it's got, like, fifteen or twenty million profiles now, but it didn't start out that way. If our skeleton's toward the short end of that thirty- to forty-year estimate, we might find him there. The older he is, the less chance CODIS has him. We'd have to resort to forensic genealogy, and that can take a lot of time."

Iris nodded, but she still looked troubled.

"DNA's causing a lot of problems for people," she said. "Adopted people finding birth parents who may or may not want to hear from them. People finding out one or both of the people who raised them aren't their biological parents after all."

"But it's also starting to let people know about stuff that could affect their health," Vern pointed out.

"Not to mention catching a lot more crooks who used to get away with murder," I said. "Quite literally."

"And you should see the work they're doing on John and Jane Does," Vern said. "Hardly a week passes without news that Dr. Blake's lab or similar places like Othram and Parabon Nanolabs have given some poor soul back their name. Seems to me it's mostly to the good. At least for everyone but criminals."

Iris nodded. She frowned and glanced over her shoulder at the door to her suite. Was she worried about what Eileen was up to there? Or—

"Mom?" Eileen came to the doorway. "Mary Catherine wants to talk to you. She's on the landline."

"Right." Iris sprang up with enviable agility and went into the house. Was it just my imagination or was she relieved to have an excuse to end our conversation?

"Tell her I had to take off." Vern ambled down the steps and turned toward his car again. But his steps were dragging. And his face looked . . . no, not just thoughtful. Anxious. Downright worried.

I fell into step beside him.

"You look troubled," I said. "Something wrong?"

He frowned. He stopped, turned back to look at the dig site, and didn't say anything at first. I waited him out.

"It's those shoes," he said finally.

"The ones they found with the skeleton?"

"Yes." He frowned. "Air Jordans. Basketball shoes."

"Not just for basketball," I said. "I think everyone and his brother was wearing those in the nineties."

"Everyone and his brother and maybe even his sister," Vern agreed. "But Air Jordans—makes you think of basketball. And makes me wonder if maybe our skeleton could be Billy Taylor."

"The name doesn't ring a bell," I said.

"No reason it should," Vern said. "He left town long before you moved here. Nearly forty years ago. At least, that's what I thought had happened. What if he didn't leave town after all? What if that's him?"

"Any reason why it should be?"

"Because I haven't heard word one from him since he left," Vern said. "And I'd have thought I would have if anyone did."

"Okay," I said. "Just who was—is—this Billy Taylor?"

"Local high school basketball hero," Vern said. "Two years older than me. He wasn't NBA tall—not even back then, when they had fewer seven-footers. Only maybe six-three or so. But he might have gotten a college scholarship. He was a great player. Fast, good ball handler, really aggressive. And pretty good at trash-talking, too, which was what got him in trouble."

"You think trash-talking got him killed?" It didn't sound all that plausible to me.

"We were playing Clay County High one week," Vern said. "By 'we' I don't mean I actually did much playing—I was only fifteen, and a sophomore, so I mostly sat on the bench. But even if I didn't play more than five minutes, I loved watching Billy play. Learned a lot from him, too—he was always great at helping the younger players. And in spite of him being a senior and the team big shot, I really think he considered me a friend."

"Sounds like a good guy," I said,

"Clay County folks hated him, though. Bad enough that we beat them, but beating them with a star player who was Black? And was really good at telling them exactly how bad they were? That did *not* go down well over there back then."

"Yikes," I said. "Yeah, not sure it would go down all that well today, over in Clay County. What happened?"

"Well, nothing much at the game," Vern said. "Maybe a little more shoving than usual on the court, with the Clay County refs pretending they didn't see anything. And some rude words shouted, of course. Someone should sit down and explain to those jackasses that their side lost the Civil War. Things didn't get bad until the day after the game. They tried to frame Billy."

"Frame him how?"

"One of the Clay County players reported his brand-new Harley missing," Vern said. "Only it wasn't missing—he and some of his friends hid it in the shed behind Billy's grandma's house. Billy lived with his grandma—his mama died when he was born, and as far as I know, old Mrs. Taylor was his only living relative. And then whoever hid the bike called in a tip to the Caerphilly police."

"And this would have been before Chief Burke's time," I said.

"Back when the Pruitts were running things." Vern's scornful tone of voice told me what he thought of the Pruitts—a family who had arrived in Caerphilly as carpetbaggers in the 1870s and proceeded to run the town as their personal fiefdom for more than a century. "The mayor was a Pruitt, and the chief of police was either a Pruitt or married to one, or maybe just thick as thieves with them, I forget which. They sent out a couple of cops to search the grandmother's house and yard."

"Where they found the planted motorcycle in the shed?" I asked.

"And not just the motorcycle," Vern said. "The jerks also planted a big stash of cocaine in the saddlebags. Or maybe they just forgot they'd left it there. Billy was well and truly ruined. He'd have had a hard time getting off even here in Caerphilly, where most everyone knew he was a good kid, hardworking, with pretty much straight A's since grade school. Over in Clay County?" He shook his head and snorted.

"You said you thought he'd left town," I said. "He got bail and vanished?"

"He wasn't eligible for bail here in Caerphilly," Vern said. "They picked him up on Clay County's warrant and locked him up, planning to hand him over in the morning. And fat chance of getting bail over there. More likely bad things would have happened."

"So how did he manage to leave town?" I asked.

"My late uncle Rollie was on the force then," Vern said. "He didn't last long, on account of not being good at keeping his mouth shut when he saw something scummy and illegal going on. At the time, he was assigned to jail duty, mostly because no one else wanted to do it. He came home from his shift and was really down at the mouth because he knew Billy was a good kid and there wasn't a thing he could do to rescue him."

Vern fell silent. After a minute or so, I prodded him.

"So what happened?"

"I stole my uncle's keys and his car and let Billy out," Vern said.

"Seriously?"

"Seriously. Security at the jail was a joke back then. I went down there around midnight. No one paid any attention to me—the guy on duty was fast asleep. I let Billy out and then I drove him down to Richmond."

"You drove him down to Richmond?" I said. "I thought you said you were only fifteen."

"Yes, so all I had was my learner's permit," he said. "But I'd been driving tractors since I was in grade school, and I was already tall enough to get away with it, as long as I didn't do anything to get stopped and have the cop ask for my license. I dropped Billy off at the Greyhound bus station with enough money to buy a ticket to anyplace in the country. Told him not to tell me where he was going, so I couldn't let it slip if they interrogated me. Which never happened. I think my uncle figured out it was me who'd done it, but the rest of them never had a clue."

"A good deed," I said.

"Yeah. I was hoping maybe he'd drop me a line when he got settled, but I wasn't mad that he didn't. Figured maybe he was still worried about what would happen if they caught up with him."

"Or maybe he didn't have your address," I suggested.

"Could be," he said. "I thought of that, figured maybe I should have tucked a slip of paper with my address into his duffel bag.

Because I didn't just drop him there on the sidewalk without even a spare pair of socks. I went by his gran's house earlier that day, told her what I was going to do, and she packed the duffel bag for him."

"You could have asked his grandmother," I suggested. "Not where he was, just whether she'd heard that he was safe."

"I did, once or twice," he said. "She said she hadn't heard from him. Never could figure out if that was true or not. Decided it was more likely she just didn't want to tell me, in case I leaked it. And then she died, about a year after he left, and there was no one around to ask."

He fell silent and we both stood there for a few minutes, watching the slow, methodical digging.

"I always wondered what happened to him," Vern said eventually. "Smart kid. Straight A's. He and his gran were hoping he could use his basketball to get a scholarship to a good college. When I thought about what happened to him, the worst thing I'd worried about was that maybe he hadn't been able to pull it off—going to college and making something of his life. It made me sad, thinking that maybe he was stuck in some dead-end job or something. I never thought anything like that could have happened to him."

He nodded toward the dig site.

"What if they followed us to Richmond and dragged him back?" he said. "Or what if he came back to see his gran and got caught? To end up like that—"

"You don't know that it's him," I said. "Could be someone else entirely."

"Hope so." He sighed.

"Have you told the chief?" I asked.

"Only that Billy was someone who disappeared back then," he said. "Not the whole story. Just enough for him to know why I'm worried."

"He'll keep you posted, then."

"Horace says they can't figure out how tall the skeleton was till they finish digging up the leg bones," Vern said. "At least I think that's what the femur, fibula, and tibia are."

"Yeah, those are the major leg bones," I said.

"Sure hope our guy turns out to be well under six feet," Vern said. "So I'll know it can't be Billy. Well, those dognappers aren't going to scare themselves. I should be going."

"Get some rest," I said. "And give Elvis a pat for me."

Vern's expression lightened at the thought that his beloved Redbone Coonhound would be waiting to greet him at home. Normally, when he was on duty, he dropped Elvis off at what he called our doggie day care, to play with the resident and visiting dogs. But we'd all decided that with so many unfamiliar dogs running around, things would be too exciting for the usual arrangement, so Elvis had probably spent a slightly lonely day and would be overjoyed when his human got home.

"Be seeing you," Vern said, and then strode toward his cruiser with something more like his usual energy.

I stood for a few minutes, pondering what Vern had told me. Under ordinary circumstances, I'd probably be dashing off to the library by now to see what else I could find out about Billy Taylor's disappearance, since the library had decades of back issues of the *Caerphilly Clarion* on microfilm. But circumstances today weren't ordinary. What if—

Just then something caught my eye. A large cardboard box had appeared on Rob and Delaney's front porch. From the brand name on the box I deduced that it had originally held either paper towels or toilet paper.

I stood and stared at it for a minute or so. Under ordinary circumstances, I'd just assume someone had dropped off another housewarming present, but with a skeleton in the back yard and threats of dognappers back at my house, the box seemed to take on a menacing aura. Should I notify Chief Burke? Get him to call out the bomb squad to investigate the suspicious package? Of course, since Caerphilly didn't have an official bomb squad, that would probably mean calling in the state police—unless one of the deputies had ambitions to become a demolitions expert. I could see Horace and Vern getting fired up for that.

I decided to take a closer look at the box myself before sounding the alarm. And it wouldn't be hard to check it out—I could see that the top flaps were loosely closed, so I could probably peer in. Or maybe get a long stick and flip them open from a distance.

As I drew closer, I realized that the box was quacking. I relaxed just a little. I'd heard of bombs ticking, but not quacking. I sidled closer to the box and peered in.

It was full of ducks.

Chapter 9

I gazed down at the ducks. Two of them. They were beige and white, and rather oddly shaped for ducks—long and skinny rather than plump. Perhaps they were malnourished?

They quacked with greater enthusiasm when they detected my presence. Perhaps they thought I was there to rescue them from the box.

"All in good time," I told them. I pulled out my phone. A quick online search for "duck breeds" produced a useful chart featuring pictures of more than a dozen ducks. Aha! The ducks in the box were almost certainly Indian Runner ducks. Prolific egg layers who stood more upright than other ducks, and ran rather than waddled. Fascinating. But it didn't explain what they were doing on Rob and Delaney's porch.

Maybe someone intended to surrender them to the shelter in time for the Mutt March and had gotten confused about where we were keeping all the animals. Unlikely—they'd have had to pass our house to get here, and what were the odds they hadn't noticed the chaos and commotion in our yard? And however suspicious I was of the possible dognappers, I couldn't figure out a way to blame them for the stealth duck infestation.

More likely whoever Rob and Delaney were planning to get their ducks from had decided to deliver them early. Yes, that was probably it. As I headed for the backyard, I called Rob. I'd let him tell the original owner of the ducks that we had nowhere to keep them yet.

"What's up?" he said. "Found any more skeletons in our backyard?"

"Just the one so far," I said. "Your ducks are here."

"Our ducks?" He sounded puzzled. "Ragnar's supposed to deliver them once the pond is ready."

"Well, it looks as if he jumped the gun. They're here."

"Bother," he said. "Look, is he still there? Can you ask him to take them back for another few days?"

"I didn't see him," I said. "I just found them in a box on your front porch. And come to think of it—you're getting your ducks from Ragnar?"

"Yes," he said. "He has Cayuga ducks."

"Let me guess," I said. "They're black."

"Of course."

Ragnar, a retired heavy metal drummer, was spending the fortune he'd earned during his career on turning his already imposing house into a castle, complete with turrets and a moat. His dedication to the Goth aesthetic was so profound that he wanted only black animals on his farm. He sometimes tolerated animals with dark-gray fur or feathers. Nothing like the ducks on their porch.

"They even lay black eggs," Rob was saying.

"I don't think these ducks came from Ragnar. They're not black."

"Dark gray?" Rob sounded hopeful.

"Beige and white." I turned and headed back to the front yard. "Maybe that's why Ragnar was giving them to you? Because he somehow acquired some ducks that didn't fit into his color scheme?"

"No way," Rob said. "He knows we want black ducks. Are you sure?"

"That they're beige and white?" I said. "Pretty sure. I'll send you a picture."

I lifted one of the box flaps and held my phone out to take a picture. Then I noticed something.

"Uh-oh," I said. "They're multiplying."

"They tend to do that," Rob said, with a snicker. "The birds and the bees, you know."

"Not this fast." I snapped a picture of the ducks. "A few minutes ago there were two of them. Now there are four. All full grown, and definitely not black," I added, as I texted him the picture.

"No," Rob said. "And I'm sure they're very nice ducks, but we want Cayugas."

"These are Indian Runners," I said. "They seem like very interesting ducks. Prolific egg layers. Often referred to as 'penguin ducks' because of their upright posture. And—"

"They're not Cayugas." Rob could be stubborn.

I sighed as I stared down at the ducks. Was someone trying to perform a good deed for Rob and Delaney by giving them some ducks? Should I tell Rob not to look a gift duck in the bill? Or was someone trying to offload unwanted ducks by dumping them here? But why would they dump them here, rather than give them to a local farmer?

"Maybe you could just take them over to the Mutt March," Rob suggested. "You're including a limited number of non-dogs, right?"

"We can't do that until we find out who owns them," I said. "What if someone stole them and dumped them here to avoid being caught with them?"

"So they might be hot ducks?" Rob was snickering at the idea.

"And you've been the victim of a drive-by ducking," I said. "Look, I'm going to get Clarence to look at them. He's the only vet in town—if they came from someone local, he'll know who it could be. And if we don't find out who owns them before the Mutt March starts, the shelter can keep them until we do."

Although, given how busy Clarence and the shelter were at the moment, I wondered if we wouldn't end up fostering them for the time being. I'd worry about that later.

And another idea occurred to me. What if the ducks weren't intended for Rob and Delaney, but for Iris? One of her friends might have heard about the planned duck pond and decided to give her the Indian Runners, since she'd have a place to keep them.

It didn't sound all that plausible, but it was worth asking.

I returned to the porch. Iris and Eileen were still inside Iris's suite. Should I interrupt them or wait until they came out? I still had half a glass of my Arnold Palmer there. I'd sip that, and tell Clarence about the ducks. If Iris and Eileen hadn't emerged by the time I'd finished that, I could knock on the door.

I realized that I was enjoying the small mystery of the ducks. And dealing with it would give me a break from the Mutt March preparations. I'd put in a full day there yesterday, though at least it hadn't been as draining as if I'd been in charge, thank goodness. Mostly washing dogs so filthy that it took two or three tubs of water to get them even close to clean. But we had more volunteers today. Surely they could do without me for at least part of the day.

I called Clarence.

"What's up, Meg?"

"Were you expecting someone to drop off a batch of Indian Runner ducks for the March?" I asked.

"Indian Runner ducks? No. Why?"

I explained about the sudden appearance of the ducks on Rob and Delaney's front porch.

"I'll come over to check them out this instant," Clarence said, before I was even halfway through my explanation. I was trying to decide whether to meet him on the front porch or detour out to the dig site to see what was happening there when I overheard a scrap of conversation from inside.

"I don't see why you have to make such a big deal about it!" Iris exclaimed.

Iris sounded—angry? Or was it anxious? Either way, call me nosy, but I wanted to find out what had set her off.

"It's just silly," Eileen was saying. "I can't imagine Rob and Delaney would mind if you kept the stuff here until we finished dealing with it. Even if they're planning on having enough kids to fill up all the bedrooms, they've only got the one now. You should just shove all our stuff in one of the unused bedrooms and—"

"That would be imposing," Iris said. "Taking advantage."

I smiled. From Iris's point of view, Eileen and her siblings had already had their chance to deal with the contents of the house. Before handing over the house to Delaney and Rob, Iris had chivvied her three children and her one adult grandchild to come down and take anything and everything they wanted. And then, with Mother's help, she'd sorted what was left. She'd rented a storage unit a few miles down the road at the Spare Attic to hold what she and Mother defined as "the good stuff," with the idea of giving her children one last chance to claim it before holding a big estate sale. And the bulk of what she no longer needed had gone to various local charities.

But I suspected Eileen's discontent was less with either the cost of moving the stuff to a storage unit or the inconvenience of going out there if she wanted to take yet another look at what her mother planned to get rid of. I suspected she was having a hard time accepting how suddenly and completely the house she'd grown up in had been emptied out and turned over to people who were, to her, comparative strangers.

And I found it ironic that Eileen was so gung-ho on storing Iris's surplus possessions in one of Rob and Delaney's spare bedrooms and yet so stubbornly resistant to accepting their offer to stay in one of those same bedrooms when she came down for a visit to her mother. And her brother, Sam, was the same way, always staying either at the Caerphilly Inn or in one of the local bed-and-breakfasts. Mary Catherine, the nun, hadn't been down in the few months since the change of ownership. It would be interesting to see if her vow of poverty made her more willing to accept a free room.

I wondered, briefly, if we should offer Eileen the use of one of the inflatable beds we kept for times when we had an unusually large number of houseguests. She could set it up in Iris's suite, which was completely separate from the rest of the house, accessible only through the door that led out onto the back porch. I'd offer it the next time she came—especially if it was during a time when the Caerphilly Inn was fully booked.

Then again, given the way they alternated congenial coexistence with affectionate but fierce squabbling, maybe being able to get away from each other at the end of the day might make for a more enjoyable visit for both.

Just then Clarence popped out of the woods, heading for the front yard. I waved at him, but decided to stay put to do a little more eavesdropping.

"You're welcome to go down to the Spare Attic and take anything you've a mind to," Iris was saying. "It's all stuff you've already turned up your nose at or said you didn't have room for, but suit yourself. I can hang on to the unit as long as you like."

"That's not the point," Eileen said.

My phone dinged. I glanced down to see a message from Clarence.

"Can you come to the front porch? Now?"

Chapter 10

The "now" made Clarence's message sound rather urgent. I texted back "OK" and stood up. Probably a good thing to make myself scarce. Eileen sounded annoyed. She'd never been anything but gracious, but I suspected at moments like this she'd probably consider me part and parcel of the interlopers who had taken over her childhood home. I'd give her and Iris some time and space to work it out.

So I headed for the front yard.

Clarence was standing on the front porch, talking to a woman dressed in lavender pants and a matching top—probably some kind of expensive athleisurewear. I recognized her as a resident of Westlake, Caerphilly's one irredeemably snooty suburb. I couldn't remember her name off the top of my head. Maybe that was my subconscious trying to protect me. Over the years, in my role as special assistant to the mayor, I'd certainly fielded plenty of her complaints against her neighbors—cranky, entitled, and utterly bogus complaints.

"What's going on here?" I asked.

"I found her putting more ducks in the box," Clarence said,

"Just dropping off a few ducks for your brother," she said, with a determined smile. "I heard he was looking for some."

"Whose ducks are they?" I asked. "How do I know you didn't steal them?"

"Good heavens," she said. "They're our ducks."

"I've never seen them in my office," Clarence said. "Who's your vet?"

"Why would I need a vet for a bunch of stupid ducks?" the woman asked.

"What would you need a vet—" Clarence began.

"Now, now," I said. "Let her talk."

"Thank you," the woman said. From her expression, she seemed to be mistaking me for an ally. "My stupid aunt gave the kids a pair of ducklings for Easter last year, and they were cute as the dickens for a while, with their fluffy little pink-and-blue feathers—"

"Dyeing their feathers is so bad for the chicks!" Clarence exclaimed.

"But then they grew up," the woman went on. "And they started breeding and we just can't keep them anymore. So I thought since your brother had a duck pond . . ."

"May have a duck pond," I said. "Right now the construction's on indefinite hold. What are we supposed to do with them in the meantime?"

"Oh, please, can't you just take them?" The woman had tears in her eyes. "Our nice backyard is just covered with duck poop, and they chase my children—my youngest has nightmares about them. Even the older children don't want them around anymore, but they get upset at the idea of taking them to a farmer who would just eat them—"

"Nonsense. They're egg ducks, not meat ducks." I made it sound as if I were an authority on domestic waterfowl, rather than someone who had just learned this interesting fact on the internet. "They'd be in no danger. I tell you what—how about if you surrender them to the shelter and we can put them up for adoption during the Mutt March?"

The speed with which she accepted this plan spoke volumes about how eager she was to get rid of the poor ducks. I wondered if she'd tried unsuccessfully to give them away to other people. Probably not surprising she'd failed, since with all her babble about poop and chasing children, she certainly had no idea how to sell potential adopters on the joys of duck ownership.

"We can certainly take care of them." Clarence's tone was uncharacteristically stern. "And we should have no trouble finding homes for them. In fact, I'll pass the word along to a couple of farmers who might be interested."

"Is this all of them?" I asked, glancing into the box, where the duck population had grown to six.

"I have a few more in my car," she said. "I parked out of sight," she added, waving in what I assumed was the general direction of her car.

"Let's take these back to your car, then," Clarence said. "And we can drive them all over to Meg's house, where we're set up to take care of them."

Actually, I wasn't sure we were set up to care for ducks back at the house, but I had every confidence that we could be once Clarence put his mind to it. He picked up the huge box with ease, and as they headed off I heard him begin to lecture her about responsibly releasing unwanted animals to the shelter rather than dumping them on unsuspecting bystanders or, worse, releasing them into the wild.

I found a quiet corner and called Rob.

"So are we still infested with bland, beige ducks?" Rob asked.

"No," I said. "I located the owner, and she's happy to release them to the shelter. Clarence already has plans to call several farmers who might be interested in taking them. Egg farmers," I added, knowing that Rob was softhearted enough that he'd probably worry otherwise, even about a flock of bland, beige ducks he'd never met.

"Great," he said. "Thanks for doing that. Not sure what Delaney would have done if we'd come home and found them."

And of course it would have been Delaney who figured out how to cope with the ducks.

"No problem," I said, and we both hung up.

I decided to see what had been happening at the dig site while I'd been dealing with the ducks.

"How's the Mutt March going?" the chief asked when I came near.

"A lot like yesterday," I said. "At least the last time I was over there. So if there's anything useful I can do to help out with this, don't hesitate to ask."

"I'll keep that in mind," he said, with a chuckle. And then his face became serious again. "I shouldn't be sitting here myself. Horace and the professor don't need my supervision."

"You seem to be getting a few things done while you're here," I said. "And wasn't this originally supposed to be your day off? A respite before the chaos of the weekend?"

"Plans change," he said. "I was going to spend today finishing that budget report I should already have submitted to the town council. I've actually managed a few minutes' work on that, in between phone calls with nearby sheriffs and police chiefs about this dognapping threat. And even if I didn't have all that hanging over me, I've been shirking the one thing I probably need to do to tackle this case properly—whether it turns out to be a murder or just a John or Jane Doe. Something I'd feel a lot happier if I'd gotten it done years ago."

Years ago? Now my curiosity was aroused. I'd always found Henry Burke to be an efficient, no-nonsense person who got things done. Was he about to reveal a guilty secret—a hidden Achilles' heel?

"So what is it?" I asked. "And is it something I could help with?"

"Dangerous words," he said. "I just might take you up on that. What I really ought to be doing is going through our old files to see if we have any missing person cases that might possibly account for our skeleton."

"I can see that," I said, nodding. "Tedious work, but potentially useful."

"It's not the tedium," he said. "Or if it was, I could get some deputies to help with it. But before anyone can go through our files, I have to organize them. And that's something I've been procrastinating on for years."

"Seriously?" I asked. "Because I always thought of you as someone who probably keeps pretty well-organized files."

"I do," he said. "My personal files, and the department's files since I came on board, are in pretty darn good shape. But I seem to be the first chief of police here who can say that. Before I came, whenever any of their file cabinets got too full, they'd box up the oldest stuff and shove it into the attic."

"Oh, no," I murmured.

"Maybe I should be glad we have that big attic over the station," he said, "or they'd have thrown it all out. But all the stuff from thirty to forty years ago is up there, shoved into whatever corner they could find, along with boxes and boxes of files going back to the Reconstruction era. Hundreds of boxes. Maybe more than a thousand. There isn't even enough room to step inside the attic, much less rummage around to find things."

"When I have a project like that, I try to nibble on it," I said. "Forget the hundreds and hundreds of boxes. Just take one, and organize that. No deadline, no pressure. Just focus on that one."

"I try that every so often." He sighed. "In fact, I made a New Year's resolution to do just that. Start with one box. I mean, how hard can it be to go through and organize one box? And then see if I can keep it going. Do one box a week, or at least one a month."

"How long did that last?" I asked.

"Box one is still sitting in a corner of my office."

"Ouch."

"A year and a half later. And the attic's still a disaster."

"You need help," I said. "You didn't create the disaster all by yourself. You can't expect to dig your way out without help. If you've got a hundred and fifty years' worth of files, dozens of people helped create the disaster."

"I can't expect my deputies to help out," the chief protested. "We're shorthanded as it is. Especially now, when the tourist season's really getting underway."

"And organizing paper isn't necessarily their forte anyway," I said. "But I can think of people who are brilliant at it, and would be willing to pitch in to help."

"I can't let just anyone have access to the police files." He was shaking his head.

"I wouldn't ask just anyone to help with this," I said. "I'm thinking of reliable people. Some of them are already Caerphilly employees—like Ms. Ellie Draper."

"She would be good at it," he admitted. "And she's trustworthy."

"I'll come up with a list of possible trustworthy volunteers, and you can vet every one of them, and maybe swear them in as temporary deputies or whatever you do when we have an emergency."

He nodded. He was looking less stressed.

"And let's enlist Randall," I suggested. "If part of the problem is that there's no room left to maneuver in the attic, I bet he can find a space big enough to spread out the boxes, and some workmen to haul them over there—under police supervision, of course."

"And then we triage it all," the chief said, with a note of enthusiasm in his voice. "We rough-sort them by decade, and then I can find the files I need to try to identify our skeleton and start with them." Then his face fell slightly. "Of course, we probably can't get started until the Mutt March is over."

"We can ask Randall and Ms. Ellie to start thinking about it," I said. "And be ready to start as soon as we've recovered from the Mutt March."

"And while I am impatient to identify our John or Jane Doe—"

"Why don't we use something unisex, like Jan Doe?" I said. "Or maybe just J. Doe?"

"That makes sense," the chief said. "And luckily it's unlikely that identifying Jan Doe will be a matter of urgency."

"Don't say that!" I exclaimed. "You probably just jinxed us. Now whoever killed poor Jan will hear that we've found the body and come back to continue his leisurely but deadly crime spree."

"Seems unlikely," he said, with a chuckle. "But I'll refrain from statements that might jinx us."

"And I'll start planning for the great file-sorting festival. What if—"

"Chief! We've found something!" Dad shouted.

Chapter 11

We glanced up to see that Dad was squatting down beside where Dr. McAuslan-Crine had been excavating the skull. Horace and the grad student were also clustered around the spot.

"Something useful, I assume." The chief stood and began picking his way through the web of string toward where they were gathered. I followed, a little tentatively, half expecting someone to order me to stay away. But no one did, and the chief and I joined the circle around the professor's excavation.

"It looks as if this isn't a natural death." Dad's voice revealed a mixture of excitement and apology. Excitement because, in addition to being the medical examiner, he was also an avid reader of crime fiction, and was never happier than when he could get involved in a real-life murder. And regret because he knew how much hassle a murder investigation was for the chief. Especially right now, when the combination of the Mutt March and the usual spring surge in tourism were already making life hectic for him and his whole department.

"You think it's murder, then," the chief said. "Why?"

Dad pointed to where Professor McAuslan-Crine had been carefully removing dirt from around a skull. The skull had a neat round hole nearly dead center in its forehead. A few cracks radiated from the hole, making it look like the center of a macabre star. If you'd asked me to draw my layperson's impression of what a bullet wound would look like on a skull, I'd have drawn it just like that.

"They shot him," the grad student muttered. "Right between the eyes."

"There could be other explanations for the hole." The chief lifted his gaze to the professor. "Don't you often find holes like that even in really old skulls? Pre-firearms-era skulls?"

"We do," Dr. McAuslan-Crine said. "Skull holes are often a sign of trephination—drilling a hole through the skull. Humans have been doing that since prehistoric times, either as a genuine medical procedure or in the belief that it would release the evil spirits they thought were causing what we would recognize today as mental illness."

"But a trephination hole wouldn't show those radiating fracture lines," Dad said. "That's a sign of an impact injury."

"Exactly." The professor nodded her agreement. "You might see a hole like that on someone struck by a spear. But in this case—bring it out and show them, Horace. We've got enough pictures of it in situ."

Horace produced a long, slender pair of tweezers—nearly a foot long. I suspected that he and Dad might call them something else when they were used for medical or forensic purposes, but they just looked like really stretched-out tweezers to me. He used them to reach into the skull—not through the spear or bullet hole but through one of the eye sockets—and pull out a lump of lead. It was slightly deformed, but still recognizable as—

"A bullet," the chief said.

I let out the breath I hadn't realized I was holding.

Horace lifted the bullet up so the chief could get a closer look at it. The rest of us studied it in silence.

"Pretty sure that's not going to turn out to be an old-timey Civil War bullet," the chief said.

Horace and the professor both shook their heads.

"I doubt it," Horace said.

"No way," Dr. McAuslan-Crine agreed.

"Small caliber, I should think," the chief said finally. "And probably from a relatively low-velocity firearm. Because you usually get an exit wound with a high-velocity weapon, and I'm not seeing one, am I?"

Horace and the professor again shook their heads in unison, and Horace focused a small pocket flashlight on the skull, as if to emphasize the lack of any other suspicious holes.

"No exit wound," Dad said. "So you're right about the low velocity. And, ironically, a shot from a high-velocity round can often be more survivable. A low-velocity round can sort of rattle around in the body—or in this case, the skull—tearing up tissue and doing a lot more damage than a clean through-and-through wound from a high-velocity projectile."

"Yes," the chief said. "Of course, given the location of this bullet hole—"

"It probably wouldn't have been survivable under any circumstances," Dad said. "And you'll note there's no sign of the bone starting to heal around the edges of the hole. He didn't survive this."

"So murder or suicide," the student said, with just a hint of ghoulish relish in his tone.

"Or terrible accident," the professor added.

"Pretty awkward way to shoot yourself," the chief said.

"Very," Dad said. "Not impossible, of course. I read a study of gunshot suicides recently, and only seven percent of the fatal wounds were in the forehead. The vast majority—seventy-three percent—were in the temple, with another sixteen percent in the mouth."

"So a forehead shot's not unheard of, but not common." The chief nodded. "That tracks with what I've seen over the years."

"Who's that?" The grad student was pointing at something. We all either turned around or looked up, but there was nothing to see. I could hear a rustling noise, though, as if someone was running through the woods.

"What did you see?" the chief asked.

"Someone watching us from back there in the woods," the student said.

"Probably a deer," Horace suggested.

"Not unless you issue binoculars to your deer around here," the student said. "Whoever it was, they were staring at us through binoculars. That's what caught my attention—a flash of light off one of the lenses."

"Which way did they go?" I asked.

"I don't know." The student shrugged. "Straight back into the woods, as far as I could tell."

"Could it be the killer returning to the scene of the crime?" Dad's tone was dramatic.

"After thirty or forty years, he just happens to show up now?" The chief shook his head. "More likely a reporter or a curious tourist who heard about our find from the *Clarion*'s website and came by to check it out."

"A little suspicious that they'd be creeping through the woods," the professor said.

"That's pretty much how they'd have to get here," the chief said. "I set up a roadblock just out of sight of Meg's house. The road dead-ends a few miles from here, at the creek, and there's not many people who need to drive beyond this point. Just a few farms, the Spare Attic, and that apartment building Rob created out of the old motel. We'll only be letting residents past the roadblock. Or people with some legitimate reason to visit one of the residents."

The "legitimate reason" part probably explained how the duck lady had been able to get by. Whoever had been stationed at the roadblock would have no reason to suspect that Rob and Delaney weren't expecting a duck delivery today.

"What about people who want to get to the Spare Attic?" I asked. The old factory, which had been turned into an off-site storage building, was at the end of the road, on the banks of the creek.

"Anyone who's got an irresistible urge to fetch their junk can show us their unit key," the chief said. "And Sammy's minding the roadblock. He'll notify me if he's not sure whether to let anyone through. So I'm pretty sure if anyone's skulking through the woods, it's someone who wants to get a look at our crime scene."

"Or a potential dognapper casing her escape route." I pulled out my phone and texted Mother.

"Unidentified person lurking in the woods behind Delaney and Rob's," I told her. "Watching crime scene with binocs. Fled when spotted. Might be headed your way."

After a few seconds, she texted back a thumbs-up. I breathed a sigh of relief. Mother would handle any threat to the dogs.

"Could be someone connected with the crime, if they're local," Horace was saying. "Thanks to the *Clarion*, everyone in town knows about the skeleton by now."

"It's possible," the chief said. "If we don't finish the excavation by nightfall, we'll plan to set a guard."

"Great!" Dad exclaimed. "Whoever's guarding could hide on the back porch and apprehend anyone who returns to the scene of the crime. Or if Vern's back on duty he could set up that portable deer blind of his in one of the bigger trees."

I could tell from the expression on the chief's face that he considered it a long shot, the idea of the killer returning to the scene of the crime. But not an impossibility. And that while he wasn't keen on making Vern crouch up in a tree all night, it was sounding like a good idea.

"Get Kevin to set up a camera or two, focused on the skeleton," I suggested. "And then your guard could hide more comfortably just inside the house and rush out here if anyone actually shows up."

"Not a bad idea," the chief said. "If Kevin has the time. I know he's pretty involved in the Mutt March."

"He'll make time if you explain what's at stake," Dad said. "That catching anyone who comes to visit our skeleton could give us the best possible clue to who he is. He or she," he added.

"He," the grad student said. "I haven't quite finished uncovering the pelvis, but enough to tell that it's male."

"Excellent," the professor said. "Let's take a look."

We all turned and regrouped around where the student had been digging. Dad and Dr. McAuslan-Crine both started nodding as soon as they peered down at the bones that jutted out of the dirt.

"Definitely a *John* Doe," Dad exclaimed. "And what's that? Right next to the ilium?"

The professor had her little laser pointer out, and used it to highlight the spot Dad was pointing to. A small bit of metal was visible.

"I was getting to that." The student sounded defensive.

"Can you get to it now?" Dad asked. "Because I think that could be a coin."

"Good idea," the professor said. "Just take it slow. Slow and careful."

We all watched as the student began digging in the indicated spot. He was definitely exaggerating the slow-and-careful part, and I could tell having such an intent audience made him nervous. I suspected Dad and the chief were just as impatient as I was at his pace. Dad was dancing from foot to foot, but the chief managed to look solemn and impassive, and didn't wince the way Dad did at the several times when Dr. McAuslan-Crine repeated her slow-and-careful mantra.

But eventually the student's careful brushing revealed the familiar profile of George Washington, with its aquiline nose and ponytail. And a date along the rim beneath the head.

"A nineteen-eighty-six quarter!" Dad exclaimed. "We have an outside date for the burial! It couldn't possibly have happened before nineteen eighty-six!"

"Let's keep digging." Horace had his camera out and was snapping pictures of the quarter from every possible angle. "With luck we'll find another coin or two. Maybe narrow it down even more."

"Make it so," Dr. McAuslan-Crine said.

Horace and the student buckled down to their digging with what I assumed was renewed enthusiasm—although it was hard to tell from their glacial pace. The chief and I watched them for a minute or two. Then he sighed.

"That pestilential budget report won't write itself," he muttered.

But clearly he wasn't eager to go back to it. He glanced toward the other end of the skeleton, as if hoping to see something that needed his attention more than the paperwork.

And he was in luck. As we watched, Dr. McAuslan-Crine carefully removed the last bits of dirt from the skull, and she and Dad began an animated discussion about how old its owner had been. The chief moved closer, the better to hear what they were saying, and I tagged along.

"Definitely under thirty," the professor was saying.

"Given the state of the sagittal, coronal, and lambdoid sutures, yes," Dad said. "Hardly any sign of that fusion has begun. He could even be in his late teens."

"He could indeed," she said.

"So does this give us a fairly solid age range?" the chief asked.

"Well, solid as far as it goes," Dad said. "Between fifteen and thirty."

The chief frowned and nodded. Clearly he'd been hoping for a narrower range. Dad and the professor sensed his disappointment.

"We'll do what we can," Dad said.

"Still a lot of variables that could come into play," Dr. McAuslan-Crine said. "But that could be as close an estimate as we can manage. He didn't make old bones, that's for sure."

The chief nodded, and returned to his lawn chair. I decided Iris was right about archaeology as a spectator sport, so I joined him, taking the chair Dad had temporarily abandoned. Although I reminded myself that I had better things to do than hang around distracting Dad and the archaeologists from their work.

But what if I took off just before they made another discovery?

Chapter 12

I was hovering, torn between staying and going. I envied the chief, who appeared to be perfectly content to stand by while Horace and the archaeologists took the lead in his investigation. Or maybe he was secretly hoping they'd turn up something to justify his neglecting the budget papers. I glanced toward where the path to home led into the woods and sighed.

"What's wrong?" he asked.

"I should go back home and help out with the Mutt March," I said.

"But you don't want to." He chuckled. "I can relate. I should go back to the station. It would be more efficient to work on these darned budget reports there. Or I could even start trying to figure out who our victim is."

"How about if I do a little research to help you out?" I said. "Since your departmental files aren't apt to be useful immediately."

"What kind of research?" He was frowning, but not shutting my idea down without hearing it, which was encouraging.

"Well, for starters, the *Clarion*'s project to put all their old issues online hasn't gotten back to the nineteen eighties yet, but the library has it all on microfilm. I could go down there and start looking through the old issues, beginning with nineteen eighty-six, and see if there are any articles about missing persons. And the same with the Caerphilly College student newspaper. If old issues aren't available electronically from that far back, I bet the college library has them on microfilm. And while I'm sure you could overcome how persnickety the college is about giving library access to anyone who's not faculty, student, or staff, I already have access, thanks to Michael."

"Both of those searches would be useful," he said. "Because yes, going through all the microfilm is going to be time consuming. Even assigning a deputy to start ferreting through the online portion of the papers' archives is going to be pretty difficult, given that on top of our regular patrol duties and the extra work associated with the Mutt March this weekend, we're going to need security both here and over in your yard. And I do know I can trust you to bring me your findings rather than doing anything stupid and dangerous, like trying to solve any of those missing person cases yourself. So if you've got the time, then yes. Go for it. Start looking into the library angle. But stick to online records and microfilm for now. And keep it discreet."

"Since any of those missing persons could have ended up back there with a bullet in his brain, I think I can manage to restrain my eagerness to go rogue," I said. "Another idea—have you considered briefing Judge Jane Shiffley? Because if any Shiffleys disappeared within the rough time frame Dr. McAuslan-Crine and Horace have laid out, she'd know about it."

"She'd be a good source on disappearances in general," he said. "Not just her own family. She takes a rather proprietary, protective interest in everything that goes on in her town."

As the chief did himself. I suppressed the urge to chuckle at this.

"I gather Vern told you his theory?" I asked.

"Theory about what?"

"About who our skeleton is. Maybe not so much a theory as a worry."

"About that friend of his," the chief said.

"Billy Taylor."

"Yes. A troubling idea, that something terrible could have happened to the poor kid in spite of what that good Samaritan did for him."

"But you can see why Vern's worried," I said. "Bad enough that his buddy disappeared like that—to think that he might have been murdered . . ."

"Of course," he said. "But this theory of his—it brings up something else. Something I probably should consult Judge Jane about."

He frowned, and seemed to be thinking about something. I waited patiently, suspecting that he'd be more apt to share whatever he was thinking about if I didn't badger him.

"Judge Jane was venting one time," he said finally. "About how bad things used to be when the Pruitts were running the town. If our skeleton comes from the late eighties or the nineties, Judge Jane was either starting out as a very junior prosecutor or working her way up in the D.A.'s office. She said she always hated it when one of the judges granted bail to a Pruitt or a Pruitt crony, because the odds were they'd skip out on it and she'd never see them again. Either that, or the county attorney, being a Pruitt himself, would make a sweetheart deal with them."

"You want to bet she remembers most of the guys who skipped out?" I asked.

"I bet she remembers every single one of them," he said, "and exactly what they were arrested for, and whether they ever showed up in town again. I should call her. I doubt if she's in court today, so I should find out how soon I can go out to her farm for a walk down memory lane."

"You don't have to go out to her farm," I said. "She's over at our house right now, helping out with the Mutt March preparations."

"Don't tell me she's washing dogs."

"No." I shook my head. "Assessing their temperaments. And probably doing a little canine-to-human matchmaking, when she runs across a dog she thinks would be a good fit for one of her friends or family members."

"I hope her friends and family members are actually planning to adopt dogs," the chief said, with a chuckle.

"Because if they're not, they might be in for a surprise on Saturday," I said.

"Indeed. I think I'll go over and talk to her now."

"I'll go with you," I said. "Time I showed my face over there, at least for a little while."

"Back in a bit," he called over to the excavators as he rose from his lawn chair. "Call me if anything else interesting comes up."

"Of course!" Dad said, before returning to a discussion he and Dr. McAuslan-Crine were having about the feasibility of doing forensic facial reconstruction on the skull they had unearthed.

I was trying to follow their discussion, but I'd noticed rather a lot of barking going on in the background. And the barking appeared to be getting closer.

"I think Dr. Jain might be the best person to ask about it," the professor was saying. "She could test out that new computer program she's been developing to do it."

"Yes!" Dad exclaimed. "I know her work very well." Of course he did.

"This all sounds—" the chief began.

Just then a dog burst out of the woods and headed toward us. A sleek, fawn-colored greyhound, running joyously with her ears flying and her tongue lolling out.

She was headed straight for us.

"Protect the dig!" Professor McAuslan-Crine shouted. She,

Horace, and the grad student all flung themselves over the areas they'd been excavating, while the chief and I stood up and began waving our arms frantically, in the hope of convincing the greyhound to change course.

And then a pack of more dogs appeared. None of them were greyhounds, and even the fastest of them had no hope of catching up, but that didn't mean they weren't having fun trying.

Luckily, at the last moment the greyhound veered to the left of the dig, and the pack followed her.

I whipped out my phone and took as many pictures as I could of the dogs as they raced by, barking wildly, and then disappeared into the woods. I figured maybe the pictures would help us make sure we recaptured all the dogs. And then I remembered the GPS tags they were all supposed to be wearing. Still, you never knew.

"Blasted mutts!" Aida appeared out of the woods, running at top speed.

"What's going on?" the chief shouted.

"Someone left a gate open." Aida stopped and bent over, hands on knees, panting. "We'll never catch them."

"Remember, they've all got GPS tags," I said. "We'll track them down eventually. Let's let Kevin know."

"And what if we see some of those GPS tags heading out of town?" Aida said. "At a speed even a greyhound couldn't manage?"

The chief was on his phone.

"Possible dognapping in progress," he was saying. "Get everyone out here, stat."

"I'm alerting Kevin," Aida said.

"Let me see what I can do." We all turned to see that Rose Noire had joined us. Unlike Aida, she didn't seem the least bit winded, although she'd gotten here almost as quickly.

"You plan on casting a spell to lure the dogs back?" Aida asked.

Rose Noire ignored her. She detoured around the edge of the

excavation and walked until she was at the edge of the woods. Then she pulled something out of her pocket and sat down on a fallen log.

"Who wants a treeeat?" she called out in a singsong voice. "Who's a good dog? Who wants a tree-eat?"

I heard the grad student chuckle. The rest of us didn't—we knew Rose Noire. She continued to croon about treats, her voice both musical and surprisingly loud.

A small scruffy dog came trotting out of the woods. He sat at Rose Noire's feet on command and was rewarded with a treat. Not just any treat, of course, but one of the homemade, all-natural, organic treats whose recipe she refused to divulge to a living soul.

A cocker spaniel and a large mixed hound appeared and received their rewards.

It took a while—maybe ten or fifteen minutes—but eventually all the dogs were clustered in a circle around Rose Noire, wagging their tails as they eagerly awaited the next round of treats. Even the greyhound was sprawled at her feet, panting and looking as if the treat were just the icing on the cake of a really good run.

By this time Josh, Jamie, and Adam had appeared with a supply of leashes, and we began snagging the dogs. Although when they tried to lead away the first few, the dogs dug in their heels and refused to leave Rose Noire's side. Eventually, when they were all leashed up, Rose Noire rose from her fallen tree and led them back to the path through the woods, tossing bits of treat over her shoulder from time to time.

"It's like the freaking Pied Piper," the grad student exclaimed.

"Kevin says we got them all," Aida said.

I breathed a sigh of relief. And I wasn't the only one.

"Exactly what happened?" the chief asked.

"There was this woman we were keeping our eyes on," Aida said. "No one knew her, and she was kind of evasive when we tried to strike up a conversation with her. She went over and pretended to be watching the dogs in the fenced-in exercise yard, but then we realized she was fiddling with the gate."

"Suspicious," the chief said.

"Very." Aida nodded. "We intercepted her, and then she took off, and we were so busy trying to follow and see where she was going that we didn't notice until the greyhound nudged the gate open. They all took off before we could close it. I should get back and keep a lookout."

The chief nodded, and she took off, almost running.

"We should see if any of Kevin's cameras got a picture of her," the chief said. "If so, we can have people keep an eye open in case she comes back. And once I get that organized, I'll have that talk with Judge Jane."

"Good plan," I said.

The chief and I set out along the path between the houses. We had to take it single file—it was well-worn, but not really wide enough for two people to safely walk abreast. As I followed the chief through the dappled shade, I was glad we'd resisted Mother's suggestions for "improving" the path. If she had her way, the rustic path would give way to a paved one, lined with handrails, illuminated by tiny lights, and featuring several benches so people could stop along the way to rest or enjoy the scenery. But Michael and I had talked with Rob and Delaney, and we'd all agreed that the path stayed the way it was. Low-key. Rustic. Oh, maybe we'd let Mother put out a bench or two eventually—but very rustic ones. There was something private and ever-so-slightly adventurous about the path. We didn't want the pedestrian equivalent of a four-lane highway spoiling our peaceful woods.

I was already finding the path invaluable as a sort of decompression zone. If I was feeling stressed by anything going on at our house, one of the easiest ways to improve my mood was to grab something that needed to be taken over to Rob and Delaney's and set out on the short walk between the two houses. Or think of something that needed fetching back to our house. The trip was particularly charming in the spring, when all the flowers were in bloom—Eastern red columbine. May apples. Jacob's ladder. Wild geranium. Bluebells. Trillium. Dogwoods. As I followed the chief along the path, I found myself wondering—not for the first time—if they had all been growing there on their own or if someone—Dad, perhaps, or Rose Noire—had been quietly putting native flowering plants where they'd be visible from the path. One of these days I'd remember to ask.

And even if whatever was stressing me was still going on when I finished my return journey, I usually felt at least a small surge of emotion when I emerged from the trees into our backyard. Was it pride? Contentment? Maybe just "all's right with the world." The Welsummer chickens would be scratching in the dirt for the feed Rose Noire had scattered. The llamas would be sticking their heads over the fence to watch whatever their humans were up to. Skulk and Lurk, our feral barn cats, would be sunning themselves on one of the picnic tables or creeping through the underbrush in search of rodents. The door to the barn would be open, inviting me to both my office and my blacksmithing workshop. Rose Noire would be puttering in her herb garden or in the kitchen. And both the resident and visiting dogs would be romping in the yard or sleeping on the tile floor of the sunroom.

Of course, usually the number of visiting canines ran to three or four at most. In addition to Vern, my cousin Horace and my friend Aida often dropped off their dogs when they were on duty, rather than leave them to pine alone at home, and Adam Burke often brought along Willie Mays, his pup, when he came over to hang out with Josh and Jamie. Having a hundred times the usual number of visiting dogs was more daunting than heartwarming. Still, as the chief and I emerged from the woods and scanned the crowd of humans and dogs, the words "there's no place like home" sprang into my mind. Of course, home wasn't much like home at the moment, but I reminded myself that the dogs were only temporary.

To my surprise, someone had put a Shiffley Construction Company sawhorse across the path, just where it emerged into our yard. And stationed beside it, in the shade of another small lawn pavilion, were another two knitting ladies.

"We're supposed to head off sightseers to your crime scene," one of them explained to the chief, without slowing a bit on the complicated sweater she was knitting.

"And if they ignore you?" I asked.

"Then we let Aida and your mother know," she said. "But so far we haven't had to do that."

"Good job," the chief said.

"Of course, we can't do anything if they sneak into the woods and detour around us," the other lady said.

"I think discouraging casual spectators is all we can expect," the chief said. "Thank you."

Almost the next person we ran into was Judge Jane Shiffley. She was looking down somewhat dubiously at a smallish fluffy dog of indeterminate parentage. Although the judge was fond of animals in general, her taste in dogs ran to hounds. Hunting dogs—especially the Redbone Coonhounds she bred and raised. Her expression suggested that she wasn't quite sure what to make of the happy little creature that was gazing up at her so adoringly and wagging his tail with such excitement. But, dammit, he was a dog. Not her idea of a proper dog, but he'd make someone a good pet. She sighed, and addressed the dog in the calm but firm tone she used with her pack.

"Sit, sir! Sit!"

The dog uttered a joyous bark and began whirling around in a circle, as if having a human paying so much attention to him gave him almost more happiness than he could bear. Certainly more than he could sit still for.

She sighed and looked up at us.

"He's going to be a handful for someone," she said.

"A good thing he's cute," I replied.

"If that's your taste," she said. "I hear you've been having some excitement next door."

"We have," the chief said. "Found a skeleton. Male between fifteen and thirty, height to be determined when they've dug up more of the leg bones. Dr. Blake's working on getting a DNA profile, but I wanted to pick your brain. See if you can remember anyone who disappeared in the right time frame."

Although I was curious to hear what suggestions Judge Jane might have, Mother had spotted my arrival and was discreetly signaling that she wanted to talk to me. So I excused myself and headed her way.

"How's it going?" I asked.

"There you are, dear," Mother said. "I was just about to call you. We've identified another suspicious person."

Chapter 13

"Another suspicious person?" I echoed. "You mean the one who let the greyhound out?"

"No, dear." Mother frowned. "We've had rather a lot of suspicious persons today. The one who released the greyhound was number two. The first one became unsettled after several people tried to converse with her and left in a hurry. Without any dogs. But she had an expired state inspection sticker, so Aida gave her a ticket for that and Kevin's checking her out. And you saw what happened with the second one. Unfortunately, she disappeared while Aida was chasing the greyhound. The new one is over there near the dog-washing station. The woman in that rather . . . retro flowered dress."

"The frumpy one?" I asked.

"Oh, dear," she said. "Isn't that a rather unkind way to describe her?"

"Yes," I said. "But it's accurate. And I wouldn't say it to her face, of course."

"Of course not." Mother was practically purring, probably because for once I was agreeing with her on a fashion issue.

And it was hard to think of an adjective other than frumpy to describe the woman's outfit. She was wearing a rather shapeless knee-length blue-flowered dress in a remarkably dated style, accessorized with a one-strand pearl necklace, a small matching hat with a wisp of blue veiling, and white gloves. The sight of it brought up memories of going to church as a child. There had always been a few matrons dressed in much the same manner. I recalled wondering if they thought their outfits were the height of style and looked down on those of us with more modern sensibilities, or if being old-fashioned and indisputably respectable was the whole point. You still saw a few such dresses at the various Caerphilly churches—especially on the ladies who came by minibus from Caerphilly Assisted Living. But who in the world went dog-shopping dressed up like an elderly churchgoing matron? And this woman wasn't exactly elderly, either. The outfit aged her, but still—I estimated she was only in her thirties. Could she possibly belong to some very conservative religious group whose dress code had been established in the thirties or forties?

And then something hit me.

"*Driving Miss Daisy*," I said. "She looks as if she walked out of a scene from *Driving Miss Daisy*."

"You're right," Mother said. "And while that was an excellently costumed historical piece—"

"Nominated for an Oscar for the costumes." Being married to a drama professor had its perks—or dangers. Thanks to the Drama Department's fondness for trivia contests, I'd memorized more Oscar, Emmy, and Tony award trivia than I cared to admit.

"And lovely costumes they were," Mother said. "For the period. Why would anyone in the twenty-first century dress like that"— Mother gave a dismissive wave in the woman's general direction— "to come to an event like this?" Her sweeping gesture took in the beehive of activity surrounding us, including the dozens of people clad in the sort of practical garb a sane person would wear if they planned to spend any amount of time in close proximity to several hundred dogs, many of them in need of baths or remedial obedience training.

"Why would anyone in the twenty-first century dress like that for any reason?" I asked. "Have your investigators figured out who she is?"

"Not yet." Mother cast another disapproving look at the frumpy woman. "Rose Noire says she has a very menacing aura."

"But that's not proof that she's a dognapper," I said.

"Of course not," Mother said. "But it does suggest she's someone we should keep a close eye on. Which we've been doing."

"Time to escalate," I said. "Let's get a picture of her and see what Kevin can do."

"That's going to be difficult," Mother said. "She seems a bit camera shy."

"You're making her sound like a very suspicious character indeed," I said. "Let me see what I can do."

I scoped out the part of the yard where the Frump was standing, with both hands primly clutching a blue leather handbag, in a pose that looked as if she might be trying to protect—or camouflage—her stomach. I studied her from afar while pretending to be completely absorbed in petting a rather phlegmatic bulldog. She had curly blond hair and was relatively short—well, shorter than my five foot ten. Maybe five foot four. My initial impression was that she was somewhat on the thin side, if not actually anorexic, but after studying her for a while I realized that was an optical illusion, caused by the way the dowdy flowered dress drooped and hung on her. Her weight was pretty normal.

"You interested in Dimples?" I started and glanced up to see the woman who had been brushing the bulldog—one of Mother's garden club friends—smiling beatifically at my interaction with her charge.

"If this is Dimples, then not really," I said. "Just feeling sorry for her. She looked as if she'd enjoy the attention. And smells as if she could use another bath," I added, wrinkling my nose slightly.

"She's had two baths already," the woman said. "She seems to have a gas problem. But Clarence says that will probably clear up with a proper diet."

"Clarence should know," I said. "And I'm sure there will be some bulldog fanciers at the parade."

The woman's face fell, as if she took my lack of enthusiasm for Dimples personally. Dimples farted noisily and then wagged her tail as if she'd done something clever. The woman sighed and leaned back to take a deep breath. I edged a little farther away.

"Courage," I said.

Then I strolled in the direction of the Frump, stopping from time to time to greet some of the workers or pet the occasional dog. I arrived at where the Frump was watching yet another dog being groomed. The volunteer groomer in question was Joyce Grossman, wife of Temple Beth-El's rabbi and a leading light in the Ladies' Interfaith Council. I sailed over and crouched down to pet the dog.

"What a cutie!" I said. Joyce frowned slightly—about the only thing you could see about the dog in question was that he had rather a lot of long, matted fur that Joyce was struggling to clip off. "At least he will be when you've finished with him," I added. "He shows promise. Let's get some before-and-after shots with him."

I whipped out my phone and pretended to be lining it up to take a selfie with Joyce and the dog. Actually, I was centering the Frump on my screen.

"I think you've got that aimed wrong," Joyce said. "You need to—"

"Don't worry—I'll crop out the background later," I said. "Smile!"

We both smiled, and the dog wagged his tail, and I snapped a couple of pictures of the Frump. And then an actual selfie, just for verisimilitude.

"Perfect!" I held the phone out so Joyce could see the selfie. Then I turned it around and waved it so the Frump could see.

"Isn't he going to be the cutest thing when she's finished with him?" I enthused.

"Oh, yes," the Frump said, eyeing me with much the same panicked expression I'd have expected to see if I'd said, "Oh, look—a baby copperhead! Right there by your foot!" Then the Frump pretended to see something across the yard that interested her, and slunk away from us.

"What was that all about?" Joyce asked, sotto voce.

"Suspicious person," I said. "Going to see if Kevin can identify her." As I spoke I texted my photos of the Frump to Kevin, with the message "suspicious person to ID."

Joyce nodded and frowned at the Frump's departing back.

"When you figure out who she is, find out where she does her clothes shopping," she said. "So we can all avoid the place."

"Probably a thrift shop," I said. "And my theory is that she knows what she's wearing is awful, but she dressed that way because she thought it would let her fit in, here in the backwaters of rural Virginia."

"I have a cousin like that," Joyce said. "Thinks there's no civilization south of the Verrazano Narrows Bridge. Drives me bonkers. I think maybe you scared her off," she added, nodding her head in the direction of the Frump. "Looks like she's circling around to head for the road. You might want to let Aida know."

"I don't think we've got any cause to detain her for questioning," I said. "No matter how many fashion crimes she's committed."

"No, but if she breaks a single traffic law on her way out of the county, one of the deputies can pull her over and give her a warning. Which would involve checking her driver's license, of course, and finding out exactly who the heck she is. Aida can set that in motion."

"Awesome," I said. "I'll tell her."

But when I found Aida, she was already on the case.

"Yes, she's definitely leaving," she was saying into her cell phone. "I'll let you know as soon as the lookout ladies tell me—wait, they just texted. Fairly new-looking silver sedan. Uh-huh. And keep it off the radio—if it's who we think it is, they could be monitoring our channels."

"The lady in the blue-flowered dress?" I asked.

"Yeah." She shifted position slightly, and I deduced she did so to make it easier to keep her eye on the Frump without appearing to stare. "We've tagged three women as suspicious. Got an ID on one of them half an hour ago, and Kevin's checking her out. Be nice to do the same with this one."

"I sent Kevin her picture," I said.

"Good job," she said. "Lord, I'll be glad when this thing is over. Don't get me wrong—I think the Mutt March is a great idea."

"But a heck of a lot of work," I said. "Speaking of which, I think I'll go put in enough dog-tending time to overcome my feelings of guilt about the fact that I haven't spent all day over here."

"If you want to do a good deed, go talk Clarence out of going to fetch any more dogs," Joyce said.

"More dogs?" I echoed. "Good heavens—why?"

"He thinks we don't have enough small dogs," she said. "Keeps fretting that a lot of the potential adopters want smaller dogs and that we need to have more of a selection."

"I'll talk to him," I said. "And point out that if we have too many small dogs, it will hurt the chances of the larger ones. It's about animal welfare, not providing an optimal shopping experience for the humans."

"You're preaching to the choir," she said. "Go tell Clarence."

I did. And managed to talk him out of going in search of more dogs—mainly by pointing out that we were already stretched to the limit to feed, house, groom, and costume the ones we had.

And then for the next few hours I pitched in. Given the unseasonably warm temperature—the thermometer hit eighty-five by early afternoon—Mother had no shortage of volunteers for the dog-washing station. And Judge Jane tactfully suggested that perhaps assessing the dogs' levels of obedience training wasn't my forte—had she decided this after watching my failure to get a lively fox terrier to obey even a single one of my commands? Or was she passing judgment on how well trained our household dogs were? Which didn't seem particularly fair, given that I hadn't been the one in charge of training any of them. Especially not Spike, who had been fully grown, with his evil temper and bad disposition well established, when Michael's mother had declared herself allergic and consigned him to our care.

I ended up being assigned to what Ms. Ellie called the "poop patrol"—collecting designated dogs from the various runs, pens, and crates and escorting them to the stretch of pasture we'd set aside to serve as the canine bathroom. And if a dog balked at producing something she could log in to her spreadsheet, I'd walk it briskly around the pasture a few times. "Until you shake the poop out of them," as Ms. Ellie put it. I was just relieved that we seemed to be past the phase of having to collect stool samples from any of the dogs so Clarence could ensure they were parasite free. Next time I cleared out my tote, I could probably get rid of the stash of plastic freezer bags I'd been carrying around so I'd know where to find one when one of the dogs produced a sample while I was in charge of it.

Clarence had cleared out one of the dog runs to hold the Indian Runner ducks. Since most of the dogs had already been washed at least once, he repurposed an old bathtub we'd been using for the larger dogs into a temporary duck pond. It was a little on the small side for nine adult ducks, but they seemed to be very good at taking turns. And I was delighted to see at least one overalls-clad farmer inspecting the flock with a critical eye before dropping by the table where Clarence was collecting paperwork from potential adopters.

The Mutt March preparations began winding down for the day at around six or so, with participants either heading home to have dinner with their families or filling plates at the buffet, which was mostly full of what Michael liked to call planned-overs, rather than leftovers, from the Shack. Although there was still plenty of work left to do on Friday, I was no longer doubting that we'd be able to finish it all. And after supper, many of those who had stayed around began shifting gears to setting up tents and sleeping bags for everyone who would be camping out to help guard the dogs. At least a dozen tents—the dogs would be well guarded. Of course, that would probably mean a less-than-restful night, not only for the campers but also for those of us who lived here—I predicted that people would be coming and going to the bathrooms and the refrigerator all night. But I was glad that Josh, Jamie, and Adam wouldn't be the only ones camping out with the dogs.

I had just returned a genial yellow Lab to her assigned run when I saw the chief walking briskly through the crowd. Heading away from the house—in fact, he appeared to be heading for the path to Delaney and Rob's house. I made sure the door to the dog run was secured and managed to catch up with him just as he was passing by the two knitters who were guarding the barricade.

"Something up?" I asked, as I fell into step behind him.

Chapter 14

"Your dad just called," the chief said. "Your grandfather's on his way with some kind of news. And whatever it is, I gather he wants the fun of telling us all in person."

I was opening my mouth to ask if he minded my tagging along, but decided against it. If he really didn't want me there, he wouldn't be shy about telling me to stay behind. And he might even welcome my presence—he'd been within earshot a few weeks ago when Mother had paid me the compliment of saying that I was really getting quite good at managing Grandfather when he became obstreperous. That talent might come in handy—if, for example, he tried to increase the drama of whatever news he had with a long, drawn-out, suspenseful introduction instead of just coming out with it.

We arrived in Rob and Delaney's backyard to find Grandfather seated in one of the lawn chairs overlooking the excavation. Dr. McAuslan-Crine was doggedly continuing to excavate the area surrounding the ribs, but Horace and the grad student had given up any pretense of working and were waiting, with visible impatience.

"Not until Chief Burke is here," Grandfather was saying. "It's only fair to let him be the first to know."

"Well, I'm here now," the chief said. "So you can put an end to the suspense and tell us whatever it is that's so exciting. I gather you succeeded in getting usable DNA out of that finger bone."

"Better than that," Grandfather exclaimed. "We've got a partial match for our skeleton!"

"But I haven't even uploaded it to CODIS yet," Horace said. "I thought you were going to tell us that you had the profile ready for that."

"I do, and you should definitely upload it," Grandfather said. "You might find a full match there, or at least another partial match or two. But I ran the profile through my DNA database down at the lab."

"You have a DNA database?" I asked. And then I glanced over at the chief, to see if he was annoyed by my jumping in. From the expression on his face, I deduced that I'd saved him the trouble of asking.

"Not a huge database," Grandfather admitted. "Mostly members of our family, as part of that big study I've been doing on us. Although I have started to add a number of profiles from my employees who want to analyze their own family heritage. And I do have a modest number of profiles from local residents who have expressed an interest in learning about their genes."

"And just which local resident is a partial match for our dead guy?" I asked. "Because if you don't tell us soon, Horace is going to explode in sheer frustration."

"Eustace Pruitt," Grandfather said.

"Our dead guy's a Pruitt?" Horace exclaimed.

"Our dead guy shares five point two four percent of his DNA

with Eustace Pruitt." Grandfather sounded triumphant. "So either a Pruitt or a close relation."

"A close relation?" I echoed. "Doesn't sound like that high of a percentage."

"It's pretty high as genealogy goes," Grandfather said. "Even first cousins only share twelve and a half percent, on average. This percentage means he's most likely a second cousin to Eustace, or maybe a first cousin once removed. I might be able to pin it down more if I had more Pruitts in my database, but he was the only one who ever showed an interest."

Knowing the Pruitts, many of them probably had good reason to keep their DNA profiles to themselves. And if his indiscretion in sharing his DNA with Grandfather led to the arrest of one of his cousins, Eustace would probably find himself persona non grata at future family gatherings. Assuming they still had family gatherings someplace other than the visitors' parking lot at the nearest penitentiary.

And maybe knowing the skeleton was a Pruitt would ease Vern's worries about his missing friend Billy.

"Can you email me the profile?" Horace said. "I should probably go down to the station ASAP and get it uploaded into CODIS."

He glanced over at the chief as he said this, and the chief nodded his agreement.

"Can do." Grandfather stared down at his phone, frowned slightly, and then tapped on the screen a couple of times. "You should have it any second now."

"Great! Thanks!" Horace said—though he continued to look at his phone for a few seconds—checking, I assumed, to make sure Grandfather had succeeded in sending his email. I hovered, ready to help if needed, but then Horace smiled, nodded, stuck his phone in his pocket, and loped toward his cruiser.

I strolled closer to check out how things were progressing at the excavation site. Or would "dig site" be the preferred term for

For Duck's Sake

a scene whose purpose had obviously changed from construction to archaeology? I'd occasionally visited local sites where Dr. McAuslan-Crine and her students had been excavating, so it all looked familiar. Familiar and mostly harmless—at least as long as I could clear my mind of the chilling image of the skull with its bullet hole.

Grandfather had joined Dad and Chief Burke in the growing cluster of lawn chairs gathered just outside the maze of string and stakes. The nearby wrought iron side table now held a supply of tall glasses, a plate of chocolate chip cookies, and a pitcher of iced tea in addition to the lemonade and the Arnold Palmers. Clearly Iris had decided to turn the dig into a social occasion, and was prepared to demonstrate the hospitality of the house to however many kibitzers showed up.

Dad was listening raptly as Grandfather explained exactly what his scientists had done to extract DNA from the finger bone. The explanation was sufficiently technical that I didn't even pretend to be trying to follow it. Nor did the chief—he was working on what I recognized as the budget paperwork he needed to turn in before the county board's next meeting. I'd done battle with the same bureaucratic nonsense a few days earlier. His wad of paper was starting to look a little frayed at the edges, probably because he'd been carrying it around for days and working on it whenever he found a few free minutes.

"Is Horace going to be gone long?" Dr. McAuslan-Crine asked. "He still has a ways to go on his section." She gestured to the plot to her right, where Horace seemed to have begun unearthing the remnants of a second athletic shoe.

"No idea," I said.

"It'll probably be dark before he can get back from uploading to CODIS," the chief said.

"I could take his place for a while if you like." Dad sounded eager.

"Continuity's preferable," she said. "Continuity, and keeping down the number of people working the chief's crime scene."

Dad nodded, but continued to cast longing glances at Horace's section of the dig.

"I don't think uploading the DNA takes all that long," I said. "And if our guy is in CODIS, we should know who he is pretty quickly."

Dad brightened at that thought.

"True," the professor said. "But I'd be astonished if you found our friend here in CODIS. The more I see of him, the more I lean to the younger end of our age range. I think when we identify him we'll find he's closer to twenty than thirty. Not sure he'd have had time to misbehave badly enough to earn himself a place in CODIS, especially if it was just getting started back then."

"I tend to agree," the chief said, looking up from his paperwork. "But let's keep our fingers crossed for a partial match, at least."

"A partial match would be excellent," Dr. McAuslan-Crine said. "Although it could be expensive, identifying him through genetic genealogy."

"Genetic genealogists don't come cheap, I gather," the chief said.

"No," she said. "Of course if you're game, I could always recruit a few grad students to take it on as a project. Could be a fun project to supervise."

"That would be excellent," the chief said.

"But it's not the genealogists who are going to break your budget," Dr. McAuslan-Crine said. "It'll be the cost of all the DNA tests you're going to have to run on the people in the family tree they build. Could take dozens of tests."

"Alas." The chief glanced down at his budget report and sighed.

"Don't worry about the DNA tests," Grandfather said. "I'll donate my lab's services to help clear this up."

"We would be eternally grateful," the chief said.

"And knowing he's a partial match to a Pruitt should help a bit," Dad said.

"And not just to a Pruitt, but to that particular Pruitt." The chief closed his eyes and pinched the bridge of his nose, as if the news had already given him a headache. "So a five-percent match is pretty high as DNA matches go?"

"Five point two four percent," Grandfather corrected.

"As Dr. Blake said, probably a second cousin or first cousin once removed," Dr. McAuslan-Crine replied. "Then again, it could be another generation or two further back if these Pruitts are a particularly inbred family."

"They might be, for all we know," the chief said.

"They probably are," I said. "Considering that most of the town didn't even want to give them the time of day, much less breed with them."

"I'm a relative newcomer to town, you know," Dr. McAuslan-Crine reminded me. "Just why were these Pruitts so unpopular?"

"They arrived in Caerphilly as carpetbaggers," I said. "Around eighteen seventy or so. Operated a textile mill that was notorious for how badly they treated their workers, even in that unenlightened era. And pretty much ran the whole town with an iron fist, up until a few years ago, when the honest locals managed to get proof of what crooks they were and ran them out of town."

"Thanks in no small part to Meg!" Dad was beaming proudly. "But that's a long story."

"And I'd like to hear it," the professor said. "Another day, though. We should focus on the challenge at hand. Do you think the Pruitts who are still in town would be cooperative with the genetic genealogy phase of the project? Getting DNA from some of them could help, and it could be invaluable to interview them about family members who might have gone missing during the relevant time frame."

"I'm not sure we have any Pruitts left in town," Dad said.

"Between the ones serving time for various crimes, the ones who managed to disappear before the chief could arrest them, and the ones who just figured out they'd be better off starting over someplace else."

"Not even this Eustace Pruitt who provided his DNA?" the professor asked.

"Alas," Dad said. "We lost him about three years ago."

"Lost him?" The grad student looked fascinated. "Someone did him in, too?"

"He did himself in," Dad said. "Hepatic cirrhosis, cardiomyopathy, pancreatitis—a perfect storm of alcoholism-related conditions."

"We do have one Pruitt left in town," the chief said. "Miss Ethelinda Pruitt. Eustace's aunt, I believe. She had already been living at Caerphilly Assisted Living for several years when all the excitement happened. I assume her family thought relocating would be too stressful for her."

From what I'd heard about Miss Ethelinda, I thought it was more likely her family were overjoyed at finding an excuse to leave her behind. I knew from the local grapevine that she made life hell for the assisted living's staff and her fellow residents. Her one redeeming feature was that she appeared to loathe her entire family at least as much as the rest of us did. When she'd first moved in, everyone tried their best not to diss the Pruitts in her hearing. Before long, though, they figured out that if anyone said anything nasty about our former would-be overlords, she'd try her best to say something even worse. So while she'd probably come in dead last if the assisted living ever held a Miss Congeniality contest, she'd earned the staff's grudging respect for clear-sightedness.

"I'm not sanguine about getting any information out of Miss Ethelinda," the chief said, with a sigh. "Remember when I was interviewing the residents about that Peeping Tom problem they were having? She wouldn't even talk to me. She seems to have gotten it into her head that the assisted living's a part of the state penal system, and that I'm the one who sent her there. Just kept saying she wasn't a stool pigeon and she was exercising her right to remain silent."

"If she won't talk to you, maybe we can find someone else who can get some information out of her," I said. "One of the staff, maybe."

"Or whoever her pastor is," the chief said.

"That would be Robyn," I said. "Miss Ethelinda shows up at Trinity Episcopal occasionally."

"Excellent," he said. "I expect the Reverend Smith could be very helpful."

"I could even try tackling her myself," I offered.

"You're welcome to try," he said. "Just don't blame me if she bites your head off. Then again, we found the Peeping Tom without Miss Pruitt's help. We'll see if we can pull this off in spite of her." He glanced over at Dr. McAuslan-Crine. "I know you've had experience with this genetic genealogy work. What do you need to get started?"

"A few cooperative Pruitts, for starters," the professor said. "So we can start building family trees."

"We'll work on that," the chief said.

"Good luck," Dad muttered.

"Didn't George Pruitt publish a book about his family back when he was mayor?" the chief asked.

"He did," I said. "I remember there being a big stink because he used town staff to do all the typing and copying and such."

"And then tried to get the town to pay for the printing," the chief added. "On the grounds that it was an important contribution to the town's history. I should think that book would be helpful, but we might have to find a Pruitt to get our hands on a copy. Not sure why anyone else would bother with it."

"The library has a copy," I said. "Or used to. I remember Ms. Ellie telling me what a tough time she had when she caught a bunch of teenagers giggling in the conference room and figured out they were defacing the Pruitt family history book with all kinds of rude remarks. Rude but accurate," I added. "She might have taken it out of circulation, but I can't see her getting rid of it."

"Good to know," the chief said. "Or we could contact the publisher and see if they still have any copies left."

"I don't think they went to a publisher," I said. "I think they just had it printed somewhere. Not locally," I added. "I'm not sure if they turned up their nose at the *Clarion*'s printshop or if whoever owned it back then was smart enough to demand payment up front, but I'm pretty sure they sent it out of town somewhere."

"We'll see what the library has, then." He glanced at his watch. "Library's probably closed by now."

"I'll hit them in the morning," I said. "And let you know what I find."

Dad sighed heavily.

"I guess I should tell Ragnar we won't be picking up those ducks anytime soon," he said.

Chapter 15

"Ragnar?" the chief echoed. "They're getting their ducks from Ragnar?" He sounded puzzled. Not surprising. Ragnar wasn't known as a purveyor of livestock.

"They wanted Cayuga ducks," Dad said. "Well, some kind of black ducks. And Ragnar has a wonderful flock of Cayugas."

"Isn't it nice to know that Delaney and Rob are channeling their inner Goth," I said.

"Cayugas are fascinating!" Dad's tone suggested that I had somehow dissed them by my lack of enthusiasm. "A heritage breed developed right here in North America—in upstate New York. They're completely black—not just the feathers, but also the bill, legs, and feet. And they even lay black eggs."

"Really?" The chief sounded surprised.

"Well, very dark eggs," Dad clarified. "Nearly black. At least at the beginning of the laying season. The eggs get paler as the season goes on. Back in the nineteenth century, they were overwhelmingly the most common meat duck in the country, but in the twentieth century the Pekin and Muscovy ducks replaced them so completely that for a while they were on the Livestock Conservancy's 'threatened' list. But they've rebounded a bit, and they've been upgraded to merely 'watch' status."

"Wait—Cayugas are meat ducks?" I asked. "I think Rob and Delaney are more interested in eggs."

"Oh, they lay eggs," Dad hastened to explain. "Just not as many as you'd get from breeds like the Pekin or Indian Runner, that have been bred for high egg production. Cayugas wouldn't be the best choice for a duck egg farm, but they should produce more than enough eggs for family use. And they'll look very elegant, swimming across that pond."

"Assuming eventually Dr. McAuslan-Crine's excavation ends and we get to dig the pond sometime this century," I said.

"Odds are good," the professor said. "This isn't looking like anything that's going to be declared a historic site or a sacred spot for an indigenous tribe. But yes, you'll need to hold off on the ducks for the time being."

Just then my cousin Rose Noire popped out of the woods, with baby Brynn securely strapped in her all-terrain stroller. I noticed that the storage area underneath the child seat was crammed with what looked like a good selection of plastic food containers.

I was startled at first—why was she bringing Brynn back so early? Then I checked my watch and realized that it wasn't the least bit early. It was nearly seven. I headed over to greet them.

"Delaney and Rob just let me know that they're on their way home," Rose Noire said. "And in case they're a little upset when they find out what's been going on right in their own backyard, I thought they might find it reassuring if Brynnie were already here."

"Good thinking," I said. "And I gather you brought dinner."

"For them, and for Iris and Eileen," she said. "Should I have brought some for everyone else?"

"No need," I said. "I'll invite the chief and the archaeologists to drop by the house for dinner when they knock off. Which will probably be pretty soon—they've only got about an hour and a half of daylight left."

"Good," she said. "Could you take care of the food while I get Brynnie settled?"

So I followed Rose Noire into the kitchen and relieved her of all the food containers. I made sure all the stuff that needed heating was on microwave-safe plates, ready to go, and stashed everything in the fridge.

Then I went back out onto the porch. The door to Iris's suite was open, and when I knocked on the frame, she appeared almost immediately.

"Rose Noire brought over supper," I said. "Country ham, pulled pork, barbecued chicken, potato salad, green beans—"

"You had me at country ham," she said. "The Shack?"

"Of course," I said. "Why don't you and Eileen come over to the kitchen? I'm heading home, but I've got everything ready to nuke as soon as Delaney and Rob get here, and over dinner you can help Rose Noire bring them up to speed on all the excitement."

"Too much excitement, if you ask me," Iris grumbled. "When are they going to haul away that blasted skeleton, anyway?"

"Not until they've finished excavating it," I said. "Which I expect will be tomorrow," I added, seeing her frown. "From what I can see, they're already more than half finished."

Back in the kitchen Brynn was asleep in the portable crib and Rose Noire was setting the big oak kitchen table for dinner. I decided she had everything under control.

"The chief is sending over a deputy to keep watch here tonight," I said. "Why don't you suggest they pull their cruiser into the barn when they get here? Might increase the chances that they'll be able to catch anyone who comes sneaking around."

"Good idea," Iris said. "Maybe we'll catch the murderer returning to the scene of his crime, like a dog to its—"

"Dinner's almost ready," Rose Noire trilled.

I wouldn't bet on the murderer turning up. More likely just overzealous gawkers, but I didn't want to dampen Iris's enthusiasm, so I wished them good night and headed back outside.

Out at the excavation, Dr. McAuslan-Crine and her student were packing up all their gear while Dad read them what his phone's weather app had to say about the chances of rain. Near zero, apparently, which was bad for everyone's garden, but meant they didn't need to take heroic measures to protect the partially excavated skeleton.

I invited them all to drop by our house for dinner. Dr. McAuslan-Crine and her student eagerly accepted the invitation and, after stowing most of their equipment in the barn, hurried back to the professor's battered pickup truck. Dad was visibly torn between accompanying them and staying behind, while the chief was still sitting in his lawn chair, sipping an Arnold Palmer and muttering over his budget papers.

"You go on," the chief said, when he realized Dad's dilemma. "I'm just staying until Vern shows up to keep watch."

So Dad happily trotted over to the path and disappeared into the woods. I took a seat in one of the lawn chairs and poured myself half a glass from the Arnold Palmer pitcher.

"Adam seems to have invited himself to camp out in your yard and help protect the dogs," the chief said. "That okay with you and Michael?"

"The more the merrier," I said. "Dare I hope that we'll have at least one deputy keeping watch tonight?"

"Yes," he said. "Goochland County was already lending us a couple of deputies to help with the Mutt March, and they're coming over early. Since Vern's up for it, I want to have him out here, and we'll have one or both of the loaners at your house."

"Good," I said. "Assuming Mother has everything under control tomorrow—"

"A safe assumption," he said.

"I thought I'd drop by the library in the morning to ask about that Pruitt family history book," I went on. "If they won't let us check it out, maybe I can make a photocopy for you."

"That would be quite helpful," the chief said.

"I'll take this stuff to the kitchen before I head home." I held up the Arnold Palmer pitcher, but he shook his head, so I added it to the tray, wished him luck with his budget report, and brought the tray back to the kitchen, where Rose Noire and Iris happily added the pitchers to the table they were setting.

"I'll see you back at the ranch," I said to Rose Noire.

"Don't you want to stay and help me break the news about the skeleton to Rob and Delaney?" Rose Noire sounded anxious. "In case they're worried about the baby?"

"They already know," I said, remembering my conversation with Rob. I thought of pointing out that if neither parent had called for reassurance, it was probably a sign of how completely they trusted leaving Brynn in Rose Noire's hands. "And if Rob and Delaney are at all nervous, remind them you'll have a deputy on guard here overnight. Probably Vern."

"That's right." This reminder seemed to completely restore Rose Noire's good humor. So I wished them good night and left the kitchen.

And speak of the devil—when I went back outside I spotted Vern ambling across the side lawn.

"Evening," I said. "Did they tell you what Grandfather's DNA test revealed about our skeleton?"

"That it's a Pruitt? Yeah. I heard." He didn't look as cheerful as I'd expected.

"Isn't that good news?" I asked. "It means the skeleton's not your friend Billy."

"Not necessarily," he said. "Makes it less likely, yes—but Billy never knew who his daddy was. No one knew. His mama wasn't around to say, and he always claimed his gran either didn't know or more likely wouldn't tell him. So how do we know he wasn't a Pruitt? By blood if not in name?"

"I never thought of that," I said. "Damn."

"And if he or his gran knew, or even suspected that his daddy was a Pruitt—well, if I found that out about myself, I sure as the devil wouldn't admit it. I always figured maybe they either didn't know who the daddy was or weren't telling because it was some lowlife from Clay County. Not sure whether being a Pruitt would be better or worse."

"About the same, if you ask me," I said. "Hope you have a quiet watch."

He nodded, and strode toward where the chief was packing up his budget papers.

I headed for home, taking it slowly, so my trip through the woods would have its maximal calming effect.

Things were quieter now. Most of the dogs were safely confined to their assigned pens, crates, runs, or kennels, after enough vigorous walks to make it reasonably likely that they'd be ready to sleep. Someone had set up a makeshift coop in the temporary duck pen, and the Indian Runners had settled down inside it. At least a dozen groups of people were either still setting up tents at strategic points around the circumference of the yard or settling down in camp chairs in front of their tents. One group back in the pasture had set up a portable grill, where they were toasting marshmallows and having an old-fashioned campfire singalong. The strains of "Kumbaya" drifted across the lawn. I hoped they'd run out of steam by bedtime, but if they didn't, at least they were pretty far from the house.

Over at one of the picnic tables, Dad was having a lively discussion with the two archaeologists. At another, Mother conferred with several women I recognized as her staunchest allies from the Garden Club and the Ladies' Interfaith Council. Including Minerva Burke, who, in addition to being Chief Burke's wife, was the director of the world-famous New Life Baptist Choir. From the way she kept glancing over at the chief with a slight frown, I suspected she was worried that he was overdoing it. After loading his plate the chief took a seat at another table, where he picked at his dinner while briefing two tall, fit young people in uniforms that were slightly different from what the Caerphilly deputies wore. Presumably they were the loaners from Goochland. The woman deputy looked familiar, which meant she was probably a repeat loaner. Was being lent out to Caerphilly a punishment or a reward? I wondered. I made a mental note to look for a chance to ask one of the visiting deputies.

I headed for yet another picnic table where Josh, Jamie, and Adam were telling Michael about the excitement of the day, in between bites of watermelon and brownies.

"Over here, Mom!" Jamie called. "I saved you some of the watermelon hearts."

I managed to join them before Josh, alerted to the presence of a favorite treat, raided the watermelon stash.

As I sat and listened to the ebb and flow of their conversation, my mind was teeming with questions. Had I really convinced Clarence that we had an adequate supply of dogs and he should focus on prepping the ones already on hand? Had Mother and her minions spotted any more suspicious persons? Had Kevin identified all the ones she'd found? And had she recruited anyone to feed tomorrow's work crew, or was I going to have to make a food run by lunchtime?

But I was too tired to do much more than think of these questions. I wanted nothing more than some quiet time with Michael and the boys, followed by a hot bath and an early bedtime.

And although I did my duty as a hostess first, making the

rounds of the various tents to ensure all our volunteer dog watchers had everything they needed, I did manage the bath—made more enjoyable by a chance to test Rose Noire's new rose-and-gardenia bath salts blend—and a bedtime that wasn't all that late.

Of course, as soon as my head hit the pillow, my brain went into overdrive.

Chapter 16

Michael was already asleep, and I reminded myself how important it was to follow his example as soon as possible. Tomorrow would be a busy day. And a pretty awful one if I couldn't manage to get some sleep. I should put in at least a little time working here at the house on the Mutt March preparations, but with luck I could use helping the chief as a reason to get away from the chaos for some reasonably long, sanity-preserving stretches of time. The idea of spending a few hours down at the air-conditioned library, looking at microfilm, was surprisingly appealing. And if I—

I reminded myself that I needed to stop thinking. Or think boring thoughts that would put me to sleep, not thoughts that made me want to hop out of bed, pick up my notebook, and begin checking off items.

I envied Michael his ability to drop off easily, no matter what the circumstances. I lay quietly, listening to his not-quite-snoring, and trying to match the speed of my breath to his. I was just drifting off to sleep when suddenly a dog barked outside. And then another. Several others. In a minute or so, the scattered barking had swelled to a resounding chorus. And I was wide awake again.

"Who let the dogs out?" Michael muttered.

"Go back to sleep," I said. "I'll go downstairs and check."

I pulled on my yoga pants, stuck my feet into my gardening crocs, and went downstairs. Rose Noire was in the kitchen, looking half asleep.

"Aida went out to look around," she said. "She'll touch base with the visiting deputies and all the human guardians. At least the ones that are awake."

"If any of them aren't awake after all this, she should check to make sure they're still alive," I said.

She yawned and nodded.

I peered out of one of the back windows. There was enough moonlight to let me see Aida moving through the yard, stopping occasionally by one or another of the tents. I focused on the closest tent—the one in the middle of our yard, where Josh, Jamie, and Adam would be sleeping. All three of them were standing in front of the tent, looking around intently, but not moving from their campsite. I'd bet anything Aida had ordered them to stay put.

"Here." Rose Noire handed me a glass of milk. "It will help you get back to sleep."

I thought of pointing out that "back to sleep" didn't apply to people who hadn't managed to drop off in the first place. Or that I didn't want to go to sleep until I was sure nothing untoward was happening in the yard. But both sounded surly, and she was trying to be kind, so I just thanked her and sipped the milk.

Eventually the barking died down, and Aida returned to the kitchen.

"Nothing to see," she said. "And all the dog watchers are sure their batches of dogs are fine."

"All's well that ends well," Rose Noire said in a determinedly cheerful tone. Then she yawned and drifted out of the kitchen. Aida sat down in a kitchen chair that she'd set just inside the back door and returned to staring out into the yard.

"Any idea what set them off?" I asked.

"Not a clue." Aida's eyes were busy, flicking around the yard. "Could be anything. Human prowler. Nearby deer. One of the dogs had a bad dream and woke up barking. I'm going to suggest we get Vern to take a look around before he goes off duty in the morning. See if he finds any suspicious tracks."

I nodded.

"Get some sleep," she said. "Long day tomorrow."

I finished my milk and followed her suggestion. On my way back upstairs I mentally rehearsed the most calming way to say that we had no idea what had set the dogs off, but Michael was fast asleep by the time I returned to bed.

I glanced at the clock. Nearly midnight. I curled up in bed and focused on breathing.

The same thing happened all over again at a quarter to one. First one dog, then several, then the whole bloody pack began barking furiously. Again, I padded downstairs to wait in the kitchen while Aida patrolled the yard and checked in with all the human campers.

And then again at 3:00 A.M.

"What's wrong?" Michael said as I was slipping out of bed. He sounded more awake now. Not a good sign.

"I think the dogs have detected an intruder again," I said.

"An intruder who didn't know we have nearly four hundred dogs who would give the alarm as soon as they scented him?" Michael chuckled. "Probably not from around here, this intruder."

"Or maybe someone who isn't that familiar with how dogs behave," I suggested.

"They should have figured it out by now," he said. "Since they've done the same thing three times in a row. Or did I sleep through a few other canine serenades?"

"No, I think you caught them all."

Then another idea came to mind.

"What if the intruder is deliberately getting close enough to set off the dogs and then running away?" I asked. "Whoever it is, they've tried three times now. One time should have been enough to show all but the most clueless interloper that approaching the house and yard undetected is not possible."

"But maybe they figure if they keep doing it, eventually we'll decide the dogs are crying wolf," Michael said. "And we'll stop coming out to check on the commotion. Should I go down and help Aida?"

"She's got two loaner deputies from Goochland County to help her," I said. "You should close your eyes again and get some sleep so at least one of us will be in shape to cope with whatever's happening around here tomorrow. I'll go downstairs and share our crying-wolf theory with Aida."

He nodded and stretched out under the covers again. I slipped my feet into the crocs—I hadn't taken off the yoga pants this time—and headed downstairs.

In the kitchen I found Aida talking on her cell phone.

"And don't use the radio," she was saying. "For all we know whoever's doing this could be listening in. Stick to cell phones."

She hung up. Then she glanced over at me, one eyebrow raised in a silent question.

"Good idea about the cell phones," I said. "And I just came down to see if I could do anything useful, so don't let me keep you from checking out this latest disturbance, because getting complacent could be exactly what the intruder wants us to do."

"That idea occurred to me, too," she said. "Really wish Vern were here."

"He's right down the road at Rob and Delaney's," I said. "You could ask him to drop by."

"No." She shook her head. "Crime scene needs guarding, too, and we're doing okay here. I just wish we had two of him, so we could have the spare one over here."

"He'll have better luck tracking the intruders when it's light."

"I know." She made a brief noise, half chuckle and half annoyed snort. "But if he were here I could ask him what kind of laws our intruder has broken. Because this whole thing is really getting on my last nerve, and it would cheer me up immensely to know we can charge the clown who's doing this with something when we catch him."

"Probably not trespassing," I said, "since we don't have any signs posted. Maybe we should do that."

"Not a bad idea," she said. "Here and at Delaney and Rob's."

"I'll look into it," I said. "At least while the dogs are here. We can put up a few signs tomorrow."

"I'd leave them permanently."

"Feels inhospitable."

"So you tell your friends and family the signs are only there to scare off the bad guys," she said. "Makes things a whole lot easier on us when someone shows up that you want to get rid of."

"I'll talk to Michael about it," I said. "And let Rob and Delaney know."

"Meanwhile, get some sleep," she said. "Tomorrow's not going to be a slow day."

I took her advice and headed upstairs.

FRIDAY, JUNE 9

Chapter 17

Either no more intruders showed up or I managed to sleep through any subsequent visits. I woke when Michael got up, not long after dawn, but decided to follow his suggestion to go back to sleep and let him cope with whatever was happening outside.

I rolled out of bed a few hours later feeling at least halfway rested and went over to the window to see what was happening in the backyard before I ventured down into it. Things looked much the same as yesterday. No worse, although this was the last day of preparation for the march. I decided to start the day with that visit to the library I'd talked to the chief about. I figured the main reason he didn't try to talk me out of it was that he was feeling more than a little stress, juggling a murder investigation on top of his budget reports and tomorrow's festival. If I waited till things slowed down, he might change his mind about accepting my help.

So instead of donning the old clothes I kept around for things like dog washing, I put on clean jeans and a presentable t-shirt before going down to let Mother know what I was up to. And before stepping outside, I slung my tote bag over my shoulder and took my keys in hand, as a sort of silent declaration that no, I would not be pitching in to help out with the dogs. At least not immediately.

"Good morning, dear," Mother said. "Your dad tells me you're going to be helping Chief Burke identify that poor young man you found in Rob and Delaney's backyard."

"That's the plan," I said. "I know Dad will feel a lot better if we can put a name to the victim. And he's a lot more necessary for the Mutt March preparations than I am." I gestured to where Dad was ministering to a depressed-looking beagle. "And I can always come back later and help with the dogs."

"You're just as important to the project," Mother said. "But at the moment, I think giving that poor young man back his name is even more important. So you do what you need to do."

"Will do," I said. "Is organizing food for all the volunteers one of the things I need to do?"

"No, dear," Mother said. "The Methodists are bringing over a covered dish lunch, and Minerva's organizing the Baptists to grill for dinner. You don't need to worry a bit. Just show up with an appetite."

I liked the sound of that.

I took a quick stroll around the yard, just to see what was going on. Cooperation had broken down in the Indian Runner duck pen, where they'd begun squabbling over whose turn it was to swim. And two more people I knew to be local farmers were lurking outside the pen, casting covetous glances at the ducks and frowning at each other. I texted Mother to suggest that Clarence might need her diplomatic skills to keep peace among the rival duck fanciers.

"Of course, dear," she texted back.

Nice to know that we could stop worrying about ducks, even if Rob turned up his nose at them.

I saw Vern out near the edge of the woods, squatting down to get a close look at something on the ground. Two other tall, lanky Shiffleys were nearby doing much the same thing. Wait—one of them was hammering signposts into the ground. Even from here I could tell they were NO TRESPASSING signs. And the young student reporter was out there furiously taking pictures. Probably a good thing. If last night's prowlers were local, knowing the Shiffleys were tracking them would probably make them rethink any return visits. And if they weren't local, the new signs would make it all the easier for the chief to throw them in jail.

I wasn't exactly going to stop worrying about the dognappers and everything else that could go wrong here, but I could probably shove my worries to the back of my mind and focus on getting useful things done.

I strolled out and got into the Twinmobile. But as I was backing out of the parking area, I found myself wondering how things were going at the crime scene, or dig site—I wasn't sure which we were calling it. So instead of heading for town, I turned the car in the other direction and drove the short distance to Delaney and Rob's.

Dr. McAuslan-Crine was hard at work, assisted not only by Horace and yesterday's grad student but also an additional two young women. I hoped that meant that they'd finish up today. But I decided not to interrupt them by asking. So I just waved, and pulled into the driveway to turn around.

As I was backing out, Eileen Rafferty appeared from behind the house and waved her arms at me. Rather frantically. I pulled back into the driveway and rolled down my window.

"What's up?" I asked.

"I was just going to call you," Eileen said. "I'm worried about Mom. This whole thing has upset her."

"Understandable," I said. "Finding a skeleton in her backyard."

"Not hers any longer," Eileen said.

"She still lives here," I said. "She's allowed to claim it."

"And it was hers when it happened. Whatever happened. And—"

She stopped and looked behind her at the house. At the door into Iris's part of the house.

I killed the motor and got out.

"What's wrong?" I asked.

"Mom was acting weird last night," she said finally. "I kept asking her what was wrong. She wouldn't talk about it. Just kept talking about old times. Stuff that happened back when Sam and Mary Catherine and I were growing up."

"Such as?"

"Such as the time Mary Catherine was dating a boy she and Dad didn't approve of. They did everything they could to discourage it."

"Am I about to hear the dramatic story of how Mary Catherine ended up becoming a nun?" I asked. "After her cruel parents parted her from her one true love?"

"Good heavens, no." She laughed. "She found her vocation pretty young and never dated much. If she ever had a one true love, it sure as heck wasn't Gus. She was flattered by the attention at first—he was a school track star. But dumb as a box of rocks. She wasn't serious about him—only went out with him a couple of times, mainly because she could see it really got to our parents. She was going through a bit of a rebellious period at the time. But then Gus turned up one night drunk—absolutely stinking. And he banged on our front door and yelled for Mary Catherine to come out and go to the movies with him."

"Yikes," I said.

"And if you ask me, Mary Catherine was a bit scared. I think she'd told him she wasn't going to see him anymore, and he hadn't taken it well. So she begged Daddy to make him go away.

Only Gus wouldn't. He kept yelling, and pounding on the door. Mom was on the phone, calling the police, and then Daddy said he'd had enough of this nonsense. He grabbed his shotgun, went to the door, opened it on the chain, and then racked the shotgun and said, 'If you don't get off my property in about one minute, I'm gonna use this.'"

"Did it work?"

"Like magic," she said. "Gus probably broke his own record for the four hundred meters getting back to his pickup. And since Mom was already on the phone with nine-one-one, she told the dispatcher what was up, and they picked Gus up for a DUI on his way back to town."

"Good riddance," I said.

"I guess so." She frowned. "Only now I'm worried. Gus was a Pruitt, you see. Augustus Pruitt."

Uh-oh.

"What if that's him?" She gestured toward the backyard. "What if the skeleton they're digging up belongs to Gus Pruitt?"

"Our John Doe wasn't killed with a shotgun," I said. "They didn't find any shotgun pellets—only a single bullet. Probably .22 caliber."

"Daddy had a rifle as well as a shotgun," Eileen said. "A really old one. I have no idea what caliber it was. Whatever you'd use for deer hunting. He used to hunt sometimes when he was younger. I have no idea what would have happened to it. Maybe he got rid of it before he died. I know I didn't want it, and Sam's pretty vocal about not wanting guns around his kids."

And obviously she didn't think she even needed to say that her sister hadn't wanted it. Were nuns even allowed to own guns? Even if they were, I couldn't imagine the formidable Mary Catherine wanting or needing one. She had that ability that the best high school principals shared with librarians—being able to strike fear and obedience into the hearts of rebellious kids with a single glance.

"Are you actually thinking that your father might have shot this Gus Pruitt?" I asked.

"No!" she said. "I can't imagine that he would ever do something like that unless . . ."

Her voice trailed off and she shook her head as if to clear it.

"Unless he had to," I suggested. "To protect himself or his family."

She nodded.

"But if it was self-defense," I began, and then stopped myself. If I'd shot an intruder in self-defense, I'd call 911 immediately. Of course, this was a hypothetical situation, since we had no guns in the house, and it would take a pretty resourceful intruder to make it past our guardian llamas, Kevin's security system, and the resident dogs. But in the unlikely event that I ever shot an intruder, I knew that Chief Burke would investigate it thoroughly and fairly. But thirty to forty years ago, even if it was self-defense, Joe Rafferty wouldn't have had an easy time if he shot a Pruitt, in a county run by Pruitts. The sheriff, the town's chief of police, the prosecuting attorney, and the judges were all either Pruitts or owned by Pruitts.

Maybe Eileen was right to worry.

"Have you talked to your mom about any of this?" I asked.

"Not yet," she said. "I tried to last night, but the subject kind of upset her, so I thought I'd talk to her today when she'd had time to calm down. Is she still over at your house?"

"Over at our house? She's not here?"

"She stormed out in the middle of dinner and never came home. I thought she headed over your way. I waited around for a while, then decided to go back to the Inn and give her some space. Her bed wasn't slept in, so I assumed she stayed over at your house—the way she does sometimes when there's construction going on here."

"Not that I know of," I said. "But I was kind of avoiding spending too much time at home yesterday, so I wouldn't get sucked into quite so many of the Mutt March preparations. Let me check with Rose Noire," I added as I pulled out my phone.

But Rose Noire hadn't seen Iris.

"Not since midday yesterday," she said.

"Can you look around for her?" I asked. "If she came over because she was having a tiff with Eileen, maybe by the time she got to our house, she'd have cooled down a little and been embarrassed by the whole thing."

"And just found a quiet corner to hide in till she wanted to go back home," Rose Noire said. "I can see her doing that."

For a couple of hours, maybe. Overnight? But I didn't want to say that in front of Eileen.

Rose Noire seemed to pick up on my unspoken anxiety.

"I'll organize a search," she said.

"Excellent," I said. "And I'll help Eileen look here if you can handle it there. Recruit the boys. And Mother."

"Immediately," Rose Noire said, and hung up.

"She's not there?" Eileen looked pale.

"Rose Noire hasn't seen her," I said. "But it's a big house, and things were pretty chaotic yesterday. She's going to look."

Eileen dashed back into the mother-in-law suite. I followed her to the door and saw that she was frantically searching for . . . something.

"She didn't take anything," she said. "Her purse is here. And her toothbrush. Which is dry. And her meds."

"So she probably wasn't planning to stay out overnight," I said. "How urgent are her meds?"

"I don't know." Eileen looked dazed. "I don't think she'll keel over immediately from skipping a dose, but . . . I just don't know."

"Put together a list of them," I said. "And we'll ask Dad. And while you're doing that, I'll call Chief Burke so he can start looking for her."

"Great!" she said, and dashed into the small en suite bathroom.

I pulled out my phone and called the chief.

"Can you put out a BOLO for Iris Rafferty?" I asked.

"What's she done now?"

Under any other circumstances that would have made me laugh. Not what you'd ask about your typical ninetysomething.

"Had a fight with her daughter and disappeared last night," I said. "Eileen's worried. She thought Iris had stormed over to our house to cool off, but Rose Noire hasn't seen her. She's organizing a search at our house, in case Iris took refuge there, but I think someone would have noticed by now if she had."

"When did Eileen last see her?"

I put the phone on speaker and called Eileen. She stuck her head out of the bathroom. I repeated the question, and Eileen frowned slightly.

"I'm not sure of the time," she said. "In the middle of supper. But we ate rather late, if you remember. It was just starting to get dark, whenever that would be."

"Let's call it between seven thirty and nine," the chief said. "I'll get the search started, and then I'll drop by to talk to Eileen and get any more information she can think of."

"Roger."

We hung up. I went over to the door, where Eileen was staring into the medicine cabinet. She started when she noticed me.

"This is what she takes every day." She tore the top sheet off of a notepad and handed it to me.

I studied it. Only three items—not a long list for a woman Iris's age. And all three were things I'd heard of—although my knowledge of prescription drugs was probably better than most people's, thanks to Dad's frequent lectures about the potential side effects of popular drugs. Hydrochlorothiazide—a diuretic often prescribed for hypertension. Levothyroxine—to boost a low thyroid. Restasis—for dry eyes. None of these sounded like things that would result in a medical emergency if she skipped a dose or two, but Dad was the expert. I took a photo of the list, texted it to Dad with a quick explanation, and tucked it into my pocket.

"Have you searched the rest of the house?" I asked.

"Just a quick peek into the downstairs," she said. "I didn't want to intrude."

"Let's do a complete search now," I said. "And try to remember any clever hiding places you and your siblings used to know as kids."

We started in the attic and searched every square inch of the house, including spaces that would be a tight fit for Spike. And although I didn't mention it to Eileen, I kept my eyes open for signs that anything bad had happened. And found nothing. No blood smears. Nothing broken. No objects out of place. Nothing obvious missing.

And no Iris.

Chapter 18

Eileen and I were finishing up our search of the basement when the doorbell rang.

"Maybe that's Mom." Eileen ran up the stairs.

I followed her, more slowly, and refrained from asking why Iris would be ringing the doorbell to the main part of the house instead of coming around to the door of her suite.

I found Eileen and the chief in the front hallway.

"Do you think Rob and Delaney would mind if I used their living room to have a talk with Ms. Rafferty?" the chief asked. "It might be a good idea to . . . er . . ."

"To treat her room as a crime scene?" Eileen said. "You're thinking maybe she was kidnapped or—"

"Even if she left completely under her own steam and is absolutely fine, y'all are worried," the chief said. "And her environment could yield clues to why she left. Or where she's gone. Best to leave it as undisturbed as we can."

"I can't imagine Rob and Delaney would have any problem with you using their living room for your interview," I said. "But let's not ask them—they'll worry like crazy if they think anything's happened to Iris. We can fill them in once we find her."

Or if we hadn't found them by the time they were due home from work—but even though we were all thinking that, none of us wanted to say it aloud. The chief nodded.

"Debbie Ann's put out that BOLO," he said. "And we've issued a Silver Alert, too, and included the adjacent counties on both. Let me know if you run across her."

"Will do," I said.

"Or if she turns up at your house," Eileen added.

"I'll make sure Rose Noire knows to do that," I said. "Call me when she turns up. Or if there's anything I can do other than keep my eyes open."

She nodded before following the chief into the living room.

I called Rose Noire again.

"Any luck?" I asked.

"She's not here," Rose Noire said. "The boys and I did a complete search of the house and yard."

"Have you let Mother know that—"

"Yes, and everyone here is keeping their eyes open. We'll let you know when we find her."

"Thanks." I liked her choice of words. When, not if.

I took off again. I was tempted to drive around and look for Iris, but between the BOLO and the Silver Alert, there would be dozens of people already doing that. And if her taking off had something to do with the skeleton, maybe helping the chief identify it was the most helpful thing I could be doing right now.

I also knew that Iris, like me, tended to take off for a long walk whenever she was angry or upset about something. More than likely, she'd turn up soon, footsore and ready to devour her share of the Methodist covered-dish lunch.

I decided to stick to my plan and head for the library.

As I passed the house, I spotted Seth Early, our across-the-street neighbor, mending one stretch of his fence, and stopped long enough to roll down my window, say good morning, and ask him to keep his eyes open for Iris.

"She hasn't gone past here in the last hour or so," he said. "Not by the road, anyway. But you know Iris. She's probably taken to the woods to get away from all the craziness at her house. I hope I'm in half as good shape as she is if I make ninety."

"You're probably right," I said.

Just then Seth's border collie, Lad, appeared, escorting a wayward sheep.

"Good boy." Seth trotted over to open a gate and watched with approval as Lad chivvied his charge into the pasture and toward the rest of the flock. Then he strode back to where my car was still paused by the fence.

"I'm looking forward to tomorrow's demonstration," I said. Lad would be showing off his sheep-herding skills down at the town square during tomorrow's post-parade festival. I still wasn't sure if Seth was serious about doing one demo with the assistance of the Pomeranians, now that Lad had been teaching them all to herd—with a surprising degree of success, considering their small size and the fact that their breed wasn't generally considered adept at the job.

"Yup," he said. "Say, what's the drill if I want to adopt another dog?"

Another dog? Was something wrong with Lad? Or had the Pomeranians' success inspired this?

"Just let Clarence know you're interested, and he'll go through the formality of doing a background check," I said. "You thinking of taking on another apprentice for Lad?"

"No, he's got the herding side of things covered," he said. "And I can always borrow a Pom or two if he needs help. But

I've been thinking of getting a couple of dogs that I can train as livestock guardians. Your dad tells me they have a couple of dogs that might be mostly if not all Great Pyrenees. That's one of the breeds that's best at protecting livestock, and he says these two look young enough to train. Only about six months old, so not even full grown."

"Sounds like a great idea to me." And I meant it. Quite apart from protecting the flock, guardian dogs might have better luck keeping Seth's Houdini-like sheep from escaping the pasture and hanging out in our house and yard. Not to mention the fact that Clarence was already worrying that either no one would want to adopt the two enormous white dogs, already close to a hundred pounds each, or that they would go to someone who wasn't really up to the challenge of even one dog that size, much less a bonded pair.

"Clarence is over in our barn again today," I added. "Drop by when you get a chance and fill out the paperwork."

Seth frowned at that. Not a big fan of paperwork, I knew.

"That way you've got first dibs if anyone else shows an interest in the dogs you want," I added. "He might even let you put a hold on them. But I'd get in quick before someone else does. You might not be the only farmer taking an interest in the Mutt March."

As I hoped, that sparked Seth's competitive instincts.

"Right." He tucked the hammer back in his toolbox and spread the top and middle strands of the barbed wire apart so he could slip through the fence. "Might as well drop by there now."

I gave him a thumbs-up and drove on.

In a minute or so I reached the line of fencing that divided Seth's sheep pastures from the Washingtons' corn fields and something occurred to me. Vern said that no one knew where his friend Billy had gone. And maybe that was true. But what if it wasn't? Thirty years ago, Billy's grandmother would have had very good reasons for not trusting local law enforcement, even in

Caerphilly. Or, for that matter, the white residents of Caerphilly in general. She might have worried about the possibility that anyone to whom she revealed where Billy had gone would be either in cahoots with the Pruitts or under their thumb. She was probably hoping that once Billy wasn't in town anymore, the Pruitts and the Clay County sheriff would just say good riddance . . . but she might have worried what would happen if they were too mad to give up. Or, worse, if they were savvy enough—or paranoid enough—to realize the possibility that their attempt to frame Billy could come back to bite them.

No, the smart thing for Billy's grandmother to do was to pretend to the world that she hadn't heard from him—even to Vern. If they mostly hung out during basketball, she might not have realized they were good friends. Even if she had, she might well have worried about the possibility that Vern would cave under pressure.

And maybe there was also the same good reason why it wasn't generally known who Billy's father was. His grandmother might have thought—not without reason—that it was safer to keep her late daughter's secret. Especially if that secret implicated someone from the self-proclaimed first family of Caerphilly.

But what if she had confided in someone—about Billy's parentage, or his whereabouts, or both? Most probably someone in the local Black community.

If anyone still around would know who Mrs. Taylor might have confided in, it would be Deacon Washington. He'd been a leading light of the New Life Baptist Church, the county's largest traditionally African-American church, for half a century, and a pillar of the Caerphilly community in general. And he was particularly passionate about mentoring young people who were disadvantaged or at risk. He'd have taken an interest in someone like Billy—a bright, talented student from a poor family. And he'd have watched over an elderly widow in straitened circumstances, like Billy's grandmother.

On impulse, I turned into the Washingtons' driveway. Maybe the deacon wouldn't tell me what he knew—assuming he knew anything. But I could try. And maybe plant the seed that he should at least tell the chief what he knew.

When I pulled up in front of the barn, I spotted Isaiah Washington, the deacon's grandson, who now ran the farm. He was unloading sacks of chicken feed from the back of his pickup, but stopped to greet me.

"Morning," he said. And then, with a grin, he added, "What brings you this way—things at home gone to the dogs?"

"Completely," I said. "So I'm looking for excuses to sneak away. Your granddad home? I wanted to ask him a couple of local history questions."

"Like if maybe he knows whose skeleton they dug up in your brother's yard? Don't be surprised," he added, seeing my expression. "I think everyone in the county's heard by now."

"Silly me," I said. "And of course they have. And yes, I wanted to let him know what little we know and ask him to search his memory to see if he can help put a name to our skeleton. We've got Iris Rafferty working on the same thing, and Judge Jane, but they move in slightly different circles."

"And you think maybe the dead guy's Black?" Isaiah asked, cutting to the chase.

"All we've got is the skeleton," I said. "So who knows? I figure we should ask all the knowledgeable old-timers if they have any ideas on the subject."

"Gramps will be tickled pink if he can help," Isaiah said. "We were talking about it over dinner last night, and he was saying what a terrible thing it was, that young man's family probably not knowing what happened to him for all these years. Go on back—last time I looked he was on his front porch, reading his library book and enjoying the day."

"Thanks," I said. "By the way—Iris Rafferty's on the lam. Her daughter Eileen's worried, and they've got a BOLO out on her, and a Silver Alert, so if you see her—"

"I'll call it in," he said. "What do you bet Eileen's been trying to talk her into going into the nursing home again and she just took off to get away from the nagging?"

"Very possible," I said. "Or maybe she just needs a little time to herself so she can process finding out that she's been living with a murder victim buried in her backyard for the past few decades."

"Good point," he said. "Understandable either way."

With that he returned to unloading his sacks, and I set out on the dirt path that led beyond the barn to what the deacon called his retirement cottage.

Chapter 19

The deacon's tiny cottage was the perfect arrangement for an elderly widower. He still had his privacy and dignity, but with plenty of family just a quick shout away if he needed anything or just wanted company.

It was reassuring to see his face light up with a smile when he spotted me approaching the cottage. He stuck a bookmark in his library book—Walter Mosley's latest—and stood up to shake my hand in welcome. I'm not sure I'd have reacted that cheerfully if someone interrupted me when I was immersed in a good book. Then again, reading time was hard for me to find. And while he still played a very active role at New Life Baptist, the deacon's schedule seemed to give him a lot more reading time than mine did.

"How's it going getting ready for the Mutt March?" he asked. "You sure you don't need me to rehearse my bit?"

"You'll have to ask Minerva about that." Minerva Burke, as

music director of the New Life Baptist Church's nationally famous choir, was organizing its entry in the parade—a float on which a small group of singers would be performing dog-themed musical numbers, accompanied by a marching formation of humans and dogs dressed in the choir's familiar red-and-gold satin robes. I wasn't sure what the deacon was supposed to be doing while riding on the float, but I was sure he needed no rehearsal time. "Or Mother—she's in overall charge of the parade preparations. I'm doing what I can to help out Chief Burke. You probably heard about the skeleton Aaron Shiffley and his bulldozer found yesterday," I added, as I took my seat in the rocking chair next to his.

"I did indeed," he said. "And I also heard he thinks he's got himself a homicide victim. Has he figured out who that poor soul is yet?"

"No," I said. "So he wants to see if we can get useful information from some of the county's longtime residents. The skeleton's male, somewhere between fifteen and thirty, and his height's still to be determined. And he's probably been buried there for thirty to forty years. Can you put your thinking cap on and let the chief know if you remember anyone who disappeared during that time frame?"

"I surely can," he said. "I'm assuming we have a reason for thinking he's from around here?"

"Yes," I said. "Thanks to the one additional bit of information Grandfather's DNA scientists figured out. He's related to the Pruitts. Most probably a second cousin to Eustace Pruitt."

"Oh, dear." The deacon frowned. "I'd say the situation is downright ironic, wouldn't you? If it's a Pruitt . . . could turn out to be someone we thought we were better off without. Someone we all breathed a sigh of relief about when we figured out he'd definitely left town. And now we're all probably going to feel guilty about how we all muttered 'good riddance' when we heard the news."

"Also ironic, now that all the Pruitts have left town, that a situation turns up when having a few of them around could be useful," I said.

He chuckled at that.

"Of course, the skeleton isn't necessarily a Pruitt," I pointed out.

"You think your granddaddy's DNA experts got it wrong?"

"No," I said. "But the DNA doesn't necessarily prove that the guy's a Pruitt. Only that he's related to them. DNA testing's uncovering a lot of family secrets these days. What if the dead guy is someone we didn't know was related to the Pruitts?"

"Good point," he said. "In fact, for all we know, the skeleton could be someone who didn't know it himself. Ironic indeed if that skeleton in your brother's backyard led to uncovering another skeleton in the Pruitts' family closet. I'll definitely put on my thinking cap and let the chief know of anyone I can think of who disappeared back then. Even if I think there's not much chance of them being a Pruitt."

"That'd be great," I said. "And while you're at it, it would be great if you can do anything to ease Vern Shiffley's mind. He's worried that the skeleton might turn out to be a friend of his who disappeared back then. A friend who's probably not a Pruitt, but he's still worried. Do you recall a kid named Billy Taylor?"

"I do indeed." Did I detect a hint of reserve creeping into the deacon's voice? "Does he have some reason for thinking Billy's the skeleton?"

"No reason, except maybe for the fact that our skeleton was buried wearing a pair of Air Jordans," I said. "Vern started worrying that it might be Billy before we found out the skeleton was kin to the Pruitts. And even when we found that out, it didn't reassure him, because by then he realized he never knew that much about Billy's family to begin with."

I could see from the deacon's face that he was still puzzled, and maybe even a bit disturbed by Vern's interest.

"The reason he's so interested—and you can't tell anyone about this," I said. "Promise to keep it to yourself."

He nodded.

"Vern helped Billy escape," I said. "From jail and then from Caerphilly. And it always kind of bothered him that he never heard anything afterward, but he figured maybe it was what Billy had to do. To protect himself. But finding the skeleton of someone about Billy's age, who was murdered at around the time Billy disappeared . . . it's brought back all his worry."

"And now he's going to fret about Billy," the deacon said. "Even if the chief can prove the skeleton's not him, it's stirred up all those old worries."

"Exactly," I said.

The deacon nodded, and stared into space for a minute or so. Into space, or maybe into the past.

"I don't know who Billy's daddy was," he said finally. "I think his gran knew, but if she did she might have taken it to her grave. All I know was that Billy's mother was . . . taken advantage of by a very bad man. But she wouldn't say who."

"And back then they couldn't do a DNA test to find out," I said.

"Even if they had been able to, I'm not sure they'd have had the nerve to go up against whoever did it," the deacon said. "Especially if it was a Pruitt. This is interesting. I always wondered how Billy managed to get away. Didn't know he and Vern were that good friends."

"I think they bonded over basketball," I said. "Plus a bit of hero worship on Vern's part. He's always been a massive basketball fan, and I gather Billy was a brilliant player."

"That he was." He smiled and nodded. "And whip-smart to boot. That was a good deed Vern did. Never even guessed it was him who did it, but I'm not surprised. He's a good man."

"I think it would ease his mind once we could find a way to prove the skeleton isn't Billy's," I said. "So he can go back to thinking

Billy's out there somewhere, living his best life, and not lying in Rob and Delaney's backyard waiting for Maudie Morton's hearse to haul him down to the funeral home. If his grandmother were still around, we could ask her, but she's not, and according to Vern, she didn't seem to have any relatives in town."

"She didn't," the deacon said. "But she must have had some somewhere. Some of the old folks might remember. I'll see what I can find out. If that skeleton is Billy, it would be a kindness to reunite him with any remaining family he might have."

"And if it's not, it would be just as much a kindness to reassure Vern that Billy did make it safely out of town," I said.

"Indeed." He smiled. "So it's Vern Shiffley we have to thank for Caerphilly's twentieth-century reenactment of the Underground Railroad. Life's full of surprises, isn't it?"

"It is indeed." I stood up, and motioned him to keep his seat. "The chief would be delighted to hear from you. And wish me luck—I'm going to drop by Caerphilly Assisted Living and see if Miss Ethelinda Pruitt can contribute anything to the mystery."

"Good heavens!" he exclaimed. "You are going above and beyond the call of duty. If it was me, I think I'd rather go wash a few dozen ornery dogs."

"I may regret volunteering to do it," I said. "But the sooner we figure out who our skeleton is, the sooner Rob and Delaney can stop worrying. And Iris. Especially Iris."

"How's she taking it?"

"She seemed a little unsettled yesterday," I said. "In fact, more than a little. I haven't talked to her yet this morning, but here's hoping she's had a good night's sleep that can work its magic."

I decided not to add to his worry by mentioning Iris's disappearance. I'd let Isaiah decide whether or not to tell him that.

"When you see her, tell her we're all thinking about her," he said. "And if there's anything we can do, she just needs to ask. And make sure she knows we're going to do everything we can to help clear up this whole thing."

"Will do," I said.

As I headed back toward my car, I noticed that he hadn't picked up his library book again. He'd reached into his pocket and taken out his phone. That cheered me. The deacon was on the case. I wasn't sure if justice for Billy or peace of mind for his longtime neighbor was the bigger motivation, but I couldn't help feeling we were a lot closer to figuring out a few of the town mysteries.

I wished Isaiah a good morning and headed for town. Next stop, the library. And after that, Miss Ethelinda. If I were a better person, I decided, I'd visit Miss Ethelinda first. Get it over with. Rip off the bandage. Maybe learn something that would help make my library research more effective.

I considered it for a moment, then took the turn that led to the library.

Chapter 20

The library parking lot was so empty that for a moment I worried that I might have missed an unscheduled closing. Had drafting Ms. Ellie and her assistants to help with the Mutt March temporarily deprived the town of access to new reading material? But then I spotted two cars, sensibly parked at the far end of the lot in the shadiest spot available. I followed their example.

When I stepped inside the library, I felt a wave of peace and well-being wash over me. Libraries and bookstores had that effect. It wasn't just the presence of books in large numbers. I also liked the calm, focused, relatively quiet atmosphere, and the company of people who were either seeking knowledge or in the business of dishing it out.

And I enjoyed the feeling of being among old friends. Many of the books now surrounding me had lived for several years in our library, during those dark days when, thanks to the Pruitt family's financial machinations, the town of Caerphilly had temporarily lost possession of its own library. Of all its public buildings, actually. Randall Shiffley, then newly elected as mayor, had set up his office in a tent on the town square. Mother and Dad had given Chief Burke the use of their barn for the police station. All over the town—and the county—barns, warehouses, and spare rooms had sheltered the various government offices until we'd finally succeeded in driving out the Pruitts and recovering our buildings from the clutches of the financial institution we all thought of as the Evil Lender.

And now the Pruitts were once more causing us trouble.

I sighed. There are few things more discouraging than having to refight a battle you thought was won. Then I squared my shoulders and looked around to see who was on duty at the main desk.

One of Ms. Ellie's student interns, alas. Not that there was anything wrong with the interns, who were invariably bright and helpful. But they tended to look down their noses at what they considered old-fashioned technology, which meant that if the microfilm reader misbehaved, they would disavow any knowledge of its workings and throw up their hands in despair.

So I decided to start my research with the Pruitts' family history book. I remembered seeing it on the shelves when it and its siblings had been living at our house—seeing it and occasionally favoring it with a rude gesture.

I strolled over to the 900s—history and geography, in the Dewey Decimal System—and trailed along the shelves until I reached the 920s—biography and genealogy. But when I arrived at the 920Ps, the book I remembered wasn't there. I scanned the nearby shelves, in case it had been misfiled—a heretical thought, under normal circumstances, but with Ms. Ellie and the more seasoned assistants spending so much time out at our house preparing for the Mutt March, something of the sort could have happened. And the volume in question wasn't an unobtrusive one—it was an inch thick, with an impressive black faux leather binding, with *The Pruitt Family* stamped in gold in the spine in an almost unreadable block-letter font. The front cover expanded that to *The Pruitt Family, First Family of Caerphilly, Virginia.*

Maybe Ms. Ellie had reclassified it as fiction, on the basis of the title. Or in Dad's beloved 360s, for criminology, given how very many illegalities the Pruitts had racked up over the decades.

Or, more likely, maybe someone else had checked it out. The library's computer system would tell me that, along with where it was filed if it wasn't checked out. So I went over to one of the computer stations and typed in the title. I'd been right about the number—it was classified in the 920s. But at the bottom of the book's entry was a message I'd never seen before. "See a librarian for assistance."

So I pulled out my phone, took a picture of the entry, and went over to the circulation desk, where the intern was sitting.

"May I help you?" she half whispered. She looked eager, which suggested that Ms. Ellie had given her some kind of useful but tedious task to perform when she was not assisting patrons.

"I'm looking for this." I held up my phone to show her the entry on the Pruitt history. She peered at it and her face grew stern.

"That doesn't circulate," she said.

"I don't really need to check it out," I said. "I'd just like to look at it."

She frowned.

"I'm happy to let you have my driver's license and all my valuables as hostages," I said. "And I can sit here right in front of you the whole time I'm looking at it."

"Oh, I'm sure you could be trusted with it," she said. "But it's locked up in a special cabinet in Ms. Ellie's office, and she's the only one who has the key. Could you possibly come back sometime when she's in?"

I choked back my impatience and was coming up with a way to thank her without sounding annoyed when she added a few words.

"Unless you could work with an electronic copy," she said.

"An electronic copy would be excellent," I said. "How do I check it out?"

"Let me have your email address and I can just send you the PDF," she said. "We have PDFs of a whole bunch of the local history and genealogy stuff. A lot of it is so irreplaceable that we don't let it circulate, but as long as something isn't under copyright there's no problem sharing the PDFs."

I rattled off my email address, and after a minute or so of rapid typing, she announced that I should have the file any time now. I glanced at my phone and saw that yes, an email from the library had arrived, with a fat attachment. I'd wait until I was back at my regular computer, though, rather than trying to look at a PDF on the tiny screen of my phone.

"Anything else?" the intern asked, in the sort of perky voice that suggested she was expecting Ms. Ellie to be pleased with her when she brought her boss up to speed on how she'd spent the day.

"Just one more thing," I said. "I need to look at the archives of the *Clarion*. From the eighties and nineties."

"Those would be on microfilm." Her tone of voice suggested that she was rather hoping the mere mention of microfilm would discourage me, the way dropping a hint about great white shark sightings might cool someone's ardor for a bracing ocean dip.

But when I appeared undaunted, she steeled herself for the ordeal. A few minutes later I was seated in the remote corner of the building where they hid the elderly microfilm reader as well as a printer you could use if you wanted a hard copy of anything you found. Several reels of microfilm, containing the *Clarion*'s weekly issues from 1986 through 1999, were at my elbow.

And both reader and printer seemed to be working nicely. Evidently Ms. Ellie had found someone who could keep them running. Someone like Kevin. In fact, given how close a friend Ms. Ellie was to the family, quite probably Kevin himself. Keeping what he referred to as legacy systems and vintage tech in good working order was one of his stranger hobbies.

In another mood, I might have found searching the microfilm tedious. But today it felt like a welcome respite from the chaos of the Mutt March preparations. And, for that matter, a nice distraction from the murder investigation, Iris's disappearance, and last night's repeated intruder alerts. And that was without even taking into consideration that the library was air-conditioned and the thermometer outside was rising toward the nineties.

In fact, my biggest challenge was keeping myself from getting distracted by reading stories that, however fascinating, couldn't possibly have anything to do with the skeleton in the duck pond. I chuckled at seeing the high school prom pictures, complete with classic examples of big 1980s hair, of people I now knew as mature, sensible adults. I indulged in a few sad moments of wistful reminiscence when I came across a story about a beloved resident who was no longer with us. I gritted my teeth whenever I saw yet another story that tried to make the Pruitts look like noble, public-spirited, charitable town benefactors.

And occasionally I ran across a story that might just possibly have something to do with the skeleton. I found an article about Billy Taylor's escape from jail—in 1987, so definitely within the time frame Horace and Dr. McAuslan-Crine had calculated. The article tried to paint Billy as a dangerous criminal, but the accompanying photo undercut the attempt. A yearbook photo, I suspected, since he was in a suit and tie. He had a twinkle in his eye, and a broad, friendly grin. And a distinctively wide gap between his two upper front teeth—a feature that might help Dad and Dr. McAuslan-Crine identify him, if he was the skeleton. Or rule him out, which would ease Vern's mind. I printed out the page. And then, after thinking about it, I printed out the rest of the issue. It might help to know what else had been going on around town when Billy had disappeared.

The short article in the next week's issue didn't add much to the story, and after that Billy disappeared from the pages of the *Clarion*.

It was while I was reading about Billy that I heard the faint ding of an arriving text. Probably someone who wanted me to come back home to help with the dogs, I thought, stifling a pang of annoyance as I pulled out my phone.

It was from Iris.

"Tell them I'm fine. Just need some time by myself. I'll come back when I'm ready."

I felt a rush of relief. It sounded like Iris. Like Iris exhibiting exactly the degree of crankiness and irritation I'd expect if, for example, Eileen was trying to use the discovery of the skeleton as grounds for renewing her quest to talk her mother into entering assisted living.

But just in case . . .

"Did you take Millicent with you?" I asked. Millicent was what she'd named her cell phone. Iris gave human names to all her wayward mechanical and electronic devices. Her television was Hector, her blender was Veronica, and her hearing aids were Frannie and Annie. It amused her—especially on those occasions when someone who had not been initiated into her naming system overheard a comment like, "Millicent's giving me fits, I haven't seen Frannie and Annie for days, and I think I managed to kill Hector last night."

But if Iris wasn't really fine—if she was being held prisoner by someone for whatever reason, and her captor was forcing her to text me to disarm everyone's suspicions, this question would give her the chance to signal that all was not well.

Her reply was reassuring.

"Duh. Of course. How else would you be hearing from me? But now I'm going back to ignoring her."

Which sounded like a completely normal response.

"Call if you need anything," I texted.

Then I took a screenshot of our conversation and texted it to the chief.

"Thanks," he texted back. "Keeping the BOLO going, though, if only to placate Eileen."

I nodded my approval and put the phone back in my pocket.

Maybe I'd been reading too many of Dad's mystery books, if I was jumping so easily to the idea that Iris might have been kidnapped.

I focused back on the microfilm. I tried to scan even the smallest article about a Pruitt. Which made for slow going on my search, since the Pruitt-era *Clarion* seemed to document even the most mundane activities of the town's self-appointed first family. Their election or appointment to nearly all of the town's important posts. Their frequent ostentatious donations to Caerphilly College, which at one point had had seven buildings and an athletic field named after various and sundry Pruitts. Their social events. Their births, deaths, and marriages.

And their occasional departures from Caerphilly—I paid special attention to those. It stood to reason that even back in the days when the Pruitts ran everything, the occasional wayward son or daughter would have made the town too hot to hold them. I found myself suspicious of an announcement that Wolfgang Pruitt had left town to pursue career opportunities on the West Coast—if they were legit, why not give at least a hint what those career opportunities might be? And why not mention what out-of-town institution of higher education Anatole Pruitt was planning to attend? Was it mere embarrassment because young Anatole had turned up his nose at Caerphilly College? Or, worse, had he failed to meet even the infamously low admissions standards the college used to evaluate what the alumni office referred to as "donor spawn"?

Since we knew our skeleton was male, I paid less attention to the departures of female Pruitts, but I did make a note to find out more information about The Young Ladies' Academy of Keswick. Was it an elite but little-known finishing school? Of course, given my almost nonexistent level of interest in finishing schools, for all I knew it could be well-known—just not to me. Might it be the sort of strict boarding school where you sent teenage girls in lieu of the military academies designed to rehabilitate their wayward brothers? I had noted the departure of more than one teenage Pruitt male to one or another of the lesser-known East Coast military academies. I even toyed with the idea that the Keswick place might be a front for a home for unwed mothers—but if that were the case, surely the Pruitts wouldn't advertise who they sent there—would they? I made an entry in my notebook to research the academy later, and then shoved it out of my mind so I could focus on Pruitts who might turn out to be our skeleton.

I kept a running list of male Pruitts who left town for whatever reason, and then made notes when most of them reappeared in later issues of the *Clarion*. Armand Pruitt, for example, returned from exile at the C. Bascom Slemp Military Academy and joined his father's CPA firm, so I demoted him from hot prospect to merely another Pruitt of approximately the right age whose present whereabouts I hadn't yet determined.

So far, though, Wolfgang and Anatole hadn't reappeared in the *Clarion*, so I kept them on the list. Although I had my doubts about Wolfgang. He appeared in a group shot, and it was easy to see that he was unusually short—maybe as short as five feet. If he were the skeleton, identifying him might be relatively easy.

I pulled out my phone and texted Dad.

"Have you found the femur and the tibia yet?"

I was turning back to the microfilm reader when a soft ding announced his reply.

"YES! And we've calculated that the deceased was between 5´11˝ and 6´2˝ tall."

Probably not Wolfgang, then. Unless he'd gone through a late growth spurt. Which was possible. I kept him in the pile, but not at the top of it.

I found a few references to Gus Pruitt in the *Clarion*'s sports pages. Eileen had called him a track star, but that was a bit of an exaggeration. He got the occasional second or third place, but usually as part of a relay team rather than as an individual runner. And then, in 1992, during what I figured out was his senior year, he disappeared from the paper's pages. Gus was definitely in the running to be our skeleton.

As was Hobart Pruitt, presumably one of his cousins. Second cousin, if the rough family tree I was sketching out in my notebook was accurate—I'd check it later against the official version in the Pruitt family history. In what struck me as unusually candid coverage of Pruitt-related news, the *Clarion* reported that Hobart had been arrested in 1990 as a suspected drug dealer, was granted bail by Judge Wilmer Pruitt—by my reckoning, his great-uncle—and then skipped town. Of course, according to his family, young Hobart was a choirboy who'd been framed by overzealous—if not actually malicious—DEA agents, and he would never have jumped bail. Something must have happened to him. They actually organized a massive search for the missing Hobart, complete with helicopters and scent dogs, to no avail. Interesting. Did they really have no idea where Hobart had gone? Or were they going a little overboard in the effort to make him look innocent? I could see them doing the latter—especially if he wasn't the only Pruitt involved in the drug-dealing ring.

By the time I reached December 31, 1999, I had a fat wad of printouts from the microfilm along with a dozen pages of scribbled notes on young male Pruitts, including five who had left town under what could turn out to be mysterious circumstances. I also had either printouts or notes about any non-Pruitts of around the right age whose departure from town made the *Clarion*. Counting

Billy, I had three of those, but Gus Pruitt, Hobart Pruitt, and Billy Taylor were my leading candidates for the skeleton.

My work wasn't over, but starting with January 1, 2000, the *Clarion*'s archives were online. It would probably be a good idea to continue scanning them for another five or ten years—but I could do that at home, in the comfort of my own office. And my eyes could use a break.

Chapter 21

Before leaving the library, I ventured into the reference section, which boasted a complete collection of the Caerphilly High School yearbooks—at least it was complete as far back as they could be possibly useful for my research. I flipped through every volume from 1980 through 2010, phone in hand, and carefully took pictures of various male Pruitts who graced their pages. Not all of them. Since I'd come to town well after the skeleton was buried, I could safely skip any Pruitts I'd either met or was absolutely sure had been spotted alive in town since my arrival.

I even took pictures of the occasional non-Pruitt whose facial features suggested he might be a Pruitt relation. The Pruitts weren't all cookie-cutter clones, but they did tend to share certain slightly unfortunate facial features. They were almost always short-changed in the chin department, and their eyes, usually pale blue, always seemed to bulge slightly. In middle age they tended to become pudgy and jowly, so these high school boys hadn't yet grown into the full Pruitt look. But still, none of them were exactly teenage heartthrob material.

Gus Pruitt, Sister Mary Catherine's one-time swain, was relatively presentable for a Pruitt. His light-brown hair was on the shaggy side, with long untidy and rather greasy-looking bangs that fell over his eyes. The style had looked better on nineties-era celebrities like the young Leonardo DiCaprio, but it wasn't bad. The scruffy goatee actually improved his looks by camouflaging the weak chin, and his eyes weren't anywhere near as protuberant as those of most of his family. Had Mary Catherine really been interested in him? Or was it one of those cases where the guy wouldn't take "get lost" for an answer?

Hobart Pruitt didn't seem to have been as lucky—although it was hard to tell from the relatively small headshot of him in his junior year. He didn't appear in the following year's senior shots, and I couldn't find any mention of him as "not pictured." Had he dropped out before graduation? Or merely avoided having a picture taken? The latter seemed plausible, since even in his teens he'd already taken on the rather frog-like appearance his luckier relatives managed to fend off until middle age.

And the other possibly vanished Pruitts, Wolfgang and Anatole, were . . . typical Pruitts.

And none of the pictures I found of Billy Taylor looked the least bit like a Pruitt. More like a young Denzel Washington. I found myself hoping the skeleton didn't turn out to be him.

I dropped by the circulation desk to thank the intern for her help and pay for all my printouts. And then I headed back to my car.

But Billy Taylor was still running through my head. Instead of starting the engine and heading for my next stop—the Caerphilly Assisted Living—I called Dad.

"It's Meg!" I heard him exclaim to someone nearby. "You're missing a lot of fun," he continued, to me. "But the chief tells me you're out getting some information that might help us identify our skeleton. Any hot prospects?"

"Maybe," I said. "Take a look at this photo."

I texted him Billy Taylor's senior picture.

He didn't say anything for a minute or so.

"He doesn't look like a Pruitt," he said finally. "Most of them look distinctly exophthalmic."

"Is that the fancy scientific word for bulging eyes?" I said.

"Yes," he said. "Quite often a symptom of thyroid issues—the tissue swelling that causes it can result from either hyperthyroidism or hypothyroidism. If the Pruitts were my patients, I'd do thyroid testing on every single one of them so I could get them on the proper medication. A wonky thyroid can cause a lot of issues—including some mental health problems. This young man's eyes look just fine, though. What makes you think he's a Pruitt?"

"We're hoping he isn't," I said. "Also hoping he's not the skeleton." I gave him the CliffsNotes version of Billy's history.

"I understand," he said when I'd finished. "I'll share this with Dr. McAuslan-Crine and see what she thinks. But I bet it will be fairly easy to determine whether or not he's the skeleton. We've got the maxilla, and we're making good progress on the teeth. And that diastema's pretty distinctive."

"The diaste—what?" I asked. I knew the maxilla was what I'd have called the upper jawbone, but the other word was unfamiliar.

"Diastema," he said, more slowly. "The gap between his front teeth."

"I never knew it had a name," I said. "But that was actually what I was thinking—that the shape of his teeth would be fairly distinctive."

"It definitely will." Dad sounded delighted with my discovery. "Do you have pictures of any other suspects?"

"A couple." I texted him my shots of Hobart and Gus.

"Now that's more like it," he said. "Classic Pruitt physiognomy. No distinctive dentition, though."

"No visible dentition at all," I said. "The one isn't smiling, and the other looks as if he's trying hard to smile without showing his teeth. Given how bad the skeleton's teeth are—"

"Good point. Someone with as much dental work as our skeleton could very well want to avoid smiling, or cultivate a closed-mouth smile. Did I tell you that Dr. Ffollett is going to come down next week to help us with the forensic odontology?"

"He'll enjoy that," I said. "See if Cordelia wants to come with him. I know she'd enjoy another visit with Brynn."

"I'll suggest it," he said. "But what I wanted to mention was that the other day he was telling me about a test they used to administer to dental students. They'd put a single tooth in a box, and the student had to stick his hand in and identify it by the shape alone. And not just whether it's an incisor or a molar, which I could probably manage, but exactly which of the thirty-two teeth it is."

"I never knew that." And I was willing to bet that Dad was already trying to train himself to perform the same feat. "But if Dr. Ffollett had to learn how to do that, think how easy it will be for him to sort out the skeleton's teeth if you let him take off the blindfold. Anyway—I'll see you later. I have a couple more errands to run."

We said our goodbyes. Then I started the car and set off to visit Miss Ethelinda Pruitt.

The Caerphilly Assisted Living was a sprawling one-story concrete-and-glass building on the outskirts of town, only a few blocks from the hospital. The residents found this proximity comforting, and every so often, if both of the county ambulances were deployed elsewhere, you could see staff members sprinting down the sidewalk pushing a wheelchair or hospital bed when they wanted to get a resident to Caerphilly General in a hurry.

Brianna Shiffley, the receptionist, a young cousin of Vern and

Randall, looked up from her slightly old-fashioned switchboard and greeted me cheerfully.

"Afternoon, Meg," she said. "What's up? Have they figured out who's buried in your brother's backyard?"

I glanced at the clock on the wall behind her. Yes, it was afternoon. Nearly one. I'd spent longer in the library than I'd realized—on top of getting a late start due to the search for Iris. Just for a moment, I wished I'd had lunch before dropping by here. Ah, well. I could start thinking about it as a reward for tackling Miss Ethelinda.

"Not yet," I said. "But they're working on it." I came close to saying "I'm working on it," but caught myself in time. "I wanted to visit one of your residents—Miss Ethelinda Pruitt. Any idea where I can find her?"

"Miss Ethelinda?" Her face showed surprise. Maybe even astonishment. "Why in the world would you—I mean . . . Oh! Does this have anything to do with the skeleton?"

It occurred to me that I had no idea if the chief had released the information that the skeleton was a Pruitt or if he wanted that held back.

"The chief's talking to a lot of the local old-timers," I said. "To see what they can remember about people who might have disappeared around the time the skeleton would have been buried. And Miss Ethelinda's probably the only person in town who could give him the Pruitt family perspective, but he doesn't think she'd be all that willing to talk to him or any of his officers, so I offered to come and see her."

"The chief's right," Brianna said. "Not all that sure she'll talk to you, either, but you're welcome to try. Room 199. Take a left in the hallway. But keep your eyes open, and if she picks up anything smaller than a shoebox, get ready to duck. She used to play fast-pitch softball, and she's still got a pretty good arm."

"Thanks for the warning," I said, before heading down the

hallway toward Miss Ethelinda's room. I quickly deduced that room number 199 was at the far end of one of the building's long hallways. Was there any significance to that? I remembered once, when Grandfather had been in the hospital, he'd been such a noisy and disruptive patient that the staff had put him at the far end of the floor he was on, with several empty rooms as a buffer between him and the rest of the patients. Had the assisted-living staff done the same thing with Miss Ethelinda?

The door of room 199 was open, but I decided that barging in unannounced would get our conversation off to a rocky start, so I knocked on the doorframe and waited. As I did, I noticed a framed cross-stitched sampler affixed to the door, right under Miss Ethelinda's name plate. It read WARNING: THIS IS PROOF I HAVE THE PATIENCE TO STAB SOMETHING 1,000 TIMES. I suppressed the giggle this sentiment inspired and knocked again.

No answer.

"Miss Pruitt?" I called out. "It's Meg Langslow. May I come in and talk to you?"

"Not much in the mood for talking," came a surprisingly loud, deep, raspy voice—the voice, I suspected, of a longtime smoker. "Can't very well stop you if you want to try."

I stepped inside and took in Miss Ethelinda's decor. My first impression was that I'd walked into a jungle. She had several dozen houseplants of all kinds, either crowding the windowsill and the top of her dresser or dangling in the window on old-fashioned macramé hangers. Most of the wall space was filled with more framed cross-stitched pictures. But the initial impression—that I'd entered the homey space of a sweet little old lady with a green thumb and a flair for needlework—vanished when I started reading the samplers, which featured sentiments like:

"Profanity makes talking fun."

"Other people ruin everything."

"It's not mean if it's hilarious."

"Hell is other people."

"Bitch, please."

And those were only the more printable ones. Did she design these herself? Or had she found a vendor who actually sold such a wide range of amusingly misanthropic messages, many of them featuring the f-bomb?

I glanced over to see that she was watching me with an expectant expression, as if she was waiting for me to express my outrage over her needlework. I decided not to play into her game.

"Fabulous needlework," I said. "Do you take commissions?"

Chapter 22

Miss Ethelinda blinked for a second, then burst into a wheezy laugh that trailed off into a cough, strengthening my hunch that she was an ex-smoker. Or maybe not even ex, despite the assisted living's strict rules against smoking, not only inside but also on the grounds. I didn't know Miss Ethelinda all that well, but it wasn't hard to see that she probably got away with pretty much anything she wanted, in spite of the staff's best efforts.

While she got her breath back, I studied her. I couldn't guess her age. Her skin was weathered and leathery, but somehow it looked more like sun damage than extreme age, and there was something youthful about her short, curly hairdo, in spite of its gray color. She was sitting in an easy chair with a garish fuchsia afghan over her lap. She was holding another piece of needlework—an unfinished sampler that so far said "What the actual f—" She had more chin than the typical Pruitt, and an atypically aquiline nose. In fact, she appeared to have lucked out in the genetic lottery and missed getting the worst of her family's usual facial features. She probably hadn't been a beauty queen as a young woman, but she'd have been the belle of any Pruitt ball and had aged into a relatively distinguished-looking little old lady.

"You here for some good reason?" she asked when she got her breath back, although her voice still sounded a little strangled. "Or just to snoop?"

On the way over, I'd planned out a couple of possible approaches. I decided to try the relatively straightforward one.

"I'm here in the hope of tapping into your knowledge of local history," I said. "They found an unidentified skeleton buried in my brother's backyard, so we're asking folks from all the old families to help us figure out who he is."

"And you're thinking I might know him?"

"We're hoping someone does. May I tell you what we know?"

She tossed her unfinished needlework onto the side table that also held a tall glass of iced tea and leaned back, in a gesture that suggested she was granting me an audience. It occurred to me that in addition to keeping quiet about Grandfather's identification of the deceased as a Pruitt, I should refrain from mentioning the bullet until I knew whether it was public knowledge.

"The skeleton's male, between fifteen and thirty," I said. "They estimated he's been there between thirty and forty years, and then they found a 1986 quarter in his pocket. So they're looking for someone who went AWOL between 1986 and around 2005."

"Who's they?"

"My dad and the archaeologist from the college." I didn't think mentioning the chief would encourage her to help.

"And you're thinking he might be a Pruitt?"

"We're asking a lot of people to search their memories," I said. "Judge Jane Shiffley, Ms. Ellie from the library, Deacon Washington of the New Life Baptist Church—"

"And I bet I'm the only Pruitt you can find." Another wheezy laugh.

"So far," I admitted.

"They've still got George down in Coffeewood, I hear," she said. "You could talk to him."

I pulled out my notebook and jotted this down. George Pruitt was Caerphilly's former mayor, and Coffeewood was a medium-security state prison in Culpeper County. This was probably information the chief could find out through official channels, but maybe hearing it from me would save him time. And besides, I wanted to look properly grateful for anything she chose to share.

"Hamish was down at Greenville," she continued. "Of course, he's probably out by now. He got off easy on account of turning state's witness against anyone he could. Pretty sure Mervyn's still down at Deerfield, but he's old as the hills and off his rocker, so they stuck him in the Looney Tunes wing. Not much use going to see him."

Deerfield, I recalled, was where the Virginia Department of Corrections had established a geriatric and assisted-living prison unit. I'd let Chief Burke worry about whether Mervyn was a useful source of information. It would probably depend on whether time had eroded his memory, or only his inhibitions.

"Damned if I know where any of the rest of them went," she said. "They pretty much ignore me. Good thing I can pay for my keep here with my own money, 'cause if they tried to bill any of my deadbeat relatives, it would come back marked 'moved, no forwarding address.'"

I wondered if she was quoting what she'd seen on letters she'd sent to absent family members. I was starting to feel a little sorry for her.

"Any candidates you can think of for our skeleton?" I asked.

She studied me for a while before answering. I did my best to wait patiently. It helped to imagine her dislike for her family fighting a duel with her hatred of everyone else in the world.

"I'll think about it," she said.

Well, at least it wasn't a flat-out refusal.

"And I'll ask my relatives when they come to visit me," she said.

Less promising, since everything I'd heard suggested that her relatives almost never set foot in Caerphilly these days.

I pondered, for a moment, asking about Gus and Hobart. And then decided that no, it was better to see what she came up with on her own. If she came up with anything.

"If you think of something, please call me." I'd already tucked one of my business cards in my pocket in anticipation of this. And I'd chosen one of the blacksmithing cards—I didn't think the card identifying me as special assistant to Mayor Shiffley would sit well with her. I pulled out the card and offered it to her.

"Hmph." She frowned, but she took it.

An idea occurred to me.

"Are any of your family still plugged into the local grapevine?" I asked.

"How should I know?" she said. "But if you're thinking maybe some of them will show up to help you identify your corpse, I wouldn't bet on it."

"Actually, I was wondering what would happen if word went out on the grapevine that you'd suddenly come into a whole lot of money," I said. "Like winning-the-lottery level of money."

"They'd all come around sucking up, trying to get their hands on some of it," she said. "And as soon as they found out there wasn't any money, they'd vamoose again."

"Yeah," I said. "But you could have a lot of fun while it lasted."

She blinked, and then a mischievous grin spread over her face.

"And you're also thinking maybe that would help you track down some of them," she said.

"The thought had crossed my mind," I admitted. "A win-win situation."

Just then an anxious-looking young woman in an aide's uniform hurried in.

"There you are, Miss Pruitt!" she chirped.

"Get lost," Miss Ethelinda growled.

"But it's time for your massage," the aide protested. "And your midday meds."

I was expecting Miss Ethelinda to dig in her heels, but the pleased expression that appeared on her face suggested that she probably liked the massage. And either liked whatever effect her meds had or was willing to put up with them to get to the massage.

"Hmph!" she snorted, but she extended her hand for the plastic water cup the aide was holding in one gloved hand and used it to swallow a small collection of pills. As I watched her wash down each pill with a sip of water, I could almost see the DNA she was depositing on the rim of the cup. And the aide was wearing gloves.

Miss Ethelinda set the plastic cup on the side table, and I stood aside to let the aide escort her out of the room.

I tried not to stare at the plastic cup until they were out of sight. Then I rummaged through my purse until I found— Yes! I still had my stash of freezer bags, left over from my doggy specimen collection duties. I plucked a couple of tissues out of a nearby box, used them to pick up the plastic cup without touching the rim, and tucked it into a freezer bag.

Of course, if Horace and Dad were here, they would point out that in most cases, brown paper bags were the only proper evidence bags—that over time, the moisture retained by a plastic bag could promote mold growth and lead to the gradual degradation of the evidence it contained. But I figured the key was "over time." I planned to make sure this evidence got to Grandfather's lab as soon as possible. I had no idea if it would be of any use in the quest to identify the skeleton, but I recalled Dr. McAuslan-Crine saying she could use "a few cooperative Pruitts." Which was an oxymoron in my book, so I figured we'd better start working on stealth DNA collection.

I thrust the bag containing the plastic cup down near the bottom of my tote and put on my most nonchalant expression as I made my way out and back to my car.

As soon as I got there, I called Grandfather.

"Am I correct in thinking you'd like to increase the number of Pruitts in your DNA database?" I asked.

"We're going to need to if we want Dr. McAuslan-Crine to figure out who that blasted skeleton belongs to," he said. "Have you found me some?"

"One," I said. "It's a start," I added, before he could protest that one wasn't going to do all that much good. "And I have a plan to get some more. Of course, keep it mum—the Pruitt in question doesn't know I've got her DNA."

"That won't make any difference to my analysts," he said. "And if it turns out to be useful DNA, the chief can figure out a way to get an official sample."

"That's what I figured," I said. "I can drop the sample off at your lab."

"How about if you bring it out to me?" he said. "I'm back at the crime scene at the moment. And then I can deliver it to the lab personally and make sure they jump right on it."

"I'll bring it right over."

Since Grandfather no longer drove, I suspected he'd wanted me to bring him the specimen so he could recruit me to ferry him back to his lab along with the plastic cup. But I needed to drop by the house, anyway—if for no other reason than to grab some lunch. In the unlikely event that the ravening hordes had completely consumed the Methodist covered-dish lunch, perhaps preparations would have begun for the Baptist cookout. Worst case, I could probably scare up something acceptable from the pantry. I'd eat, and then hunt down Grandfather.

As I was reaching to start the car, I heard the faint ding of an arriving text. I pulled out my phone to see who it was. Mother.

"Have you had any luck tracking down Iris?"

I felt a surge of both worry and annoyance. Worry that Iris must still be missing, and annoyance that Mother seemed to be expecting me to find her. Did she not know that the chief had put out a BOLO?

I took a deep breath before replying. And I started by texting her the screenshot of my exchange with Iris.

"I got this from her, saying she was fine," I texted. "But she didn't say where she was. Have you found out anything?" Back in her court.

Instead of replying, she sent me a picture of a note:

"Don't worry," it said. "Back soon."

No signature, but I recognized Iris's bold, sprawling handwriting.

I frowned. My first reaction was a feeling of relief. This, plus the text conversation I'd had with her, seemed pretty clear evidence that Iris had left under her own steam.

"Who found this?" I asked. "And when?"

"Eileen," Mother texted back. "Just now, but she has no idea when it was left. Could have been anytime between last night and five minutes ago. She's worried. She thinks that it doesn't sound like her mother and she must have written it under duress."

It sounded exactly like Iris to me. Short and straight to the point, as if she was dashing off to do whatever it was she wanted to do and not bothering to explain. And she'd be annoyed if we complained that her lack of communication had caused anyone distress. "You'd think I was a toddler," she'd grumble. I'd seen this play out before between Iris and her children.

"Have you shared that with Chief Burke?" I texted back. "He has a BOLO out for her, you know."

"Yes," she said. "But keep your eyes open."

So before heading for home, I drove around town a bit, trying to cruise by any place Iris was fond of going, like the bakery and

Muriel's Diner. Although since Iris had sold her car and given up her driver's license, she'd have had to catch a ride from someone to get to any of them, so I didn't think my efforts were going to be all that useful. I eventually gave up and headed for home, still fretting not just over where Iris was but also why she'd pulled this disappearing act. It had to have something to do with the skeleton.

At least at home I could find something to do that would distract me from worrying about Iris.

Chapter 23

An astonishing number of cars were parked all along both sides of the road leading up to our house. I resigned myself to the likelihood that the covered-dish lunch was long gone—and the single thin plume of smoke rising from the yard suggested that the cookout preparations had only just begun. But it cheered me to see how many volunteers had turned out for this last day of parade preparations. Even if my absence had been noted, no one could logically claim I'd sabotaged the event.

And when I reached the kitchen, I found that Mother and Rose Noire had saved me a generous sampling of the covered dishes—Mrs. Dahlgren's savory beef stew, Reverend Trask's spicy curried chicken, and a salad that must have been assembled by committee, since I couldn't imagine a single cook having the time and patience to slice and dice nearly three dozen fresh ingredients.

As I was sitting down at the kitchen table to dig in, my phone rang. It was Delaney.

"Afternoon," I said.

"Afternoon," she replied. "Did you borrow my bike?"

"No," I said. "Why would I? Mine's in perfect working order. At least as far as I know, it is—all the places I needed to go today were far enough away that I didn't even consider biking to them."

"Damn," she said. "I was hoping maybe you'd had a flat tire or something and borrowed mine. I was going to use it for taking some of the bigger dogs on a nice brisk run, but it's gone. I guess I should report it as stolen."

"Is Rob's bike still there?" I asked.

"Yes," she said. "Right in the barn, beside the empty space where mine should be. Which is weird, because his is much fancier than mine. Must have been a pretty clueless thief."

Or maybe a thief who wanted the slightly smaller of the two bikes. A thief who wanted to use the bike rather than sell it.

"Tell the chief about it," I said. "And let him know it disappeared around the same time Iris did."

A short silence.

"You think Iris stole my bike? Why? And what do you mean, disappeared? Where has she gone?"

"Iris would probably say she only borrowed it," I said. "And obviously so she could go someplace that was farther than she wanted to walk, but exactly where that is—your guess is as good as mine. Give the chief a good description of your bike. If they find it, I bet they'll find Iris, or vice versa."

"Weird," she said. "I'll call him right now."

I returned to my plate, but a lot of the joy had gone out of it. I studied my phone for a minute or so, then shifted my fork to my left hand and texted Kevin.

"Did you install cameras at Rob and Delaney's yesterday?" I asked.

Since Kevin rarely strayed far from his electronic devices, I wasn't surprised to get a rapid reply.

"Yes. Around eight p.m."

"Would they have covered the barn?"

A pause.

"No, just the dig site. Why?"

"You heard that Iris is missing?"

"Yes."

"She may have taken off on Delaney's bike."

"Seriously?"

"It disappeared about the same time she did."

"I'll see if any of my cameras caught anything. Or any others I can monitor."

I wondered what other cameras he meant. I wouldn't put it past Kevin to have figured out how to hack into any number of cameras—the various Ring, Nest, and Blink doorbell cameras local homeowners had installed around town, along with any web-enabled cameras belonging to local businesses. It was information. And Kevin was all about information. I'd lost track of how many times he'd intoned his favorite quote from Ursula LeGuin's *The Left Hand of Darkness*: "When action grows unprofitable, gather information; when information grows unprofitable, sleep."

I returned to eating, keeping an eye on my phone in case Kevin found anything worth sharing. But he hadn't by the time I finished most of my late lunch. So, muttering to myself that a watched phone never dings, I decided to go outside with the several perfectly ripe slices of watermelon that were my dessert.

I saw Ms. Ellie sitting at one of the picnic tables, sipping a glass of lemonade. I couldn't quite tell if she was taking a break from her labors, or keeping an eye on the many volunteers scurrying around her. Probably a little of both. I joined her.

"The chief tells me you dropped by my library this morning to research people who might be our skeleton," she said. "How did it go?"

"Your intern was very helpful," I said. "She gave me a PDF of the Pruitt family history. I'm going to start digging through that tonight and making a list of all the Pruitts who could possibly fall within the age range of our skeleton. And then we can figure out which of them are still around, or at least were still around well after whatever Dad and Dr. McAuslan-Crine decide was the latest possible date for him to have been buried there."

"It won't be complete, you know," Ms. Ellie said.

"I know," I said. "I wouldn't expect them to include anyone who was biologically a Pruitt but born out of wedlock, for example. Even if they knew about them. DNA testing is turning up a lot of that these days."

"True," she said. "But the Pruitts who put together that book also tended to leave out anyone they decided was a black sheep. Anyone who got convicted of a crime or left town under a cloud or interfered with whatever shenanigans the family was trying to pull off back when they were running things."

My mood sank.

"Oh, great," I said. "In other words, they probably left out exactly the guys we'd most want to know about. So the family history isn't going to be the least bit of use."

"Oh, it'll be of some use." She chuckled at my reaction. "Not as much use as it could be if they were honest. Or if they were competent genealogists who always checked their sources and never jumped to conclusions. It wouldn't just be people you and I would consider dodgy that they left out. Anyone they disapproved of. For example, I happen to know they left out an unfortunate cousin who went to work for the justice department back when FDR was president. Not big fans of the New Deal, the Pruitts. But it's still going to be useful. For one thing, it'll let you tick off a lot of the possibilities. You can knock off anyone who was still around marrying and fathering children and such within the last ten to fifteen years. And for another thing, the ones they left out are going to be the very ones you want to take the closest look at. They can delete the black sheep from their silly little puff piece of a family history, but they can't delete them from the official state birth records—which are a lot easier to access these days. Not only from the state, but they're all online at Ancestry.com and places like that."

"Here I thought I had a leg up on the project," I said. "I may have to leave it to Dr. McAuslan-Crine after all. She's thinking of getting the students in one of her summer session courses to tackle the project."

"You should definitely share the PDF with her," Ms. Ellie said.

"And make sure she knows it's a puff piece."

"She's a smart cookie. She'll know that. She's worked with unreliable amateur genealogies before. Just make sure she knows that it's not just a case that the authors weren't professional genealogists. She should know that they were hell-bent on cleaning up the family reputation. She can take it from there. And it might be a useful lesson for her students. A project that would help them learn about the importance of vetting your sources."

"A good thing I talked to you before turning this over to her. Although since I don't have her email address, I'll turn it over to Dad and Grandfather—with a warning about its probable unreliability."

She nodded her approval.

"You probably saved me from embarrassing myself," I said.

"I bet you'd have figured it out pretty quickly yourself," she replied. "When you noticed that some of the Pruitts who left town had also vanished from the pages of the family history. Oops—I think I need to go over there and keep the peace."

She rose and hurried off toward the barn. I turned to see what emerging problem she'd spotted. A stocky, fortyish woman in jeans and a pastel pink t-shirt was haranguing Clarence. Her face was beet red with anger, and she was shaking her finger in his face. I watched as Ms. Ellie steered the woman away from Clarence.

Clarence looked relieved. The beet-faced woman was now shaking her finger in Ms. Ellie's face.

"It won't do her any good."

I turned to see that Judge Jane, carrying a glass of iced tea, had joined me at the picnic table.

"If you mean the woman who's currently earning the wrath of Ms. Ellie, I agree," I said. "Do you have any idea why she's so upset with Clarence?"

"He told her she can't have a dog unless she goes through the usual background check," Judge Jane said. "No idea if she's the dogfighting connection we've been worried about or just an entitled idiot. Either way, the more she kicks up a fuss about what's become a pretty standard measure to protect animals, the less chance she has of getting one. So the chief tells me you've been searching old issues of the *Clarion* for Pruitts who might have turned into our skeleton. Any hot prospects?"

"A few." I fished the stack of printouts out of my tote and held them up.

"That many?" She looked dismayed.

"Only half a dozen," I said. "But whenever I found a possible missing person, I printed out the whole issue, so I could see what else was going on at the same time. Put the disappearance in context." I showed her that I'd used paper clips to divide the printouts by the issue date.

"Good thinking," she said. "Mind if I take a look?"

I set the printouts in front of her. She moved her reading glasses from the top of her head to her nose, picked up the top sheet, and began studying it.

"Gus Pruitt," she said. "Now, that puzzled me. Something definitely happened with him."

Not what I wanted to hear. If the skeleton was Gus, did Iris have a good reason to be unsettled by it? A reason to make herself scarce?

"Gus actually got a track-and-field scholarship to someplace," the judge went on. "Only a partial scholarship, and it wasn't anyplace I'd ever heard of, but still, his family were mighty proud of it. Far as I know, they hadn't even bribed the place with a donation. And then suddenly *poof!* He was gone. Taking a little time off to find himself, or so they said. Hope he eventually found himself, because nobody else ever could. The kid was on probation for DUI and underage drinking. When he stopped showing up for supervision, his probation officer tried to get him hauled in on a violation. His family claimed they had no idea where he was and swore they'd tell the court if he showed up. But they never did. And the police never found him—or maybe never even tried, since the Pruitts were more or less running the department back then. It just all petered out."

"So he could be the skeleton."

"He could. No idea why someone would want to bump him off. He was no angel, but I can't think why anyone would want to shoot him. Mostly what he got in trouble for was underage drinking. I'm not even sure he'd turned eighteen by the time he disappeared."

She continued slowly flipping through the sheets.

"Now that was a time."

Chapter 24

Judge Jane was holding up one of the pages I'd printed out—a copy of the *Clarion*'s front page with the heading "Spare Attic Heist."

It wasn't an article I'd deliberately focused on—I'd only printed it out because it was in the same issue as one of the disappearing Pruitts. Although it had sounded interesting, and I'd made a mental note to read it when I had more time. I leaned over her shoulder and did so now. Evidently thieves had struck overnight at the Spare Attic, breaking into storage units, stealing valuables, and vandalizing much of what they didn't steal.

"Yikes," I said. "Pretty major crime wave for Caerphilly."

"Very much so," she said, with a rueful smile. "Everyone who had a unit out there was in an uproar about why there wasn't better security. A lot of people thought it was an inside job, but it turned out to be two layabouts from Clay County. A Dingle and a Peebles, if memory serves."

I was shuffling through the stacks of printouts, because I recalled printing out a follow-up article. "Your memory serves pretty nicely, as usual," I said, when I found it. "Victor Dingle and John Wayne Peebles."

"Yup." She nodded as she scanned the article. "I prosecuted that. Police had them dead to rights. They'd just shoved everything they'd taken into the hayloft at Vic Dingle's uncle's barn. Funny, though. I was kind of surprised when it turned out to be them."

"You had them pegged as law-abiding citizens?"

"Them? Heavens, no." She snorted in derision. "Hardened juvenile delinquents, from what I'd seen. But I'd kind of expected them to graduate to drug trafficking, not grand theft. They'd already done time in juvenile detention for drug-related offenses. Hadn't been out all that long when they pulled the Spare Attic stunt. And neither of them was exactly a rocket scientist, so I kind of expected them to stick to what they knew."

"And they were sent to prison," I said. "For twenty years each. Isn't that kind of a stiff sentence for a first adult offense?"

"It was," she said. "If they served the whole time. I doubt they did. After the Truth in Sentencing laws came into effect in 1995, they'd have had to serve eighty-five percent of their sentences, but back then? Juries were giving felons outrageously long sentences just to make sure they did any time at all. Plus, I think the length of the sentence was partly because of how much stuff they took—it must have added up to fifteen or twenty thousand dollars' worth, on top of which they did a fair amount of damage to the building itself. And of course, back then the Spare Attic belonged to one of the Pruitts."

"Yeah, that kind of explains it," I said. "As much revenge as justice."

"But I don't think there were any Pruitts on the parole board, so odds were they got out in well under twenty years. And you're right about the crime wave. Look what else happened about that time."

She held up another page.

"Hobart Pruitt," I read. "One of my candidates for the skeleton. Vanished while out on bail for drug-trafficking charges. Doesn't say what drug."

"Cocaine," she said. "We had a lot of that back then, between the wilder young Pruitts and the less-reputable citizens of Clay County. I remember when Hobart skipped bail and left town. I'd have said good riddance, but it really galls me that we didn't get the chance to send him up. He was a very bad dude. And he disappeared the same week as the Great Spare Attic Heist. I never realized those two things happened so close together. Were they in the same issue of the *Clarion*?"

"The Spare Attic heist article appeared in the next issue after the one with Hobart's disappearance," I said. "I printed it out because it had a short follow-up about Hobart."

"Yes, that was quite the crime wave," she said. "We should remind Henry Burke of this, next time he complains about how busy he is."

"It might actually be useful to him," I said. "A lot of locals would have a good idea what they were doing when the Spare Attic heist happened. That might give the chief some clues about what else was happening in town around the time Hobart Pruitt disappeared."

"Good point," she said. "Most locals would have done their best to forget about him."

"Do you remember much about him?"

"Oh, yes," she said. "He was rude and arrogant. Showed up in court wearing track pants that sagged halfway down his rear end, so the whole world could see his underwear."

"I was thinking more of things that might help them figure out if the skeleton belongs to him," I said. "Like his height. And what were his teeth like?"

"Hmm." She thought for a moment. "Tall side of average. Maybe five eleven, six feet. Don't remember anything about his teeth. Is there anything weird about the skeleton's teeth?"

"You'd have to ask Dad," I said. "Or the chief. I just figure the teeth are probably one of the few identifying features you'd see on a skeleton."

"You know, that's curiously depressing," she said. "Thinking that skeleton could be Hobart. And I'm not sure why. I can't say I gave him much thought over the last few decades, but when I did, it was usually to fret about what a hardened criminal he was at what I seem to remember was a pretty young age."

"Only twenty-three," I said, glancing at the article.

"Yes," she said. "At the time, it just made me mad—that Judge Pruitt, who should have recused himself on account of the family connection, gave him bail, which meant that instead of stopping him we as good as turned him loose to cause trouble somewhere else."

"But did we?" I asked.

"Exactly," she said. "What if he didn't skip bail? What if he's your skeleton? How are we supposed to feel about that?"

I didn't much like the "your skeleton" bit. A few minutes ago, she'd been calling him "our skeleton." But I didn't protest.

"And if he's the skeleton," she went on, "it would explain why his family never managed to drag him back so they could try to get his bail refunded. They certainly tried hard enough. And made a big fuss about how much all their unsuccessful efforts had cost."

"That sounds like them."

"Yes. Always focused on the money side of things, the Pruitts." She flipped to the next stack of papers.

"Billy Taylor." She nodded. "Hope it's not him. Good kid. Whoever broke him out of jail did a good deed, if you ask me."

"You have no idea who did it?" I asked.

"Well, I didn't, if that's what you're thinking," she said. "Although I like to think maybe I'd have gotten up my nerve to try if I'd had any chance of pulling it off. The family always figured maybe it was my cousin Rollie, who was working as a deputy then. I think the Pruitts thought so, too—they fired him not long after that. But we managed to keep them from going after him."

"How did you manage that?" I asked.

"Gave him an alibi for when someone rescued the Taylor kid," she said. "When they hauled Rollie in for questioning, he was smart enough to say he wanted a lawyer and I was the only one he could think of. I told them no way Rollie let Billy go, because that night he and my daddy both fell asleep in those old broken-down La-Z-Boys in the basement after drinking too many beers while watching basketball. And Daddy was sharp enough to back me up."

"Interesting," I said. "Did he ever admit that he'd done it?"

"He told us he hadn't done it, and didn't know who did, but he was grateful we spoke up for him, because there was no way he could prove he was home alone and fast asleep."

"How would you feel if you figured out he had done it?" I asked.

"I didn't know he hadn't," she said. "But even if he'd told me he'd done it, I'd have helped him. I just knew that whoever rescued Billy was on the side of the angels."

"Would he get in trouble if it came out now that he'd done it?"

"Don't think so," she said. "He passed on a few years after that, and if he did do it, that's between him and the man upstairs now. And if anyone tried to charge me with giving false information to the police—well, Daddy's gone, too, so I'm not sure how they'd prove it. And besides, whatever they charged him with would probably be a misdemeanor—or could be bargained down to one by a good attorney—and there's a statute of limitations on those, you know."

"So if some person or persons unknown helped Taylor leave

town, they could probably admit what they'd done without fear of retribution."

"Yup."

Good to know that if anything happened that put Vern in the position of having to confess what he'd done, his good deed probably wouldn't come back to hurt him.

She returned to her careful perusal of my printouts while I ate the rest of my watermelon.

"I think you've got the likeliest candidates pegged," she said a few minutes later, gathering up my printouts and tapping them into a neat pile. "No idea how you're going to prove it's one or another of them, though. Law enforcement did a decent job of searching for them back when they disappeared—Hobart in particular, since it was the DEA and the state police on top of local law enforcement. By now the scent has gone pretty darn cold."

"If we can narrow it down to only a few possibilities, we could try hunting down their dental records," I suggested.

"If your possibilities were Pruitts, they'd have gone to Dr. Braxton Pruitt," she said. "Nothing if not loyal to their own, the Pruitts. And Braxton shut down his practice and left town a year or two before the big dustup that took the rest of his family."

"If he retired, we could figure out who took over his practice."

"He didn't retire," she said. "Someone blew the whistle on him. Turns out he flunked out of dental school and only got his license by submitting forged documents. I doubt if he handed over his records to another dentist. If he was smart he burned them all. Last I heard the State Board of Dentistry was still gunning for him."

"Nothing's ever easy when Pruitts are involved, is it?" I said.

"Then they'll have to identify the skeleton through genetic genealogy. Dr. McAuslan-Crine's going to work on it. We track down any relatives we can find of the young men who went missing, compare their DNA with that of the skeleton, and eventually she should be able to figure out which one it is. Which reminds me—I need to find my grandfather—have you seen him?"

"Last I heard, he was next door telling the archaeologists how to do their job," she said.

"I'll go and rescue them, then," I said.

Chapter 25

I headed for the path to Rob and Delaney's, picking my way through the crowd, dodging Dobermans and patting puppies as I went. A few of the volunteers were still giving dogs haircuts or baths—possibly, in a few cases, second or third baths. But most of the dogs now seemed to be clean and well-groomed, so the rescuers were focused on costumes and, where necessary, remedial leash training.

I passed by where Clarence was communing with the two probable Great Pyrenees dogs, petting one with each hand. They were so enormous they almost managed to dwarf Clarence, even though at six foot six he was two inches taller than Michael and twice as wide. But somehow the Pyrs, as he called them, seemed completely unthreatening, in spite of their size—probably because they had the kind of faces that made them look as if they were perpetually smiling, with mellow dispositions to match. I had a hard time imagining them going up against anything that would bother the sheep, but then Caerphilly wasn't infested with wolves or mountain lions or whatever else would prey on sheep in the wild. And who knew how fierce the Pyrs would be if something threatened one of their charges? Our normally mild-mannered llamas could get quite feisty if they detected something they thought was a threat to any of our resident critters. Besides, I got the idea Seth was more worried about human sheep rustlers than four-legged predators, and even if all they did was bark at intruders, the dogs would probably be an effective deterrent to that. I found myself hoping Seth would adopt them. They'd make nice canine neighbors.

"So have you convinced Seth that their livestock guardian potential is up to snuff?" I asked.

"Yes, indeed," Clarence said. "Of course, we'll never know for sure if they're purebred Great Pyrenees, but they've definitely got quite a lot of Pyr in them. They've got the temperament. And the double dewclaws on their hind legs."

He reached down and lifted up one of the rear legs of the closer dog. If I did that to Spike, I'd end up in the emergency room, but the Pyr just shifted his balance to make it easier for Clarence and wagged his tail, as if delighted by any attention.

And sure enough, where many dogs would have a single dewclaw—or even no dewclaw at all—this one had a curiously shaped dewclaw that branched into two.

"That's kind of weird looking," I said. If it had been anyone but Clarence talking, I'd have assumed they invented the double dewclaw thing to increase the adoptability of a dog with a minor deformity. But Clarence wasn't sneaky like that.

"Perfectly normal for the breed," Clarence said. "The theory is that it helps them get slightly better footing in the snowy mountains where they originated. Works a little bit like a snowshoe."

I refrained from spoiling Clarence's mood by pointing out how infrequently snowshoes were needed in Caerphilly. And I had to smile as I watched him scratching behind two sets of large, fluffy white ears. Clearly Clarence was eager to have the two gentle giants as permanent patients. I wondered if there was anything I could do to increase the likelihood that Seth Early would take them on. Perhaps I could interest Dad in the idea.

Or would that be dangerous? Dad had livestock of his own—a modest but growing collection of heritage-breed sheep and cows. What if he, too, took a notion to provide guardian dogs for his charges, and snatched the Pyrs out from under Seth's nose?

I should probably wait and see if Seth needed encouraging. For now, I shoved the whole problem away for later consideration. I spotted Grandfather and Dad emerging from the woods, and headed over to meet them.

"There you are!" Dad said. "I hear you've started collecting Pruitt DNA samples for us."

"Only the one sample." I dug into my tote, pulled out the bag with the plastic cup in it, and handed it to Grandfather. "Miss Ethelinda drank from this."

"Excellent!" He held it up for closer inspection. "We can take it over to the lab right now and get the technicians started on it."

To my relief, Dad assumed the "we" in question meant Grandfather and him.

"Great!" he said. "I love watching that whole process. We'll keep you posted."

Grandfather handed him the plastic bag and began striding across the yard toward the driveway, with Dad bouncing along behind him.

I surveyed the activity around me. Everything looked busy, but not frantic. I could probably find someplace to make myself useful, but I wasn't urgently needed. And I couldn't help fretting about Iris. I decided to go over to Delaney and Rob's. Maybe if I poked around some more I could get a clue to where she had gone. Or why she'd gone in the first place. She'd seemed curiously negative on the topic of DNA—was she worried about what he'd find? Or merely alarmed about DNA's potentially pervasive effect on all our privacy?

And in addition to looking for Iris—or clues to where she'd gone—I could see if Dr. McAuslan-Crine and her students were still excavating or if they'd removed the skeleton to . . . wherever you took unidentified skeletons when you found them. If it had been a complete body, they'd have taken it to the hospital morgue for Dad to autopsy. But a skeleton? What would they be doing with him?

My curiosity was aroused, so I walked briskly down the path between the houses. To my satisfaction, Dr. McAuslan-Crine and two students were still there—although there was nothing but dirt at their excavation site.

"You took Mr. Bones away," I said, in a tone of mock protest. "Just when I was starting to like having him around."

"If you find yourself missing him too much, you can drop by our lab and visit him," the professor said. "We'll be taking care of him for the time being."

"For the time being," I echoed. "What happens to him in the long term, then?"

"Best case, we identify him and reunite him with his family," she said, "so they can give him a proper burial with his kin. If we can't identify him, then we'll eventually be handing him over to the Virginia Department of Historic Resources down in Richmond. The state archaeologist and her staff are in charge whenever someone finds an unidentified skeleton. They make sure they're properly removed from the ground and try to find homes for them."

"Homes?" I echoed. "They don't just bury them?"

"We try to find their relatives or descendants," she said. "For example, if we determine the bones belong to an indigenous person, we try to reunite them with their tribe. If a skeleton's found in a defunct churchyard, we try to hunt down the descendants of the congregation, since the odds are good that the unidentified person was related to some of them. And nowadays, using DNA, we're a lot more successful at finding living people who are actually related to them."

"And if you can't find anyone to reunite a skeleton with?"

"Then it stays in the state archaeologist's keeping until we can," she said. "Indefinitely, in some cases. Her goal—hers and her staff's—would be eventually to identify all of them and give them a proper burial, but if they can't do that, they keep them safe. Unlikely our friend will end up there, though, since we've already got a partial identity on him. They were pleased to hear that."

"They already know about our skeleton, then?"

"Oh, yes," she said. "I notified them before we even started excavating, and I've been keeping them posted. I think they had a little celebration when I told them about the partial DNA match. Last I heard, they already had around a hundred and fifty full or partial sets of human remains in their custody. They hate having to add to their number, and it lifts their spirits whenever they find a real home for one of them."

"I never knew about any of this," I said. "I certainly hope never to become an unidentified skeleton, but it's nice to know I'd be well treated if that ever happened."

"Didn't used to be that way," she said. "You used to see a lot of skeletons on display in museums—if they weren't dumped in a cardboard coffin in an unmarked grave. We treat human remains with a lot more respect these days. Well, that's it for us." She straightened up and stretched her back as if to ease out the kinks from so much stooping and digging.

"Have you finished here, then?" I nodded toward the excavation site. "Or are you going to keep going a bit to see if you can find any more objects that might give us a clue to what happened and when?"

"We're planning to come back on Monday and dig a little more," she said. "If we hadn't finished with the skeleton, I might have brought my students out tomorrow and Sunday, but . . ." She shrugged.

"But any inanimate objects you haven't found yet have been buried there for a good thirty or forty years already," I said. "Another few days won't hurt."

"Exactly," she said. "And we've done our best to spread the word that we don't expect to find any valuable relics, which should fend off the pothunters."

"Pothunters?" I echoed.

"Nonarchaeologists who go around digging up historical sites and stealing anything valuable they can find," she said. "The bane of our profession. Although frankly, if you go back a century, or even a few decades, it can be hard to see the difference between what the pothunters do and what we used to do. All those Victorians in their pith helmets digging up the Egyptian pyramids and the ruins of Knossos and Troy, and hauling away the valuable stuff to European museums. These days there's a big debate about whether any of us should be taking away anything at all."

"Seems unlikely that anyone would expect to find anything valuable here," I said.

"I'd still be happier if we had a guard up for a while longer," she said.

"Kevin put up some cameras," I said. "And there will be a deputy or two next door to keep an eye on the dogs. If anyone comes snooping around here, they can check it out."

"Better than nothing," she said. "And I'm probably worrying unnecessarily. Well, I'm off. See you Monday. Or maybe tomorrow at the parade."

She slung a couple of tools over her shoulder, like a soldier carrying a rifle, and marched toward where her students were already waiting by her battered pickup.

I headed for the back porch. Spike was there, enjoying a patch of late afternoon sunshine and studiously ignoring me. The door to Iris's suite was partly open. Elated, I hurried over to peer in, and saw only Eileen, lying atop the neatly made bed with an ice pack over her eyes. She lifted one corner of it to peer at me.

"Sorry," I said. "I saw the open door and thought maybe your mom had returned."

"No." She let the ice pack fall back in place. "No sign of her. She's probably still alive. I got a text from her an hour ago. Told me to stop worrying about her and go home. Not planning on going anywhere except maybe back to the Inn when I can manage it. Stress gives me migraines."

"Did you tell the chief?" I asked. "About the text?"

"What can he do?" she said. "I texted her back and she didn't answer me. I doubt if she'll answer him, either."

"No," I said. "But he could contact the phone company. They might be able to trace where she is. Not necessarily precisely enough to find her, but you could tell whether she's texting from Timbuktu or from the floor above you at the Inn."

She lifted the corner of the ice pack again and peered at me.

"They can do that?"

I reminded myself that she didn't do criminal law.

"I think so," I said. "Kevin could tell you for sure, but it's worth trying." Should I mention that Iris had also texted me? Maybe not. I couldn't remember if I'd told Eileen about it, and if I hadn't, she might be upset by the omission.

"I should call the chief." From the way she said it—and the drawn expression on her face—I deduced that just sitting up would be a major effort.

"I'll do it," I said. "Text me a screenshot of the message she sent you, so we know the time, and I'll tell him all about it."

"You're an angel." She reached for her phone, held it up over her face, and squinted at it with one eye. She tapped for a bit, and in a few seconds a ding from my phone announced the arrival of the screenshot.

"Perfect," I said. "Now take care of your head and let the rest of us worry about your mom."

"Thank you," she half whispered. She had already replaced the ice pack.

I went back out to the porch and pulled the door almost closed. Then I sat down in one of the rocking chairs and called the chief.

"Iris just texted her daughter," I said, keeping my voice low to avoid disturbing Eileen. "At four twenty-three. Maybe the phone company can help us find her."

And then I sent the screenshot.

"It never occurred to Eileen that we might find this useful?" he said.

"Evidently not," I replied.

"And she waits till very near to the close of business on Friday to share it," he said. "Blast. I'll get a data request started. Although they still haven't gotten back to me about the text you sent me earlier today. At this point, we might not hear from them till Monday. I darn well hope we find Iris before then."

"We'll keep looking," I said. "That's all we can do."

"Actually, we can do a bit more," he said. "I'm going to bring in some scent dogs and see what they can do. Horace is going to try tomorrow, after the parade is over, with a couple of the Pomeranians he's been training. And if they don't find anything, York County's going to lend us their bloodhound on Sunday."

"Great," I said. "I'll keep my fingers crossed."

"We'll need it. At least these occasional calls and texts let us know she's still alive and kicking. And not far away."

"How do you know that?" I asked.

"Kevin's been working on it," he said. "He thinks the phone company might be able to give us a lot more information. All he can tell is that her phone seems to be hitting the same couple of cell phone towers it normally uses. Same one your phones use. You sure there isn't a secret room somewhere in that house?"

"Not that I know of," I said. "And I think if there was, Randall would have found it while he was working on the house. And mentioned it."

"Maybe I'll ask him to take a look around, just in case."

"Good idea," I said.

And we ended the call.

According to my phone, it was 5:45. I leaned back in the rocking chair and closed my eyes. Where had the day gone? No wonder I was so tired. Although it wasn't so much a physical tiredness, like the satisfied ache I'd feel after spending the day in my forge. More the frazzled feeling I'd always get when I spent the whole day running around without feeling that I'd accomplished all that much. And my eyes were still a little tired from all the microfilm.

Still, I was in better shape than Eileen. I pulled out my phone again. I should rope in Dad. Since Mother also suffered from migraines, Dad had long ago turned himself into an expert in doing as much as could be done for them. And I was too tired to remember if Rose Noire's natural remedies for migraine were more beneficial than annoying, but Dad would know, and could draft her help if needed.

"Eileen Rafferty's got a migraine," I texted him. "Any chance you could drop by Iris's place and check on her once you've delivered Grandfather and the DNA?"

"Of course!" he texted back.

I leaned back and closed my eyes. I should head home soon, but the temptation to rest my eyes for just a few more minutes was irresistible. And if anyone gave me a hard time about shirking whatever was still going on with the dogs, I could always say I was keeping an eye on Eileen.

It was so still that I heard the faint rustling of the leaves as someone approached the house.

Chapter 26

I opened my eyes and was relieved to see Vern ambling across the yard toward me. Since Vern was notorious for being able to creep up silently on deer or whatever else he was hunting, I more than half suspected that he'd scuffed his feet deliberately, to avoid startling me.

"I see our Pruitt's gone," he said, as he drew near.

"Dr. McAuslan-Crine took him back to her lab," I said. "Find anything interesting back there in the woods?"

"You could say that." He stopped at the bottom of the porch steps. "Must have been like Grand Central Station back there last night. Not that I've ever seen Grand Central Station, mind you, but that's what people always say."

"You mean there were tons of people wandering around in our woods last night?" The thought roused me from my lethargy, and I sat up straight.

"At least three people," he said. "And that's three more than I'd expect to find out there in the middle of the night. It's nowhere near hunting season, and I can't think of a reason why someone would creep into this yard or yours from the woods, instead of coming to the front door like an honest citizen."

"Grandfather sometimes takes people out there on owling expeditions," I said. "But I don't think he was up to that last night."

"And if he was doing it, he'd start and end in this yard or yours," Vern pointed out.

"So where did our trespassers start and end?" I asked.

"Trespassers." He chuckled. "Yeah, that's what they were. One trespasser was probably a woman, from the size of shoe prints. I'd estimate a women's size five, which is pretty darn small."

"I haven't been a size five since I was five years old," I said.

"Ms. Size Five parked down by the Spare Attic and snuck through the woods, going past here until she got to the stretch of woods behind your yard. Spent some time creeping around back there before heading back toward her car—at which point, she met up with the other two. I'm calling them Mr. Big Work Boots and Mr. Worn Out Sneakers. They parked a Chevy truck with nearly bald tires on the town side of your house, on that old dirt road that leads into the woods across from the Washingtons' north pasture. Ended up back there." He jerked his thumb over his shoulder to indicate the woods behind him.

"Did they come close enough for Kevin's cameras to catch them?"

"No." He shook his head. "Maybe they spotted the cameras, or me up there on the porch, because all they did was lurk back there in the trees for however long it would have taken one or both of them to smoke six Marlboro Reds. Then the solo creeper showed up—not sure if it was planned or if she stumbled across them while heading back to her car. Some kind of scuffle or altercation took place, after which she took off running back to her car and they made a beeline for theirs."

"You got all that from their tracks? I'm impressed. You didn't happen to collect those cigarette butts, did you?"

He reached into his pocket and pulled out a handful of small brown paper bags.

"Horace has got me carrying around these itty-bitty bags he likes so much," he said. "In case I run into any useful bits of evidence. Had to use up my whole supply on the cigarette butts, but I figured if your granddaddy is still taking an interest in the case, we might be able to convince him to test these butts for DNA without charging the department an arm and a leg."

"And that might let you figure out who's been sneaking around in the woods," I said. "If you can drop them off at his lab, I'll call Dad and get him to help me talk Grandfather into testing them."

"I'll head over there now." He nodded in farewell and ambled through the side yard, heading for his cruiser.

I took out my phone and was about to call Dad. But a wave of tiredness washed over me—and just then I heard a faint snore from Eileen. I knew that if Mother could manage to fall asleep in spite of a migraine, she'd usually wake up refreshed and restored. With luck it worked the same way for Eileen. I tiptoed over to the door, made sure it wasn't locked, since Dad would be dropping by to check on her, and pulled it closed. And then I sent Dad a quick text saying "Vern's dropping off more evidence for DNA testing—can you help make sure it's prioritized?"

Spike had lifted his head and was watching me. I picked up his leash and held it up where he could see it, as a hint that I could escort him home if he wanted. He tucked his head back under his paws. Okay, he could stay until the boys came to get him. Or he could stay overnight. I made sure the screen door was securely closed behind me, so he wouldn't wander off, and headed for home.

I was halfway home when Dad's enthusiastic "of course!!!" arrived in my phone.

When I got back to our yard, I made a beeline for the barn. I unlocked my office, turned on my laptop, and opened up the email from the library intern—the one with the electronic copy of the Pruitt family history. Then I forwarded it to everyone I could think of who might possibly find it useful: Dad, Grandfather, Chief Burke, Horace, and Kevin. I included a warning that the accuracy of the contents was highly suspect and added in a request that someone forward the file—and the warning—to Dr. McAuslan-Crine.

Then I logged into the *Clarion*'s website and spent some time poking around in the online archives—so much easier than the microfilm. I didn't find any other reports of young Pruitts disappearing mysteriously, and confirmed that one of the young men who'd left town without much explanation in 1998—a non-Pruitt I'd added to the list just in case—had reappeared in 2003. His five-year absence remained unexplained, though, so I saved a copy of the article, just out of curiosity. I kept going in the archives until 2010, which I figured was well out of the range Horace and Dr. McAuslan-Crine had calculated for the skeleton's demise. I didn't find any more Pruitt disappearances, or any sign that Hobart, Gus, or any of the others had reappeared. So I woke up my printer, scanned my microfilm findings, and sent them to the same five people.

The dinner bell rang when I was in the middle of all this, but I'd eaten so late—and so heavily—that I wasn't yet hungry. Not even for the New Life Baptist cookout. I texted Rose Noire to ask her to save me some for later. As I locked up my office door, I fought back a tremendous yawn. The way I felt, later might mean breakfast.

It was dark when I walked outside, and I realized that once again I'd been so caught up in my online sleuthing that several hours had flown past.

Things were winding down. All the dogs had been fed and recently walked and were bedded down in their crates, pens, and runs. And the cats, rabbits, ducks, parrots, geckos, and other non-canine potential adoptees had all been properly tended. Quite a few volunteers were camping in the yard again, both to protect the dogs and to make sure there were plenty of hands available for walks as needed. And maybe a few who shared my night-owl habits were staying over so they wouldn't have to drive all the way from home in the morning for the start of the parade. The pooper-scooper crew had almost finished hauling away the evidence so the canine restroom would be clear for use in the morning. A few groups were still sitting around campfires in front of their tents, but most had already turned in. I greeted anyone who was still awake, and usually stopped to exchange a quiet word or two. I was doing it partly since it seemed like the least I could do as their ostensible hostess, and partly because I was keeping my eyes open to see if Iris was trying to hide in plain sight by joining one of these groups. I had a flashlight with me, the better to peer into any spaces where I thought Iris—or any aspiring dognappers—might be lurking. But I hadn't needed it yet since someone—probably Mother—had arranged to have a number of strings of tiny lights installed in places where they'd help illuminate the paths to the house and the porta potties.

On my way back to the house, I went by the tent where Josh, Jamie, and Adam were going to be sleeping. They were standing in front of it, talking about something. When they saw me they raced over to join me.

"Have you seen Spike?" Jamie asked.

"We've looked everywhere," Josh said.

"Even in all the dog runs," Adam added.

"Last I heard he was over at Rob and Delaney's," I said. "Did you look there?"

"I brought him back from there before dinner," Josh said.

"If you had him loose out here in the yard, he might have headed back there on his own," I said. "You know how he hates having to be near all these other dogs."

"Why didn't we think of that?" Adam asked.

"Mom's pretty good at figuring Spike out," Jamie said.

"I bet that's it," Josh said. "We should go get him."

"Why don't you guys get ready for bed?" I noticed they were still in their day clothes. "Do your teeth, change into whatever you're sleeping in. I was planning to go over there anyway, to check on a couple of things. I can bring him back with me."

"That would be great," Josh said.

They all darted into the tent. I went inside to grab the little container of oil for the screen door hinges. As I headed for the trail between the houses, I saw the three boys emerging from their tent with toothbrushes and bundles of garments and heading for the back door.

I turned on my flashlight and entered the woods.

It was peaceful in the woods. About halfway between the houses, a faint motion startled me. I stopped and I looked up to see the flat white face of a barn owl, sitting in a nearby tree. We stared at each other for a minute or so, and then the owl took flight, so soundlessly that I tapped the handle of my flashlight with the fingernails of my free hand, just to make sure my ears were still working. I knew that owls were famed for their silent flight, but the real thing still always surprised me.

I made a mental note to tell Grandfather, since any encounter with an owl, even secondhand, seemed to raise his spirits. And maybe I should ask Vern if the presence of owls said anything about whether or not there were intruders creeping through the woods. Would they avoid intruders, or hover near them to defend their territory?

Being birds of prey, they'd probably just ignore anything too large to be dinner and fly off, as that one had just done. And with that thought, I resumed my journey toward the relative security of Delaney and Rob's house.

Which was dark. I wondered if they had gone to bed or if they were still over at our house, showing off Brynn to some of the relatives who'd come to town for the Mutt March. I was hoping to see Eileen pacing up and down as she waited for Iris to return—or better yet, Eileen interrogating Iris about where she'd been all this time. No luck. Perhaps Eileen was still battling her migraine.

I had been keeping my flashlight beam aimed at the ground and turned it off before I exited the woods. I wasn't sure why—to avoid scaring away any suspicious characters? To avoid alerting them to my presence? Or maybe just because I didn't need it. The nearly full moon gave plenty of light for me to find my way on what had become such a familiar route.

Maybe I was being melodramatic, but I couldn't shake the thought that perhaps someone might be lurking nearby, waiting for darkness to fall before sneaking into the yard . . . but who? Dognappers planning to use Rob and Delaney's yard as a base to stage a raid? Pothunters with designs on the dig? Someone who wanted to find out what was happening with the skeleton and had some guilty reason for not just coming right out and asking? Iris sneaking home for something? The last seemed the most likely somehow. Or maybe I was just letting my imagination run wild.

When I approached the screened porch, Spike emerged from under the steps and fixed me with a petulant stare. I'd been right about him heading back here for peace and quiet.

"It would be nice if you could avoid getting lost when everyone's on edge about possible dognappers," I said, softly.

By way of an answer he hopped up onto the bottom step and looked up at me with a peevish expression.

"Oh, so you want to come inside?" He didn't answer, but when I opened the porch door he followed me inside and curled up in his favorite place in the far corner.

I took out the oil container and did the screen door hinges. While I was doing that, I spotted a note taped to the door to Iris's suite. I strode over to read it.

"Mother," it said. "Worrying about you has given me a migraine. I have gone back to the Inn. If you come back and find this, please call me immediately! No matter how late it is!"

Something occurred to me. I let myself into the kitchen, without turning on the lights, and called Eileen's number.

"Have you found her?" she said, instead of hello.

"Not yet," I said. "And sorry to bother you when you're under the weather, but I thought of something that might help us find her. You left a note on your mother's door. Did you also leave her a voicemail to say you'd gone back to the Inn?"

"Yes." Her tone added "of course."

"When?"

"Not that long ago," she said. "Half an hour at most."

"Good," I said. "I'm going to lurk here on the porch for a while. See if she decides to sneak back while she knows you're not here."

"That would be just like her," Eileen said. "Call me if you find her. I don't care what time. I know I won't sleep."

"How about if I text you?" I said. "That way, in the unlikely event you do manage to drop off in spite of worrying about her, you can get the rest you'll need to deal with her in the morning."

"That works." She actually laughed at the idea. "Thank you."

I slipped back outside and settled down in one of the rocking chairs—one that was in the same shadowy corner of the porch where Spike was snoozing. I set down my flashlight where I could grab it if I needed it. I pulled out my phone and made sure it was in its night mode, but even that could be spotted if someone were casing the place before approaching. So after texting Josh and Jamie to say that I'd found Spike and would drop him off at their tent later, and then letting Michael know I'd be home in a little while, I turned it off.

The night was quiet and peaceful. My thoughts weren't. I reminded myself that I'd done a good day's work, researching possible candidates for the Pruitt skeleton. I wasn't exactly sure what

Kevin and Dr. McAuslan-Crine would be doing with the information I'd found about vanished Pruitts. I assumed they'd study the Pruitt family history and the state birth records to figure out which Pruitts who were still among the living were most closely related to Gus and Hobart. And then, since all of the Pruitts other than Miss Ethelinda had left town, the chief would try to track them down to ask for a DNA sample. What would he do if they balked? Was there any way he could compel them? Or would he end up having one of his deputies tracking them until they got a chance to do what I'd done with Miss Ethelinda? I'd heard of detectives doing that in some of the true-crime cases Kevin reported on in his *Virginia Crime Time* podcast.

For now, I'd probably done as much as I could. As much as any civilian could. And now that my brain wasn't busy with Pruitts, I'd started wondering if I should have spent my day differently. Like maybe looking for Iris. Which was silly. The chief had a BOLO out on her, and by now I suspected the entire population of Caerphilly was on the lookout for her. Finding her wasn't my sole responsibility. I wasn't even particularly qualified for doing it.

So why did I feel so guilty about the fact that she was still missing?

Just then Spike erupted into hoarse but savage barking, and hurled himself against the screen door's wooden frame. But the hurling didn't look like the frantic, mindless reaction of a dog so overcome by his prey drive that he was reckless of the consequences. More like a very deliberate demand that he be let out to pursue his unseen enemy.

"Shush," I murmured, as I scanned the darkened yard outside the porch. "Whatever you're barking at is bound to be bigger than you are. Don't tempt fate."

Spike didn't always pay attention to the word "shush," but he must have picked up on the stress in my tone, because this time he did. He subsided into muted growls and continued to stare out into the darkness.

I peered in the same direction, but I couldn't see anything. I wondered what, if anything, he saw. Clarence was fond of explaining that dogs' eyes, like human ones, were equipped with both rods and cones—eye cells that performed different but complementary functions. Humans had a greater number of cones, which made us better at seeing color and details, while dogs, who had more rods, were better at detecting motion and seeing in dim light. So it was possible that Spike was seeing something I couldn't. Or that he was barking at something his keen canine sense of smell had detected—barking at it and straining to catch a glimpse of it.

And it was also entirely possible that he was feeling bored and cranky, and barking just to entertain himself. After all, this was Spike.

I shifted my phone into my left hand and picked up my flashlight. Should I go out and see what Spike was barking at? Or should I call in to report it so whichever deputy was nearby could check it out? I wasn't exactly keen on making that call. "Spike is barking at something" didn't exactly sound like an emergency situation. More like "what else is new?"

While I was still waffling over what to do, Spike erupted into motion, hurling himself at the screen door with such force that he ripped the screen out of the doorframe and went charging toward the woods.

"Stop! Bad dog! Come back!" I yelled as I grabbed my flashlight, thumbed it on, and raced after him. Not that I expected him to listen, but shouting at him helped relieve my irritation. He ignored me as he galloped past the dig site and deeper into the woods.

He had a head start, but my legs were longer. I had almost caught up with him and was leaning down to grab him when suddenly I felt the ground give way beneath me and I was falling.

Chapter 27

I landed hard and managed to knee myself in the stomach, knocking the wind out of me. Spike uttered one startled squeal from someplace nearby, so I deduced that he'd fallen with me. As if embarrassed by his momentary weakness, he growled vehemently from just in front of me. I wanted to snap "Shut up!" at him, followed by "And no treats for a week if you bite me!" But at the moment I couldn't have managed a single syllable, so I focused on thinking the words fiercely as I sat, eyes closed, struggling to breathe.

After a few seconds I opened my eyes again, sat up, and looked around. My flashlight had fallen to the ground, a little behind my right hip. It was just out of reach, unless I turned slightly, which wasn't appealing at the moment. But it gave enough light for me to see that Spike was standing squarely on all four stubby little legs and gazing around with an expression of annoyance. He looked fine. Whatever we'd fallen into was small enough that I could reach out and touch him if I wanted to, but that would be a bad idea if he was still in a cranky mood from his fall. Any second now he would probably start barking to demand that I get him out of . . . where the hell were we, anyway?

It looked as if we'd fallen into some kid's underground fort.

When I was growing up, my friends and I had spent many summer hours off in the woods, building such forts. We'd find a likely-looking clearing and dig a hole, usually around three or four feet deep. More like a trench than a hole, actually—it could be as long as we had the time and energy to dig, but it had to be narrow enough for us to roof it with whatever logs and fallen branches we could find nearby. We'd start by laying the largest ones parallel to each other across the trench, a foot or so apart, like beams. Then we'd add on medium-sized branches perpendicular to the beams, and more layers of branches atop that. With every layer, the branches got smaller and smaller, and we'd finish it off with a thick layer of pine needles, like a thatched roof. We'd leave at least one hole for people to crawl in and out—and yes, it usually was crawling. Digging a hole big enough for even the smallest of us to stand upright in was beyond our juvenile excavation capabilities.

I didn't remember much about what we actually did with these forts when we'd constructed them—all I remembered was building them and then crawling in and out of them. Oh, and digging each other out when a portion of the roof collapsed, which happened often. The whole point, at least to me, was the building. We were always trying to dig the main trench an inch or two deeper, adding on side passages, and regularly, when the roof began collapsing too often, dragging off all the logs and branches and starting the roof anew.

This hole was a bit deeper than most of our forts—about six feet deep, and three in diameter. And the roof I'd fallen through wasn't made of logs and branches—more like scrap lumber. Mostly rough, faded one-by-two boards, with a few one-by-fours, and inch-wide gaps between them. It looked as if whoever built this thing had spread some garden netting on top of the boards, and then covered the whole thing over with leaves.

I fingered the splintered end of one of the boards. They were untreated wood, and more than one showed visible signs of rotting. Not surprising, given the fact that they had been out here for who knew how long in noticeably damp conditions. Only surprising that no one had fallen through before this—and thank goodness Spike and I had been the ones to fall, not someone like Grandfather, with more brittle bones. Or Brynn, once she began toddling—Delaney would be on the warpath about that. Even I was lucky to have escaped without apparent injury—this pit was an ER visit waiting to happen. Whoever had built the roof—or maybe trapdoor was the right term for it—had definitely done a pretty lousy job. I was no master carpenter, but on top of opting for treated wood I'd have known enough to use two-by-fours, at least, for something that was obviously intended for people to walk on without realizing that there was a hiding place underneath. It was only a matter of time before someone found that out as I had—the hard way.

I'd been leaning against one side of the hole, waiting until I got my wind completely back. I was starting to feel better, so I wriggled myself a little more upright. I reached back to pick up my flashlight—and my hand touched metal.

"That's weird," I muttered. I squirmed a little more, until I could turn my head (and flashlight) to see what was behind me—ignoring the faint growl from Spike, who evidently didn't like my derriere encroaching on his personal space.

The side of the hole I'd been leaning against wasn't dirt—it was a cinder-block wall, with a metal door in the middle of it. The door was about four feet high—no, more like five. The floor of the hole was full of leaves and dirt, which had slightly cushioned our fall, and now obscured the bottom foot or so of the door.

I played the flashlight beam over the door. No sign of hinges, so presumably it opened inward. On the left side, an industrial-sized hasp was securely welded to the door and the frame, with an enormous padlock securing it.

And when I brushed away the leaves around the bottom of the door, I encountered something metallic. The rusty remnants of a second padlock that looked as if it had been cut off with a blowtorch.

I rapped the door with my knuckles. By the sound of it, this wasn't a thin sheet-metal door, like the outside cellar doors at our house. It was heavy. Solid steel.

Who had built this underground bunker? Was that the right word? And why had they built it? It had to have been the Raffertys—no one else had lived here for more than a century, and I didn't think this construction was anywhere near that old.

And then something teased my memory. I'd seen something like this door before. But where?

Then it came to me. Several years ago I'd helped Randall Shiffley organize an estate sale at the farm that had belonged to one of his elderly great-uncles. Fordyce Shiffley had been a Marine sharpshooter in World War II, after which he had come home and settled in to lead what Randall called a carefree bachelor existence for the rest of his ninety-eight years. He'd raised horses and beef cattle, competed nationally in marksmanship contests, hunted deer and other game in and out of season, distilled his own moonshine long before that became legal, and lived in cheerful squalor with a rowdy pack of hunting dogs and an undetermined number of feral barn cats—two of whom had eventually come home with me to perform rodent control in our barn. Randall, his nearest kin and favorite great-nephew, had inherited the farm, but I'd never quite figured out if the financial gain had outweighed the immense amount of work he'd had to do on the place.

When we'd started clearing out the house—which wouldn't have looked out of place on one of those TV shows about hoarding—Randall had begged all his helpers to keep their eyes out for stray keys, because he couldn't find the key to his uncle's gun room. Eventually, when the key he'd been looking for never showed, he'd used a blowtorch on the padlock that secured the door in question, and I was one of the few people he allowed to see what he found inside.

The gun room was in a converted fallout shelter, an eight-by-twelve-foot underground concrete room that Fordyce had retrofitted with racks, drawers, and display cases for his guns. Several hundred of them, from what I could see. When you added in the ammunition shelves, the gun-cleaning station, and the setup for loading his own cartridges, the whole place was pretty overwhelming.

"Any idea what country he was planning to invade?" I remembered asking.

"I'm just relieved it's only guns," Randall had said. "I was more than half expecting a few hundred gallons of moonshine."

And the door to the fallout shelter turned gun room had looked a lot like this door—even down to the addition of a hasp and padlock on the outside—added, no doubt, when the door's purpose changed from locking out would-be freeloaders to locking up valuables.

But Joe Rafferty hadn't been a gun collector. From what Eileen had said, he'd owned a shotgun and a hunting rifle, but that was pretty common for farmers, and he wouldn't have needed a giant underground gun room to store them in. Wouldn't have wanted to keep them back here in the woods, if one reason for owning them was to protect his family and his livestock. If there was an underground bunker behind the cinder blocks and the heavy door, what had he and Iris used it for? Maybe Joe Rafferty had shared Fordyce Shiffley's interest in moonshine? Or had he also built a fallout shelter during the panicky early days of the Cold War and then, not needing a secure storage area, just covered it up and abandoned it?

I'd find out when Iris reappeared. When, not if. Iris probably had some good reason for disappearing. But enough was enough. So maybe tomorrow, instead of hunting down more vanished Pruitts, I'd spend the day tracking her down. And then asking her if this underground whatever-it-was had something to do with her disappearance.

No, not tomorrow. Tomorrow was the Mutt March. But if she didn't reappear tomorrow—

Spike growled softly. A growl of complaint, not menace, but it focused my attention back on our current predicament.

"Yeah, I know," I said. "I'll work on getting us out of here."

Easier said than done. Jumping up and trying to grab the top of the hole didn't work. If I managed to get a grip on the rim of the hole, the dirt crumbled in my hands and rained down on my feet and the disgruntled Spike. I reached up and tested the remnants of the roof. Definitely more like a trapdoor, I decided. And not going to be helpful for our escape—just touching it brought more leaves and bits of rotten wood raining down on us, to Spike's increased annoyance. So I carefully pulled down the rest of the trapdoor, doing my best to avoid causing more falling debris, or at least to keep what fell from hitting Spike. I piled the remnants of the trapdoor along one side of the hole, being careful to make sure there were no sharp ends or nails pointing up that could impale me if I fell on them. Because I could already see that any effort to get out of the hole was probably going to involve some falling.

Unless, of course, I called for help. Duh. I reached for the pocket where I kept my phone.

It wasn't there. My hand found the little can of household oil instead.

I remembered that I'd been carrying the phone in my hand when I took off after Spike. In my left hand, with the flashlight in my right. Evidently I'd dropped it. But had it fallen inside or outside of the hole?

I aimed the flashlight down and began searching for it. I even risked life and limb by encouraging Spike to move a foot or so, in case he'd landed on it.

No luck.

"Just great," I muttered.

I was resisting the familiar but useless temptation to search every square inch of the ground all over again when I heard a familiar sound. The tinkling ringtone I'd assigned to Josh. It was coming from somewhere above my head. Searching the hole again would be useless.

I tried seeing if I could chimney up—bracing my back against one side of the hole and my feet against the other and gradually inching up. But the hole was a little too wide. Michael's legs might have been long enough for him to do it, but at six foot four his legs were half a foot longer than mine. Chimneying was a no-go for me.

I thought of banging the spare padlock against the metal of the door to make noise, while shining my flashlight up to guide any would-be rescuers. But something stopped me. What if whoever saw and heard my signals wasn't a potential rescuer?

We'd had nighttime prowlers at our house last night, and Spike had definitely been chasing something here. Were last night's intruders, as we assumed, would-be dognappers? Or did they have something to do with the skeleton? Or with this hidden bunker? And perhaps more to the point, Iris was upset about something. Had she merely disappeared to dodge potentially awkward questions about the dead guy we'd found in her old backyard? Or was she scared of something? Something or someone? And should I be scared as well?

I decided to keep a low profile for now. If someone came looking for me—most likely the boys, if they grew impatient for me to return Spike—they'd probably make enough noise for me to tell who they were. I wasn't keen on them walking into whatever danger might be lurking here in the yard, but at least I could be pretty sure they'd travel in a pack. Safety in numbers. Or I might hear Rob and Delaney returning. In the meantime, instead of waiting helplessly to be rescued, I'd make a start at rescuing myself. It would take a while, but I was pretty sure I could dig my way out. I could start at the side of the hole opposite the door and begin digging to create a sloping ramp. Eventually I could walk out. Even better, eventually Spike could walk out, which would be a lot safer than trying to pick him up and carry him.

So I selected the least dilapidated chunk of one-by-two lumber I could find and began digging.

It was easier going than I expected, Easier than I remembered from the last time I'd done any serious digging in our backyard, when planting a dozen apple trees had done me in for a week. And I'd had a well-maintained shovel for that. Could the terrain possibly be that different here? I doubted it. Digging here was so easy that I began to suspect that I wasn't digging undisturbed ground but clearing out where someone had filled in part of the hole.

That suspicion was confirmed when I struck something hard. And not a rock. A concrete surface. I redoubled my efforts, focusing on the area around the concrete.

The concrete was a step. Underneath the suspiciously loose dirt I was digging, I was probably going to find a set of concrete stairs leading up to the surface. It made sense that whoever built the fallout shelter would have had to have some kind of stairs or ladder to get down to it. Once I cleared off the steps, Spike and I could easily climb them.

I returned to digging with new vigor. Occasionally I'd hear my phone ringing up on the surface, Josh's ringtone alternating with Jamie's.

I was more than halfway finished uncovering the steps when I heard voices from above.

Chapter 28

I froze, and glanced at Spike, willing him to silence until I could figure out who was approaching. What if—

"Mom! Where are you? Mom!"

The boys.

"Meg!"

And Michael.

"Down here!" I shouted. I grabbed my flashlight and aimed it upward. A few seconds later Jamie's face appeared over the edge of the pit.

"Mom," he said. "What are you doing down there?"

"Trying to dig my way out," I said. "Why don't you see if you can find a rope or a ladder or something. Spike and I would both appreciate being rescued."

Jamie ran off, shouting that he'd found me. A minute later, Michael's face peered over the side of the hole.

"You okay?" He looked anxious.

"I will be as soon as you guys get me out of here."

"One ladder coming up."

His face disappeared, and I heard him talking to someone.

"She's fine," he said. "Tell the Goochland deputies to stay put and guard the dogs."

Josh's face appeared.

"Ladder coming down," he said. "Want me to take care of carrying Spike out?"

"Please," I said. "He's a little cranky. I think he thinks it's my fault he's down here, and I'd like to keep all my fingers. And we know he'd never bite you or Jamie."

The end of a ladder appeared over the top of the hole, and slowly descended until it touched the bottom of the hole. I made sure it was stable, then quickly climbed up. Spike began barking, of course—did the silly dog think I was abandoning him? But Josh scurried down the ladder and brought him up to the surface. Spike shut up and allowed Josh and Jamie to make a fuss over him.

Michael gave me a quick, fierce hug.

"Are you sure you're okay?" Chief Burke said, from somewhere behind me.

"I'm fine," I said, turning to face him. "But I'm afraid I just uncovered another mystery to add to your case. Take a look at what I found down there."

He peered over the edge of the hole, frowned, and climbed down the ladder.

"Was this area disturbed when you found it?" he called up.

"Since I found it by falling into it, I have no idea," I said. "And I rummaged through all the leaves and debris looking for my phone, so if it wasn't disturbed when I got there, it was by the time I figured out I'd dropped the phone up here."

"The lock looks to me as if it's been rusted shut," he said. "Does it look that way to you?"

"From what I could see, yes," I said.

He emerged from the hole. Michael took his place and peered at the lock.

"Looks that way to me, too," he called up.

"I'd still feel better if we could get into that . . . whatever it is," the chief said.

"I'm betting it's an old fallout shelter," I said. "Of course, Iris never mentioned anything about having a fallout shelter, but maybe it's been covered up so long she forgot it was there."

"Or maybe she didn't know about it," Michael said, as he climbed up the ladder again. "Maybe Joe or his father had it before she moved out here."

"Maybe," the chief said. "Or maybe she has some reason for not mentioning it. And maybe I'm overreacting, but Iris is still missing, and even if that door hasn't been opened in years, what if there's another entrance? Let's call Randall and see how fast he can get someone out here with a blowtorch."

"We don't need to wait for Randall," I said. "Josh! Jamie! Can one of you run back to the barn and bring us the blowtorch that's in my forge?"

The boys exchanged a look. Then, without a word, Josh took off running toward the path into the woods while Jamie continued to comfort Spike.

"Is Iris's daughter here?" the chief asked.

"She's over at the Inn," I said.

"It's not that late," he said, glancing at his watch. "Let's see if she can come back out here. Can you call her?"

"I can as soon as I find my phone," I said. "Can someone call it?"

"I will," Jamie said.

"But don't you want to just call her yourself?" I asked the chief. "To ask her about whatever that is?"

My phone jingled with Jamie's ring, and I pounced on it.

"I want to see how she reacts when we show her this," the chief said. "And I don't want her to have time to think up an explanation. So if you could lure her out here thinking she's helping you . . ."

"I can try," I said, and began dialing. "And I assume I should keep my mouth shut about our find."

"Please." The chief was peering into the hole again.

"Do you suspect Eileen of something?" Michael asked.

"Not particularly," the chief said. "But I don't know her that well, and her mother's disappearance is pretty darned peculiar, so . . ."

Eileen answered my call on the first ring, so I motioned them for silence and put her on speaker.

"Have you found her?" Eileen demanded.

"No," I said. "But I've found something that might be a clue. It's a little hard to explain—can you come out here? And then—"

"On my way." She hung up.

"That was easier than I expected," I said.

"Thanks," the chief said.

"Grandpa?" Adam rather hesitantly approached where we were all standing around the hole. "Do you think Ms. Iris is down there?"

"If I had to bet on it, I'd say no." The chief put a reassuring arm around his grandson's shoulder. "Not unless there's another entrance to . . . whatever it is. But just in case I'm wrong, I want to get into that thing and check it out."

"In case she's trapped down there?"

"She left a voicemail for her daughter an hour or so ago," I said. "So if she's trapped down there, it hasn't been for too long."

The chief nodded. Adam looked less worried.

Just then Josh came running back, carrying my blowtorch. And to my delight, he'd also brought along the safety equipment I'd forgotten to mention—the heavy gloves and the tinted face shield. After a brief discussion, Michael and I agreed that while I was the more seasoned blowtorch user, his skills were up to the task at hand, and I might be more valuable standing guard by the road to alert the chief to Eileen's arrival and lull any suspicions she might have about why we'd invited her over.

So Michael tackled the padlock, under the supervision of the chief and the three boys. Jamie and Josh offered him quite a lot of advice that, while accurate, probably wasn't necessary. Unlike the boys, Michael hadn't been taking metalworking lessons from me, but he was pretty handy with most tools, thanks to years of working backstage on sets and props.

Horace arrived a few minutes later, and then, as he was getting out of his cruiser, Eileen pulled up at a speed that might have gotten her a warning under other circumstances.

"Horace, can you escort Ms. Rafferty back here?" the chief called.

"What's going on?" Eileen asked.

"Easier to show you," I said, gesturing toward where the chief and the boys were standing. Eileen didn't wait for Horace to do any escorting.

"Have you found my mother?" she demanded as she ran to where the chief was standing.

"No," the chief said. "But we've found something puzzling, and we'd like to see if it could possibly have anything to do with her disappearance. Tell me about that."

He gestured down at the hole, where Michael's efforts were generating a small shower of sparks.

"Tell you about it?" she echoed. "What is it?"

"We think it's a fallout shelter," the chief said.

"A what?"

"A fallout shelter," he repeated. "Back in the sixties, when people were very nervous about the—"

"I know what a fallout shelter is." Her voice was cross. "But what is it doing back here? I thought Rob and Delaney were building a duck pond. Was that just cover for building a fallout shelter? You know, so no one will know it's there and try to barge in if they ever have to use it?"

"As far as I know, they're only doing a duck pond," I said. "And it looks as if the fallout shelter's been here for quite a while."

"Were you aware of its existence?" the chief asked.

"No," she said. "Of course not. I don't know anything about a fallout shelter. And I can't imagine my parents wanting to build one. If—"

Then she fell silent. The noise of the blowtorch stopped, and I heard a clink that I assumed was the padlock bumping against the metal door as it fell. We all remained focused on Eileen.

"Granddaddy, now," she said, in a more thoughtful tone. "He passed when I was pretty little. Nineteen sixty-five I think, or thereabouts. I don't remember all that much about him, except that we all tried to steer clear when he watched the news on TV. He'd always find someone or something to be mad at—everything from Congress and the IRS to the county extension agent. And he really got worked up about what he called the dad-blamed Russkies. I wonder if they upset him so much that he built himself a fallout shelter. That would have been the era, right? The early sixties?"

"I expect so," I said.

"If this house were in town, we could look in the archives," the chief said. "And maybe find the building permit for it. But I bet out here he wouldn't have bothered with that."

"No way," she said. "Even if he were in town he'd have tried to avoid getting one. I can hear him now. 'The gubmint has no call to stick its nose in our business.' Stubborn old cuss." I could hear affection along with exasperation in her tone, and maybe even a little admiration. "So how big is it? And what does it look like inside?"

"No idea," I said. "All I saw was the locked door."

I gestured toward the hole, and she peered down at where Michael was standing, with the blowtorch in his hand and the face shield tipped up. He was, wisely, waiting for the blowtorch to cool before setting it down.

"Did the archaeologists find this?" Eileen asked.

"No, I did," I said. "The hard way—by falling into it. There was a sort of trapdoor concealing the entrance. You never noticed it?"

"No," she said. "I've never seen any of that before."

"Let's open it up," the chief said. "Just to see that there's nothing inside we need to worry about." The rusty padlock Michael had just removed reassured us that no one could have gotten through the steel door lately, but clearly the chief was still worried about the possibility of a second entrance that Iris could have used. "Horace, will you do the honors?"

Michael and Horace exchanged places, and we all clustered around the rim of the hole. Horace took his flashlight in his left hand and fixed it on the metal door. He gave the door a push.

Nothing happened.

A series of increasingly more forceful pushes did nothing. Finally, Michael joined him in the hole, and they both put their shoulders to the door, which swung open with an ear-piercing creak.

Horace retrieved his flashlight and shone it into the open doorway.

"Holy Toledo," he said. "I think we're going to need the feds."

Chapter 29

"The feds?" the chief echoed. "Michael, if you wouldn't mind?"

Michael and the chief switched places—although not until Michael had paused long enough to take a look through the open doorway.

"Pretty obvious from the cobwebs that no one's been in there for years," he said, in an undertone, when he joined me.

"The feds," Horace repeated, when the chief reached his side. "Like the DEA and maybe the ATF."

"Possibly the DEA." The chief took a step closer to the doorway, but instead of stepping inside he leaned in as far as he could. I almost expected Horace to have to grab him to keep him from falling over. Then he straightened up and turned back to the ladder. "I doubt if the ATF would be all that interested in a single vintage firearm, no matter how state of the art it might have been a few decades ago. Start taking pictures," he added over his shoulder to Horace. "I need to make some phone calls."

"What's going on?" Eileen asked.

"Horace, send me a picture or two that I can show Ms. Rafferty." When the chief reached the top of the ladder he pulled out his phone, waited a few seconds, then held it up for Eileen to see. "You're asking a good question," he said. "Any idea what's going on here?"

I peered over Eileen's shoulder. The picture showed that the whole room was festooned with spiderwebs, but against the wall you could make out a set of metal utility shelves, similar to the ones we had in our basement for holding extra supplies of food, cleaning supplies, and other household goods. The shelves were empty except for the second shelf from the top, which held a stack of three foil-wrapped objects, and the third, on which a sleek, black gun rested.

Eileen was shaking her head. The chief pulled up a second picture, a wider shot showing that one whole wall of the underground chamber was lined with shelves—all empty except for the one we'd already seen in the close-up.

"What is that?" she asked. "And what is it doing here under our yard? Our former yard," she corrected, with a sharp glance at me.

"That's what we're going to find out," the chief said.

"Of course we won't know till we test them," Horace said. "But those foil packages do rather resemble the way drug dealers package cocaine or heroin."

"Drug dealers?" Eileen muttered.

"Meg, can you take Ms. Rafferty inside?" the chief asked. "Fix her some tea or something, and I'll join you in a few minutes."

"Sure," I said. "And maybe if we promise to tell the boys everything that happens later on, we can convince them to head back to their tent and go to bed."

"Good idea." The chief turned to Josh, Jamie, and Adam. "You did a good job, helping rescue your mom. Now I am trusting you three not to say anything to anyone until I tell you it's okay."

All three boys nodded solemnly.

"Now go and try to get some sleep. Finding this thing, whatever it is, doesn't cancel the Mutt March, and Doc Clarence is going to need your help for that more than ever."

"Okay," Josh said. "You want me to put the tools back?"

I glanced at the chief, who frowned slightly.

"Your dad and I can bring them back when the chief is sure we won't need them for anything else," I said.

Josh nodded. The three of them—four, if you included Spike—headed for the path through the woods, moving slowly, but following orders.

"Text me when you're safely back at your tent," I called after them.

Jamie gave me a thumbs-up and they disappeared into the woods.

I reached for Eileen's arm, but she avoided my hand and strode toward the house. I followed, a little more slowly. I glanced back to see that the chief was on his cell phone.

"Hope I didn't wake you," he was saying to someone.

Who did he need other than Horace? Not Dad, since there didn't appear to be a body for him to examine.

None of my business, I told myself, and followed Eileen into the house.

We settled down in Rob and Delaney's kitchen. I pulled out my phone and texted Rob. Although he and Delaney were now technically settled into their new house, there was still a perfectly fine queen-sized bed in the room they'd been occupying in our house, and they would retreat to it whenever the latest round of renovations grew noisy or smelly.

"Why don't you and Delaney and Brynn stay over at our house tonight," I typed. "More police action here. Nothing dangerous but could keep you awake."

He texted back almost immediately.

"OK."

Just then a picture arrived—a selfie of the three boys and Spike standing in front of their tent. I clicked on the thumbs-up. Then I turned back to Eileen.

"Before you put the kettle on, I don't need tea." She sat down at the kitchen table, scowling. "I just want to know what's happening here."

"You and me both," I said.

"You said you were going to hide here to see if Mom came back," she said. "And instead you end up uncovering a drug smuggler's hideout. How did that happen?"

So to while away the time until the chief came in, I gave her a blow-by-blow account of my accidental discovery of the entrance pit, and my subsequent efforts to escape. The chief came in when I was about halfway through, but he motioned for me to continue.

"This is unbelievable," Eileen said when I'd finished.

"And you had no idea the fallout shelter was down there?" the chief asked.

"Absolutely no idea." She shook her head.

"I have just a few more questions, if you don't mind." He glanced up at me, and I deduced that was my clue to leave them alone.

"I should be heading home," I said as I stood up. "The Mutt March must go on, no matter how many more local mysteries we uncover."

"Speaking of the Mutt March," he said. "Minerva has me down to drive the New Life float in the parade, and I'm afraid I'll be rather busy tomorrow. And the only reason I agreed to do it was that she couldn't find anyone else who knew how to drive a truck with standard transmission and hadn't already been recruited by one of the other floats. Any chance I could draft you to fill in for me? Or does your mother have you already assigned to a vital task?"

"She already has me assigned as general dogsbody to troubleshoot and fill in where needed," I said. "I think making sure the choir gets safely from the rally point to the town square would be a reasonable troubleshooting assignment."

"I'll tell Minerva you're game, then. And thanks."

"Rob and family will be staying over at our house tonight," I said. "So could whoever's last out pull the door to?"

They both nodded, and I went back out. To my surprise, Horace and Michael, who had been standing by the fallout shelter, had been joined by Vern and Aida, and they were all sitting in rockers on the porch, talking quietly.

"You're leaving the den of iniquity unguarded?" I asked.

"Sammy's sitting down there in the hole," Vern said. "He's going to stay there overnight, in case someone comes snooping."

"And I'm going to bed down here on the porch," Aida said. "Ready to rescue Sammy if the need arises."

"Vern measured the entrance and got in touch with Randall," Michael said. "Who is making a new trapdoor even as we speak and will drop by with it as soon as possible. I thought we could stay here until he arrives with it."

"We figure if someone was sneaking around back there looking for the fallout shelter, maybe the Scourge of Caerphilly scared them off before they spotted it," Aida said, using her favorite nickname for Spike. "So if we can get it covered up again, maybe they'll have another go at it tomorrow night and we can nab them."

"But why would someone even know to look for the fallout shelter?" I asked. "From what I could see, it's probably been hidden back there at least as long as the skeleton."

"Could have something to do with finding the skeleton," Vern said.

"How?" I asked. "You think some middle-aged drug dealer heard about the skeleton and said, 'Oh, wow, it totally slipped my mind that I hid a bunch of my merchandise in an abandoned fallout shelter in that very same backyard. Maybe I should go back and collect it before the archaeologists start digging in that direction.' I'm not buying it."

"Not when you put it like that," Vern said.

"But I bet they're connected somehow," Aida said. "Maybe someone out there heard about the skeleton and said, 'Hmm. So that's where they buried so-and-so's body. I wonder if they hid his stash nearby?'"

"Now that I could buy," Vern said.

"I'm taking off to do some research," Horace said. "To see if I can identify that gun and figure out whether it could be the weapon someone used to bump off our skeleton."

"I doubt it," Vern said. "Looked like a MAC-10 to me, which takes .45 caliber ammo, and the slug we found in the skeleton was a .22."

"Good to know," Horace said. "I'll start by looking up MAC-10s. Thanks."

"Time for us to head home." Michael stood up and stretched. "Unless you want to stay around for any reason?"

"No, I need my sleep," I said. "Looks as if I'll be chauffeuring the New Life Baptist choir tomorrow while the chief deals with our new find."

We stowed the blowtorch and safety gear in the barn, in case the chief needed anything else blasted open anytime soon, and took the path toward home.

"It'll be a relief to get back to our normal number of dogs," Michael said as we trudged along.

"That could take a few days," I said. "Depending on how many potential adopters still need to be checked out."

"Still, I'm hoping we come back with a lot fewer dogs than we'll be taking to town," he said.

"Amen."

I hoped not too many people had actually dropped off to sleep, since our arrival in the backyard set off a few dozen of the more vigilant dogs. But various volunteers quickly hurried to shush and reassure them, and things quieted down once we went inside. We made sure we could get a quick start in the morning. Michael laid out all the parts of his costume—he would be marching as Darth Vader in the boys' *Star Wars*–themed parade entry. I made sure I had clean clothes ready to fall into.

I seriously considered whether to use a pair of earplugs to improve my chances of getting a good night's sleep. And then decided no. If anything happened in the night—here or next door—I wanted to know about it.

SATURDAY, JUNE 10

Chapter 30

Either there were no disturbances in the night or I slept through them. When I woke up—earlier than usual—the backyard was already a hive of activity. Michael was taking a quick shower—though I wondered why, when he was about to don a costume in which he knew he'd be sweating buckets.

I decided to dash over to Delaney and Rob's house to see what had happened overnight.

I found Dad there, sitting on the porch, interrogating Aida about the night's events.

"Meg can tell you more than I can," Aida said, with a yawn. "If it's okay with you, I'm going to try to catch a few hours of sleep before the parade starts."

"What an exciting find!" Dad exclaimed, turning to me. "Tell me how it happened!"

So I related my discovery of the hidden fallout shelter, to his great delight. Halfway through my narration, we heard a rustling noise among the leaves at the back of the yard. The trapdoor popped off of the hole I'd fallen into and Sammy, the deputy who'd been guarding it, emerged.

"Aha!" Dad exclaimed. "Now's my chance to take a look down there."

He hurried out to the hole, while Sammy trudged toward the house.

"You going off duty?" I asked.

"No." He shook his head. "Bathroom break. Can you keep an eye on it for a minute?"

"Dad and I both," I said.

He glanced back to where Dad was climbing down the ladder into the hole and sighed.

"I figure he knows not to cross the crime-scene tape the chief put over the door into the shelter," he said. "Gonna need you to help cover up the trapdoor when I go back down. No use having me lie in wait when any fool can see the trapdoor in the middle of a patch with no leaves from a mile off."

"What if I glued a bunch of the branches and leaves to the top of the trapdoor for camouflage?" I suggested. "Then you can pull it closed after yourself and it will look just fine. I think the old trapdoor had something like that."

He blinked.

"Yeah," he said. "That'd be helpful. Any chance—"

"Consider it done."

I knew Delaney had a crafting station in the barn, so I snagged her glue gun and set to work festooning the nice, sturdy new trapdoor with an assortment of leaves and small sticks. I made sure that a lot of the vegetation overlapped the edge of the door, the better to blend in with the leaf-strewn area around the hole. By the time I was finished, as long as Sammy made sure the ground around the hole was reasonably well-covered with leaves, he could pull the trapdoor down after himself and be well hidden.

The chief arrived while I was working on the trapdoor. He frowned when he saw Sammy standing outside the hole.

"Dr. Langlow is inspecting the scene." Sammy spoke quickly, before the chief could say anything, and gestured toward the hole.

"I see."

"Chief?" Dad's head popped up out of the hole. "I thought I heard your voice. Fascinating, isn't it?"

"I admit, this case continues to surprise me." The chief sounded tired.

"I thought you said you found drugs and weapons there," Dad said.

"We found several foil-wrapped packages," the chief said. "Horace's field test was positive for cocaine, so they're now secured in our evidence room. Along with the firearm we found."

"So if our drug dealer shows up to reclaim his property, he'll be disappointed," Dad said.

"I rather suspect if its owner were alive, the cocaine wouldn't be here," the chief said.

"And of course, the cocaine won't have survived all this time unchanged," Dad said. "It degrades over time."

"What do you mean by 'degrades'?" the chief asked. "Would it become less toxic, or more? Or would it change into something else entirely? Something that isn't a Schedule Two controlled substance?"

"Now, that I'll have to look up." Dad's face took on the eager, cheerful look it always wore when he was about to embark on a research project—particularly one that involved both medicine and crime. "I could talk to Professor Zahray at the college. This would be right up her alley. If you're in touch with the DEA, of course, you might see what they know. But I bet the professor can come up with the answer before they do."

"That would be helpful," the chief said.

"I'll get right on it!"

"Of course, it could all be pretty theoretical," the chief said. "Since we have no idea who to charge for possession of those few pounds of what might not even be cocaine anymore."

"But I'll talk to the professor," Dad said. "So you've got all the information you need when you do find the owner of the drugs."

He hurried away, pulling out his phone as he walked.

"If you ask me, we probably already found the owner of the drugs," I said. "Our skeleton."

"I have a feeling you're right." The chief sighed, and headed back toward his car.

Sammy was arranging the leaves so they covered everything but the hole on which the trapdoor would go. I was gluing a few final fronds to one edge of the trapdoor when Grandfather appeared and stared down at what I was doing.

"What is that thing?" he asked.

"A trapdoor," I said. "A replacement for the one Spike and I fell through last night." I held it up and waved it around so he could take a better look. And refrained from adding "what the heck does it *look* like?" Maybe his question had been reasonable—after all, he hadn't been here for the excitement, and I might have trapdoors on the brain.

"Looks a little like a tasseled wobbegong to me," Grandfather said. At least that was what I thought he'd said.

"Okay," I said. "I'll bite. What's a tasseled wobbegong?"

"*Eucrossorhinus dasypogon*," he said, unhelpfully. "A species of carpet shark. Lives in coral reefs off the coast of New Guinea and Northern Australia. Actually a rather fascinating species."

I didn't bother to ask what was fascinating about it. I knew no power on Earth could prevent him from telling me.

"They're flat," he said, as if that explained it.

"Like flounders?"

"More like rays," he said. "Which are close relatives of sharks, you know. They're very well camouflaged, so during the daytime they lurk on the ocean floor or in underwater caves. And they're opportunistic ambush predators—they like to lie in wait for unsuspecting prey to swim by. Sometimes they remain completely motionless except for wiggling their caudal fins. Looks a lot like a small fish flailing in the water, and when a predator tries to pounce on the small fish, bingo! Dinner for the wobbegong."

He was holding his right hand up over his head and fluttering his fingers, in what I assumed was intended as an imitation of a wobbegong wiggling its caudal fin.

"I'm still not sure what this has to do with our trapdoor," I said.

"The most unusual thing about them is their bearded appearance," he said. "They have a fringe of fleshy skin lobes around the entire front of their heads."

"Like tentacles?"

"Tentacles are usually prehensile," he said. "These are just inert skin flaps. They might undulate in the current. They probably resemble some kind of marine vegetation and help with the camouflage. Anyway, your trapdoor looks a lot like a lurking wobbegong. You know, the way you've got the leaves and vines sort of trailing off all around the edges."

He fiddled with his phone, then held it up to show me a picture of a tasseled wobbegong. Not a particularly decorative example of marine life. I'd have assumed I was looking at a patch of vegetation, or maybe a large sloppily made pizza that had landed on the ocean floor, if not for the two bulging eyes popping up in the middle of it. And yes, the fringes around the entire front of the creature were pretty distinctive. The whole effect was distinctly creepy, like something H. P. Lovecraft would have invented.

And he was right. My leaf-covered trapdoor did look a bit like his wobbegong. Maybe he could teach Sammy how to wiggle his hand like a caudal fin.

"Are you thinking of getting some wobbegongs for your zoo?" I asked.

"No, dammit." He sighed and fiddled with his phone. "They can get up to nearly two meters long. None of the marine habitats I have are anywhere near big enough for them. But they are impressive, aren't they?"

He held up his phone again to show me another wobbegong picture. This one had a wide gaping mouth that seemed to take up at least two-thirds of the width of its flat, round body. If wobbegongs were six feet long, this one was probably almost as wide, and that would make the mouth between three and four feet long.

"Stick to starfish and koi," I said. "That thing looks as if it would like to chow down on your zookeepers. Actually, our trapdoor does have one thing in common with your wobbegong. We're hoping to use it to ambush whoever has been creeping around in the woods at night. We're not sure if they're after the dogs or if they think there was something valuable buried with our skeleton, but if they missed seeing me fall into the trapdoor, maybe we can lure them in if we make it all look just the way it did before."

"Sounds like fun," he said.

"Your definition of fun never ceases to surprise me."

I picked up the trapdoor and carried it over to hand it to Sammy, who was arranging leaves around the perimeter of the hole.

"Fantastic," he said. "I was starting to think having me guard the place was going to be pretty useless, unless the chief assigned another deputy to tidy up every time I had to make a sortie out of the hole. But this will make it a lot smoother."

"We should get back to your house." Grandfather turned and began striding toward the path. "I need to get my wolves ready for the parade."

Chapter 31

"We can head over there in— Wait." I scrambled to keep up with him. "Why are you bringing your wolves? Please tell me you're not putting some of them up for adoption."

"Of course not," he said. "They're going to ride on the zoo's float, and we'll have a dozen or so of the more wolf-like dogs marching along with it—any ones that look as if they have a lot of shepherd or husky or malamute in them. And then we'll have the wolves on display in the town square all afternoon. We figure at least some of the folks who get all fired up over *Canis lupus* will be interested in dogs who hark back to their wild ancestors."

"Anything for the dogs," I said, as I followed him down the path.

Back in the yard, squads of volunteers were giving the dogs last-minute walks or grooming before boarding the fleet of cars, trucks, and buses that would ferry them to the Caerphilly High School football field. Since the school was on the outskirts of town and had ample parking, we'd chosen it for the parade's rally point. From there, the parade would follow a sort of spiral route, circling first around the outlying streets and gradually closing in until it finally arrived at the town square. In several places along the parade route, we'd had banks of bleachers set up. The idea was that the parade units that gave performances—such as the high school marching band, the local dance academy, and the New Life Baptist Choir—would halt at each of these points and do their best number for an appreciative audience of tourists.

I was puzzled by one thing. Josh, Jamie, and Adam were running around attaching strips of ribbon to all the dogs' collars. Red and blue ribbons. Had Mother decreed some sort of color scheme for the march? It didn't seem likely, if for no other reason that Mother would never have chosen those colors. If the ribbons were, say, lavender and pale coral, perhaps, but primary colors weren't usually her thing. And these looked more like prize ribbons than decorations.

I strolled over to where they were working on a throng of lively terriers to ask what the deal was.

"So I agree that all the dogs are winners," I said. "But how can they possibly all have won both first and second prize?"

"These aren't prize ribbons," Josh said. "If someone spots a dog they want, in the parade or once we get them to the town square, they can run up and grab the blue ribbon from its collar and have dibs. And then if the blue-ribbon holder doesn't get through the vetting process or changes their mind, the red-ribbon holder gets the next choice."

He held up one of the ribbons, and I could see that it had the dog's number and picture stapled to it.

"That's pretty cool," I said. "A lot of work, though."

"Grandma and Ms. Ellie thought it up," Josh said. "And we helped make the ribbons yesterday afternoon. Now if we can just get all the dogs tagged before they leave the yard."

"I'll stop distracting you," I said.

Grandfather had joined the group of his employees who would be marching in the parade. He seemed to be inspecting the pack of dogs they'd be leading with a stern frown, as if not entirely convinced that some of them were sufficiently wolflike.

I went over to eavesdrop.

"But these are the most wolflike ones we could find," Manoj was saying. "And we need to have enough dogs to make a good impression. We do not want to be the least impressive parade entry."

"The high school drama club made a few sheep costumes before they joined forces with the college Drama Department and decided they wanted their dogs to march as dinosaurs," I suggested. "How about if I have them bring the spare sheep costumes over? You can turn the dogs that aren't wolfish enough into wolves in sheep's clothing and you'll still have the numbers to make a good impression."

This suggestion pleased both Grandfather and the zoo staff, so I introduced them to the drama club members and left them to sort things out. I had other things on my mind.

I hurried inside to make sure Spike and the Pomeranians, both resident and visiting, were safely confined to their crates, and that the crates all bore signs announcing that the occupants were "Waterston Family Dogs! Not Eligible for the Mutt March!" We'd had an unfortunate incident the first day of march prep when a well-meaning volunteer had tried to give Spike a bath. Luckily she'd been wearing very heavy rubber gloves, so he hadn't technically broken skin, but it was still pretty traumatic for her, and I noticed she hadn't come back the next day. By now most of the volunteers had learned to be wary of Spike, but the Poms loved everyone and would probably be delighted if someone took them out to join the canine exodus.

I had a moment of panic when I found that none of the crates were in the living room, where I'd left them. But it occurred to me to check with Kevin, since one of the missing crates would have contained Widget, his Pom. To my relief, I found that he'd hauled Spike and all of the Poms down to his computer-infested lair in the basement. The row of crates along one wall of the room were all empty, since Spike and the Poms were either sleeping on the wide counter where Kevin's computers and their gear lived or sitting in front of one of the monitors, watching a Road Runner cartoon.

"I'm going to keep an eye on them," he said. "In case any dog-nappers think we'd have all gone off to the parade and left our own dogs unguarded."

"Good thinking," I said. "But are you okay with missing the parade?"

"I won't completely miss it," he said. "I've got cameras set up in a bunch of key points along the route. I'll probably see more of it than you do if you're marching. Are you?"

"I'll be driving the New Life Baptist truck," I said. "Since the chief's going to be pretty busy today. You actually went around and set up cameras all over town so you could watch the parade without leaving your lair?"

"Actually, I set them up in places where I thought we might spot Iris," he said. "I got Rose Noire to tell me some of the places she likes to go. Of course, we're not sure how she'd get to any of them without someone giving her a ride."

"She may have borrowed Delaney's bike," I said. "So keep your eyes out for that, too."

He nodded.

"I'm actually going to be pretty busy during the parade," he said. "I want to monitor those dogfighting message boards to see if anyone posts anything suspicious there. Plus, I'll be keeping my eye on all the GPS trackers the dogs are wearing."

"Seriously?" I asked. "All of them?"

He typed something on his keyboard and a graphic appeared on one of the large nearby monitors. I recognized it as a map of Caerphilly County. In the lower left-hand corner, which I deduced was our house, was a tight knot of blue-and-red blinking dots. A smaller cluster had formed closer to the center of town—presumably at the high school football field—and groups of between two and a dozen could be seen slowly moving from our house to the high school.

"If any of them leave the parade route, I can sound the alarm," he said. "It'll be a relief when this is over and I can get back to tracking down Pruitts."

"Which Pruitts?" I asked.

"Any of them I can find," he said with a shrug. "Since we have no idea which branch of the family tree our skeleton came from."

"Excellent," I said. "Have you run across—let's see—Wolfgang? Anatole? Armand? Hobart? Or Gus?"

"Wolfgang's doing fifteen to life up at Coffeewood," he said. "Armed robbery. And Armand managed to do himself in about ten years ago up in Roanoke, although I don't yet know how. The obituary just said that he was suddenly taken from us. And obviously he's not our skeleton, so there's no great rush to find out, but I'm curious. Haven't run across anything about the others. Nothing about their present whereabouts, that is."

"Let me know if you do find anything interesting," I said. "Or if you spot Iris on any of your parade cams."

"Yeah, the chief already asked me to keep an eye out for her." He frowned. "She was so excited about the Mutt March. Kind of hard to believe she won't try to get to someplace where she can watch it."

"That's what I'm hoping," I said. "Laters."

I climbed back up to the kitchen. I snagged one of our minicoolers, filled it with bottles of cold water, and went out to look for transportation to the parade rallying point. Michael was using the Twinmobile, our vintage van, to transport loads of dogs and volunteers over to the high school. I managed to squeeze myself and my cooler into his latest load—nearly a dozen terriers dressed in Ewok costumes—and spent the trip to town being licked with great enthusiasm by most of the tail-wagging Ewoks while trying to clear my head so I'd have at least a fighting chance of enjoying the event.

The presence of the Ewoks reminded me of what one of Rose Noire's yoga gurus called the Jedi mind-clearing technique. She'd urge her pupils to take all the busy thoughts that were crowding their brains and imagine them appearing in yellow letters on a black screen, and then moving away and vanishing into the distance, like the opening crawl of a *Star Wars* movie. Sometimes the technique worked, and sometimes it just left me humming the *Star Wars* theme music for the rest of the day. It probably worked better if you gave your mind a stern order to visualize your worries, instead of conjuring up the familiar "It is a period of civil war. Rebel spaceships, striking from a hidden base, have won their first victory against the evil Galactic Empire."

I tried it now, imagining skeletons, fallout shelters, foil-wrapped cocaine bricks, chinless Pruitts, and visions of a kidnapped Iris slowly rolling off into the distance. It didn't work all that well, but the effort kept my mind occupied until we got to the rallying point, and with luck I could soon lose myself in getting ready to play my part in the parade.

Michael and I unloaded our Ewoks near the home goalposts, where Josh and Jamie and a group of their classmates were collecting their charges. I helped Michael don his Darth Vader costume. Then I hurried over to the end of the parking lot where the choir members were gathering around a gaily decorated flatbed truck.

The chief hadn't told me that my assignment as driver for the New Life Baptist float would include wearing a shaggy dog costume made of polyester fake fur. I started sweating profusely the second they zipped me into it, so I peeled it off and renegotiated my job responsibilities. Since I had no plan to hop out of the truck at any time during the parade, and only someone in a helicopter could see what I was wearing on the lower half of my body once I was behind the truck's steering wheel, I convinced them that it would work if I pulled on only the top half of the costume and left it unzipped, with the bottom half draped down between the driver's seat and the stick shift. And it was still going to be pretty miserable, but luckily this time of year I kept an old swimsuit in the Twinmobile, in case of impromptu visits to lakes or pools, so I snagged that. And Randall had hauled one of the fancy porta potties over to the field, so I used that as a dressing room to don the swimsuit before pulling on the shaggy dog costume again.

"But what are you going to do when we get to the town square?" Minerva asked, with a worried look.

"I'll stay in the truck until you're all unloaded," I said. "And then I'll drive off and park somewhere out of sight."

She wasn't thrilled by the idea, but was savvy enough to realize the wisdom of taking precautions against the float's driver having heatstroke. Thank goodness the chief had already convinced them that he couldn't possibly drive the truck with his hands encased in the fuzzy paws the costume had come with. I stowed my regular clothes in the passenger seat so I could change back into them when I shed the dog outfit. And I made sure I could easily reach my mini cooler.

The truck was all gussied up with red-and-gold bunting, to match the choir's robes. They'd installed a U-shaped four-tiered platform in its bed, which would let the choir either sit or stand, half facing the onlookers and half facing Minerva, who would be standing at a lectern right behind the cab, from which she could direct the choir—and give instructions to me as needed. In addition to two dozen choir members on the float, we had a dozen or so assorted dogs in red-and-gold costumes sitting at the feet of the singers—senior dogs and puppies that we didn't think should be forced to walk the whole way. Another thirty-odd members of the choir would be marching in formation beside or behind the truck, singing along while leading more costumed dogs.

As the parade's noon starting time approached, Ms. Ellie took a place by one of the parking lot entrances with a clipboard and a referee's whistle in hand. With her two assistant librarians as runners, she began marshaling the different floats and units into the agreed-upon order and sending them slowly rolling toward town.

First up was the high school marching band, followed by the float from the Caerphilly Garden Club. Most of the adoptable birds were displayed in cages hanging from the several vine-and-flower-covered arches on the bed of the garden club's float, along with blossom-decked cages that contained some of the more decorative cats. Mother and several of her cronies were riding on this float, dressed in long, flowing pastel gowns and wearing picture hats festooned with silk flowers and ribbons. They were already practicing the wave they'd be displaying for the crowd—an accurate re-creation of the sort of regal yet wrist-protective gesture Queen Elizabeth II had been famous for. Half a dozen girls in princess dresses were marching ahead of or behind the float, leading dogs and carrying baskets of flower petals that they could toss at the crowds once we got close enough to town to see crowds.

The theater arts squadron came next—the high school drama club plus quite a few of Michael's drama department students, escorting several dozen dogs dressed in remarkably clever dinosaur costumes, all marching around a life-sized papier-mâché T. rex with tiny red bulbs to represent its eyes. At intervals, they'd throw a switch that opened the T. rex's tooth-studded jaw and triggered a ferocious roar that set every dog in the formation to barking or howling furiously.

Next up were Seth Early and Lad, escorting a dozen of their best Lincoln sheep, followed rather ironically by Grandfather's wolf-themed float. I had my doubts about the wisdom of putting the wolves that close to the sheep, but I had to admit that it seemed to fire up the wolves to an enthusiastic display of pacing and snarling in their enormous cages, and it was obvious that the sheep felt perfectly safe in Lad's care.

More floats followed. Rancid Dread, Caerphilly's own homegrown metal band, was giving an enthusiastic performance atop their float, accompanied by a squadron of dogs in costumes and makeup that made them look like refugees from a KISS concert.

A squadron of blue-and-white Shiffley Construction vehicles was next—several trucks, a cement mixer, a boom lift, and Aaron Shiffley on the fateful bulldozer—all festooned with dogs and flanked by even more dogs, all wearing miniature hard hats and t-shirts with the company's logo.

After that came the float from the Caerphilly Dance Studio, featuring a sort of dance-off between half a dozen ballerinas and an equal number of tap dancers. A bevy of dogs wearing pink, lavender, and baby blue tulle tutus trotted along with it.

A float from Flugleman's Feed Store and Garden Supply followed, piled high with produce—presumably the idea was that the seeds, tools, and fertilizers sold in the store were responsible for the large size and healthy appearance of all the fruits and vegetables. It also carried several of the Flugleman grandchildren and their friends, armed with buckets of the store's locally made all-organic dog treats that they'd be flinging at the crowd. The dozen or so dogs trotting alongside in shirts with the store's logo on the side were already looking up hopefully at the treat buckets.

And next came the choir. I eased the truck slowly into motion and fell in behind the feed store float.

Chapter 32

As soon as the truck hit the road, Minerva tapped her conductor's baton and the choir launched into its first number—a full-throated rendition of "(How Much Is) That Doggie in the Window?" Not that we had much of an audience yet, but Minerva wanted the singers to be already making a joyful noise as soon as we encountered the first listeners, and I think she considered the first few miles to be the equivalent of a dress rehearsal.

They followed up their first number with "Me and You and a Dog Named Boo," the Monkees' "Gonna Buy Me a Dog," and "B-I-N-G-O." Deacon Washington, as the lead singer on "Who Let the Dogs Out" was definitely going to be a show stealer, topped only by Aida's daughter, Kayla, whose rendition of "Hound Dog" would have made both Elvis Presley and Big Mama Thornton proud.

Unfortunately, that was the extent of the canine-themed repertoire the choir had been able to come up with, so I resigned myself to the possibility that I'd get a little tired of those six songs by the time we reached the town square. But that wouldn't bother the tourists, who'd be lucky if they got to hear two whole songs as the parade rumbled slowly but steadily on.

Whoever came up with the marching order evidently considered the choir one of the parade's star attractions, since we were third from the last. Immediately behind us was the boys' *Star Wars* formation. They had more dogs than any other unit, most of them costumed as Ewoks, with a few of the larger ones garbed as Wookies. Josh, Jamie, and Adam marched at the front—costumed as Han Solo, Luke Skywalker, and Lando Calrissian, respectively. I knew the costume shop at the college had helped with the costumes for the dozen imperial stormtroopers who marched behind them, and I suspected Kevin had helped create the mechanical R2-D2 unit that beeped furiously as it zoomed in circles around the marchers. Michael, as Darth Vader, brought up the rear, marching on specially designed platform boots that added at least a foot to his already impressive height, waving a light saber that flashed a sinister blood red.

Bringing up the rear were Clarence Rutledge and Mayor Randall Shiffley, riding in a vehicle that almost always played a starring role in local parades and processions—Judge Jane Shiffley's 1965 Mustang convertible, bright red and in mint condition. If anyone else had owned that car, they might have balked at letting anyone else drive it, much less filling it with at least a dozen of the shaggiest, happiest dogs available. Judge Jane had been delighted, and had given orders to the official parade photographer—the college student who'd covered our finding the skeleton for both the *Clarion* and the college rag—to take plenty of pictures.

We rumbled along for a little while, singing, dancing, waving, and making music for our own enjoyment. But before too long we spotted the first tourists lining the roadway and cheering. Soon we were passing through an almost unbroken wall of tourists on either side of the road. Many of them were waving Mutt March flags—small triangular red-and-gold pennants decorated with cartoon pictures of dogs and attached to bamboo sticks. Randall had had them printed up by the hundreds and had scattered boxes of them at strategic points throughout town.

All along the route, people were leaping into the air to catch the gaily wrapped dog treats and clapping along with the various musical numbers. Many people had brought along their own dogs, and quite a few of them fell into step and marched along with the parade for a while. Some dropped out after a few blocks, but quite a few seemed determined to keep going until we reached the town square.

I had been a little worried about how the dogs would react to the crowd, but it soon became obvious that someone—probably Judge Jane and Clarence—had done a good job of assessing the dogs' temperaments. Any shy or reactive dogs must have been assigned to ride on the floats—or possibly sent down to Caroline Willner's resident dog expert for therapy. All of the dogs flanking the floats—and thus accessible to strangers who wanted to pet them—seemed to be cheerful, friendly, exuberant dogs who were energized by the cheering, waving crowds. It was all some of the handlers could do to keep their charges from darting over to lick the faces of the onlookers. And all along the route, people were constantly darting out to pet the dogs or snag one of the blue or red ribbons.

Most of the blue ribbons had already been claimed by the time we hit the halfway mark—a stop in front of the college administration building, where a wide green stretch of lawn made space for a row of bleachers—and the red ribbons were going fast.

There was hardly a ribbon in sight by the time we reached the next-to-last stopping point—the street in front of the New Life Baptist Church. Not only were there bleachers in the parking lot for the tourists to enjoy the various shows in comfort, but when we pulled to a stop there, nearly a hundred additional choir members emerged from the church in an upbeat procession, their red-and-gold robes fluttering behind them as they strode toward the truck to join their voices to those of the singers on the float.

I cut the motor, set the hand brake, and fished another cold bottle of water out of my mini cooler. I figured I was doing my part for the performance by nodding my head in time to the music—vigorous nods that made the costume's droopy ears flap around in what people seemed to find an amusing manner. And as I sipped and nodded, I scanned the crowd, enjoying the sight of so many smiling, clapping, cheering onlookers.

Onlookers and, with luck, future contented dog parents.

Then, as the augmented choir neared the end of "Who Let the Dogs Out"—with Deacon Washington dancing and singing as if he were nineteen instead of ninety, and hadn't already done this routine at least a dozen times—I spotted something interesting. Two very familiar male faces. Not men I knew, exactly, but men who looked remarkably like older versions of those weak-chinned, pop-eyed Pruitts I'd seen so many of during my research in the *Clarion*'s archives and the Caerphilly High School yearbooks.

Interesting. Hadn't the chief said that Miss Ethelinda was the only Pruitt left in town? Had he overlooked these two? More likely they'd returned to town for some reason. Quite a coincidence that they showed up right now, so soon after we'd unearthed the skeleton of one of their relatives, under circumstances that were getting increasingly mysterious.

And like the chief, I wasn't a big believer in coincidences.

I pulled out my phone and, without missing a beat in my head wagging and ear flapping, texted the chief.

"We're stopped in front of the New Life Baptist Church," I typed. "Just spotted two guys in the crowd who look a lot like Pruitts. Thought you'd like to know."

"Roger," he texted back.

Not a very satisfactory reply, since it didn't let me know whether he was glad to get the news and was sending some of his deputies to intercept the Pruitts, or whether he was merely acknowledging that he'd gotten my message and rolling his eyes at the irrelevance of it.

So I kept my eye on the Pruitts.

They didn't seem to be as cheerful as most of the onlookers. They weren't smiling or clapping or bouncing their heads to the music. They were peering around as if trying to find something. Something or someone.

Then one of them lifted his head, as if he'd spotted something. He cuffed the other on the shoulder and pointed to their left. They both began moving in that direction, shouldering their way through the crowd a little rudely. I turned and tried to figure out what they were heading for. All I saw were spectators, lined up three or four deep along the side of the street.

Wait—someone had started moving rapidly away from them through the crowd. I could only see the back of their head above the kids and mostly shorter people who made up the crowd at that point. It was a tall woman or a man on the tall side of average, with a neatly cropped head of gray hair.

Was it Iris? From this distance, it looked a lot like her.

Whoever it was, the Pruitts were definitely in hot pursuit. As I watched, the two Pruitts caught up with her, and each of them grabbed one of her arms.

My first impulse was to hop out of the truck cab and give chase—but I couldn't abandon the choir. And besides, the Pruitts and Iris were already disappearing into the crowd.

I pulled out my phone again.

"I think I just spotted Iris Rafferty," I texted to the chief. "The Pruitts I saw seem to have grabbed her and dragged her off."

"Which way were they headed?" he texted back. "North or south?"

"No idea. Away from the center of town, whichever that is."

"That would be south. Roger. Let me know if you spot them again."

"Will do."

The air around me was full of the glorious sound of the choir, providing a backup to Kayla's dynamite rendition of "Hound Dog." But instead of losing myself in the music, I was frantically scanning the crowds, hoping to catch sight of Iris. Or the Pruitts.

I was slightly reassured when I spotted a cruiser whizzing by a few blocks down the street behind us, lights flashing. And probably siren wailing, though I couldn't hear it over the choir.

And before I knew it, the song was over, and Minerva was tapping on the back window of the truck cab, signaling me to start the engine.

"Find her," I muttered to myself as I turned the key. "Just find her before . . ."

Before what? I didn't want to think about it. I eased the truck into motion. Next stop, the town square. Suddenly I had to force myself to keep to the parade's snail-like pace.

Chapter 33

I fretted all through the slow trip from the church to the town square, but I forced myself to focus on my driving. Which was a good thing, since this part of the parade route was the most perilous. It had the biggest crowds, and tourists kept darting out into the road, either to snag one of the few remaining red ribbons or to find an optimal spot for taking photos of the parade. One middle-aged man with a video camera lumbered out into the middle of the road, planted himself there, six feet from the truck's front bumper, and stood stock still, evidently shooting video of us. I had to stop the truck to avoid hitting him. I tapped gently on the horn, then less gently, and finally just leaned on it—to no avail. I glanced around to see if there was a deputy nearby, but they were probably all off chasing Pruitts. The cameraman didn't even seem to notice that anything was wrong until three of his friends darted out and dragged him back onto the sidewalk, still obsessively taking his video as I eased the truck into motion again.

I breathed a sigh of relief when I'd unloaded the last choir member and could put the truck back in gear and head for the parking lot behind the courthouse, which was cordoned off for parade-related vehicles. As soon as I'd set the hand brake, I stripped off the sweat-soaked dog costume and threw it onto the passenger seat. I chugged half a bottle of water and then, feeling a little more like myself, grabbed the costume and folded it neatly. Of course, it would have to go straight into the laundry, but I didn't want the Baptists thinking Mother had raised me to mistreat borrowed objects, however unprepossessing.

I scanned the parking lot and then spotted something that raised my spirits. At bedtime last night, Michael had mentioned that while ferrying dogs to the high school, he could probably enlist someone's help to drop both the Twinmobile and my old car off here, so we'd have wheels when the parade was over. I'd thought of jotting a reminder in my notebook, and had been too tired to turn on the light and open it. So I'd forgotten—but he hadn't. I spotted both vehicles at the far end of the parking lot, in one of the few shady patches.

Then I pulled out my phone and—

Who could I call to find out what was happening with Iris and her Pruitt pursuers? The chief had better things to do than brief me, and the same went for his deputies. And most of the other people who could normally be counted on for the latest local news were probably over in the town square, caring for the dogs, manning the various booths and stalls, or watching the first of the acts that would be performing onstage during the afternoon's festivities.

I dialed Kevin. I suspected on a day like this he'd be monitoring the police radio in addition to his GPS map and the dogfighting forums he'd targeted.

"What's up?" he said, by way of a greeting.

"I reported spotting two Pruitts who seemed to be dragging Iris off," I said.

"Heard about that," he said.

"Great," I said. "Have you heard what's happening?"

"Horace and Aida collared them a few minutes ago."

"And did they also find Iris?"

"Apparently. I heard Aida call for backup so they could take all three of them down to the station in separate cars. They didn't mention Iris by name—just called her the complainant."

"They probably wouldn't want to identify her on the radio," I said. "Thanks. I'll think up a reason to drop by the police station before I head over to the town square."

"Let me know if you find out anything interesting," he said.

"And you do the same."

"Roger."

We hung up and I looked around for a place to change. I could put my t-shirt and jeans on over the swimsuit, but it was as wet as if I'd actually taken a dip in it, and, given the high humidity, I didn't think it would dry off all that soon. Luckily Randall's luxury porta potty was still there and, even luckier, the crowds of tourists hadn't yet found it. I used it to change into my dry clothes.

As I emerged from the porta potty, I heard the highly amplified opening chords of "Daybreak Cataclysm," one of Rancid Dread's signature numbers. At least that was my most plausible guess about what the title was. The Rancid Dread lead singer had a reasonably good voice, but he couldn't enunciate for beans. "Down by the Catacombs" was another possibility. It actually sounded more like "Don't Buy Catalogs" than either of them, but I had a hard time imagining a heavy metal band singing about catalogs. One of these days I'd go online, to whatever streaming service they uploaded their music to, and find out if I'd guessed right.

In the meantime, hearing them starting up banished any doubt I had about whether to head straight for the town square or detour by the police station. Fifteen or twenty blocks away was the perfect distance for listening to Rancid Dread. And if the chief or any of his officers looked askance at my turning up at the station, I could always explain that I was trying to preserve my hearing. And my sanity.

So I took off to walk the few blocks between the parking lot and the police station. I passed the occasional band of tourists heading in the other direction—toward the town square. One group very helpfully told me that I was going in the wrong direction. I thanked them and assured them that I'd be going down there as soon as I ran a quick errand. I didn't want to disparage the Rancid Dreads by revealing my real motive.

When I walked into the police station, I was surprised to find the public waiting area empty except for George, the civilian employee who staffed the front desk. But of course anyone they'd arrested would be back in an interrogation room or a jail cell, and the officers would be either guarding them or back in town patrolling the festival. And George greeted me with an air of suppressed excitement that made me optimistic about my chances of finding out what was going on.

"I hear they caught those Pruitts I spotted," I said. I'd never found subtlety all that effective with George.

"They did!" he exclaimed. "Good job spotting them. Of course, it's driving us crazy, not being able to interview them yet."

"They lawyered up?" I asked.

"They're trying to," he said. "We've got callbacks out to all the local defense attorneys, but so far we haven't gotten hold of any of them. Not surprising—not just a Saturday but a Saturday with a big festival going on."

"Is Iris okay?"

"Iris?" He looked puzzled. "Iris Rafferty?"

"Yes," I said. "When I spotted the Pruitts, it looked as if they had grabbed her and were dragging her off."

"Oh," he said. "That wasn't Iris. It was their aunt or cousin or whatever. Miss Ethelinda."

Disappointment hit me hard.

"Damn," I said. "I couldn't decide whether to be relieved that I'd spotted Miss Ethelinda or worried that the Pruitts were hassling her for some reason. Now I'm just worried."

It also occurred to me that maybe whatever the Pruitts had done was my fault. I'd been half joking when I suggested that Miss Ethelinda spread a rumor that she'd won the lottery and see if any greedy relatives showed up. What if she'd actually done it? Who knows what those two might have done to her if I hadn't happened to spot them in the crowd? Or if they'd managed to whisk her away before the police caught them?

My face must have reflected what I was thinking.

"Don't worry," George said. "Miss Ethelinda's fine. And Ms. Iris will be, too. She's been sending her daughter messages this whole time, so we're pretty sure nothing has happened to her. And they're bringing in the bloodhounds tomorrow. And I hear Horace is going to try to take the Poms out this afternoon, as soon as things aren't quite so crazy with the festival."

"Yes, I heard." I decided not to ask why they were bringing in bloodhounds if they were so sure she was fine. "But I still feel bad about getting everyone's hopes up." Not to mention possibly setting Miss Ethelinda up for her greedy relatives. Not that I was going to reveal that to George—although maybe I'd confess it to the chief.

"An understandable mistake," he said. "Ms. Iris and Miss Ethelinda are about the same height, and they have the same hairdo."

"So Miss Ethelinda did a runner from the assisted living again," I said. "Was she sneaking out to see the parade?"

"She was sneaking out to get away from her relatives," he said. "I don't think she was watching the parade so much as using the crowds for cover. Those two cousins of hers showed up and, when they asked to see her, the staff showed them back to her room. Then there was a big row, and she had them kicked out, and they were threatening that if the staff didn't let them back in, they'd come back with their power of attorney and make them hand her over, and while all that was going on, she flew the coop."

"Power of attorney?" The guilt came surging back—it was sounding more and more as if Miss Ethelinda had followed my suggestion. A suggestion that had backfired. "I can't imagine her giving any of her family a power of attorney."

"That's what the staff at the assisted living thought," he said. "They didn't have one on file, so they told the cousins to come back with a copy of it and then they'd talk. And Miss Ethelinda flat-out told us that she hadn't given anyone a power of attorney, and she'd sooner give one to Satan himself than any of that lot. She was pointing to her two cousins at the time."

"Good for her," I said. "I could get to like Miss Ethelinda."

"So could I, as long as it's from a distance," he said. "I'll like her a whole lot better when she's back where she belongs at the assisted living. They're short-staffed today, and it could be a while before they have anyone they can send to pick her up. She just wants us to turn her loose so she can walk home, but the chief doesn't want to."

"Sounds like a bad idea in this heat," I said.

"Yeah." He frowned. "We stretched out the paperwork as much as we could on the charges she's filing against her cousins."

"Any interesting charges?"

"Assault and battery and kidnapping, so far," he said. "The chief and the town attorney are brainstorming on what else might apply. Then the chief had the brilliant idea of getting your dad to come over so she can be medically checked out before he turns her loose, and she's all for that. Wants someone to verify that her cousins grabbed her so hard they left bruises. Which we already took pictures of, but she likes the idea of having a real medical opinion."

"I'm sure Dad was delighted at the opportunity."

"Yes, and he's on his way, but we're trying to get him to stall a bit until we can organize a ride for her. He'd do it if he had his car, but he left it back at your house."

"How about if I volunteer to take Miss Ethelinda home?" I suggested. "Back to the assisted living, that is. My car's only a few blocks away. I could fetch it while you're waiting for Dad. And if she balks, maybe he would even come with us."

"She might like that, having a doctor hovering over her," he said. "You go fetch the car and I'll slip the word to your dad."

So I half ran to the parking lot and collected my ancient but trusty blue Toyota. By the time I got back to the police station, Dad had arrived and he and Miss Ethelinda were in the entrance area. Dad had his medical bag out, and appeared to be arguing with his rebellious patient.

"But you never know," he was saying. "Those roughnecks could have caused internal injuries. If we do an MRI—"

"They've taken pretty pictures of my bruises," Miss Ethelinda said. "That should be fine."

"But at the hospital—" Dad glanced at me, and I deduced what he was trying to accomplish.

"Good heavens," I said. "If she doesn't want to go to the hospital, just leave her in peace." I turned to Miss Ethelinda. "If you don't want to go to the hospital, I could take you back to the assisted living. And you could let them know how annoyed you are that they let those creeps get past them to bother you."

"But Meg—" Dad began, although I could tell from his expression that he was greatly relieved, and only putting up a protest for form's sake.

"Yes, that sounds like exactly what I'd like to do," she said. "Good to set them straight right away. Where's your car?"

"In the parking lot," I said. "Want me to bring it around to the front door?"

"I can walk just fine," she said. "Lead the way."

So Miss Ethelinda and I walked briskly out to my car, followed by Dad, who fussed over her enough to keep her motivated to leave him behind. I refrained from trying to help her into the car, only standing near enough that I could catch her if she tripped or fell. And then I assured Dad that I'd see her safely to her room and got behind the wheel.

"You don't need to tuck me into bed," she said. "Just drop me off at the entrance."

"I figured as much," I said. "Although maybe I should go in long enough to tell the staff you've had a thorough medical exam and just need to be left alone."

"Good idea." She snorted with what might have been amusement, or maybe just exasperation.

"Who were those two clowns?" I asked. "Were they really relatives of yours?"

"Unfortunately yes," she said. "Drysdale and Anatole Pruitt. My feckless brother's two most useless grandsons. Not the kind of relatives I'm likely to brag on."

"Any idea why they were bothering you?" I tried to make the question sound innocent, as if I was baffled by why anyone would harass such a sweet old lady. "You didn't follow that suggestion of mine, did you? About starting a rumor that you'd won the lottery?"

"I thought of that," she said. "But I decided maybe fear would motivate them just as well as greed. I called a couple of the worst family gossips and let them know I was planning to tell the police anything and everything I knew."

"And that brought them running?"

"Hard to say." She frowned. "They might have been heading here already. They seemed to think I'd have some idea where their cousin Hobart the drug dealer stored his merchandise."

I didn't quite manage to keep a straight face when she said that. The fact that I didn't run the car off the road probably qualified as a miracle.

"And I told them they should look in their own backyards," she went on. "Or Hobart's daddy's backyard. You ask me, that boy must have been a mole or a gopher in a past life, or maybe a squirrel. Always going on about hiding stuff underground. He had this stupid idea that scent dogs couldn't find something if it was underground."

"What kind of stuff?" I asked.

"I figure it was drugs mostly," she said. "You don't see a whole lot of high school dropouts driving brand-new Trans Ams unless they've got some kind of illegal racket going on. And he didn't seem to care about getting other people in trouble by hiding his stuff where the cops could think it was theirs. His grandma finally had to put a lock on the door to her root cellar to stop him from hiding his trash behind her preserves."

"We just uncovered an abandoned fallout shelter in Rob and Delaney's backyard," I said. "Sounds like the kind of thing Hobart would like. You think maybe he'd have tried to use that?"

"Maybe," she said. "If he knew it was there. Who knows? It wouldn't have been his first choice. He thought a fallout shelter was a cool idea, but he wanted his own. He had this whole big plan for digging a fallout shelter that you got to from a trapdoor in the floor of his daddy's equipment shed. And just in case the cops found the fallout shelter, it wasn't going to be anything more than a real fallout shelter—the merchandise was going to be in a secret hidey-hole underneath it—a hidey-hole big enough that he could get in there, too, if someone was after him."

"Like another whole mini fallout shelter underneath the main fallout shelter?" I asked.

"Yeah," she said. "He had impressive plans for that shelter. Completely impractical plans, but impressive."

"Interesting," I said. "But it seems to me that if the cops found the fallout shelter and the drugs weren't there, they'd do a pretty thorough search for any secret hiding places. They'd be looking for secret stashes."

"Hobart thought of that," she said. "He was going to put the trap-door to the secret hidey-hole underneath the main shelter's chemical toilet. He figured he could make that look so disgusting they wouldn't even want to touch it, much less search underneath it."

I nodded, but I didn't think Hobart's plan would have stopped Caerphilly's present-day law enforcement officers. I couldn't imagine Vern failing to find it, or Horace balking at searching in and around the chemical toilet. But perhaps the Pruitt-era police were less diligent. Or more squeamish.

And the thought certainly amused Miss Ethelinda. She was wheezing with mirth.

"Did he ever try to dig it?" I asked.

"Yeah." She started chuckling in earnest. "He borrowed his uncle's backhoe one day and tried to dig in the shed. Found out it had cee-ment under what he thought was a dirt floor. That's when he really ticked off his daddy. He already had the backhoe, so he decided he could dig his fallout shelter in the backyard. Figured he'd hide the entrance underneath a fountain or a birdbath or something."

"His daddy didn't like the idea?"

"His daddy hit the roof when he came home and found Hobart had destroyed half their septic field. After that, no one would let Hobart anywhere near their yards or their barns. He was always a smart cookie, Hobart, but not right in the head."

I decided not to share my opinion—that if Hobart really was such a smart cookie, why hadn't he applied his brains to some lawful enterprise? Did he seriously think he was smarter than the cops?

He probably did. And maybe he wasn't wrong, given that back then most of the cops were his fellow Pruitts.

But I didn't think this was a sentiment I should share with Miss Ethelinda.

"So Hobart never got his fallout shelter?" I asked.

"Not as far as I know," she said. "Not long after the septic field fiasco he got himself arrested as a drug dealer, and then skipped out on his bail. His daddy was mad as a hornet about that. Losing all that money."

"Really? I'd have assumed his father would be willing to sacrifice a little money to save his pride and joy from a long prison term. To save the family reputation, even if he was still mad about the septic field."

"Well, yeah," she said. "If that was the only way to keep him out of the slammer. But the family bigwigs were already working out how to make the evidence against him disappear. They were going to hang it all on his two accomplices. A couple of lowlifes from Clay County. Would have been considerably cheaper, given how high the judge had set the bail, and he'd have been able to stay in town. We all figured that was why he never came back—'cause he knew his daddy was furious. Plus he had those outstanding charges against him. After his daddy passed, a couple of years later, the rest of the family kind of gave up trying to get the charges dropped. Probably a good thing he stayed away for good."

"His family never heard from him again?" I asked.

"Not a peep," she said. "Made for all kinds of headaches when they had to probate his daddy's will. He wasn't really in it—his daddy pretty much cut him out after the septic field thing. Left him a 1910 silver dollar and the whole wide world to make his living in—that's what it said in the will. But it would have been better to leave him out altogether. They went to a deal of trouble and spent a lot more than a dollar trying to find him. No need to park," she added, since we were arriving at the assisted living's front entrance. "Just pull up to the front door. They'll scamper out and start fussing over me as soon as they spot us."

Chapter 34

Miss Ethelinda was right. Three staff members were hurrying out to greet us—one pushing a wheelchair, which, after an initial protest, Miss Ethelinda condescended to sit in.

"Just to make you happy," she said to the hovering aides. "So you can go home and tell your families you actually did a lick of work today."

They were so relieved to see her back safe and sound that they didn't even seem to resent the insult. Or maybe they were used to insults from her.

"And if those two cousins of yours show up again, we won't even let them in the front door," the nurse in charge said.

"Won't see *them* anymore," Miss Ethelinda said. "Police have them locked up for kidnapping and a bunch of other felonies."

"Really?" The nurse looked up at me for confirmation. I nodded.

"They'll probably get years in prison for that," Miss Ethelinda said, in a satisfied tone. "Won't they?"

She was looking up at me.

"Up to ten years for kidnapping," I said. Not that I was an expert on the code of Virginia, but Vern was, and I recalled what he'd said one time when they were throwing the book at someone who'd forced me out into a snowstorm at gunpoint and without a coat.

"Mercy," said one of the aides, as she began to wheel her charge inside.

"And if they think I won't testify against them 'cause they're family, they've got another thing coming," she said, over her shoulder. "You tell them that."

"I will if I see them," I said.

I felt an enormous sense of relief at getting Miss Ethelinda safely off my hands. As soon as I could break free of the nurse, who insisted on thanking me effusively, I hurried back to my car and called the chief.

"What's up, Meg?" He sounded a little testy, as if I was interrupting something that was probably more important.

"How much did Miss Ethelinda tell you about her cousin Hobart Pruitt?" I asked.

"Hobart wasn't one of the ones bothering her," he said. "Drysdale and Anatole were their names."

"I know," I said. "If Hobart's name never came up—"

"It did not."

"Then she didn't mention how Hobart, the drug dealer, had an obsession with fallout shelters and tried to dig one in his family's backyard so he'd have a place to hide his illicit goods."

A slight pause.

"She didn't mention anything of the kind," he said. "Why don't you fill me in on exactly what she told you?"

So I did, in as much detail as I could remember—and adding in my own speculations. About Hobart's curious obsession with fallout shelters—could that have arisen after he somehow stumbled across the Raffertys' abandoned shelter? And my worry that Miss Ethelinda's taciturnity about Hobart's disappearance arose from knowing some dark family secret that she couldn't bring herself to reveal, no matter how annoyed she was with her kin. And the possibility that Anatole and Drysdale had shown up because she'd spread the rumor to her family that she was going to talk with the police. I even managed to slip in a confession that she might have gotten that idea from me.

Maybe I was imagining the sound of his pen scratching over the pages of his notebook. I didn't imagine the several times he told me to hold on a second while he caught up.

"Okay, now what little she told me about Anatole and Drysdale starts to make sense," he said. "All she would say was that they were threatening to hurt her unless she told them the whereabouts of some kind of lost property or family treasure. And she claimed to have no idea what they were talking about, much less where it would be. It seems she may have been a little disingenuous."

"Disingenuous?" I echoed. "I'd have said a bald-faced liar. I don't have the Pruitt family tree memorized. Do you have any idea where all of these characters fit into it?"

"Let me check the expanded and corrected version Kevin has helped me put together," he said. "Whoever wrote the family history left out Hobart altogether, but his birth record was easy enough to find. Anatole and Drysdale are brothers. Their father and Hobart's were brothers, so Hobart is or was their first cousin. And both fathers were sons of Miss Ethelinda's late brother. Technically they're all three her grandnephews. And that makes all three of them second cousins to Eustace Pruitt, the one your granddaddy has in his DNA database."

"And Grandfather said the skeleton was probably a second cousin to Eustace," I said. "So the skeleton could be Hobart."

"He very well could be. Not jumping to conclusions here, but Kevin's prioritizing tracking down Pruitts from that particular branch of the family tree. Hobart's father is long dead, but Kevin can't find a death record on his mother, and he had three siblings. And that DNA from Miss Ethelinda you got was helpful, too. Your granddaddy threw around a lot of technical terms and percentages, but I got your father to translate for me. Apparently her DNA's completely consistent with being our skeleton's great-aunt. Not absolute proof it's Hobart, but it's looking more likely all the time. And if we can't get Drysdale and Anatole to give us DNA samples voluntarily, we'll see what we can do with a court order. Or stealth."

"That's good news."

"Of course, that raises up as many questions as it answers," he said. "Your information does help explain how Hobart could have known about the fallout shelter—but not how he ended up buried beside it. And how do the Raffertys fit into all this? I have a sneaking feeling Ms. Iris could give us some answers if we could find her."

He didn't add that maybe dodging his questions was the reason she'd disappeared. He didn't have to.

"And that's not even mentioning the biggest question of all," I said. "Who killed Hobart?"

"Exactly."

"Are Anatole and Drysdale on the suspect list?" I asked.

"At the moment they pretty much *are* the suspect list," he said. "But that's mainly because they showed up as soon as we found the skeleton and tried to badger Miss Ethelinda into telling them where Hobart hid his drug stash."

"Which is suspicious," I said.

"But a long way from conclusive evidence. And it's going to be pretty tough digging up evidence on a case that's more than thirty years old."

"You hear about a lot of that happening these days," I said. "Cold cases even older than this being solved."

"Usually because there's DNA evidence," he said. "Horace and your granddaddy's experts are going over every bit of evidence we've got to see if they can get some trace DNA. The quarter, the Air Jordans, the bullet, the cocaine and gun we found in the fallout shelter. Every inch of the fallout shelter."

"If there's anything there, they'll find it."

"But there may not be anything to find. Well, even if we can't prove Drysdale and Anatole killed their cousin Hobart, at least we'll be able to take them out of circulation for a while, thanks to what they tried to pull off with Miss Ethelinda."

"On a different topic," I began. "Well, not all that different—what was Hobart's father's name?"

"Wilfred Pruitt."

"Sounds familiar."

"It's unlikely that you could have met him. He died before either of us came to Caerphilly,"

"I figured as much," I said. "I probably just saw an article about him when I was searching through the microfilm at the library."

"Sounds likely," he said. "And if it had been anything interesting you'd have made a copy of it."

Was that a suggestion that perhaps I'd dumped a few too many microfilm printouts on him, or a compliment on my thoroughness? I decided to assume the latter.

"Anyway, thanks for the information," he said.

We hung up and I was reaching to start my car when I spotted something interesting. At the far end of the assisted-living building, Miss Ethelinda was leaning out of a window. Was she about to go on the lam again?

I got out of my car and strolled down the sidewalk until I was outside her window.

"Hi again," I said.

"You hear that caterwauling?" she asked. "What are they doing down at the town square—slaughtering hogs?"

I had to suppress a giggle. I'd almost blocked out the distant yet highly audible caterwauling, as she called it, but I knew at once what she meant.

"That's Rancid Dread," I said. "Local heavy metal band." I decided she wouldn't be interested in learning that the song they were playing went by the catchy title of "Alone in the Morgue with My Zombies."

"People pay money to hear that?"

"Not usually," I said. "At least not in great numbers. They're donating their performance to the Mutt March."

"Wish they'd donate some earplugs," she said. "What are you doing still here?"

"I had a question for you," I said. "Wilfred Pruitt—Hobart's father—what did he do for a living?"

"As little as he could get away with," she said. "Mainly he owned and managed that hot-sheets motel down by the creek. Ran it for twenty, maybe twenty-five years. Even lived there most of the time, in that rundown house behind it, the one Hurricane Isabel knocked to smithereens some twenty years ago. Why?"

"Just curiosity," I said. "I couldn't help wondering how much Hobart lost by getting himself disinherited."

"Damn little," she said. "The place was losing money hand over fist. Wilfred Junior finally found some fool he could talk into buying the place."

I nodded. I knew that part of the story. The fool in question hadn't been able to make the place pay, either, and had managed to get himself bumped off a few years later, while playing Santa in the town Christmas parade. Rob bought the motel from his estate, had it gutted, and turned it into affordable housing for many of his junior staff. But I remembered that during the sale process, a Pruitt had popped up claiming that he hadn't been paid in full when he'd sold the motel, and that Rob therefore owed him several hundred thousand dollars. Our cousin Festus had taken care of that, but I'd bet anything Rob would still remember the name Wilfred Pruitt, and not fondly.

"Was the septic field Hobart wrecked just for the house?" I asked. "Or—"

"For the whole motel," she said. "They had to close down for weeks. Old Wilfred was fit to be tied."

"Interesting," I said. And it was. I had the feeling Miss Ethelinda could share a lot of Caerphilly lore if someone she trusted—or at least didn't hate—encouraged her. "You know a lot about the local history—have you ever considered letting them record you for the Caerphilly Oral History Project?"

"Never heard of it," she said. "Who's doing it?"

"It's through the library," I said. I didn't think telling her it was one of Randall Shiffley's ideas would encourage her participation. "I can have Ms. Ellie drop by to tell you about it."

"Sounds good. Always like visitors, as long as they're not related to me."

"Great," I said. "See you later."

I half expected her to say something snarky, like "Not if I see you first," but she just nodded and slammed her window shut.

As I headed back to the car, I digested what she'd told me. The Whispering Pines, as the former hot-sheets motel had been called, was only a few miles down the road from our house—right beside the Spare Attic. If Hobart's family had lived behind it, he had probably spent time exploring the neighborhood as a kid. That could explain how he knew about the fallout shelter in the Raffertys' backyard.

Though not why the Raffertys would have let him use it. Or why Iris had gone AWOL.

When I reached my car, I pulled out my phone and texted the chief.

"Wilfred Pruitt used to run the Whispering Pines motel," I texted. "Hobart may have lived there as a kid."

He didn't answer immediately. I hoped that meant that at least one local defense attorney had returned his calls so he could start interviewing the Pruitts he'd arrested. It wasn't until I was pulling into the participants' parking lot that I saw his reply.

"Thanks. Useful."

I waited for a few minutes, hoping he'd say more. Maybe not "Hurray! That last little bit of information solved the case." Even "it's starting to look as if those two Pruitts might know more about their cousin Hobart then they're admitting" would be nice.

But after waiting a few minutes, I gave up. I might as well go and try to enjoy the festival.

Chapter 35

I left my car in the lot and headed for the town square. I could tell that Rancid Dread was wrapping up their performance—I heard the not-exactly dulcet strains of "Guiltmonger," which had gotten enough downloads on Spotify and all the other streaming platforms that the band proudly referred to it as their hit. By the time I reached the festival, another act would be performing. The high school band, or the dance academy, or maybe the sheepherding demonstration with Seth Early and Lad.

And then I did my best to enjoy the festival—in spite of my double worries about Iris's absence and the possibility that dognappers might still be lurking with evil intent, I ate several hot dogs. I cheered Lad's superb herding demonstration. I applauded the high school band and the dance academy. And all the time I tried to look calm and casual as I scrutinized every face in the crowd.

I found I could ease my anxiety by spending most of my time helping out in the adoption tent. Not only could I keep my eyes on the dogs, I could also do my best to impress upon the adopters the importance of making sure their dogs were safe. And given how much Iris had been looking forward to the Mutt March, I couldn't help hoping that even if she was on the run, she might try to find a chance to drop by and see the dogs.

And the adoption tent really did need volunteers, especially to help with the complicated paperwork and logistics. Preapproved blue-ribbon holders could take their dogs home immediately, after posing for a "Gotcha!" picture with the lucky adoptee. Volunteers worked with the would-be adoptees who weren't preapproved, helping them fill out the paperwork and getting the vetting process in motion. Mother and I teamed up to deal with the occasional dustup when preapproved red-ribbon holders thought they should get priority over unapproved blue ribbons. If anyone tried to balk at the vetting requirement, we sicced Grandfather and Dad on them. Grandfather would hold forth with great passion about the evils of dogfighting and the horrors he'd seen, while Dad reassured the recalcitrant ones.

"Of course, we don't suspect *you*," he would say, in his most earnest tone. "But we have to have a process—so we've got a way to refuse when someone dodgy wants to adopt."

And all the while Ms. Ellie and her fellow librarians were busy with their iPads: logging in all the information on the blue-and-red ribbon holders. Logging out dogs who were leaving with their new families. We had a few moments of excitement late in the afternoon, when we heard that a cocker spaniel had been taken away without authorization, but soon afterward word went around that everything was okay. I suspected one of the volunteers had forgotten to reclaim the cocker's GPS tag and they were avoiding making a big fuss over it so whoever had done it wouldn't be embarrassed. Me, I'd have made a fuss, so everyone was less likely to forget about the proper procedure.

About the only thing that completely drove worry out of my

mind was the last act of the day—the New Life Baptist Choir, full strength, and singing some of their normal repertoire instead of the earlier limited selection of dog-themed songs. It was hard to listen to their rendition of "His Eye Is on the Sparrow" without starting to think that yes, everything would turn out okay. And their performance drew nearly everyone's eyes—and ears—to the stage, which made it easier for us to shut down the adoption center and load the dogs onto the vans and trucks that would be transporting them back to our yard. Although to my delight, less than half of them would be making the return journey, and all but seven of those had would-be adopters lined up. Even if a few people didn't pass the background check, the Mutt March was a smashing success.

Or, as Grandfather remarked, "We moved a lot of dogs."

I decided to leave Mother and Ms. Ellie to close up shop in the town square while I went home to make sure everything was going as it should. The Mutt March might be over, but we still had nearly two hundred dogs who needed to be fed, walked, and watched over.

Thank goodness for Jamie, Josh, and Adam, who shared my concern that our eager volunteers might be less enthusiastic about yet another night of standing guard. They'd recruited forty or fifty of their friends for a celebratory campout, which more than made up for the number of adult volunteers who bailed on us. Michael did a run for provisions to the Shack and Luigi's, Caerphilly's favorite pizza place. By sundown the dogs were all settled. The same couldn't be said for the campers, but they'd been well fed and were showing distinct signs of slowing down, and I was optimistic about our chances of a quiet night.

Unless any of our prowlers showed up again.

"Odds are the prowlers were Drysdale and Anatole Pruitt," Vern said when I voiced that concern. "And last I heard, they weren't getting out of jail anytime soon."

"Don't worry," Horace added. He was sitting at one of our picnic tables, feasting on fried chicken and pepperoni pizza. "Even if some dognappers show up, Sammy's going to be patrolling the yard. And if it's okay with you, I was going to sack out in one of your spare bedrooms. Me and the pup."

"You're always welcome to stay," I said. "With or without Watson."

Horace's Pomeranian looked up at the sound of his name and thumped his tail gently before sighing and going back to sleep. He looked like a dog who had eaten his fill of fried chicken.

"And I'll be doing the same thing over at Rob and Delaney's," Vern said, over the ear of corn he was nibbling. "Anything happens, we'll have plenty of backup."

"I thought Aida was going to be here tonight," I said. "Not that she hasn't put in a full day already, but I was saving her favorite guest room for her."

"The chief has her on some kind of special assignment," Horace said.

"Special assignment?" If I'd been a dog, my ears would have perked up at that.

"Actually, I think he called it a special assignment so the rest of us wouldn't get jealous," Vern said. "She's been putting in long hours the last few days."

"We all have," Horace pointed out.

"But she's had the worst of it," Vern said. "She was looking pretty ragged, so I figure the chief ordered her to go home and get some real sleep. By the way, Horace—the chief said you were going to try taking some of the Poms out this afternoon to see if they could track down Iris. Any luck?"

"No." He shook his head. "I took Winnie and Whatever—they're the best for search work. They started strong—led us down the road at a run until they got to the creek. Then they kind of wandered up and down the banks on both sides, looking puzzled."

"I thought it was a myth that crossing water foils tracking dogs," I said.

"Actually, just splashing through water doesn't do much," Vern said. "Scent doesn't lie on the ground, it sort of hovers above it, like a cloud. A good tracking dog can follow that cloud across anything as small as Caerphilly Creek. It's wind that can be a problem. Disperses the cloud."

"They were doing fine until they got down to the creek," Horace said. "Then they sniffed all the way around the Pines, going up to every unit door, and all around the Spare Attic. Ran around sniffing every rock in the parking lot, then when I took them across the creek, they did much the same thing—ran around in circles in somebody's pasture."

"Looks as if Ms. Iris did a good job of what you call scent massing," Vern said.

"Don't you mean scent masking?" Horace asked.

"No," Vern said. "Scent massing. No foolproof way to mask a scent. If you know you're going to have trained dogs tracking you, you spend as much time as you dare laying down a whole lot of your scent in as big an area as possible. Like running around the perimeter of the parking lot and then gradually spiraling in toward the center, so the whole thing has your scent. Confuses the dogs, and they start running around in circles, and most of the time either they get frustrated and give up or their handler decides they've lost it and breaks off the search. Sounds as if she handled it just the way I would."

"But once you did your scent massing, where would you go?" Horace asked.

"I'd probably take to the creek for a while," Vern said. "To avoid leaving footprints that human trackers could spot. Moving downstream, of course, so any debris I kicked up would drift away from any pursuers instead of back to them. And then I might repeat the process a time or two. Create side trails, do some scent massing around them. And when I either thought I'd done enough or knew I was running out of time, I'd retrace my steps and take one of the side trails to put some distance between me and whoever was after me. Preferably by getting into a car or a boat or something like that."

"That's what you'd do," I said. "But you're a seasoned tracker. How in the world would Iris know how to do any of that?"

"She was there front and center when I gave my talk about tracking down at the library a few months ago," Vern said, with a sheepish look. "I guess she's a quick study."

"Oh, great," I said. "You taught her how to elude detection. If they invite you out to give a talk at the assisted living, pick another topic, will you? I don't want Miss Ethelinda learning any of this stuff."

"I'll keep that in mind," he said. "I figure I'll go out tomorrow with the bloodhound and its handler. Human trackers and scent dogs use different clues. It's pretty hard to hide your trail from both at the same time."

I left them to their late dinners.

I dropped by the family tent. Michael had decided to sleep out with the boys, ostensibly because camping out would be fun. I suspected that after all his exertions today, he'd much rather be tucked up in our very comfortable bed after a long, steaming hot shower, but we didn't want to leave the dogs and campers with no adult supervision. But the boys informed me, in an apologetic but firm tone, that their tent was for guys only. There were a dozen or so girl campers in another part of the yard, but luckily for me, Rose Noire and one of her herbalist friends had volunteered to take them under their wings, and I knew that, unlike Michael, they were sincere in their enthusiasm for spending the night in a tent—or, if the night remained clear, under the stars.

I went inside and collapsed into one of the kitchen chairs. I was tired—dog tired—but I wasn't sure how much luck I'd have getting to sleep. My body might be on its last legs, but my brain was spinning wildly.

I was imagining Iris stealing Delaney's bike, riding out to the end of the road, and then following Vern's instructions about scent massing and walking down streams. And why?

What if she'd made all those confusing trails to cover up the fact that she'd circled back to hide in the Spare Attic?

She had a unit at the Spare Attic—the unit full of the stuff she'd moved out of the house so it wouldn't be in Delaney and Rob's way. Horace may have done a quick search in the Spare Attic, but had he done a thorough inspection of every unit? Not just Iris's unit, but all of those she might have had the time to break into if she was hiding out there?

It wouldn't be a bad place to hide. It was temperature controlled and had a spartan but functional half bathroom. There was a side entrance where a fugitive could come and go without being seen from the Pines next door.

And even if she wasn't hiding at the Spare Attic full time, she might be dropping by to use the toilet and appreciate the cooler air inside.

I pulled out my phone and texted Horace and Vern.

"Iris has a unit at the Spare Attic," I said. "I'm going to see if she's been there lately."

"Be careful," Horace said. "Text us if you find anything interesting."

Vern just gave my message a thumbs-up.

Chapter 36

I grabbed my keys and headed out to my car, but when I was almost there something occurred to me: it could get pretty quiet out there by the creek. Iris would hear a car coming. She might even see it if she'd found a vantage point where she could inspect any new arrivals.

So instead of getting into my car, I wheeled my bicycle out of the barn and set out toward the creek.

The sky was cloudless and the moon was nearly full, so I had no trouble seeing, even without turning on my bike's headlight. And when I got to the last turn in the road and was still out of sight from the Spare Attic, I dismounted, hid my bike in the bushes, and proceeded on foot, keeping to the edge of the woods that surrounded the Spare Attic. It was probably overkill. Odds were Iris was someplace else entirely. My vision of her hiding in her unit, ducking inside a large packing box whenever someone came to retrieve or deliver belongings in their units, eating cold food out of cans—melodrama. It would probably turn out that she'd biked here and then rendezvoused with a friend with a car and was now hiding out . . . somewhere else.

But it would drive me crazy if I didn't look.

And if Drysdale and Anatole Pruitt were the reason she'd run away, maybe she'd be glad to hear that they'd been arrested. So if she wasn't there, I could slip a note to that effect under the door of her unit, in case she dropped by.

So I kept circling around at the edge of the woods until I could approach the Spare Attic from the side away from the Pines—the side that was mostly a solid brick wall. Back when the building had been a textile mill, all the furnaces and chimneys and such had been up against this wall, while the other three walls had huge glass windows that allowed the Pruitts who owned it to skimp on artificial lighting during the workers' daytime shifts.

Since I'd been helping Iris haul things to her unit and sort through her stuff when she got it there, I had both a building key and a spare key to her unit. If she was here, she might hear me when I let myself in, but she wouldn't have time to do much.

"And won't you look stupid when you swing open the door to her unit and find nothing but a lot of old furniture and vintage china?" I told myself as I tiptoed up the steps to the side door.

I kept it as quiet as possible, unlocking the door, easing it open, and tiptoeing inside. No lights were on, but by this time my eyes had adjusted to the moonlight that spilled through the soaring glass windows. The compressor for the air-conditioning system was humming a little more loudly than seemed optimal. I made a mental note to notify Randall Shiffley, since the HVAC division of his construction company almost certainly had the maintenance contract. But if the system was acting up, it had picked a convenient time for it. As far as I could tell, the humming completely masked the slight sound the door made when I opened it and then eased it closed.

When they'd converted the former textile factory into storage units, they'd built a freestanding metal-and-concrete structure in the center of the old factory floor, with about eight feet between it and the outer walls. The units were made of metal fencing materials. The uprights and posts I'd have described as heavy steel pipes—if there was a technical construction-industry name for them when they were part of a fence, I didn't know it—and the walls of the units were chain link. People who didn't want passersby to see what they were storing—either because it was valuable and they were afraid of theft or because it was junk they were embarrassed to be seen keeping—sometimes hung curtains to give themselves more privacy. This somewhat reduced the natural light available to the inner units, but anyone who really cared about that could usually trade up to an outer unit without much delay. In a rural county where nearly everyone had plenty of storage space in their basements, attics, barns, and sheds, the demand for storage units was never overwhelming.

Iris's unit was inside, but just barely. Only one unit stood between her and the floor-to-ceiling windows, and the owner of that unit hadn't cared about privacy.

If I took the nearby stairway up one flight I'd be almost right outside Iris's unit. But if she had detected the faint noises of my arrival, she'd be looking in that direction. Expecting whoever she'd heard to approach from that direction. So I slipped through the shadows until I was in the central corridor between units on the ground floor, and crept along toward the second set of stairs, at the other end of the building. I tiptoed up the stairs to the second floor, and walked quietly down that central corridor.

About halfway down the corridor I spotted a light ahead. Not a very bright light. And I estimated that it was coming from Iris's unit.

I slowed down and made sure every step was completely quiet as I drew near.

Iris was sitting in a folding lawn chair and holding a book with a tiny booklight clipped to it. She had her feet up on a small packing box, and a second, slightly larger box at her side supported a can of Diet Dr Pepper and an open, half-eaten tin of sardines. The door to her unit was open. She had a small desk fan clipped to the chain link fence and pointed at her head, with its power cord stretching up to one of the overhead electrical outlets.

"The menu's better back at our house," I said. "Unless you actually prefer sardines to ribs and fried chicken."

She started, and then tried to pretend she hadn't.

"I needed peace and quiet," she said. "I had a lot of deep thinking to do."

I glanced at the book she'd been reading—Georgette Heyer's *Sylvester, or the Wicked Uncle.*

"You can't think all the time," she said, when she saw I'd noticed the book.

"Of course not," I said. "Sometimes it's good to tuck important topics away to marinate while you do something else."

"Exactly," she said.

"So what deep thoughts have you been marinating?"

"A bit late for heavy conversation, isn't it?"

I glanced at my watch.

"Not even ten o'clock."

"It's been a long day." She gave an unconvincing yawn.

"Well, if you don't want to share your deep thoughts, I'd be happy to give you a couple of mine. You want to hear my theory on why you suddenly went on the lam?"

"No." She sighed. "I'll tell you why I 'went on the lam,' as you call it. That first night after the skeleton turned up, I saw these two guys lurking back there at the edge of the woods."

"Did you tell Vern?"

"No." She frowned. "At first I figured if I'd spotted them, no way he hadn't. Then I realized they probably knew the chief would leave someone on guard. And they were hiding in the underbrush in a place where my suite would keep someone on the porch from seeing them. At first I was kind of smug, thinking how it never occurred to them that someone might be watching from the suite. Then I decided maybe they wanted to be seen. Knew I'd be watching from the windows of the suite and wanted to send me a message."

"What message?" I asked. "And who did you think was trying to send it?"

"Pruitts," she said. "There was this Pruitt kid who kept hunting on our land. Joe wasn't against hunting, but he never gave this kid permission. Came right out and told him not to."

"Because he was a Pruitt?"

"Because he was careless," she said. "Wounded one of our cows once, and put a bullet through the screen porch another time. Joe warned him off, but then after a couple of years he started up again, and this time Joe had an inspiration. Told the Pruitt powers that be that the state game wardens were sniffing around. Pruitts didn't have any hold over them. And not long afterward the state police arrested the kid as a dealer, and the kid jumped bail and skipped town. At least that was the story they told everybody. I was worried that the Pruitts would blame Joe for the kid's arrest, but he must have convinced them he had nothing to do with it."

"We're talking Hobart Pruitt, I assume," I said. "You thought his own family had done away with him?"

"No!" she exclaimed. "Not then, at least. We only figured the powers that be convinced him he needed to leave town, and all the fuss they made looking for him was just a show. But what if we were wrong? What if they did kill one of their own so he wouldn't take them down with him? And what if they thought I knew, and when they heard Hobart's remains had been found, they wanted to warn me not to talk?"

"Would it make you feel better to know that the chief just

arrested two Pruitts?" I asked. "Anatole and Drysdale—Hobart's first cousins."

"That's good to hear," she said. "Arrested for what?"

"Trying to kidnap their aunt Ethelinda, for a start," I said. "But if you tell your chief what you just told me, maybe he'd be able to pry something more important out of them."

She nodded tentatively.

"On a not-unrelated topic," I said, "I've been wondering why you never told us about the fallout shelter in your former yard."

She winced slightly, then nodded.

"It's not really in the yard," she said. "More like back in the woods. And I'd sort of forgotten."

I wasn't buying it. And her face told me that she wasn't really expecting me to. I frowned and waited.

"Okay." She sighed, took her feet off the footrest box and shoved it closer to me.

I accepted the unspoken invitation and sat down.

"I knew there *had* been a fallout shelter," she said. "But I remembered it being a lot farther back in the woods. And I had no idea it was still there."

My face probably showed that I was skeptical.

"It was Joe's daddy's notion," she said. "I remember Joe cursing the editors of *Life* magazine for putting out this real scary cover with a guy in a radiation suit and an article about how President Kennedy wanted all Americans to build themselves fallout shelters. Papa Rafferty was always a big fan of Kennedy's—first Catholic president and all. He got fired up to build a fallout shelter for his family."

I nodded to signal that I understood.

"And this was before Joe and I were married," she continued. "We were dating, and probably already planning the wedding, but I wasn't living out here when they dug the thing. Joe wasn't even supposed to have told me about it, since I wasn't yet family."

"Did Mr. Rafferty have a builder do it, or did he do it himself?" I asked, although I suspected I knew the answer.

"Himself," she said. "Mostly himself, with help from his two brothers on the heavy stuff. He didn't want anyone else to know about it, so no one could try to barge in if we ever actually needed to use it. Joe said it was a crazy idea and refused to pitch in. The shelter itself was all finished by the time we got married and I moved out here. They'd done a really good job of camouflaging the entrance. Planted a bunch of vines around the trapdoor and on it, so it was pretty hard to find the darned thing even if you knew where to look for it. And we never talked about it. I didn't think much about it. Didn't want to. Out of sight, out of mind."

"We're talking back in the sixties, right?" I asked.

"That's right—1962 or thereabouts. And like I said, I didn't want to think about it. At least at first. I figured if the old coot was right, and we ever needed the thing, we had it, and if we never needed it, it wasn't doing anyone any harm back there in the woods. In fact, it was kind of a blessing sometimes—when Papa Rafferty was in a bad mood, he'd go out there, shut himself in, and sulk for a while. It kind of turned into what they call a man cave nowadays. Only problem was that he never did get the ventilation system working all that well, so he couldn't stay out there indefinitely."

"If that was the case, it wouldn't have done much good as a fallout shelter anyway," I pointed out.

"No," she said. "Once I figured that out, I stopped thinking it was good for anything except keeping him out of our hair a lot of the time. But then Eileen came along, and I started looking at things in a whole different light—the way Rob and Delaney are these days."

I nodded my understanding. Brynn's arrival had triggered an orgy of childproofing. Every electrical outlet was now protected with a childproof cover. Every door and cabinet had some kind of childproof device securing it, and they'd used an industrial quantity of Bubble Wrap to pad every sharp edge or corner in the whole house. Michael and I had gone through a similar exercise after the boys were born—although not quite to the extent Delaney and Rob had. First-time visitors had been known to ask if they hadn't finished taking the padding off the furniture after their move or if they were already preparing to move out.

"It suddenly hit me that we had that darned fallout shelter not all that far from where Eileen would be playing," she said. "And you know how good kids are at finding any place you don't want them to go. The shelter wasn't just useless—it was dangerous. Designed so you could lock yourself inside, in case all your neighbors who hadn't built their own shelters showed up and tried to barge in. And without a fully functional ventilation system. I started having nightmares about Eileen crawling out there, accidentally locking herself in, and suffocating."

"I think I'd have felt the same way," I said.

"I wanted them to get rid of it," she said. "Fill it in. Only thing I managed to talk them into while Papa Rafferty was alive was welding a heavy-duty hasp onto the door so we could padlock it closed from the outside. But a couple years later, when the old man died, I told Joe I wanted the darned thing filled in. And he told me he had done it."

Her expression suggested that if her late husband were still alive, they'd be having words about the fallout shelter.

"We don't know that he didn't," I said. "For all I know, someone could have completely filled it in, and then someone else came along and cleared it out again."

"Without us noticing?"

She had a point there.

"They did fill in the concrete stairs," I said. "And maybe the whole entrance hole. And it does look as if someone hacked off the original padlock and put on a new one. New*er*, anyway—it still looks pretty old."

"Joe might have had to do that, if he couldn't find where his daddy hid the key to the padlock," Iris said. "Papa Rafferty died in November 1965, so it would have been around that time, or maybe in early 1966."

I nodded. It was entirely possible that Joe had hacked off the old padlock and then filled in the defective fallout shelter. But if that were the case, why bother with a new padlock? To me, it seemed more likely Joe had decided that leaving the existing padlock in place and filling in the entrance would work just as well as filling in the whole thing.

And was it a coincidence that a murder had taken place twenty or thirty years later only a few yards away from the entrance to the fallout shelter?

Like the chief, I wasn't a big believer in coincidences.

"Did your kids know about the fallout shelter?" I asked.

"Not that I know of," she said. "Eileen was just a toddler when Joe covered it up, and the other two weren't even born yet. And we'd have had no reason to talk about it. Every reason not to get their curiosity up, frankly. Last thing we'd have wanted was the kids digging holes out in the woods, looking for it. And before you ask, I can't imagine either of Joe's uncles telling anyone they helped dig it."

"They might have told their children," I suggested. "So they'd know where to go if they ever needed a fallout shelter."

"Seamus never married, and Brian and his wife never had kids, and they're all long gone. So as far as I know, I'm the only one still breathing who remembers when Papa Rafferty built it."

"What about when Joe filled it in?" I asked. "Did he have help on that?"

"Not that I know of," she said. "My sister was having her first, and I went to help her out. I stayed a week or ten days, and took Eileen with me. She was pretty little—three, maybe, and getting into everything, and I knew there was no way Joe could watch her all day and still run the farm. And I gave him an ultimatum that I wanted the fallout shelter filled in while I was gone. And I thought he'd done it."

"Filled in the whole shelter in a week, while running the farm?" I said.

"Yeah," she said. "I should have realized he hadn't really had time to do the whole thing. And— Wait a sec."

She frowned and seemed lost in thought.

"He hurt his back doing it," she said. "And I asked him why the dickens he hadn't hired someone to help him do it, or maybe do it for him. And he fussed about throwing good money after bad and he didn't need to pay some fool to throw a few shovel loads of dirt in a hole."

"It would have taken more than a few shovel loads," I said.

"You better believe it." She chuckled. "He probably had to have someone deliver a truckload of fill dirt, even to take care of the entrance. Multiple truckloads for the whole thing. And what if he hurt his back in the middle of doing it and hired someone else to finish it?"

"Who would he have hired?" I asked.

"If he wanted a good job done, one of the Shiffleys," she said. "But since he didn't even think it needed doing in the first place, he'd have hired cheap day labor. There's always a supply of brainless louts in Clay County."

"Hey! Watch who you're calling a brainless lout!" came a voice from behind me.

I whirled. Iris started and looked up. And we found ourselves staring into the barrels of two guns.

Chapter 37

"Keep your hands where we can see them," the shorter gunman said.

"What are you worried about?" said the other. "Two women, one of them old as dirt. I think we can handle them if they try to give us any trouble."

Actually, I wasn't sure they could without the guns. The two men were both middle-aged, and neither seemed particularly fit. The taller one looked like an athlete gone to seed. He had a prominent beer belly and his doughy arms and thighs had probably once been muscular. He had a pack of cigarettes in his shirt pocket—Marlboro Reds, like the butts Vern had found back in the woods. The shorter one was rather scrawny, with a ragged goatee that somehow increased his already strong resemblance to a rodent. If they grew overconfident enough to put down their guns . . .

"We need to know what you did with our merchandise," Beer Belly said.

"What merchandise?" I asked.

"The merchandise you found when you dug up the fallout shelter."

"The cocaine?" They both flinched when I said that. "I rather thought that was Hobart Pruitt's merchandise."

"We were his partners," Beer Belly said. "And he's dead, so it's ours now."

I'd always found it slightly implausible when the detectives in one of Dad's beloved mysteries suddenly went "aha!" and announced that they'd put the clues together and solved the case. But that's exactly what seemed to have happened in my brain—although I didn't feel the impulse to exclaim "aha!"

"How would you know he was dead?" I asked. "Most people are pretty sure he skipped out on his bail and left town."

"They wouldn't be so sure unless they were the ones who did it," Iris said.

"No way," Beer Belly said. The Rodent just shook his head, but he looked worried.

"My thoughts exactly," I said. "And I'm pretty sure I know what happened. You didn't trust Hobart and you were sneaking around. Spying on him."

"We pretty much figured he was planning to double-cross us," the Rodent agreed.

"Shut up, Vic," Beer Belly snapped.

Vic? I remembered the *Clarion*'s article on the burglaries here at the Spare Attic. Of course.

"Iris, may I introduce Victor Dingle and John Wayne Peebles," I said. "Hobart Pruitt's partners in crime and the perpetrators of the Great Spare Attic Heist."

Vic started at that, and John Wayne scowled as if displeased.

"Never heard of them," she said. "I remember Hobart, though. Complete waste of space, and the terror of the neighborhood. We as good as had a party when we heard he'd left town."

"Only he hadn't left town," I said. "He drove out here to the Spare Attic and parked his car. And his two accomplices confronted him, and there was some kind of altercation."

"He said he'd show us where he stashed the merchandise," Vic said. "And then he tried to lead us out into the woods and lose us."

"I said shut up," John Wayne repeated.

"And you got mad and shot him," I said.

"Not me," Vic muttered.

"You ransacked his pockets and took his keys," I said. "You'd convinced yourselves he'd hidden the cocaine in his unit in the Spare Attic. And when you didn't find it in his unit, you broke into a whole lot of other units. I'm not sure if you actually thought he'd have hidden it in someone else's unit or if you just wanted to grab a few valuables to make your break-in worthwhile. Didn't really matter. You got caught with the stuff you'd stolen and sent to prison. How much of that twenty-year sentence did you serve anyway?"

"Too damn long," John Wayne growled. "Since I wasn't a stool pigeon."

"That was a bum rap," Vic said. "I never told anyone anything. The parole board just doesn't like it when you mouth off at them."

"And you were worried when we dug up Hobart," I said. "Afraid maybe there was some evidence that would show who killed him."

"After all this time?" John Wayne said. But he didn't sound all that confident, and Vic looked downright anxious.

"And then when the word went out that we'd dug up an old fallout shelter in the Raffertys' former yard, you realized that maybe Hobart hadn't been trying to double-cross you. Maybe he really had been trying to lead you to where he'd stashed the merchandise. And you bumped him off when you were only a few steps from his hiding place."

"We were sure it was here at the Spare Attic," Vic said. "He had a padlock key on his key ring. Only key he had other than his house key and his car key. We tried it on every padlock here. No dice. And then we spent way too much time sneaking around to all his relatives' houses, looking for padlocks we could try it on."

"Just drop it," John Wayne muttered.

"Maybe if we hadn't spent so damn much time on that, we'd have managed to find a better hiding place for the stuff we picked up in here." Vic's tone—and John Wayne's, for that matter—suggested that this was an old argument, but not one that had lost its heat.

"Water under the bridge," John Wayne said. "And the mystery's solved. He hid the merchandise in his neighbors' fallout shelter. So where is it now?"

"Down at the police station," I said.

"Not all of it," John Wayne said. "I heard the police only seized a couple of keys. Where'd the rest of it go?"

"How do you know there was any more?" I asked.

"Hobart was a big-time dealer," John Wayne said. "A player. He was bragging on how he could barely fit all of his merchandise in the trunk of his Trans Am."

"Sounds just like Hobart," Iris said. "He was nothing but talk. How do you know he had any drugs at all?"

"He showed us," John Wayne said.

"Only that one key," Vic said. "She could be right. When did Hobart ever come through on anything he promised?"

"He showed us," John Wayne insisted. "So if most of his merchandise was gone by the time the police showed up, someone else must have taken it. So where is it?"

He scowled, looking back and forth between Iris and me.

"Don't do anything drastic," Vic advised. Was he warning John Wayne or us?

I was beginning to suspect that Vic was the brains of this pair, though only by default. And that, unfortunately, telling John

Wayne not to do something probably increased the likelihood that he'd do it.

Horace and Vern knew I was coming here. Surely if I didn't show up they'd come looking for me eventually. If we could stall them until one of them showed up . . .

But I wasn't optimistic about our chances of stalling John Wayne Peebles. Patience didn't seem to be his strong suit.

And the look on Vic's face seemed to confirm my impression. It was a look of anxious resignation, as if he'd seen this scenario play out before, but had no more idea how to stop what was coming than he'd had thirty-some years ago, when John Wayne had shot Hobert Pruitt mere yards from the prize they were after.

My brother, Rob, had always been fond of hypothetical questions, like "would you rather die by drowning or by bleeding to death?" I usually declined to play. But if he ever tried a round of "how would you least like to die?" I knew what my answer would be: getting shot by a thug whose IQ barely exceeded the speed limit, and who would undoubtedly be caught and convicted in short order. Not that I wanted to die at the hands of an elusive criminal mastermind, either. But having John Wayne Pruitt as my cause of death?

"Not going to happen," I muttered to myself.

I was still casting around for a way to stall when Iris spoke up.

"I give up," she said. "I'm too old for this. Just take my keys. They're in my purse."

She gestured to where her purse hung from the chain link wall on an S hook, near Vic's left elbow.

"What good are your keys supposed to do me?" John Wayne said.

"If you want the rest of Hobart's cocaine, you're going to need my keys," she said.

My mouth fell open in shock. Was this the truth, or some kind of weird ploy?

"That's more like it." John Wayne was looking smug. "Where have you got the stuff?"

"In the barn," she said.

"Iris," I began. "Are you sure you want to—"

"Shut up," John Wayne said.

"There's an old feed closet in the back corner. I was keeping some of my stuff there—stuff I couldn't fit in here."

She wasn't making up the feed closet. But it wasn't filled with Iris's stuff. Kevin had appropriated it to use as an electronics closet, filling it with routers and servers and some of the gear associated with the solar panels he'd installed on the roof of the barn. Knowing Kevin, he'd probably installed some sort of alarm system to keep people from meddling with his pricey toys, and getting to it would definitely involve walking through the camera field he'd recently set up to monitor the excavation site.

But had it occurred to her that once John Wayne thought he knew the location of the drugs he believed Hobart had been hiding, he would have no reason to keep us alive?

"She's trying to trick you," I said. "The feed closet—"

"I said shut up," John Wayne said. He glanced over at Vic. "Get the keys."

Vic tucked his gun in his waistband—okay, that was progress—and took a few steps over to where the purse hung. He took the purse down, opened the flap, and peered in cautiously, as if expecting a trap.

"Sometime this century," John Wayne snarled.

Vic reached in and took out Iris's key ring. He held it up with a puzzled look on his face.

"Wow," he said. "There must be a hundred keys on there."

He was exaggerating—but it did look as if there were upwards of twenty keys on the ring.

"Which key is it?" John Wayne said.

"Mercy," Iris said. "You can't just try the likely-looking ones till you hit on it?"

"No. You tell us." He gestured with his gun.

Iris sighed, and held out her hand for the key ring. Vic handed it to her, then leaned back against the chain link and stuck his hands in his pockets. I glanced at John Wayne, half expecting him to order Vic to get his gun out again, but he was focused on Iris.

"Okay . . . not this one." She held up a key. "That's for the Buick. No idea why I still have that—I sold the Buick five years ago." She selected the next key and studied it.

"I think that's for the sanctuary at St. Byblig's," she said. "For when I help out with arranging the flowers."

"We don't need to break into the church," John Wayne said.

"Pretty sure they'd let us in if we showed up looking presentable tomorrow morning," Vic added.

"And pretty sure they didn't hide a ton of cocaine there," John Wayne added. "So why would we bother?"

Just then I saw what Iris was up to. Along with the twenty-odd keys, her giant-sized key ring also held a St. Christopher medal, a mini flashlight, a tiny squeeze bottle of hand sanitizer, half a dozen plastic store discount program tags—and a tiny spray can. Mace or tear gas, probably.

"I'm trying." Iris deliberately made her voice quaver and her hands shake, doing an excellent imitation of a frail little old lady. "Now this one." She held up another key and frowned as if she hadn't ever noticed it on her key ring before.

"We haven't got all night," John Wayne snapped.

"You're not helping, you know," Vic said.

"Who asked you?" John Wayne turned his head slightly toward his annoying ally.

Iris grabbed the little spray can and fired a stream of its liquid contents at John Wayne. Her aim was good—she got him right in the eyes. He bellowed in pain and clawed his eyes with his left hand. I lunged forward and grabbed the gun from his loosened grip. Meanwhile Iris turned the spray can and aimed another generous squirt at Vic—who dropped to the ground and curled up into a fetal position, shrieking like a banshee. John Wayne seemed to have forgotten about the loss of his gun. He was lurching around, clawing his eyes, and cursing nonstop. I gave him top marks for volume and breath control, but zero for originality. Was the f-bomb the only swear word he knew?

"Let's get out of here," Iris said.

"Good idea." I reached down and plucked the gun from Vic's waistband. Iris picked up the box she'd been using as a footstool and jammed it down over John Wayne's head. As she did, I tripped him and he keeled over onto the floor.

"Don't forget your keys," I said, as I stepped over John Wayne's torso.

She held them up and jingled them slightly.

We stepped out of her unit, and I pulled the door to. She deftly selected a key from the bunch and locked the padlock on the unit door.

"How long does that stuff last?" I asked, referring to the two writhing thugs.

"Beats me," she said. "Never felt the need to test it on myself."

"Why don't we put something solid between us and them?" I suggested. "In case one of them was clever enough to bring a spare gun."

"I'd be impressed if both of those clowns remembered to bring bullets," she said. "But better safe than sorry."

So we walked down the central aisle a little ways, until we reached a unit full of lumber, pipes, and assorted building supplies. Iris pulled out her key ring, matter-of-factly selected a key, and opened the door.

"Does the owner of this unit know you've got their key?" I asked, as we took shelter behind a stack of four-by-fours.

"Key?" Iris said. "I could have sworn this unit just happened to be open."

"Ah." I took out my phone as I spoke. "I guess my imagination is running wild. Must be the shock of encountering those two reprobates."

"Just dial nine-one-one already," she said. "I'm looking forward to sleeping in my own bed tonight."

SUNDAY, JUNE 11

Chapter 38

"More sausage?" Although Rose Noire regularly overcame her vegetarian scruples far enough to cook meat for her less-enlightened family members, she didn't normally urge us to have seconds or thirds of it. Perhaps the fact that I'd survived mortal danger last night was making her more solicitous than usual. She'd certainly outdone herself with the lavish brunch she was serving.

"Please," I said.

"If there's plenty." Horace held out his plate.

"Yes, ma'am," Vern said.

Rose Noire beamed and began piling all our plates with more of the organic, pasture-raised artisanal sausage we bought from a pig farmer friend of Dad's. I was glad she remembered that Horace and Vern had also had a late night, dashing out to the Spare Attic to arrest Vic Dingle and John Wayne Peebles, and then helping process the scene while Sammy and the chief took their prisoners down to the jail.

"So where's Aida?" I asked. I'd been puzzled not to see her out at the crime scene last night, and Horace's explanation—that the chief had sent her out of town on a confidential mission—provoked more questions than it answered.

"Did Kevin tell you that he found Gus Pruitt?" Horace asked, through a mouthful of toast. "Did five years for an armed robbery he pulled over in Tappahannock, and when he got out, he moved to Richmond and started going by his middle name. He's A. Melvin Pruitt now."

"Nice to know Gus is still among the living," I said. "So we don't have to worry that Aaron Shiffley will dig him up when he starts working on the duck pond again."

"Of course, we already knew from all the Pruitts' dental records that Gus wasn't our skeleton," Vern said.

"Last I heard you were still looking for the dental records," I said.

"While Miss Ethelinda was down at the station yesterday, she gave us everything she knew about where her relatives went when they left Caerphilly. The chief tracked down Braxton's widow, and she was happy to unload a couple of boxes full of his old records. Gus's records didn't match the skeleton, but Hobart's did."

I nodded. Was fetching those Aida's confidential mission? And would those boxes of dental records be added to all the other boxes of files we'd be helping the chief sort? Probably. But not something I had to worry about today.

"Any idea when Clarence and Ms. Ellie will get here?" Vern asked. "Sammy says people are lining up to see if they can collect their dogs."

"Ms. Ellie said she'd head out here as soon as services were over at Trinity," I said.

"I thought they were over," Vern said. "You're here."

"I decided to come straight home afterward," I said. "Everyone else stayed for the coffee hour to catch up on the local gossip."

"And you already know all the local gossip," Vern said, with a nod.

"Heck, I *am* most of the local gossip this morning," I said. "They'll be along soon. I thought Clarence was already here. Somewhere. Want me to go look for him?"

"If you could," Vern said. "And I'll go help keep the adopters in line until Clarence opens up shop. Sammy's too mild-mannered. They'll walk all over him."

He grabbed the two sausages remaining on his plate and strode out the back door. I followed his example. When I stepped out into the backyard, I almost ran into Dad, still dressed in the reasonably presentable clothes he'd worn to church.

"I have wonderful news!" Dad said. "You know those two Great Pyrenees puppies Seth Early is adopting?"

"He's definitely adopting them, then?" I asked. "That's good news."

"Yes," he said. "And I have to admit, I was a little torn about that. I was kind of thinking it would be nice to have a couple of guardian dogs for our cows and sheep. Of course, Seth probably needs them a lot more than we do, and your mother was a little . . . concerned about the idea."

I suspected Mother was probably dead set against having two enormous shaggy dogs added to the household, and that Dad had tried in vain to convince her that the dogs would be mostly living outdoors, with the herds and flocks they protected, not getting underfoot and shedding on her decor.

"So I did what I could to help Seth get them," Dad said. "But guess what? Clarence has found two more Pyrs! Full siblings to the ones Seth is taking."

"Found them?" I echoed. "He got the first two from the shelter in Abingdon, right? How did he manage to overlook several hundred more pounds of adoptable dog?"

"They weren't in the shelter when he went there," Dad explained.

"Someone had adopted them, but when they found out they were only six months old and still growing, they decided even one Pyr was twice as much dog as they could handle. They returned them to the shelter. And the shelter asked Clarence if he could find a home for them, and Clarence thought of us. Isn't that great?"

Dad beamed. I wondered if he'd shared these joyous tidings with Mother yet.

"Before you get their hopes up," I began. "Clarence and the Abingdon shelter, that is—"

"I've already talked to your mother," Dad said. "We're going to build them a doghouse out by the pasture—Randall's sending over someone to do that next week. And Clarence is going to help with the training. They will definitely be completely outdoor dogs."

"So Mother's okay with it?"

"It helped that they're quite handsome dogs," he said. "And will look good at a distance."

"Nobly guarding the sheep and cows that she also finds decorative at a distance," I said. "So everything's settled."

"Well, not everything," he said. "I need to come up with suitable names for them."

Surely after managing to convince Mother to let him adopt several hundred pounds of dog, he couldn't be daunted by the task of coming up with names. In fact . . .

"Why not ask Mother what she thinks you should name them?" I suggested. "Suitably elegant names she would enjoy sharing with visitors. That way she'll feel invested in the whole guardian-dog thing."

"What a great idea! I'll go ask her right now."

Good. That meant Mother had arrived and could help Vern keep order.

"Why don't you change your clothes first?" I suggested. "You did bring some old clothes you can wear while you're working with the dogs, didn't you?" I knew Mother would fret if she thought Dad was about to ruin yet another relatively new suit.

"Right!" He looked down as if surprised to see what he was wearing. "I've got my gardening clothes in the trunk."

He dashed off.

I headed for the barn, where I hoped I'd find Clarence.

Sure enough, he was there. But he didn't exactly look like a man who had just successfully found homes for several hundred deserving dogs. He looked . . . glum.

"Why the long face?" I asked. "The Mutt March was a great success."

"It was," he said. "Nearly every animal that appeared in the parade either got adopted or is on hold while we finish vetting their future families. Only seven got overlooked, and I have a couple of red-ribbon folks coming by to inspect them this afternoon."

"That's great news." And it was—why did he look so miserable?

"But it's not enough." He sighed heavily. "The two dozen shelters we helped will be full again before you know it, and there are thousands of other shelters and rescue organizations all over the country that have the same problem. We can't possibly help all the dogs and cats who need rescuing."

"No," I said. "But we helped these ones. And we'll help others."

"I don't think we can pull this off more than once a year." He shook his head. "It was a lot more work than I expected."

"I think you're right about only doing it once a year," I replied. "But it will be easier next time. We'll know what we're doing. And with luck we won't have a thirty-five-year-old murder investigation complicating things. And in the meantime, we can try other things."

"Like what?"

"I heard about a shelter in Texas that came up with a unique program," I said. "They figured out that a lot of grown-ups really enjoy playing Pokémon Go."

"Pokémon Go?" Clarence sounded puzzled.

"It's a game where you walk around your neighborhood battling or befriending imaginary creatures that you can only see on your phone," I said. "I don't quite understand it myself—get the boys to show you sometime."

"They play it?"

"Not really," I said. "They tell me they've outgrown it. A lot of grown-ups still like it, though, only they don't want to look like fools, wandering around staring at their phones and . . . well, doing whatever it is you do when you're playing. Maybe it involves waving your arms around or your phone or something. Ask the boys. I gather it can look pretty silly to someone who isn't familiar with the game. Anyway, this shelter started a program where you can rent a dog for five dollars an hour and take it for a walk as camouflage for your Pokémon Go playing. The shelter figured that even if only a few people took them up on it, the program would turn out to be a win for everyone—a few of the dogs would get walked a little more often, the shelter would earn a bit of money, and a small number of Pokémon Go players would feel a little less embarrassed."

"And people actually took them up on this?"

"They have a waiting list of people who want to rent dogs," I said. "They're bringing in dogs from other shelters to meet demand. And they've made so much money they no longer have to charge adoption fees."

"Nice," Clarence said.

"They also encourage the walkers to post pictures of themselves with the dogs on social media, and now the shelter is getting people coming in asking to adopt a particular dog. If the dog's still available—they've already had cases where people say, 'Hey, I didn't think I wanted a dog, but I've changed my mind—can I adopt this dog I've been walking?' I'd call that a success."

"You think we could pull that off here?" he asked.

"Why not?" I said. "It won't cost anything to try. And it would take a whole lot less effort than the Mutt March."

"Let's do it!" He looked cheerful for a second, then his frown returned. "Assuming we can get someone to handle the organizing side of things. You know that's not my forte."

"Let me talk to Ms. Ellie," I said. "I have a feeling she might be willing."

"Good. I bet she'll do it if you ask her."

Actually, she might be willing under any circumstances. Ms. Ellie was a proven dog lover, having adopted one of the litter of seven Pomeranians Clarence had brought into our lives.

"By the way," I said, "whatever happened to those Indian Runner ducks the Westlake lady tried to pawn off on Delaney and Rob? I don't recall seeing them during the Mutt March."

"That's because I found them a home the same day you turned them over to me," he said. "They're now the newest residents at All Quacked Up—that all-organic, free-range egg farm one of Vern's cousins runs."

"Perfect," I said.

"By the way." He picked up a piece of paper from his table and frowned at it. "This Dr. McAuslan-Crine. She wants to adopt a dog."

"Good," I said. "I imagine she'll be a good dog parent."

"But she's English," he said. "Do you know if she's planning to go back there anytime soon? Because I know it can be complicated taking a dog to another country, and then there's the devastating emotional effect on the dog if she gives it back to the shelter."

"I wouldn't worry," I said. "She's got a tenured position at the college, she bought a house on a ten-acre farm north of town, and she just started a major excavation that will probably take years, given how slowly archaeologists work. I think she's good for the long haul."

"That's reassuring." He smiled as he set the paper—presumably Dr. McAuslan-Crine's application—back on the table.

"Getting back to the business at hand," I said. "Vern says the potential adopters are lining up outside. You ready to start seeing them?"

"Bring them on!" He looked a lot more cheerful.

I strolled out to the road, where Vern was marshaling the aspiring adopters into an orderly line. I told him Clarence was opening up shop and then hastily stepped aside to avoid getting trampled.

"Quite a production."

I looked around to see Miss Ethelinda Pruitt standing nearby, watching the stampede.

"You here about a dog?" I asked.

"As if," she said. "One of the aides put her name down for some kind of yappy little dog. Had to bring a bunch of paperwork out to suit His Lordship the Vet. Talked her into bringing me along in case she needed a character witness. I've got a favor to ask you."

"Let's hear it." Call me untrusting, but something made me wary of saying "okay" or "sure" or anything that could be taken as agreement before I heard what she was asking.

"I'm still ticked about the way those rascal cousins of mine showed up at that place where they stowed me," she said. "Trying to convince the keepers that they had a power of attorney over me. Which was a flat-out lie. I haven't given a power of attorney to anyone, as those no-good jerks know full well. And I have no idea what they were going to do to me when they got the information they wanted—or figured out I didn't know it—but it couldn't have been good."

"I'm sorry," I said. "It was probably my fault they showed up—since you were following my suggestion about spreading a rumor."

"I didn't have to take your suggestion," she said. "But I liked it. And it ended up getting them thrown in the slammer where they belonged, so it worked out in the end."

"It was a good thing the staff knew they were lying. Did you ever figure out what they wanted from you?"

"They were after Hobart's drugs, of course," she said. "No idea why they thought I'd know. I didn't have any more use for Hobart than for them."

It occurred to me that maybe it was also my fault. Almost as soon as the body had been found, I'd made a beeline out to talk to Miss Ethelinda. Maybe I'd led them to her. Well, not led them exactly—they already knew where she was. But led them to believe she had useful knowledge.

Not a theory I was going to share with Miss Ethelinda.

"And who knows what could have happened if the staff hadn't fended them off?" she said. "None of the staff are exactly rocket scientists. Dumb as a box of rocks, some of them. Oh, most of them are nice enough, but if I can regularly pull the wool over their eyes, imagine what my cousins could have gotten away with if they'd kept trying."

"That is worrisome," I agreed.

"So I figure maybe I need to have someone who does have a power of attorney," she said.

I nodded my approval. I could refer her to my cousin Festus Hollingsworth. His forte was suing evil corporations and getting unjustly convicted people exonerated, but he also did a brisk business in simple legal documents for friends and family. He could easily draw up a power-of-attorney document for her.

"But I can't hand over the power of attorney to just anyone," she said. "I need to find someone who wouldn't have anything to gain by doing me in. Also it's got to be someone trustworthy. I figure everyone in my family is out on both of those counts. And it has to be someone smart enough to handle anything my family throws at them, and tough enough to go toe-to-toe with them if they try to fight it. I figure you'll do."

My jaw fell open at that last sentence.

"Me?" I said. "You hardly know me."

"No," she said. "And you hardly know me. Better that way, if you ask me. No sentiment, no nonsense. None of that 'oh, I can't bear to lose her—maybe she'll come out of it' if I get sick and pulling the plug is the right thing to do. And I'm betting it won't ever come to that—we tend to go quick, my branch of the family. Most likely, all you'll ever need to do is say "hell, no" a time or two to my worthless relatives. And I want it drawn up so even you don't have any say unless I'm absolutely out of my gourd or maybe in a coma. For emergencies only."

"I'm flattered," I said. "But may I think about it for a while?"

"Think away," she said. "But don't take too long. I'm not getting any younger. Oh, and I figure I should give you some kind of reward—just not one that would give you a motive to off me. So how about this: you agree to do it, and I'll change my will to leave a big old donation to whatever charity you favor."

"Like maybe the Caerphilly Animal Shelter?" I suggested.

"Good choice." She gave a brisk nod. "I can live with that."

"Okay," I said. "One more thing, and you've got a deal."

"What's that?"

"You throw in one of your samplers," I said. "And I get to pick which one."

"Deal!" She cackled loudly. "You can have two if you like. I'm running out of wall space anyway. You know any lawyers who could get it done cheap? I hear those free, do-it-yourself legal documents are worth exactly what you pay for them."

"I know an excellent lawyer who will almost certainly give you the highly attractive friend-and-family discount if I ask him," I said. "And he'll draw up a good, solid legal document that your greedy relatives can't poke any holes in. I can have him drop by to see you tomorrow."

"Good!" she said.

"And make sure he gives you his card," I said. "And keep it

where you can find it if any unwanted family members show up. Scaring them off would be part of the service."

At least it would be under the deal I'd make with Festus.

She gave me a thumbs-up and strolled off toward the llama pen.

I went back inside to see if there were any sausages left over. There weren't, but I settled for a big plate of the organic fresh fruit salad Rose Noire had fixed, as part of her attempt to win over the resident carnivores.

The doorbell rang, and I realized I was probably the only person here not out helping with the dogs. So I strolled through to the front hall, set my plate down on the hall table, and opened the door.

A tall, middle-aged Black man stood on the porch. He was dressed in a well-tailored gray pinstripe suit and his close-cropped hair had flecks of gray at the temples. Distinguished looking. Also vaguely familiar looking.

"They told me down at the police station that I could find Deputy Vern Shiffley here." He had a nice voice. Resonant. The sort of voice that would be a great asset to a drama student.

But who was he and why was he looking for Vern?

He noticed my hesitation, and held out a business card.

"I'm an old friend of Vern's," he said.

I glanced down at the card: W. Lincoln Taylor, Attorney-at-Law, with a downtown San Francisco address.

It only took a second or two.

"You're Billy Taylor," I said.

Chapter 39

"I am indeed." Taylor smiled, and looked a little more like his high school yearbook photo. It was a warm smile, and revealed the diastema, as Dad would call it. "At least I was back in the day. I go by my middle name these days. Lincoln—Link for short. Have since I left Caerphilly. Taylor being one of the top twenty most common last names in the country, I figured that would be enough to keep the Pruitts from finding me. Seems to have worked. And I bet you're Festus Hollingsworth's cousin Meg."

"You know Festus?"

"Know and admire him," he said. "And we've even worked together a time or two, when one of his cases had tendrils in California."

"Come in," I said, opening the door wider and stepping back so he could enter. "I think Vern will be glad to see you. And delighted to know that you seem to have landed on your feet after you left Caerphilly."

"I lucked out," he said. "My gran slipped a letter into the duffel bag she packed for Vern to bring me. Gave me the address and phone number of a childhood friend of hers who'd moved out to Oakland, California. And a letter to take to the friend, explaining what happened. And her friend did us proud. She not only took me in, she made sure I stayed in school."

"Vern will be impressed," I said. "He told me he was always worried that the Pruitts might have kept you from fulfilling your potential. He's in the backyard."

I led him through the house and toward the back door.

"Was there a reason you came back to Caerphilly at this particular time?" I asked.

"I keep an eye on the *Clarion*'s website," he said. "Saw an article that listed me as one possible identity for the skeleton you folks dug up, and since I had to be on the East Coast for a case next week, I thought I'd come out a bit early, report myself as still among the living, and see the excitement firsthand."

We went out the back door and saw Vern standing in the middle of the yard, keeping an eye on the line of potential adopters.

"Vern," I said. "Someone asking for you."

Vern turned and ambled closer, with a polite, neutral expression on his face. Then, when he was a few yards away, he stopped short and his mouth fell open.

"Long time no see," Taylor said, with a grin.

"Billy?" Vern said.

"No other."

After a couple of seconds of staring, they simultaneously took a few steps toward each other and did one of those guy-type greetings that starts out as a handshake and then turns into a vigorous backslapping hug.

"I see they never found out about your juvenile career as an accomplice after the fact," Taylor said. "Grew up to be a deputy, like you were always hoping to."

"I can't believe you remember that," Vern said. "And you look as if you've done all right for yourself. You wanted to be a crusading attorney—how'd that work out?"

"Managed to squeak into Stanford Law School," he said. "And been trying to make good use of my JD ever since. But I always kind of kept my eye on what was happening back here in Caerphilly. Damn near stormed back a couple of times when the Pruitts got up to something especially sleazy, but I didn't want to risk them trying to resurrect those old phony charges. Cheered out loud when I heard Festus Hollingsworth was down here helping battle them, and I popped open a bottle of champagne when I heard you good folk had chased them out of town."

"Why don't you two sit down and catch up?" I said. "I see Mother just arrived. I think between the two of us, she and I can probably ride herd on the line."

They sat down at one of the picnic tables and began talking a mile a minute. Mother, still elegantly dressed in a pale pink linen suit, came over and gave me a peck on the cheek.

"You must still be tired, dear," she said. "Why don't you relax and let us help Clarence?"

Us? I glanced over and saw a posse of Mother's trusted allies marching purposefully across the lawn toward us. Some, like Mother, were still in their Sunday-go-to-meeting clothes, while others had already changed into more practical dog-tending garb.

"I won't say no," I said.

"What do you think of Sebastian?" she asked.

"Who's Sebastian?"

"As a name, dear," she said. "For one of our Great Pyrenees puppies."

"Oh, right. Sounds great to me." And the "our" bit sounded even better.

"I rather like it. But there's no rush. We need to find just the right names for them. Now you go and rest, dear."

She floated off toward the barn. I settled in one of the Adirondack chairs that dotted the yard in twos and threes. I was sure there were plenty of useful things I could have been doing, but there were also plenty of people arriving to do them. The aftermath of the Mutt March could carry on without me for a little while.

"You could just go take a nap."

I looked up to see the chief smiling down at me.

"I want to at least pretend that I'm standing by to pitch in as needed," I said. "You look as if you could use a nap yourself."

"And I just might go and take one." He took a seat in the Adirondack chair next to mine. "It could be a while before I can interrogate any of my prisoners. At the moment, Drysdale and Anatole Pruitt are still conferring with the attorneys we finally found for them, and who knows how long it will take to secure legal representation for Mr. Peebles and Mr. Dingle. So I thought I'd drop off Adam to help with the dogs and see how you and Ms. Rafferty are doing."

"I'll be doing just fine if you promise me none of those jerks will be back on the streets anytime soon."

"No way," he said. "With the two Pruitts we might eventually bargain them down to a few misdemeanors if they undertake never to set foot in Caerphilly County again when their jail sentences are over. Assuming that's acceptable to Miss Ethelinda."

We both glanced over to where Miss Ethelinda was intently studying the llamas, who were studying her back with equal intensity.

"I assume they were after Hobart's drug stash," I said. "A good thing for them those two thugs from Clay County showed up and all but confessed to the murder."

"A good thing for us, too," he said. "I could have wasted a lot of time trying to prove they'd murdered their cousin. Might have overlooked the real killers."

"I'm sure you'd have figured it out." And I wasn't just saying it to make him feel better.

"Of course, we still have work to do on them," he said. "We can probably convict them of Hobart Pruitt's murder on the strength of your testimony and Ms. Rafferty's. But I have a feeling Mr. Peebles was the one who actually fired the shot, and we'll have a much stronger case if we can convince Mr. Dingle to testify against him."

"Maybe I'm naïve," I said, "but I get the impression Vic Dingle might be tired of playing sidekick and punching bag to John Wayne. And I also wouldn't be surprised if Vic feels some guilt about Hobart's murder—even if all he did was help cover it up."

"That's how I read it, too," he said. "And he's already dropped a hint or two along those lines. So once we get some attorneys in for them, we'll see what we can work out. Oh—and on another topic entirely, Randall has found a place for us to sort all those decades of back files."

"Let me guess: someone's barn?" I tried to sound enthusiastic, but I knew a barn wouldn't be air-conditioned. And what were the chances that its owner would let us fill it with boxes of files and then wait until cool weather to start dealing with them?

"Better," he said. "Ragnar's going to lend us a couple of big rooms out at his castle."

"Excellent!" I didn't have to fake enthusiasm now. Ragnar probably had enough space out at the castle to sort any collection of papers up to and including the National Archives, and he was passionate about the comfort of his guests. Whoever volunteered to help with the sorting would probably enjoy not only an air-conditioned space but also gourmet meals from Alice, Ragnar's legendary cook. And Ragnar wouldn't put pressure on anyone to hurry with the project. I knew of people who'd shown up for one of his parties and were still in residence years later. And most of the people I could see recruiting to help with the project were people whose company he adored. The files would have a happy home for as long as needed.

"Randall's workmen are going to show up at eight a.m. tomorrow morning to start hauling all the boxes out there," he added.

"Now all you have to worry about is your budget report," I said. "And if you need help with it, let me know. I managed to fill out my version of it without tearing out all my hair."

"A day or so ago, I'd have taken you up on that," he said. "But then Friday afternoon I mentioned to your mother how I was struggling with the budget report and she lent me one of your cousins. A CPA who showed up on her orders to help with the Mutt March, but was not just willing but eager to change course and spend the day down at the station filling out my report."

"That's fabulous," I said. "Although I'm going to find out why she didn't recruit him to help me."

"Apparently she thinks you're good with numbers," he said. "Whereas she knows from talking to Minerva that I'm not. And—"

He glanced down at his pocket, took out his phone, and examined it.

"Well, well," he said. "I should be going. Looks as if Drysdale Pruitt is ready to talk. Let me know when you need us to pick up Adam."

"He's welcome to stay as long as he likes," I said. "If you're busy—and I know Minerva probably is—he can even camp out with Josh and Jamie again tonight."

"If you're not tired of having him, that's a great idea. Thanks."

He strode off toward the front yard.

I was just settling back into my chair when Vern let out a loud whoop.

"Got 'em!" he exclaimed.

I pried myself out of my chair and strolled over to where he was looking at his phone with a big grin on his face.

"Another malefactor brought to justice?" I asked.

"A whole pack of the nastiest malefactors on the planet," he said. "You remember that lady you took a picture of in your yard?"

"The one I dubbed The Frump?" I asked.

"Yeah, that fits," he said. "That dress she was wearing was so far out of style my gran would've turned up her nose at it. Seems she managed to take advantage of the crowds and confusion down in the town square to get her hands on a dog. Aida spotted her leaving town with a cocker spaniel in her back seat. Driving like a bat out of hell, so Aida's first thought was to arrest her for reckless driving and rescue the dog along the way. But then she decided maybe it could be useful to see where she went. So she notified Kevin to keep an eye on where the cocker spaniel's GPS was going, so they could track him down even if the woman evaded her, and then she settled in to tail the Frump."

"Let me guess," I said. "The Frump led Aida straight to a dogfight."

"You got it. And once Aida figured out what county they were in, the chief got in touch with the local sheriff there, and they raided the place. Rounded up a whole passel of nasty animal abusers."

"Good show," Taylor said.

"Is the cocker spaniel all right?" I demanded.

"He's fine, and so are a whole lot of other innocent critters." He frowned slightly. "But I better go tell Clarence and call Ms. Caroline. I kind of volunteered that Clarence would take care of all of the bait dogs. Give 'em any medical care they need and find them safe homes. And I'll be transporting the fighting dogs down to the Willner Wildlife Sanctuary. Rehabbing former fighting dogs is one of the things Ms. Caroline's friend specializes in. And if she doesn't have room for them all, she's got a lot of contacts in the field—she can find someplace that does. Yep—Aida's smart thinking is making life a thousand percent better for those poor dogs."

"You need help transporting some of the dogs, let me know," Taylor said. "Always glad to help make life better for animals, and the trip would give us more time to catch up."

"You're on," Vern said.

"All's well that ends well," I said. Although I wondered how many bait dogs had been rescued, and whether Clarence had room for them all down at the shelter or whether they'd be joining the pack at our house in the short term.

"At least it will end well, once we can get all those dogs transported," Vern said. "The county they were arrested in—no need to name them and shame them, because it's not their fault those dogfighters set up shop there. And they were already trying to get the goods on the slimeballs. Anyway, they have their hands full with a jail full of humans, and their animal shelter's full, too. Randall's going to lend me a couple of trucks to transport the dogs up here or down to Ms. Caroline's place. I don't suppose you could think of anyone who might be willing to spend a couple of hours rescuing some deserving dogs?"

He seemed to be looking at me.

"Someone who knows how to drive a truck with a stick shift?" I said. "I could be persuaded. And I could probably talk Michael and the boys into coming along to help, as long as you put us in charge of the former bait dogs. I don't want the boys near any unrehabilitated fighting dogs."

"Works for me," he said.

"Okay," I said. "Just give me a few minutes to clear the idea with Michael."

"Give me a call when you know, and I can have Randall drop off a truck you can use."

I looked around until I spotted Michael and the boys back in the pasture behind our yard. A couple of workmen from the Shiffley Construction Company had dropped by to take down some of the temporary dog runs, since the pack was less than half its original size and shrinking by the minute as approved adopters emerged from the barn with their new dogs.

But what were Josh, Jamie, Adam, and Michael up to? They seemed to be erecting a tent. A rather large tent.

Wait—they weren't erecting a tent. They'd set up an above-ground pool—an impressively large one—and were using a hose to fill it with water.

"How much longer till it's ready?"

I turned to see Clarence standing behind me. He was carrying one side of a very large crate. Three of Randall's workmen were supporting the other side.

"What are you getting the pool ready for?" I asked.

"Actually, it's not a pool," Clarence said, with a broad grin. "It's a temporary duck pond. Your dad was impatient to claim the Cayugas. He was worried that Ragnar would want to unload this batch and forget he'd promised them to Rob and Delaney, and then who knows how long they'd have to wait for the next batch."

I peered into the crate. Yes, it was full of ducks. A pair of adult ducks, whose glossy feathers weren't actually coal black—more like black with iridescent blue-and-green highlights. And a mass of little ducklings with fluffy dark gray feathers, who milled around too fast for me to count them. Easily a dozen. The high-pitched cheeping of the ducklings was punctuated occasionally by a much deeper quack from one of their parents.

I glanced back at the pool, where several more Shiffley construction workers were knocking together a wooden platform around the perimeter of the pool.

"I think it's ready enough," Michael said. "We need a couple more inches of water, but I think we can turn them loose and let them get settled in."

Clarence and the workmen set down the crate, and Clarence opened the door, reached in, and took out one of the adults. He strode over to the pool and carefully set the duck down on the surface of the water. It quacked a few times, flapped its wings, and began exploring the perimeter of the pool.

"Let me grab the mother," Clarence said. "She might be a little feisty. And then you guys pick up the ducklings—very carefully!—and place them gently in the water."

Within minutes, the adult Cayugas and their fifteen ducklings were gliding in formation from one end of the pool to the other.

"Ragnar sent some duck feed to get you started," Clarence said. "Let me go fetch it from my van."

We all stood for a few moments, watching the ducks. I had the sinking feeling that the boys were already beginning to suffer from duck envy. Maybe I should just give in. Get Ragnar to put us on the list for his next batch of Cayugas. Tell Randall that when he sent Aaron back out to finish Rob and Delaney's duck pond, he might as well dig another one back here for us.

Or maybe the boys would be satisfied with having ducks at what they now called their other house.

Time would tell. In the meantime . . .

"Hey, guys," I said. "Why don't we give the ducks a little peace and quiet to let them get settled? And meanwhile . . . anyone want to come and help me rescue another big batch of dogs?"

Acknowledgments

Thanks once again to everyone at St. Martin's/Minotaur, including (but not limited to) Claire Cheek, Hector DeJean, Stephen Erickson, Nicola Ferguson, Meryl Gross, Paul Hochman, Kayla Janas, Andrew Martin, Sarah Melnyk, and especially my editor, Pete Wolverton. And thanks also to the Art Department another beautiful cover.

More thanks to my agent, Ellen Geiger, and all the folks at the Frances Goldin Literary Agency for taking care of the business side of things so I can concentrate on writing.

Special thanks to Dr. Donahue and Dr. Moiseiwitsch, who taught me all kinds of cool facts about teeth. Any dental errors that appear were obviously things I wasn't savvy enough to ask them.

And very special thanks to the family of the late Madeleine McAuslan-Crine, who let me use her name in the book. She was an animal lover and an avid reader, and when I heard that reading my latest Christmas book had become part of her annual Christmas celebrations, I knew I had to name a really cool character after her.

Many thanks to the friends who brainstorm and critique with me, give me good ideas, or help keep me sane while I'm writing: Stuart, Aidan, and Liam Andrews; Deborah Blake; Chris Cowan; Ellen Crosby; Kathy Deligianis; Margery Flax; Suzanne Frisbee; John Gilstrap; Barb Goffman; Joni Langevoort; David Niemi; Alan Orloff; Dan Stashower, Art Taylor; Robin Templeton; and Dina Willner. And thanks to all the TeaBuds for two decades of friendship.

Above all, thanks to the readers who make all of this possible.

About the Author

Joe Henson, NYC

Donna Andrews has won the Anthony, Barry, and three Agatha Awards, an RT Book Reviews Award for best first novel, and four Lefty and two Toby Bromberg Awards for funniest mystery. She is a member of the Mystery Writers of America, Sisters in Crime, and Novelists, Inc. Andrews lives in Reston, Virginia. *For Duck's Sake* is the thirty-seventh book in the Meg Langslow series.